# The End *and* the Beginning

"A sad, poignant tale of two young boys caught up in Hitler's machine, risking their lives to get away from the panic of the last days of World War II. K. J. Holdom has crafted a stunning story of this time, brilliantly weaving dual time periods and the tragic consequences when families are torn apart."

**Heather Morris**, #1 internationally bestselling author
of *The Tattooist of Auschwitz*

"A haunting, beautiful story of friendship and loyalty, of laughter between tears, and of a steadfast trust in survival based on childhood innocence. The prose is poetry, the imagery crystal, the truth unimaginable."

**Genevieve Graham**, #1 bestselling author of *The Secret Keeper*
and *On Isabella Street*

"K. J. Holdom casts new light on the harrowing final days of World War II and the blurred lines of 'Us vs. Them.' This narrative intertwines the heartrending struggles of a family caught between contested borders, resonating with timely concerns of displacement and the urgent need for global safety and stability. Lyrical prose and a deeply moving conclusion add depth to this evocative story."

**Ellen Keith**, bestselling author of *The Dutch Orphan*

"Tracing one family's impossible quest to reunite amid the chaos and anarchy of the crumbling Third Reich, *The End and the Beginning* is a tale of devotion and faith, of lost innocence and grit, proving ultimately that heroism is not only found on battlefields but in the hearts of ordinary children. In superb, cinematic prose, K. J. Holdom depicts the unforgiving cost of war but also our boundless capacity to endure, to remember, to hope. I adored every page."

**Roxanne Veletzos**, internationally bestselling author
of *The Girl They Left Behind*

# The End
## *and*
# the
# Beginning

*a novel*

## K. J. HOLDOM

PUBLISHED BY SIMON & SCHUSTER
New York   Amsterdam/Antwerp   London
Toronto   Sydney/Melbourne   New Delhi

SIMON &
SCHUSTER
CANADA

A Division of Simon & Schuster, LLC
166 King Street East, Suite 300
Toronto, Ontario M5A 1J3

*For Edmund*

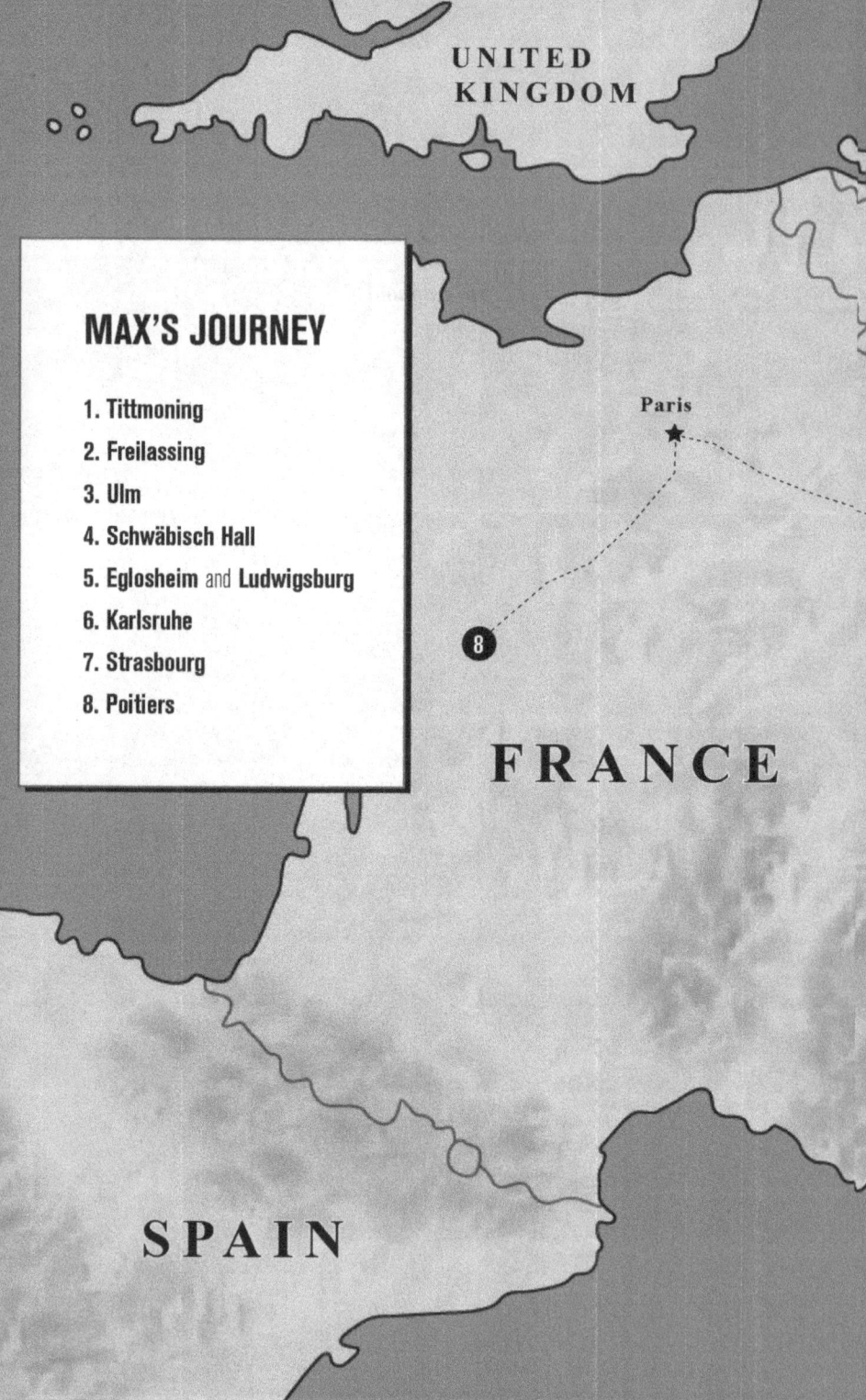

UNITED
KINGDOM

## MAX'S JOURNEY

1. Tittmoning
2. Freilassing
3. Ulm
4. Schwäbisch Hall
5. Eglosheim and Ludwigsburg
6. Karlsruhe
7. Strasbourg
8. Poitiers

Paris

8

FRANCE

SPAIN

# The End
## *and*
## the
## Beginning

# PROLOGUE

Warndt Forest
Franco-Prussian border
1815

The bones of the young soldier lie deep.

His woollen tunic is dissolved into the earth; so too the belt that gathered it and the flesh that filled it well enough to turn the head of the miller's daughter. All that remains of his polearm is a chunk of rust-gnawed iron that could not cleave so much as a dock weed now.

This far down, the soil carries a taste of that time: of iron and spruce, smoke and blood, of the land known as Lotharingia, the Middle Kingdom. This ribboning territory stretched so far—from Frisia in the north to Spoleto in the south—that few of its subjects had ever laid eyes on the prickly monarch their land was named for.

The dead soldier was one of the blessed, having pilfered a rare coin from a dead compatriot who had greatly exaggerated the contents of the pouch strapped to his leg.

The coin was no less a treasure for being the only one the liar had carried.

Beaten from pure silver in the Royal Mint at Metz, the denier was worth enough to buy a month's supply of bread, a healthy piglet, or a week of attention from a wide-hipped prostitute.

It was also stamped with the image of Lothar, grandson to Charlemagne.

Assuming that the artist seeks to flatter, Lothar's must have been a difficult face to render princely—bug-eyed, thick-eared, with an unpleasant upward curl to the lip.

Whatever the truth about the king's features, the young soldier was transfixed by this image in the short time before he suffered a poleaxe to the temple and was rolled into a shallow grave by men who never thought to investigate the pockets of such a sorry-looking corpse.

And there the coin lay for ten centuries.

The ground rose, the flesh shrank, the bones sank, and the blood ran and ran and ran in forest and fields above, but the coin had not seen its last war, nor its last pair of young hands.

At some point, the root of a young beech tree caught it up and guided it back to the surface.

It is here that an old Mosellan coal miner weeping over Napoleon Bonaparte's disastrous defeat is distracted from his misery by a sharp brightness next to his right knee.

PART ONE

Silver

# 1

Far above the bones of the Lotharingian soldier lies the sparkling village of Lauterbach. Snow has hidden the soot on its roofs and streets just in time for the celebrations. Behind frosted windows, coal miners and steel workers pull corks on the Mosel, give the miners' greeting—*Glück auf!*—and salute until their shoulders ache.

The votes have been counted.

The Saar will return to the Fatherland after fifteen long years. No more French administration. No more French language force-fed to the children at school. No more Saar francs and gendarmes and German coal being siphoned into French pockets.

*Glück auf. Prost. Sieg Heil!*

Two hundred metres to the east, in an upstairs bedroom halfway up the Hauptstrasse, three cousins huddle with a damp dog in a wigwam made from stripped branches and two rough woollen blankets.

Max Bernot, who is nearly four years old, pulls from his pocket a small silver coin.

"It's bent," says Anna, his sister, who is six, and knows things. "And dirty."

"What's that?" says his cousin Little Josef.

"Uncle Charles gave it to me."

"Well then, what's the secret?" says Anna.

The boy searches his mind for the particular words his uncle had used—a marvellous story of a land, a crown, a great and terrible war—before Charles had flipped the coin, spinning it so fast that king and cross blurred and merged and the coin had no sides but was both heads and tails at once.

"It came from a king a long, long, long time ago," he says, and is pleased with this summary. "It's real silver so it's treasure, and I should never sell it even if I'm naked on the street."

His sister and cousin laugh, which is not his intention, because Charles had been serious on this point, but there is no time to choose better words because Anna has opened her hand to reveal a pink bonbon tin.

"Poison," Anna whispers, and rattles the tin at Josef. Max snatches it out of her hand and opens the lid to reveal five red berries plucked from the Christmas wreath.

"Mama told you not to—" Max says, but Anna speaks across him.

"I *know*," she says. "So that's *two* secrets. Poison and forbidden."

Max brings the tin to his nose, curious at how poison might smell. A whiff of smoke and meat confounds his nostrils. He hands it back to her.

"Why does it smell like speck?"

"It doesn't," she says. "Your turn, Little Josef."

Little Josef pulls from his pocket a small paper flag ripped from its stick. A boot print stains the top right corner of the swastika.

"Forbidden," he says.

"Holy Christ and all of the saints," whispers Anna. Max and Josef slam hands across mouths as if it were they, and not she, who have uttered this blasphemy. Argos flips to his front, paws braced, alert to the disturbance.

Anna recovers herself. "It's ripped," she says. "Someone has stood on it."

Little Josef's face has reddened, and he looks ready to cry.

Anna flicks a plait behind her shoulder and sighs. "It will have to do," she says. "Now, Argos will choose the best one, as we decided the last time we played."

Max has no such recollection. He looks to Little Josef for confirmation and sees that his cousin is as clueless as he is about this baffling rule change. The dog rests its snout on Anna's tin, and she confirms herself the winner once again.

Downstairs, Marguerite Bernot is threatening a pale basil seedling in her speckless kitchen.

"One more week, then it's the chop," she growls. She is about to make a scissors gesture with her fingers when the kitchen door flings open and brings with it a blast of arctic air, a rush of snowflakes, and three stamping figures.

"Door!" Marguerite backs up to the bench to shield the plant from the chill. Her husband, Anton, pulls the door to, and the trio crowd around the stove, pulling off their gloves. Puddles are already forming under their boots.

"And so?" she says.

Anton sends her a look. And so. It is decided.

"Will you not reconsider, Anton?" his brother, Josef, says. "I fear for you."

"Don't fear for me, little brother. In two weeks' time the sun will rise, I will get out of my bed, scratch my head, put my trousers on one leg at a time, and go to work. We're ordinary people."

The woodstove discharges a loud crack, and Josef's wife, Cécile, jumps. A bolt of pain arcs through Marguerite's skull. Is this the new Saarland? Hearing a bullet in the crack of a stove fire?

"They were parading a gallows through Saarbrücken yesterday," says Cécile. As if that will weaken Anton's resolve. There is a thump from upstairs where the children are using every blanket in the house to make a wigwam, oblivious to the seismic changes around them. Marguerite is tempted to run up there and climb in with them.

"Anton," says Josef. A sigh in two syllables. He looks bewildered. How had they got it so wrong? He runs coal-stained palms up and down his unshaven face. "We go tomorrow. France is already dragging its feet on issuing visas. Some are saying the border will close."

Fires are burning all along the German border. Word is that Hitler ordered the Brownshirts to behave themselves in the buildup to the vote, but the beatings and vandalism have continued, even with all the world watching and international troops in the region to supervise the voting. The home addresses of known status quo campaigners have been plastered to lampposts throughout Saarbrücken. Even before the votes were counted, the thugs were banging on doors to collect their illegal questionnaires: *Did you vote? If not, why not? If so, how?* Now that the result is in, nothing will hold them back. A mob has gathered outside the socialist headquarters. Spies are trolling the queues at the French embassy.

Marguerite casts her eye around her kitchen—soup pan, ladle, and sieve shining on designated hooks—and it all seems weightless, free to lift from its moorings and float into the air, carrying her with it.

"Reconsider. Come with us," says Josef.

"I won't be chased out of my home," says Anton. "Hitler won't last."

"Anton," says Marguerite. "Could we not—"

"This is our home," says Anton. "If the Fascists arrest every Saarland miner who was ever a unionist or member of the Social Democratic Party, then who will be left to work the mines, Marguerite? Tell me that. They need us. They *need* us."

Has the world ever known two more stubborn men than the brothers Bernot? She would have better luck persuading the pig to grow an extra leg than talking Anton into leaving Saarland.

"Politicians come and go, and so will Hitler," he says in a gentler tone. "In the end, Saarland belongs to Germany."

"Never mind who is at the helm?"

"Our home, our land, Josef."

Cécile weeps and Marguerite lifts a lock of sticky brown hair out of the corner of her mouth.

"*Ça ira. Ça ira.*" It will be fine, it will be fine. She speaks French to her sister-in-law sometimes, instead of the Platt—the patois that unites them with their German husbands, that has united everyone here since before there was a Germany, before there was even a France.

The snow falls and the adults talk in circles and the children squabble and thump upstairs, while outside, past the blanketed vegetable garden and chicken house, past the ice skeletons of plum trees, past the sleeping potato fields, hundreds of shivering figures pick their way west through the great Warndt Forest, boots creaking on snow, coats snatched by fingers of larch, clambering their way through bracken and bramble, frozen creeks and cut wire, across the border to France.

What do they have that Marguerite does not, these night-walkers— these refugees from the German interior? A knack of the Gypsies. They can see the future.

# 2

Night retreats from a snow-hushed travellers' inn. *Listen*. A wooden spoon taps against a pot. A woodstove cracks and hisses. Milk tings into the frozen depths of a metal pail, and a chicken scolds its neighbour, then settles back to sleep.

Is there a more peaceful place in all the Reich? No whirr and crump of mortars, no howl of tanks, no thunk of gravediggers' shovels here. Even the prickling skies are quiet.

Careful boot prints connect courtyard to cowshed, where the Polish dairy maid rests on a milking stool, cheek against steaming flank, whispering sadnesses in her mother tongue.

In the kitchen, the proprietress and her daughter prepare a farmer's breakfast for the twenty-three resident boys of Children's Relocation to the Countryside number 42/3. This will be their last meal here, so it must be special: boiled potato fried in egg and fresh-whipped butter with a smattering of fried onion. The speck ran out long ago, and the pigs were stolen during a storm the previous autumn.

The waft of onions and butter climbs the stairs to tease the stomachs of the *Pimpfe*—little farts, as the younger members of Hitler Youth are known—who groan and unwind themselves from sleep. They are mostly aged thirteen. Some have made fourteen. This is the day these little farts become men. They will travel west, to Stuttgart.

They will carry out rudimentary military training. They will wear uniforms, if available, and a weapon, or at least a shovel. They will join the Volkssturm and fight for their country.

These are the children of the Thousand-Year Reich.

Twenty-two of twenty-three are preparing to prove to their Führer, themselves, and their fathers, living or dead, just how hard and fast and brave they can be.

One of them has other ideas.

"I won't fight for Gruber," whispers Max Bernot.

"Gruber is a prick," says Hans-Peter Schlesier. "We fight for Germany, not him."

They have volunteered to muck out the cowshed, and now that the pretty Polish girl has taken the milk to the kitchen, they are free to talk. Max hands Hans a rake and takes up a shovel. The grip burns with cold.

"I don't want to die for nothing, Hans."

"It's not nothing, our country."

"Is it our country? Or is it theirs? Hitler and the SS and the Grubers." Max leans the shovel against a timber rail and tries to blow some warmth back into his hands.

"Then we fight for each other," says Hans. "For our friends, our mothers."

"Why are we being told to fight? We couldn't grow a beard between us."

"Speak for yourself."

"Six whiskers on your top lip doesn't make a beard, Hans."

"If we don't fight, then what?" says Hans. "There's a fucking war on." He thrusts the rake at Max, who sidesteps and watches it topple into the damp straw.

"Home," says Max. "We go home."

A shadow crosses Hans's face. "I need to fight," he says. "I want to fight."

"And if it kills you?"

"Death is not part of the plan."

"Victory or extermination. Have you forgotten that?"

Hans shrugs. "Victory, then."

"It's not funny," says Max. "What am I supposed to tell your mother if you get your head blown off?"

But it is his own mother he thinks of, that bitter night when the letter arrived summoning him to the train station at Neunkirchen. He had begged her not to send him, to let him hide until the American tanks arrived, but she would not be swayed. "You will do as you are told," she said. She wanted him gone. She could not bear to look at him. He should have found the courage to speak to her in that moment, to make her see that she was wrong about him, but his heart was splitting.

"Then I go without you," Max says, holding up a hand when Hans tries to speak. He forces a smile onto his face. "No hard feelings."

Hans closes his eyes and stands there for a long time. He leans over to pick up the rake, and when he straightens there is a sad smile on his face. "All right," he whispers.

"All right what?"

"I'll come."

"Just like that?"

"You won't make it a hundred metres without me."

"Says you."

"Says me."

"They'll hunt us," says Max.

"They might," says Hans.

"All the way to Lauterbach."

"They might."

"They'll hang us."

"Who really cares about a pair of Saarfrench boys?"

Hans shakes the dark hair out of his eyes and his smile is huge and damp, and Max sees that his friend's eternal optimism is also a kind of blindness.

"What about Manfred and Stephen. What about Rudy—"

"They want to fight. So let them fight."

"And Horst?"

Hans shrugs again.

"Hans, what about Horst?"

"He'd never have the guts."

Max feels for the silver coin wrapped in his trouser pocket and calls up the bewildered face of his uncle Charles, his godfather, feet scrabbling in dirt, a red stain spreading from the waistband of his ruined trousers. He remembers Mama's scream, and the *look* she had given him. Max could crawl into a dark place and never come out. He had tried later to dredge up the words to convince her that she was mistaken. Three languages to choose from, books full of words, and could he find a single one to start with?

Only when he was on the train did they present themselves. He wanted to whisper them, press them through the glass, through the bitter air and roiling steam, into her ears, her eyes, her heart. But the train was moving, the platform was slipping away, and she was shrinking, no bigger now than a painted figure at a miniature train station. Man striding with package, guard stumbling over trolley, soldier lighting cigarette, mother and daughter waving at the train.

Too late.

Five hundred kilometres of ruined land, a murderous sky, and two great armies lie between them now, but he will cross all of it to speak with her just once, to release the words that pound against his skull with every beat of his heart.

*It wasn't me.*

"Ask them yourself," says Hans.

Max blinks himself back to the dormitory, the camp, the certainty and insanity of the plan. He presses down on the coin edge. Flesh and fabric yield until there is only metal and bone and pain.

"Go on," says Hans. "Ask how many want to desert with us, then see what happens."

Max does not need to be reminded of the drooped heads of the three men hanging from lamp poles at the ruined rail station in Munich: stained cobbles under dangling feet, hands roped behind backs, placards suspended over chests.

*Deserteur. Plünderer. Defätist.*

At least, Max thinks, I will not be a looter.

# 3

Elversberg, Saarland
March 1945

Marguerite Bernot kneels on a rug in Mrs. Liszt's salon, six pins pressed between her lips, hemming an old dress on her ungrateful daughter.

"Rotten lettuce," Anna says, shifting her weight from one restless foot to another.

Marguerite cannot argue about the colour. "For lack of thrushes, one eats blackbirds," she says through the side of her mouth. Anna makes a face and plucks the excess fabric away from her bust. Marguerite stabs a section of hem. "If you ate the food put in front of you, you'd have more than a pair of fried eggs under there. When I was—"

"When you were my age, you were not eating bread with sawdust in it."

"At your age, we were grateful to have any sort of bread, as you should be today. Stop moving, child."

"I am sixteen years old."

"And so?"

"Not a child," says Anna. It's true she stands head and shoulders taller than Marguerite, taller than most women would care to be, but she wears it well. If there is one thing years of marching have taught her, it is how to stand. And now that the puppy fat has melted from her cheeks, her hazel eyes seem bigger, her jaw more refined. She has even grown into her nose—another trait inherited from her father. *Not a child.* Indeed, not a child. Yet here she stands yawning like a toddler

15

with her stockings ripped—in service to the Reich, no doubt. She's been scouring the forest south of the township again, collecting early spring herbs and willow bark. God knows what the apothecary makes of it all—let alone with it. A handful of tinctures and compresses? Hardly a replacement for real medicine. Hardly enough to stem the ocean of blood spilling all over the country or bring back the poor women and children of their own village who had scrambled off a crowded refugee train at Sankt Wendel and into an air-raid shelter that became a living hell.

"What's wrong?" says Anna.

Marguerite shakes the thoughts free and draws another pin. She will not bring it up because Anna will deviate, as she always does, to outrage—all that smoke and fire to distract from the pain of loss. Marguerite does not want to have to listen to it again because she is tired. Her bones feel weighted with lead. Her daughter has a heart— Marguerite knows this—but at times she makes a good job of hiding it. If Anna ever mentions Charles, it is only to rail against the criminals who would be shot if the sainted Führer knew what they had done. To Anna, the Führer can do no wrong. Marguerite bites her tongue on this matter, as she has done for so long, since it became dangerous to speak her mind on so many matters in front of her own children. If only she had Max's knack for getting around Anna's prickles. Instead, she seems only to make her daughter furious.

"What is it, Mother?"

"Thinking about your brother," says Marguerite.

"What do you think he's doing now?" says Anna. "Up a tree with Hans-Peter? Skiing? Piloting a glider?"

"Cleaning toilets, peeling potatoes. The usual things boys do in camps." If he has survived the journey to Bavaria, and has somewhere warm to sleep, then God has a soft spot for Marguerite Bernot.

"Can you imagine what he'll do if he's invited to the Berghof?" says Anna. "He'll probably trip over himself and land on one of the Führer's dogs."

"Anna."

"He'll have no idea what to say."

"It's an evacuation camp—not a school trip to Berchtesgaden."

"It's not evacuation. It's a *relocation to the countryside* camp."

"Changing the name does not change the fact."

"Heinrich Grott met the Führer when he was at his KLV camp."

"So we have heard."

"Are you saying it's not true?"

"Heinrich's mother never mentioned it," says Marguerite. And if it were true, she would never have stopped. She pins the last section of fabric and spikes the remaining pins in the cushion. "Off with it and get started on the sewing. Your stitchwork needs practice."

"Skiing would be a lot more interesting than sewing," says Anna. She drags the dress over her head without regard for the pins.

"Hush, ladies, he's on!" Mrs. Liszt turns up the radio dial, but it's not Hitler's voice scratching out into the room. It's Goebbels again, rattling on about the enemy seeking the biological extermination of the German people. They haven't heard from Hitler in weeks. Into the void have crept the stories: a second assassination attempt, a mystery illness, escape to Switzerland.

The radio could be tuned so easily to the BBC German Service to hear the truth about the fronts, to hear the daily list of German prisoners, but Marguerite will not risk it, even when the old woman has gone to bed. Mrs. Liszt has made them welcome, has asked no questions about Marguerite's accent, but God help them if they are caught listening to an enemy radio service.

Marguerite often dreams she is back on that frozen, terrifying road, the day after the order was given to evacuate their home in the Red Zone in early December. She is invisible in her dreams. On the day, she might as well have been, trying to wave down a lift for herself and the children on overloaded wagons, buses crammed with bewildered hospital patients. All day, air-raid alerts ran up and down the line. The planes came only once, and she and the children sheltered in a ditch. They made way for horse-drawn infantry carriers, tank destroyers,

half-track guns covered with camouflage netting—all headed west—
and for ambulances and trucks piled high with coffins. By the time
they reached the outskirts of Neunkirchen, where they were to be billeted, they were half-dead of cold and fear.

The widow Liszt had hailed them from the roadside at Elversberg
just as it was getting dark. Would they like somewhere to rest? She was
a generous host, fussing over the children's damp hair and pale faces,
pushing hard black bread and jam into their fists with arthritic fingers,
loading the fire with precious coal. She took hold of Marguerite's
hands, flinched at the cold, and rushed off to fetch a quilt.

"The mothers bear such a burden," she'd said, wrapping it around
Marguerite's shoulders. "The men are out there making all the noise,
but who keeps the children safe?"

It was too much. Marguerite had to stuff the quilt into her mouth.

"Did you hear that, Anna?" Mrs. Liszt says. "Mr. Goebbels is saying it
can be done. We just have to hold on."

Anna lets the dress fall and off she rushes, littering pins. A child
again.

"Hurry, Mother," she calls. "There are to be new offensive armies.
We're going to beat them. The Führer himself said it to Goebbels. The
day before yesterday, the Führer said it to him."

"Of course he did," Marguerite says.

And from where are these new armies going to appear? Please God,
let Max be safe. Far from Hitler's reach, bundled up in a Bavarian chalet
learning to ski by day, playing chess by night, cradled by mountains.

She should never have let him go.

# 4

After breakfast, Max lines up to shake the hand of the proprietress, but Mrs. Giesel hugs him instead, reaching up to press her buttery cheek to his.

"My young strafe-dodger," she says, and holds him at arm's length to search his face. This close he can make out the pale eyebrows and lashes that are usually invisible against the weathered skin of her round face, a fine white line that snags the corner of her left nostril. Whatever could make a scar like that? When she smiles, she bites down on her lips. She does not like to show her teeth. "Bon courage but not too bon, my Saarfrench lad. You've already used up one of your lives."

He presents her with a small stack of postcards.

"Will you send these for me when the post is running?"

She turns over the top card, and her face changes. She flicks through the remainder.

"But there are no messages, Max. You've gone to the trouble of writing her name and address and licking a stamp. Would you not write a few lines at least?"

He forces a smile and reaches for an explanation.

"They're only for her scrapbook," he says. "I sent plenty before the post stopped."

She presses the cards back into his hands.

"A mother likes to have a little news," she says, and squeezes his

19

arm. "*Write* to her. It will take a day or two to get to Stuttgart, plenty of time on the train. Write *something*, Max, then send them yourself."

He joins the other boys before she can see the shame burning across his face, and marches out, side by side with Hans, led by the youth leader Gruber and trailed by the asthmatic teacher, Weck.

Even now, the doctor sneers at him across the years. *Coward.* The word reaches him here under the gold-washed skies of Bavaria as clearly as if he were in the classroom at the brand-new Adolf Hitler School in Ludweiler. A tin full of eyes. The nurse's secret smile. A trespasser in his blood.

*The sky was trapped in the doctor's glasses. He remembers that. There were clouds, a forest on a hill, a church needle, a bird on the fly. What age was he? Five? Six?*

*"Another Saarfranzosen, Nurse," the doctor had said. "You think this one understands German?"*

*The spectacles rose and fell each time the doctor curled his top lip and wrinkled his nose to peer into a face he seemed to find disappointing. The nurse reached up to adjust her cap, blinding in the afternoon sun, and a whorl of chalk dust scattered minuscule fireflies.*

*The doctor released Max's chin and his head tipped forward.*

*"You understand German?" The doctor took up a rectangular steel case and lifted a hinged cover to expose sixteen glass eyes, each a different colour, all fixing Max with the same expression of alarm.*

*"Yes, Doctor. I speak German. I am German," he said. "My father and grandparents and great-grandparents are from the Saar. My grandfather fought in the Great War. My father was too young."*

*This is what his mother had taught him to say.*

*"What? What's he saying?" The doctor winked at the nurse and his shiny bird eyes slid down to where the bib of her apron pulled across her chest. She dropped her hand from the cap, scooped up a clipboard, and tapped it against her chin.*

*"He is German, Doctor."*

"And yet he has a French family name and slurs his words like an Alsatian peasant."

The eyes in the container were calling Max. Pleading, cold marbles of blue, brown, grey, and green. He blinked. Blinked again.

"Stop that. Wider. Look at me."

The doctor tapped at one of the eyes in the box. The one labelled 14. It was the blue of deep snow, ringed with navy. A barely visible ring of hazel burst out from the black of the pupil. Farther along the row, the eye at number three was the colour of freshly watered earth, the colour of his godfather Charles's eyes.

The nurse smelled like soap. Her eyes were number eleven. Grey-blue with a smudged ring of brown around the pupil. She noticed and gave him a secret smile.

The doctor held a tool that looked like pincers; its cold metal edges took hold of Max's forehead.

"And your mother?"

Max hesitated and tried to see the eyes in the box. It was important to give the correct answers. He must speak only German— not the Platt, and not French.

"My mother is from Saint-Avold, but she has lived in Saarland since she married my father, Doctor."

"What does he say?" The doctor used a knuckle to nudge his spectacles northward and peered through them at Max.

"His mother is French," said the nurse, consulting the chart. "Moselle."

The doctor snorted and read out a number. "Of course, you appreciate the problem with French blood, Nurse?" He put the instrument down and flicked over a page with a sharp snap. He was close enough for Max to smell his sour breath. "It is contaminated with the blood of the African colonies thanks to French whores who fall on their backs for a black man."

The words swung in the air, the meaning out of reach, but the malice clear. Max swallowed and imagined a Zeppelin in the top right corner of the doctor's glasses.

*"After the Great War, the French, your mother's people, sent troops from their colonies to occupy the Rhineland. Having decimated their own bloodline, they set about destroying ours."*

Max steered the Zeppelin between the clouds and sliced a gentle arc toward the doctor's nose. A tiny barrel bomb detached from the undercarriage. Tip, topple, tumble. Its slow passage continued down, down, down. It soon fell clear of the spectacles and erupted in the cropped bristles above the doctor's lip. The moustache ignited. Flames spread upward to the hairs sticking out of the nostrils. The doctor breathed fire.

"Now," said the doctor. "We are here to examine you, young Max Bernot. No obvious physical signs, but inferiority can be expressed in so many ways. Cowardice is the classic marker. That and a taste for the perverse, the degenerate."

Could this unpleasant stranger know about the jazz records in Uncle Josef's living room on the French side of the border?

"Look at him, Nurse," the doctor had said, snorting like a sow. "What a picture. Shall we grant him his Aryan Certificate?"

The nurse did not reply. It occurred to Max that she did not like this man.

"Take care, Bernot," the doctor said, scratching a few words onto the report. "Don't fall prey to your base instincts. I would not want a reason to revise my findings."

Max could guess what that meant.

Sixteen eyeballs watched him with alarm.

"I will be good, Herr Doktor," he said. He had glanced at the nurse, reached out to the box of eyes, and closed the lid.

A tug on his arm brings Max back to the cold.

"Move it," says Hans. "Gruber will go mad." The church spires and roofs of Tittmoning rise from the grey. *I will be good.* Max had made the oath to the doctor and to himself. *Good and loyal and brave.* And now look at him: shaking like a kitten.

The train is late, so he joins Hans in jogging around the shelter

to bring the feeling back to his feet. The eldest of their classmates—
Rudy, Manfred, and Karl—kick icicles off a low-hanging shed roof.
Adolf and Stephan pore over the faded and peeling notices on the station noticeboard, hands deep in their pockets, rocking on their boots.
Between announcements of metal collection dates and new curfews,
there is a hand-drawn stick figure of the Führer, and beneath it the
word *Vermisst*. Missing. The image would have shocked him once.

Little Horst shivers into his collar, shifting his weight from one spar-
row leg to another. He's doing that odd thing with his face—squinting
first with one eye, then the other, making a seesaw of his cheeks. Max
had thought it a nervous tic until he noticed that this was Horst's way
of inching his spectacles back up his nose, using his cheeks rather than
his finger. Not that the distinction mattered to Gruber, who promptly
nicknamed him Blinky Boy.

"All right, Horst?" says Max, trying to sound cheerful.

Horst says nothing. Does he suspect something? A bloom of heat
travels up Max's face. How can they leave Horst with Gruber?

Hans appears with a large piece of puddle ice held up in front of
his face.

"Maxi, Maxi, look in the mirror."

Max obliges and sees Hans's grin through the ice, which cracks,
then shatters.

"Oh shit, Max, this is bad," says Hans, shaking the remaining shards
from his hands. "Only the very worst kind of ugly will break a mirror."

Horst is sniggering, but his lips are blue. He seems even scrawnier
than when they first arrived here.

"I'll show you ugly," Max says, and snatches up a piece of ice. Hans
is already running.

There is no train.

Two hours later the mayor and a party official arrive and inform
Weck that a truck will arrive mid-morning to transport the boys thirty
kilometres south to Freilassing, at the foot of the Alps, where they will
catch a westbound train. Gruber returns from the toilet to discover

that these important men have left without speaking to him, and his already crowded features pucker into fury.

"Have you ever noticed that Gruber's face resembles a cat's arse?" whispers Hans, and performs an imitation of one, arm flicking behind his head like a tail. The laugh is out before Max can stop it, but when Gruber looks across, his eyes settle not on Max, but on Manfred and Karl, who are carving penises into the snow. Their punishment is to stand to attention for fifteen minutes, doubled to thirty when Karl tries to pull his frozen hands inside his coat sleeves.

There is no truck. The boys begin to complain of hunger and Weck hands each boy a sweet white bread roll baked by Mrs. Giesel for the journey. Max had not tasted white bread for more than a year before coming to Bavaria. He suspects that Mrs. Giesel has been risking arrest for weeks by trading butter for flour on the black market for the benefit of the boys in her care. He sends her a silent thank-you.

In the early afternoon, a car pulls up and two SS men approach. Max's traitorous heart batters his ribs, but Hans is right next to him, and up go the eyebrows. If Hans's neck were on the block and the guillotine on its way down, he would expect salvation. Still, he's right. For now, they are guilty of nothing but imaginings.

The officers consult with the troop leader and teacher and invent new orders. The troop will *march* the thirty kilometres south to Freilassing, at the foot of the mountains, where there are reportedly trains in abundance.

Gruber, enraged by the delays and wasted mileage and changes of plan and the distracted air of the SS men, sets out at a fierce pace, doling out punishments for talking, for straggling, for having a stupid face. The teacher follows, wheezing, shoulders rounded against the cold.

A cheery truck driver with space to spare offers to take a few passengers—he has a boy in the Hitler Youth himself, you know—but Gruber cuts off the driver mid-sentence. He will not split the troop. He makes the same speech to a young uniformed woman wrestling a clangorous motorcar to a halt beside them. She grinds the gears and the car shunts forward with its four empty seats.

Max's heart pounds at each missed opportunity.

After the first couple of hours, Gruber's pace settles and he sticks to the front of the troop, barking orders now and then. The boys trot through the snow, fists in coat pockets, a flock of wingless crows. Only the teacher Weck breaks the rhythm, hurrying up and down the length of the line, wheezing and coughing, counting and recounting the boys. Max wants to point out this alarming vigilance, but Hans is caught up at the rear, and it is not worth risking Gruber's temper to fall back.

They snake southward, shadows inching toward the ranges on their left, teeth of the Alps rising ahead. Every intersection is jammed. Ancient wagons pass through with improvised canopies. An old man with a fat sore across his cheek squats on the roadside licking the inside of a can, ignored by travellers hauling carts loaded with suitcases. Most travellers take the lanes heading west, but a few switch southward with the troop—imagining that the urgent pace implies a worthy destination.

The smell of cooking meat reaches them long before Max sees smoke rising from within a hive of refugees. Beyond, a bomb-hit wagon smoulders. Two horses lie in mud swirled with blood and soot. Thick swathes of flesh have been cut from their flanks. Their wild eyes are frosted over, but the ear of one stands at a lively angle. A pain cuts into Max's side, but this is not the worst. The bodies of a family are lined up under a quilt. Six pairs of shoeless feet peek out. The smallest would fit into Max's palm, in socks scarred with colourful darning. If he broke out from his line, Max could step over and pull the quilt down to cover those poor frozen feet. But he doesn't have the courage.

He weaves through the slow-moving hordes and feels their exhaustion, the weight in their steps. A woman with a baby wrapped onto her chest, face hidden in a red scarf, pauses and squints ahead. He follows her gaze, but there are only lines of refugees, white fields, patches of dark forest, and deepening sky.

A hand settles on his shoulder.

"Anything to eat, Max?" Hans is at his side, grinning hopefully.

Max shakes his head, registering now the depths of his hunger, but Hans's smile broadens as he digs into his own trouser pocket and brings out two of Mrs. Giesel's miraculous white bread rolls—flatter than usual, but promising a world of soft deliciousness.

"How did you get your hands on those?" says Max.

"I told you the Polish girl had a thing for me," says Hans, handing one over.

"The Polish girl doesn't even know your name," Max says through his mouthful, and knocks his shoulder against Hans's by way of thank-you—not just for the roll, but for lifting his spirits. Hans has been doing that since the day they met.

*Max was supposed to go straight back to class after the racial-hygiene check. Instead, he locked himself in a toilet cubicle. Cowardice. Inferior. French whores. The doctor's words hissed at him.*

*The sound of a wet sneeze reached him, then a scuffle of a boot. Max pulled the chain and opened the door to see five cold white sinks lined up under five dark silver taps. No one but the contaminated Maximilian Bernot and his reflection. The soap, swollen with water, squelched between his fingers. He squeezed.*

*A boy about the same age stepped out of a cubicle, swiped dark hair out of his eyes, and looked at Max across the mirror.*

*"You hiding too?" He was speaking in Platt.*

*Max shook his head and opened the tap and tried to scrape the thick soap off his fingers.*

*"Do I have an inferior nose?" The boy's nose looked the same as his own, but dotted with brown speckles.*

*Foam was threatening to fill the sink, so Max tried to push it toward the plughole. The top of his head itched, but his hands were covered in soap bubbles and he could not get to it.*

"*The doctor said it was inferior,*" *the boy said, frowning and licking his finger and rubbing at the freckles. Max wanted to give up making the foam disappear and run away before he was caught—but the boy looked like someone you could trust.*

*"I have an African in my blood," Max whispered.*

*The boy's eyes widened. "Is he swimming up your leg right now?" His arms cartwheeled in a poor imitation of swimming. "He must be tiny. Or could it be a girl?"*

*That made Max smile, the thought of a tiny dark-skinned girl, cheeks full of air, frowning with the effort of swimming up through a winding tunnel of red inside him. He checked the mirror: no outward signs of the trespasser. His eyes and hair and skin were still pale.*

*The boy took a long step toward him, avoiding stepping on the cracks between the black and white tiles, to examine the overflowing suds. He pushed air out of his lips and acknowledged the scale of the foam problem.*

*"Don't worry," he said. He pulled up his sleeves, scooped up a tower of suds, and ran, arms outstretched, into a cubicle, where he shook his hands at the toilet. Most of the suds lay in a soggy trail of outrage on the floor. Max and the boy stared at each other, then collapsed into laughter. The boy held up his hand.*

*"New plan," he said, widening his eyes. He threw his hands in the air as though pursued by a bull, and bolted for the door, with Max close behind.*

*The boy was called Hans-Peter, but Max could call him Hans.*

*"Do you have a dog?" Max asked, wiping his hands on the back of his shorts when they were a safe distance down the corridor.*

*"My mother doesn't like dogs for reason of the insupportable smell, and I don't have a father to pay for luxuries like dogs."*

*"What's 'insupportable'?" Max said.*

*"Doggish," said Hans. "Unpleasant."*

*"What happened to your father?" Max asked.*

*"Lion attack," said Hans.*

*"Oof."*

*"Don't worry,"* said Hans. *"I was too young to remember. He threw me to safety."*

They paused at a poster from which a fair-haired adolescent stared out, dwarfed by a backdrop of the Führer's face. Youth serves the Führer, it said. All ten-year-olds into the Jungvolk.

*"Will they want us now, do you think?"* said Hans.

Max could see himself as a Pimpf in that smart brown shirt, knife at his side, belt buckle gleaming. He would be brave and loyal and strong. When his time came, he would travel on a train high into the Austrian Alps and be presented for inspection at Hitler's mountain retreat. The Führer's serious brown eyes would settle on him, Max Bernot of Lauterbach, with infinite tenderness, it being a well-known fact that Adolf Hitler loved children as much as he adored animals.

# 5

Marguerite does not see Karl Hinckel pull up in the black Mercedes. It is the other women who alert her to it, falling away from her as you might a carrier of the plague.

Later she will blame the coat, although she is mistaken in this. Too blue, too bright, too smart, too French. He must have seen her long before she saw him, but she had her mind on other things out there, having walked for an hour and a half in the rain from Elversberg to queue for coupons outside the People's Welfare Office. The wind was snatching her hair from her hat, and all her attention was on trying to keep her hair in and the cold out and the umbrella together.

"Marguerite? Is that you?" he repeats. She scrapes the hair out of her eye and peers into the open rear window. She is no student of National Socialist Party military insignia, but he must be doing well for himself to be so daubed in gold—cap, lapels, buttons, and buckle. Even the swastika on his armband is embellished with golden oak leaves and a fine gold border.

The curiosity of the other women presses in. Are they imagining her an informer? A mistress? The injustice rises like a fever. She would like to tell them, to tell him, that he is mistaken, that she does not know him, because his interest in her cannot be good. It has never been good.

"It's cold out there," he says, and slides to his left. "Come and sit."

She cranes forward to check the line. Only eight women ahead. She cannot go back to Anna and Mrs. Liszt empty-handed. The only food left in the house is a bowl of sprouting potatoes.

"Ladies," he calls, past Marguerite. "Will you kindly hold this woman's place?"

The women nod without meeting his eye. There was a time when a few of them would have flickered their lashes at a blue-eyed official wearing so much brass. Now they watch him the way sheep watch a scraggy dog. What woman has not shopped on the black market to feed her children? What woman has not expressed out loud, even just to her mother, her wish for the Western Allies to hurry it up and get here ahead of the Russians? Crimes and penalties shift with the wind. It all depends on the nature of the Nazi that blows in.

The uniformed driver—face like a torn sausage—gets out and opens the rear door.

Had her mother-in-law not chided her about this coat when she bought it a decade ago? *Auffällig,* she had scolded. Conspicuous. In other words: French. Why had she worn it? Because the day is bleak and the war is never-ending and her family is scattered like seeds to the wind. Because she doesn't know who is alive and who is dead, and the coat is a comfort and an exquisite shade of blue.

The driver tilts his head at the car: a gesture that says if she will not put herself in, he will put her in, and the longer she makes him wait out here, the more firmly he will do it.

Marguerite takes a step, and her left heel catches on a cobblestone. The driver lunges and spins her around. The crook of his elbow crushes her throat.

"Steady," he whispers, hot breath in her ear, spittle on her cheek. She tries to twist away, but her arms are pinned and her pulse pounds in her throat, her face, her scalp, her eyes. No air. Is this how she will die? In a godforsaken queue, in the arms of a thug?

"Thank you, Gunter," says Hinckel. "I believe Miss Guibert lost her footing." The pressure on her neck releases, but not the pain, and the driver steers her into the car. Every breath of blessed air burns, but she is alive, and even in her agony, she feels the relief as her body sinks into the warmth of that leather seat.

"Mrs.," she stutters, and chokes again.

"I didn't catch that, Marguerite."

"It's Mrs.," she manages. "Mrs. Bernot."

"Oh, I see," he says. "You married a Frenchman?"

"German," she says, breaking into another fit of coughing. If she could speak, it might be tempting to elaborate on Anton's family history, but the complex interlacing of bloodlines on the border does not sit well with Nazi ideas about purity, and she does not wish to make conversation with Karl Hinckel.

"You look just the same," he says.

He is an easy liar. Aside from the fact there are tears and mucus streaming down her face, she looks exactly like a woman who has scrubbed and laundered and worked in garden and field for two decades. There is dirt under her nails, and age is beginning to sketch its mark into her skin. The welfare office will close soon. She can't leave without her coupons.

"You are living here in Neunkirchen?" he says.

"Your driver choked me." She coughs again, feels inside her bag for a handkerchief.

"He was over-vigilant, it's true. Sadly there have been one or two minor incidents that have made Gunter quite protective. Gunter, apologise to Mrs. Bernot."

The driver does as he is told and turns to flash a meaty smile at her. Vile creature.

"How long as it been?" Hinckel says.

Twenty years. It has been twenty years, and it could have been longer. Damn this coat, damn her own stupid vanity. What does he *want*?

"The office will close soon," she says. Her voice is returning.

"I fear you have lost your spark, Marguerite."

"Hunger will do that to a person. And being choked half to death by a gorilla."

Hinckel smiles. "There she is."

31

"You don't know me," she says, and this is a mistake. Anger flashes across his face before he has it under control again. Still have your temper, Karl Hinckel.

"In fact, you are just the person I need. Gunter, Mrs. *Bernot* used to be a secretary—a very good one in fact. Rather a different breed to the ones we have experienced lately."

"A happy coincidence, Herr Bereichsleiter."

Marguerite feels for the door handle.

"How would you describe the last one, Gunter?" says Hinckel. "In terms of temperament."

"I don't have your talent with words, sir."

Marguerite presses her weight down and the handle descends silently. Not locked.

"Humour me," says Hinckel.

"Lacking grit, I'd say, sir," says Gunter. "More suited to the theatrical life."

"There you are. A very precise summing up."

Marguerite presses her shoulder against the door, just a little. It gives. A finger of freezing air reaches through the opening to lift the hair at the back of her neck. All she has to do is push the door half a metre more and she can step out, step away.

"In any case, Marguerite, the last secretary is gone." Hinckel's gloved hand waves a small circle in the air, as if the wretched woman evaporated. It is not hard to guess who made her disappear.

"I have to go," she says. The burn in her throat has settled into a deep ache. She pushes the door a fraction more. Droplets appear on the arm of her coat.

Hinckel reaches across her and pulls the door closed. She shrinks back and he withdraws his arm, but his face is too close. She can feel the heat of it, breathes in the scent of good soap. No Reich-issued ersatz soap for Karl Hinckel.

"It really is very good to see you after all this time," he says. She turns her head away and he sits back at last. "I am in the process of relocating to Heilbronn, and while that is some distance from here, the house has the advantage of a rural setting. The job won't be difficult for someone with your experience."

*No. A thousand times no.* But Karl Hinckel does not like the word no, so she searches for a gentler alternative.

"I am not a secretary anymore," she says. "I am a housewife. I grow potatoes."

"Potatoes?"

"If there weren't American tanks ripping up our fields right now, my husband and I would be preparing for spring planting."

He watches her for a long moment.

"Your fields are where?"

"On the border. West of the Saar River."

"You never could make up your mind whether you were French or German."

"There was a time we didn't have to choose."

"In any case," he says. "I will have someone pick you up—"

"I can't just pack up and go to Heilbronn. My family—"

"Your husband, this *Monsieur Bernot*, he is here with you?" He's making his calculations. If her husband is not serving in the German army, what is wrong with him?

"My husband is serving on the Westwall. My daughter is here with me, and—" No, Max is none of his business. "We are billeted with an elderly widow who depends on us."

"An only child?" he says.

"I beg your pardon?"

"It must be a lonely childhood for a girl without a sister," he says. "Or brother."

The base of her spine contracts. Does he *know* she has a son? There is no connection between Karl Hinckel's world and hers, nor has there been for nearly twenty years.

*Enough,* Marguerite. All those years ago she had imagined all manner of things that proved to be wrong, quite wrong.

"My husband and I have a son," she says. "But he has been relocated."

Karl Hinckel didn't even know her married name, and even if he did, how would he have found her? The evacuation was a shambles. She is supposed to be residing with a family in Neunkirchen, but it was Mrs. Liszt who came forward and offered them a room as they trudged through Elversberg on Neunkirchen's western outskirts that terrible day—terrified and freezing. They asked no questions. They had simply walked off with her.

"Marguerite?"

"I'm sorry?"

"Where has your son been relocated to?"

"He is in the care of the *Kinderlandverschickung.* I have no idea where they sent him."

"Excellent," he says. "Then he is in safe hands and we have only you and your daughter to worry about."

"Perhaps I have not been clear," she says.

"A live-in arrangement will work best."

"I appreciate the kind offer, but I cannot accept."

"The house is not yet back to its best, but there are plenty of rooms and a well-stocked pantry. You will dine with us, of course. We are accustomed to new faces at the table. At our previous houses we have often fed and housed those in need of temporary shelter."

"It is years since I did secretarial work."

"You might indulge my wife a few French lessons in your time off. We have enjoyed several trips to France in brighter days—Paris is a splendid city, *n'est-ce pas?*"

She thinks, Paris is a liberated city.

She thinks, Bite your lip, Marguerite. Don't challenge the lion in his lair.

And now hunger is dismantling her thoughts. What about this well-stocked pantry and its shelves of preserved pears and apples and confiture? There might be oranges in there, a whole crate of oranges alongside cheeses in a cool box, with litre upon litre of fresh milk. She must concentrate, must extract herself from this car, from him, but what else might lie in that pantry to put some flesh on Anna? Dried meat hanging from hooks, sacks of potatoes, flour and yeast and salt to make fat loaves of bread? Her mouth fills, but she will not swallow and show him her hunger. Would it be so bad to work for him for a short time? The Allied tanks are coming. It cannot be more than a few weeks, surely.

"Perhaps we might track down that son of yours," Hinckel says. "As a special favour. I think you will find me a generous employer. Would that be fair to say, Gunter?"

"More than fair, sir," says Gunter.

"What's the boy's name?" says Hinckel.

She does not trust his smile. Is it possible he could bring Max back to her? Only if he sees an advantage to himself. But what of it? If she could only get Max within reach, keep him safe just until the front passes and the war is over, then all will be well. This is what mothers do. They keep their children safe.

A voice deeper inside her scoffs. *You should never have let him go.*

"Marguerite?" says Hinckel. "The boy's name."

"Max," she says. "My son's name is Max Bernot."

The women have held her place in the line, but now there is more space for the wind and rain to get at her. She curses Hinckel and the women and the weather. Her hair pulls free to slap at her, and she curses her hair as well. She will not cry. Not here. But the strength is draining out of her and joining the filthy water washing through the street. She wants her son back. She wants her husband back. She wants to go home and for the war to be over and to be concerned with nothing more troubling than a turn in the breeze that will dust her washing in soot from the ironworks.

A pressure on her coat sleeve makes her flinch. The young woman behind her appears concerned. There is a firmness in the touch that communicates a message. Perhaps nothing more than sympathy. Perhaps a more dangerous idea: that the war will be over soon, that men like Hinckel will be stripped of power. Whatever it might be, such a message is not safe to give or receive, so Marguerite eases her arm from the woman's hold and lifts her face to the rain.

# 6

Freilassing, Bavaria
March 1945

Freilassing is in blackout when they arrive—the only light is in the glow of cigarettes, the quick sweep of a torch, the glare from the firebox of a train that sounds ready to depart. A fat moth flits in Max's face, and he brushes it away.

Blisters needle the soles of his feet, drenched inside his boots. Now that he has stopped marching, the chill creeps back in. Angry shouts rise above the shriek of the train, and he can make out guards patrolling the platform, dragging off stragglers desperate to board. Gruber is up on his tiptoes again, trying to make himself taller. His weasel eyes are so intent on the guards and their fists and rifles that his mouth has fallen open. Max imagines a moth flitting into that damp chasm, lodging itself in the youth leader's throat. He sees Gruber blustering and choking on the dry, furry body, the delicate wings. But no, it's a cruel thought. He won't wish that on a moth.

The teacher calls the troop together and bids them stay while he searches for a party official. A few metres in the other direction, a match flares, and the face of a tall, helmeted soldier appears. An eagle-embossed crescent hangs from a heavy chain around his neck. Feldgendarmerie. He's military police, better known as chain dogs, and his eyes have settled on Max.

Gruber pushes forward and blurts his requirements—food, water, a toilet, a train.

36

"Your situation," the chain dog says, "is not unique."

Gruber is oblivious to the officer's irritation, and the hush that has settled around them. Has he failed to notice the hundreds of people gathered along the platform and walls of the station?

"We have orders to travel to Stuttgart to join the People's Storm, Herr Feldgendarm," says Gruber, and presents his papers. The officer frowns, takes a more careful look at Gruber.

"*Saarland?*"

"Correct, sir."

"What is a troop of Westwall Gypsy girls and sheep-fuckers doing so far from home?"

"Proud Germans, sir, and no Gypsies or girls among us," says Gruber. He's been staring straight ahead but risks a glance at the officer. "I can't swear to the safety of the sheep around one or two of the border boys."

"You did not answer my question."

The smile drops from Gruber's face. "Children's Relocation to the Countryside, sir."

"You are how many?"

"Twenty-three, sir, and me."

"Age?"

"Seventeen, sir. They are fourteen, and ready to fight." Gruber is a liar.

Only Rudy, Manfred, Karl, and Hans are fourteen. Horst is twelve. The rest, including Max, are thirteen, though in Max's case, only for a few more days.

The teacher returns, a panting silhouette against the flash of the firebox, and introduces himself. His wheezing is worse than ever.

"Good," says the officer. "We have a train leaving now. We can take a few more *Flakhelfer* to go north to Frankfurt an der Oder. The rest will follow on the next troop mover."

"With respect, Herr Feldgendarm," says Weck. "We have orders to take these boys to Stuttgart."

"These are your counterorders," the officer says. "The Führer has declared Frankfurt an der Oder a fortress town."

"But some of these boys are only twelve."

"Papers," says the officer, with a glance at Gruber. Weck fishes inside his coat. Is it the unsteady light, or is his hand shaking?

"I see the need in the east," says Weck, "but is it not equally desperate in the west, where these boys are from? Their youth might suit them more to ditch-digging—"

"We want to slaughter Russians, not hide in a ditch," says Gruber. His scrunched-up features, exaggerated in the low light, give him a rattish look. *He's* the one who belongs in a ditch. Somewhere dark and damp.

"You are an invalid?" the officer says to Weck.

"Asthma. It is noted."

"Asthma," repeats the officer, as if it were contagious. "This is why you have not yet enlisted?"

"I developed asthma during the last war," says Weck. The officer inspects the erratic rise and fall of Weck's chest.

"This is the second war you have avoided?" says the officer. Gruber smirks.

"You misunderstand, sir. I was a soldier," says Weck. "There was a gas attack. Lung damage. Everything is noted there in my papers."

"Papers?" The officer holds them between his fingers as if they were soiled. "The enemy is upon us, Weck."

"If I am called, I will fight, but these boys—"

"You are called."

"Understood." Weck makes a formal nod. "But in regard to—"

"He doesn't speak for us," says Gruber.

"*Enough*," says Weck, and there is real force in his voice. Enough to silence Gruber. "Herr Feldgendarm, if we send children to war, who will we be fighting for, precisely? Who will be left to rebuild—" His breath runs out.

The smile crawls back across Gruber's face, and the officer turns his attention to the youth leader. Just like that, the power drains from one into the other.

Hans has a powerful grip on Max's arm, pulling him back into the darkness. Max shakes himself free. *Not here, not yet.* This is not the plan. They are to travel to Stuttgart with the troop. They are to break away there, in the west. Not here, in the mountains, which is as far from home as it is possible to be in Germany. Not here, under Gruber's nose, and their teacher so vigilant, and the chain dog with the power of God.

It is men like this one who knotted the rope for the dead men at Munich, who painted the slogans, who strung them up when they were still living, breathing humans.

"*Max*," says Hans.

Max is distracted by a flash of light on the arm of a pair of spectacles. A cheek lifts. *Horst.* He is moving toward them, searching the darkness for them.

Horst will not give them away. The risk, far greater, is that Horst wants to step into the shadows with them. If he does, it will be over because Gruber will look for Horst. Gruber *always* looks for Horst. Yet how can they leave him here to be put on a train? Horst cannot be sent to face Russian tanks and machine guns and bayonets.

Behind Horst's head, lit up by the firebox flame, the chain dog is calling.

"I will take five on this train. The remainder can take the troop movers moving out shortly."

Gruber raises his arm. The other boys join. Their roars carry blood and courage. To fight is to live. To die is to win. Sacrifice is victory.

Over the heads of his classmates, the gloved finger of the SS officer lifts. It pauses there, in the shivering light. The train howls its readiness to depart. Max takes a step back.

"You," the officer says. The finger descends toward a head that might be Rudy's. It lifts and descends again. Max reverses a second step, and a third. "You, you, you, you."

Five shadows that include the teacher, Gruber, Rudy, and Manfred mount the train. Gruber pauses in the doorway, searching the shadows, searching for Horst. Here is where it ends. Horst is close now, determined. He doesn't understand that if he joins them, they will all be caught.

A flash of pain crosses Horst's face. He can see straight into Max's cowardly heart.

*Max sees Horst as he was three days ago, naked in the snowy courtyard of the Children's Relocation to the Countryside Camp, the skin of his chest and arms mapped in blue. His head was nodding—the cold making a fool of him—and his hands were cupped over his penis. At Gruber's command, Max and Hans had joined the other boys to form a semicircle.*

*"Give him some encouragement, boys," Gruber had said. A few boys cheered, and Max hated them for it.*

*"Down you get, Blinky Boy," said Gruber. "And this time I want to see you try. Five more, then you can take your skinny legs and your tiny penis inside and cry for your mama."*

*What was that flicker on Horst's chest, between his ribs? A fluttering. A hidden finger inside him tapping out a quick rhythm. Tippity tap. Tippity tap. It was Horst's heart. Tippity tap. Tippity tap. Too delicate, too exposed. That strip of pale skin was all that stood between the world and Horst's fragile heart.*

*Horst's face had contorted, and Max felt the heat of his shame. For weeks they had been in this camp with Gruber the fool; Gruber the thug; Gruber the dreamer, who thought Germany was winning this war, who stumbled over the dry passages of* Mein Kampf *each morning, pretending to find them riveting; Gruber who enjoyed hurting people.*

*Horst dropped to his knees, stretched his hands into the muddy snow. He was piked in the middle to keep his groin away from the filthy slush.*

*"Flatten that back," said Gruber.*

*Horst lowered his backside. His trembling arms would never hold. He lowered himself ten, twenty centimetres, and stopped.*

*"Chilly out here," said Gruber, smacking his gloved hands together. "Hurry it up now." Heat rushed into Max's chest, and*

*he wanted to shove Gruber's face deep into the snow and hold it there.*

*Horst's arms juddered, but they held. His torso lifted, slowly, slowly. Rudy whistled and Horst lowered himself again.*

*Max shrugged off his backpack and dropped down beside him.*

*"Four to go," he said to Horst with what he hoped was a reassuring smile, but Horst's eyes were wide—a warning there.*

*Pain erupted in Max's side. His face and hair were full of snow. Gruber's second kick landed on his hip. His cheek burned, his hands ached, and he collapsed to his hands and knees.*

*"Note the natural stance of the French, boys," said Gruber.*

*Max spat snow from his mouth and got himself back into position. He nodded at Horst, and saw a new determination in his face. Together they lowered themselves into the snow, together they lifted, and this time Gruber left them to it.*

And now Horst is upright before Max, heart hidden beneath his jacket but his thoughts plain to see. He is not wanted, and he knows it.

"Horst," Max whispers. Gruber is forcing his way through the crowd, making straight for them. Horst's face relaxes into a smile.

"Godspeed," he whispers. He pivots and slips away. A few moments later: a shout, a shove, a noisy complaint. Horst is running. Gruber changes direction. Horst makes good headway, but Gruber has him soon enough.

Max and Hans exchange a look. They fall back another step. A few moments later there is a scuffle and shout at the train. The teacher sags and boards. Gruber pushes Horst up the stairs and follows him inside. He has lost his cap and a line of blood runs from his temple. The chain dog marches the remaining boys away down the platform.

Hans pulls Max down to a crouch. Max braces for the shout, the grip on his collar, but those around them are occupied with keeping warm, keeping their possessions close, getting some rest. There is no teacher, no youth leader to count heads and notice two missing boys.

Squatting among unfamiliar legs, Max pictures a train hurtling through the night, carrying his friends to the front. Will they be flak helpers, carrying and loading shells into the big guns, or messengers, or given rifles and grenades of their own? He sees Horst running into battle. Will Horst be the hero? He is the least likely candidate, but isn't that how the best stories go? The one who sacrifices himself to save his friends?

Perhaps Horst already made his sacrifice tonight. He saw what Max thought about him slipping into the dark with them. He must have understood that the problem was not Horst himself but Gruber's appetite for torturing him. Maybe the distinction is not important. Horst left and made a fuss so he, and not they, would be caught. Was that not heroic? And now Horst will go to war and a bullet will tear through that pale skin between his ribs.

*After Horst's humiliation in the icy courtyard, Max had taken him to the dormitory. Hans chattered while Max helped Horst fasten the buttons of his undershirt, eased the socks up his pale feet, and avoided his eye to spare Horst the shame. A hot rage was expanding within him.*

*"Hans, stay with him. I have to go outside."*

*Max threw on his coat and struck out into the field toward a sprawling oak, black against the bright sky. The fierce energy felt ready to explode out of him, and he used it to propel himself through the heavy snow.*

*He felt them before he heard them. A rumble in his chest. A low growl, but immense in power. There it was: a stain inking the blue. Hundreds of high-altitude, grim birds of prey, beaks pinched shut, wings outstretched.*

*The growl became a roar that swamped the field, the air, the sky. His bones ached with cold. He should move. He should move now, but there was such beauty in those deadly grids; the bombers flying wingtip to wingtip in perfect formation. How many were there? Five hundred? Seven? A thousand? Line after line, they crowded the skies. His chest throbbed.*

*A squadron of twelve tilted and fell away, splitting off in threes, dropping altitude. P-51 Mustangs. Single-seat, single-engine North American fighters. Exquisite, gleaming, pulsating. The upper wing of one aircraft flashed bright as it curved in a wide arc and settled into a dive, headed straight for him.*

*He ran, though he might as well have been underwater, hauling each boot out of the snow and plunging it as far forward as it would reach.*

*The Mustang lined up over the target made by his dragging steps. His chest burned. The coat drew him down. Could he shake it off? He tried to loosen the buttons as he ran, but his fingers were clumsy. The air burned two bitter lines down his face. Is this who he was? Who he would be for the remaining moments of his life? Saarfrench? Westwall Gypsy? Weak, scared, inferior?*

*The war was lost. He understood that now, out there in the snow, lined up in the sights of an American cannon. The war was lost. German victory was a lie. German superiority was a lie. Everything was a lie. The life he knew, the world he understood, the future he dreamed about—all of it shattered.*

*He had nothing, was nothing.*

*He stopped running and faced his attacker, feet planted, arms spread wide. The plane flattened out, rocketing toward him.*

*Just as the wingtips threatened to skim the snow, a hammering buffeted his ears and rattled his sternum. A screen of white sheered up into a spineless tower as countless bullets shuddered into the frozen earth. The machine blotted out the sun. Max's arms fell to his sides and he roared. All trace of his voice was lost in the howl of the engines and the battering gun.*

*He was not afraid.*

*The hammering stopped and a darkness passed over him. He spun around to see the airplane pulling out of the dive and banking right. Inside the cockpit—so close that droplets of condensation were visible on the inside of the glass—he glimpsed a face mask and thick sheepskin collar, the index finger of a gloved hand raised in his direction. The plane lifted into the sun to join the swarm moving north.*

*Alive. Alive. And oh, the blessed relief of it.*

*Hans and Manfred high-stepped through the snow, coats flying, bootlaces untied, pulling on gloves. More boys followed, shouting, waving hats. And there, not far behind—Horst, dragging his skinny legs through the snow.*

*"Are you hit?" Hans was panting and grabbing the front of Max's coat, patting him down for bullet holes.*

*"How many were there?" Manfred said, squinting back into the sky.*

*Rudy was bent in half, gasping. "Hundreds. Thousands."*

*Karl swung a fake punch at Max. He ducked, laughing.*

*"You almost bought it, idiot," Hans said. "What were you doing out here?"*

*"Strafe-dodging," said Horst. The colour back in his cheeks, his spectacles hanging crooked, face lit with laughter because what could be funnier than Max Bernot alive in the snow? Max threw his arm around Horst's shoulders and together they roared at the sky.*

*He was lifted by these boys, this brotherhood. He joined them as they dropped to their knees and dug for shells, filling their pockets with bloodless metal. He had wanted the moment to last forever, because the end was coming. For their country, and maybe for them.*

"All right, Max?" The whites of Hans's eyes glow in the half-light of the train station in Freilassing. The train carrying Gruber and Horst and Weck to the front has already departed.

"All right," says Max. He is glad of the press of Hans's forearm against his own, because if Hans had called his bluff, he would never have had the courage to do this alone.

# 7

Heilbronn, Baden-Württemberg
March 1945

In the rear of the Mercedes, Marguerite and Anna travel through an avenue of leafless oaks. They won't produce buds for another month yet. The house is a layer cake in pink and cream. Three circular dormer windows rise from the tiled roof like half-lidded eyes. Twin stairways curve up to the entrance, supported on the hands of chortling cherubs.

It has taken most of the day to get here. The driver had tried to pull rank at every holdup, but Adolf Hitler could not have got through faster. The road was jammed with refugees and military traffic, ambulances and bogged-down guns. At least it was warm in the car—a world away from the evacuation in December.

Whose home had this been before Hinckel claimed it? Was it a calm haven from the world? Or had it been filled with bustling silks and sparkling crystal, elegant conversation, large dinners, and small scandals?

Now the house looks cold, watchful.

Anna stares across the vast lawn leading to a wood on one side, a wintered-over garden on the other. What girl has not dreamed of visiting such a place: a grand house with its own road and forest, fields and grounds fine enough for a prince. Her daughter breathes it all in, as if it is her birthright. At least she has the sense not to say so—she had said plenty last night when Marguerite had told her where they were going.

"A Bereichsleiter?" Anna had said. "Why does he want to employ you?"

The question was a fair one, but Marguerite had bridled at the tone. It was impossible for Anna to imagine Marguerite's former life, paid for her work, admired for her proficiency in those short years before she married Anton. There were other things Marguerite was admired for too, but Anna has enough trouble imagining her mother as young.

"Because I can do the job," Marguerite had said. "And he needed someone on short notice."

"Just how important is a Bereichsleiter?"

"More important than his rank is the fact he has food. It's only for a few weeks, until the front passes and we can get home."

"Don't talk like that," Anna said.

"Like what? It's as good a place as any to wait it out."

"Germany is fighting back," Anna said. "The Führer says—"

*"The Führer says."*

Anna had flinched and Marguerite heard the contempt in her own voice. She softened her tone.

"Have you forgotten what those men did to Charles?"

"Those men were criminals, Mother. When Hitler finds out what they have done, he will—"

"Those men were agents of your beloved Führer, armed by him, authorised by— What do you mean *finds out*?"

"I have written to him."

"You have *written* to him?"

"What? I had to do something."

Marguerite's laugh had come out cold as the north wind.

"Anna, those men were Hitler's men. They act in his name."

"If he knew—"

"If he knew he would not care."

"He would have them shot."

Her daughter was so assured, her mind so poisoned that she could look right past the truth and invent a lie without even knowing it. Marguerite did not wish to look at her anymore.

"Can we just agree to tread carefully? You have seen what these men are capable of, and Karl Hinckel is one of them, so we will go there, and eat, and build our strength, and say as little as possible, and as soon as it is safe, we will go home."

They had never been hungry in wartime until this, their second evacuation. Their fields and vegetable gardens, the chickens and rabbits and pigs, had provided enough to carry them through—even with all the authorities took. They were most often able to top up what they produced with bread acquired legally or otherwise. But in Neunkirchen, they were strangers, produced nothing. Most merchants no longer honoured food coupons. Marguerite's money was dwindling, and even the black market was horribly short of supplies.

"He might be able to do something about Charles," Anna said.

"Adolf Hitler is too busy losing a war to read letters from a school-girl."

"I mean this Bereichsleiter of yours."

Marguerite had been about to snap at the inference, but her daughter was staring in the mirror, dress held up to her chin, face tilted just so. She could imagine her thoughts.

*A Bereichsleiter.*

A maid who might be Russian—her German is so unfortunate that it is hard to be sure—leads them up two wide flights of stairs and a wallpapered corridor covered in bright rectangles where paintings used to be. A few portraits remain: of men and women dressed in finery and sharing an expansiveness to the face that suggests an appetite for company, food, and humour. These are not Hinckel's people.

"This room for you," the maid says to Marguerite, leading them into a large bedroom reeking of damp and furniture polish. The geometric fans of the bed quilt were just the thing before the war. A worn chaise longue in rose-coloured velvet rests under the window where a person might be tempted to sit if not for that dark stain spreading out from beneath a bright tapestry cushion. That stain brings back Charles, the black rose unfurling into his shirt. She recoils from the memory and addresses the maid.

"Where is my daughter to sleep?"

"I show." The maid heads out the door and Marguerite calls her back.

"No, no. I mean in here. With me."

The maid is confused.

"It's all right," says Anna, fixing a smile on the maid. "I am happy with my own room. Show me."

Marguerite turns her own smile on the maid. "I am sure we can bring another bed or mattress into this room, yes?"

The girl searches them for understanding.

"My room, please," Anna says. Marguerite will not make a scene in front of this stranger and Anna knows it.

The second room is at the far end of the corridor—the same aging luxury as Marguerite's, the same powerful smell of wood polish that cannot disguise the damp. The key is on the inside of the door, at least.

"Is there nothing closer?" says Marguerite.

The maid stares, lost, so Marguerite walks her back into the corridor, points at the door next to her own room.

"What is in there?"

The girl opens the door and stands back. A wall of cold hits Marguerite, carrying with it the dank taste of rot. Something dark scuttles across the floor. The furniture is pushed to the far side of the room, ghostly forms under weather-stained sheets. One of the windows is broken; the shutter beyond swings in the breeze, and the finger of a huge oak wends through the opening. That branch, no thicker than a thumb, sends a shiver through her. How many years since this house was abandoned? It might as well be a century. What has become of her own house? Is the cherry tree pushing through the kitchen window? Are fat rats waddling down the hall? Has a mortar shell transformed it into a pile of bricks and shingles?

"Yes?" says the maid, and there is amusement in her face, but more than that—a shrewdness—before the girl lowers her eyes.

"No," Marguerite replies. She gestures at another closed door.

"What about that one?"

The maid lifts a shoulder.

"Same," she says.

Marguerite returns to Anna's room to pocket the key from the inside of her door.

"What are you doing with that?" her daughter says.

"If you insist on having your own room, I can at least make sure you are safe at night."

"I can lock it myself."

"And if you forget?"

"You want to lock me into my room?"

Yes, she does—not to imprison her but to protect her, but this is not a conversation to have in front of the Russian, who is not much older than Anna. She may not understand the words, but sees well enough what is going on.

"Look, Mama." Anna is at the window. "A greenhouse. It's heavenly."

She's right. It's grand enough to be at home in a public garden, although on a smaller scale. Domed roof, a mass of iron scrollwork, countless panes of glass, and—it's hard to tell because weather and neglect have taken their toll—stained glass detailing all across the roof. This was someone's pride and joy.

"I'm going down," says Anna.

"You are not going down."

"Mother."

"We have no business wandering around that garden."

"What harm can it do?"

*"Leave it."*

Marguerite unbuttons her coat, and the maid steps forward to reach for it. She had forgotten the girl.

"I can manage, thank you."

The maid frowns. Is she puzzling over the status of these new arrivals? She is not the only one. Is Marguerite an employee, a guest, or a prisoner? Hinckel's chauffeur is downstairs smoking with two uniformed thugs, and there are other armed men: two at the gate and at least another in the grounds. Is Marguerite free to leave, or would they stop her?

"I am sure you have more important work to do," says Anna to the maid. "We can take care of ourselves."

"Stop jabbering at the poor girl," says Marguerite. "She has no idea what you are talking about."

The maid smiles. Her teeth are the colour of weak tea. Her beauty is startling—high, round cheeks, dark, almost black eyes, and that mouth. Marguerite presses her own lips between her teeth and feels only flat, fleshless ribbons.

"Okay," says the maid, and points to the floor. "Dinner. You come there before eight. Okay? He does not like when people are late."

Marguerite feels a headache descending and decides to try the stained chaise longue after all. It is not as comfortable as it looks.

# 8

Freilassing, Bavaria
March 1945

A torch beam tracks over the crowd at the train station, blinding Max. Have they been discovered? The light sweeps away. He waits for his eyes to adjust and continues on, Hans at his shoulder.

"Mind where you go," an old man barks.

Max can just make him out, buried in a blanket. A woman with two young children makes space for them next to a wall. They unpack tarpaulins and blankets, wrap themselves up, and Max feels the dragging weight of his own body. Hidden away here in the darkness, it is possible to breathe, but his stomach is knotted tight. Low voices rise and fall. A snorer saws out a gentle rhythm, and the pacing of the guards' boots on the platform are as measured as the tick of a clock.

"I am German," someone says in an accent that doesn't sound at all German.

It is still dark. How long has he slept? He shifts his weight—he has lost all feeling in his backside. The man is pleading. He is ethnic German. He was in a reserved occupation in Poland, manufacturing missiles. His house was burned. His papers were burned. He is too injured to fight. He has lost his family. He is fleeing the Bolsheviks. The official is doubtful. Where is this man intending to go? Who will he stay with? Does he have a name and address? How will he support himself? The man does not know. He does not know. He does not know.

Max hears the same story many times through the night. They are

51

from Silesia, Bohemia, Monrovia, Slovakia—exotic, eastern-sounding places. But they are German too. No, they have never been to Germany. No, they know no one. No, they do not know where they are going. Just west. They are all going west.

*He dreams he is back in Saarland, but not at home. He is in the great city of Saarbrücken, crouched among the crowd, his fists pressed into his eyes.*

*"What is it?" Papa is saying. "Max?"*

*"I'm afraid," he says. The roar is terrible. Bigger and louder than even the ironworks.*

*He is almost four years old, and the rain is coming down in ropes. Adolf Hitler is marching his troops into Saarbrücken to take the city back for Germany.*

*Papa tries to pull Max's fists away from his ears. A man squeezing past them laughs.*

*Zee-Hi. Zee-Hi. Zee-Hi.*

*"Let the little one through."*

*A long road opens up on either side of him, shining with water, lined with people. The low sky is slashed red and black. Flags flap like laundry on zigzagging lines above the street, off windowsills and bouncing poles, down the sides of immense buildings. Adolf Hitler, the stern man with the moustache like a thumbprint, is wrapped around lampposts, pasted onto brick walls, stuck onto windows, garlanded with flowers.*

*People lean out of windows and balconies, wave from rooftops. Church bells ring, discordant and joyful. A woman with a fat mole on her nose shoves a flag into his hand. His own flag. He shakes it and it flutters and snaps. Everyone shakes theirs back at him and he laughs.*

*Legs crisscross left and right, black and brown. Shoes and trousers. Socks and shorts. Skirts and boots. Guns and knives.*

*Zee-Hi. Zee-Hi. Zee-Hi.*

*Max closes his eyes and pokes out his tongue to catch a rain-*

*drop. He breathes in the metal taste of the rain and the coal smoke and feels his father's heavy hand on his shoulder. Voices rise in song to sweep around him and fill his chest with golden light. He swells. If he were to lift his arms he would float upward.*

*He opens his eyes. A troop of drummer boys approaches. Max knows what to do. He raises his right arm. His arms and legs pump high, high in the air for a few, long, glorious moments. The faces of strangers are full of joy. They love his marching. They love him.*

*Something has hold of his shirt, dragging him backward. Papa, of course. He whirls, expecting pride or amusement on his father's face, but there is only anger. Terrible anger. The air goes out of him.*

*Papa's eyes close briefly, then he hoists Max into his arms. Strong arms hold him close until he can breathe again. Papa whispers into his hair.*

*"I just wanted you to see. I didn't want—"*

*But the words wash away in the rain and the glorious singing, and it is from this new vantage point, in his father's arms, shuddering and breathless, tears and rain collecting at his chin, that he sees Adolf Hitler gliding through the crowd in an open-top car.*

*That was all it took. The city, the faces, the posters, the chants, the march, the flags, the rain—the steady, intoxicating rain. A door inside him had opened, and Adolf Hitler had climbed in. For almost ten years he had remained there.*

Max wakes to see the frowning faces of a German Maiden's League girl and an older woman. He is still at the station at Freilassing. The girl shines from top to bottom: braids, chin, buttons, shoes. Even her nose is a shining miniature ski jump. He nudges Hans, who straightens up, scratches his hair, and sneezes.

"How many nights have you been here?" the woman says. She has the cheeks of someone who has never said no to cheese. Max risks a glance at Hans and settles on a version of the truth.

"Only one," he says. "We were separated from our troop."

"You're headed where?"

"Stuttgart. To join the Volkssturm."

"What is that accent?" she says. They tell her and her eyebrows lift.

"*Saarfranzosen*! Bless me. What are two young Saarfrench doing so far from home?"

"Not French, German," says Hans. "Can't speak a word of French." And it's not much of an exaggeration. Max and Hans speak the Platt to each other, German to everyone else.

Hans explains the evacuation, the relocation, the camp, the march to Freilassing. "It was dark," he says. "There were people everywhere—"

"And you find yourselves lost—"

"We are trying to catch our troop—"

"Stuttgart, is it? And it is there that you will join the Volkssturm," she says. "And save us from the advancing armies?"

"Mother," says the girl.

"With a tin cup and a spoon?"

"Mother."

"We have our daggers," says Hans, and sneezes again.

"*Gesundheit*," the woman says. "Forgive me. With a tin cup and a spoon and your mighty daggers."

"Guns will be provided," says Hans. "And uniforms. We will annihilate the enemy and spit on their corpses." He is possibly overdoing it.

"I've heard about the uniforms," the woman says.

"Mother," says the girl. There is a crumb on her lower lip. A morsel of biscuit, perhaps. Max has an urge to lift it off with his fingertip and slip it onto his tongue. He would like to taste that sugariness and hold it against the roof of his mouth until it melts.

"Would I be right in thinking that Stuttgart is very much in the direction of Saarland?" says the woman.

"Is it?" says Hans, raising his eyebrows.

"Could be," says Max.

The woman's eyes roll north, but she proves a useful ally. Before the hour is out, she has refilled their water tanks, provided them with soup and bread, and found them a westbound supply train. She leads them around a guardrail and introduces them to a man in a People's Storm uniform beside a strafed freight car.

"These are the boys," she says. "They will work hard all the way to Ulm. I will see to the paperwork."

"Ulm?" he says. "I'd be surprised if this train gets as far as Traunstein." He levels his good eye on Max and Hans. The other is colourless—a ghastly white marble in his head.

For a moment Max is back in the doctor's office at the Adolf Hitler school with a tin full of horrified, lidless eyes.

"Traunstein will be an excellent start," she says. "Wait here."

The freight car is loaded with cement bags—some intact, others burst open. The one-eyed man orders them to rig a tarpaulin over the damaged metal roof.

"Once you get moving, tip the ruined ones off the side," he says. "We have enough of a fuel problem without carrying deadweight. Check before you tip—all manner of fools loitering beside the tracks these days."

He salutes and is gone.

"What about that eye?" says Max. "Why doesn't he cover it up?"

"Don't turn around," says Hans. "*Don't*. It's the chain dog from last night. Quick, take this."

Max reaches for the cement bag, but the weight is a shock, and hot threads of panic have weakened his limbs. He listens for the footfalls of the Feldgendarm but hears only the scrape of a stoker's shovel.

"You."

Max feels a loosening deep in his abdomen. He glances at Hans, and together they set down the bag and salute.

"What are you doing up there?" The guard sounds more curious than accusatory.

"Volkssturm orders, sir," says Hans.

"This train is about to leave."

"We are to travel with it and offload the damaged bags, sir," says Hans.

"Who gave this order? Where is your youth leader?"

"Lost our troop, sir," says Hans.

"Lost your *troop*."

"I got sick, sir," says Hans. "Ate something bad, had to find some-where to—to—" He mimes puking, staggering. He's overdoing it again. "Max here was helping me, then we couldn't find the other boys."

Is there a chance the story might hold? Because this man above all others knows exactly where a troop of boys disappeared to in the dead of night. He is the one who sent them there.

"When was this exactly?"

Hans looks to Max, his confidence crumbling.

"Who did you report to?" demands the officer.

"Uh," says Hans.

"Women's Welfare League." The woman is back, breathing hard. Her face is pink, and a row of sweat beads have popped up across her cheeks. The Feldgendarm regards her from top to bottom, lingering at the top.

"You know these two?"

"Of course. They have been assigned to clean up this mess and report to the People's Storm at Ulm."

"On whose authority?"

She hands him a slip of paper and glances at Max. A warning—but of what?

"And what will they do once they get to Ulm?" the officer says.

"That's Ulm's problem. From where I stand, it's two fewer heads to feed and water. Which reminds me—have you any updates on that supply train? We are scraping the bottom—"

The train whistle swallows her words, and the officer gives her a careful look.

The car jolts backward a metre. The woman looks ready to speak, then thinks better of it. Even Hans is biting his lip. If they insist on one thing, the Feldgendarm will be obliged to do the other. All three of them—the woman, Max, and Hans—become studies in indiffer-ence.

The car jolts again, this time forward. The guards are checking doors.

The chain dog returns the papers and doesn't seem to notice the tremor in Max's hand.

Voices rise farther down the platform to where half a dozen travellers are charging a passenger car and the guards surge to drive them off. The chain dog swivels to help, just as the train begins to crawl. The League woman hurries alongside.

"Report to the Welfare League the moment you arrive in Ulm. They might be able to help," she calls. She reaches into the basket slung over her elbow and tosses up a packet of milk biscuits. "Make yourselves an alcove in there. More rain coming. Be safe."

They call their thanks over the hiss of steam. She raises her hand. Thirty, forty metres beyond, the Feldgendarm straightens, and his eyes are on Max. He breaks into a jog. *What has he remembered?* Panic wraps itself around Max's throat.

Two sets of fingers appear on the doorframe. A woman is pulling herself along the wall of the freight car, scarf trailing from her neck, teeth bared. A heavy suitcase is jammed between her body and the wall. The chain dog sprints, roaring at her to get down.

Max lunges and grabs for the woman's arms. She cries out and her body jolts. The suitcase has pitched off to one side and she's trying to hold it with her knees.

"Let it go," shouts Max. Hans reaches across him, to help drag the woman on board. The chain dog has stopped running. The suitcase falls away, and the woman snatches at it. She keels back, lands heavily on her backside, and rolls, as the suitcase bounces once, twice, and bursts open. Inside, a huge grey doll is folded up, its stockinged knees bent up to its forehead.

Not a doll.

The train gathers speed, and he loses sight of the woman as she rolls onto her hands and knees and starts crawling toward her ghastly luggage.

Max falls back onto a pile of cement bags. The image of the dead child's face, grey and slack, is replaced with Charles's.

"I tried, Hans. I wasn't strong enough."

"Max."

"I couldn't hold on."

"*Max*," says Hans. "She let go."

Hans presses on his shoulders to sit him down out of the wind and starts lugging bags to create a wall. Max should help, but his body feels as if it has been opened up and filled with the contents of those bags.

"Come on," says Hans, and half lifts, half drags him into the windbreak he has created under an undamaged portion of roof. "Look at it. A veritable Paris Ritz without a breath of wind and invisible to prying eyes. Go on. You can say it. I'm brilliant."

Max can only nod. Hans is indeed brilliant. He shines, and Max would not have made it this far without him. They are on a train travelling west. Home. And now he sees Horst, surrounded by empty space where his friends should be. He might already have reached Frankfurt an der Oder, named by the Führer a *Festung*—fortress town—because it must block the Red Army's passage to Berlin. Can there be any hope for Horst? Can there be hope for any of them?

# 9

Heilbronn, Baden-Württemberg
March 1945

At five minutes before the hour, Marguerite takes a mahogany chair at a dining table that seats twenty but is set for four. The room is stifling and reeks of perfumed paper, but all the *Papier d'Armenie* in the world cannot disguise the faint but penetrating odour of dead animal. Under the floor, or in the walls.

A linen napkin is pleated into a fan on her plate—a tempting cushion for her throbbing forehead.

Anna pauses at the doorway, admiring the shining silver, the fine crystal glasses, and the fancy napkins. Does she notice the stale air? Probably not. She looks tired. The dress is hanging off her.

"Sit," says Marguerite.

Her daughter disappears behind an enormous crystal vase into which someone has shoved lengths of cherry branches dotted in bud. A wall clock marks out the seconds, each reluctant twang followed by a noisy click, while a minuscule praying mantis, a rebellious shade of green, rocks back and forth on a stem, its legs like bright blades of grass.

The Russian maid is fussing with the table setting at the head, using her apron to scrub at a mark on a fork. The clock sounds the first crashing note of the hour and the fork clatters onto the floor. Marguerite's head rings. The maid retrieves the fork. Her eyes are on the door. Again, the clock chimes. If the girl puts the soiled fork back on the table, Marguerite and Anna are witnesses to the offence. There is no time to fetch a replacement. The girl looks panicked.

The clock strikes a third time, and Anna is up, her own fork in hand. She presses it into the incomplete table setting, snatches the other from the maid and, before the sixth chime, is back in her chair. Marguerite leans sideways to see her daughter, the rescuer. Anna is studying her napkin but there is a boldness to her posture that makes Marguerite want to say, Careful how you go, Anna. Also, that's my girl.

Hinckel is at the door in uniform as ever, and though she has been expecting him, his presence sends a cold shock through her. She was mad to come here. The maid takes two steps in reverse. The clock clanks out the seconds, each sending more pain into Marguerite's skull.

"Liesl," Hinckel says to the maid. "I believe you have forgotten the wine." The girl's head drops and she clasps her hands together—the stance of a novice—and off she trots.

Hinckel takes off his cap, places it on the sideboard, and runs his fingertips across hair that requires no adjustment—it's parted with precision, scraped into submission. He's been at the mirror just now, she's sure of it, and she almost laughs. Then she thinks of Anton and his stubborn curls and collier's stripes, and could weep. By comparison, Hinckel is varnished—from his obedient hair and fresh-razored jaw down to the bright buttons and medals on his jacket, to the tall, black leather boots. Look at his belt, polished to a high shine and buckled more firmly than must be comfortable, but accentuating the length of the leg, the breadth of the shoulders. Hinckel settles into his chair, shakes his napkin across his lap, and appraises the table.

"All the opportunity to learn and still the Slavs fail to grasp the fundamentals," he says. "How very nice to meet you, Anna. Marguerite, Gunter tells me the drive was uneventful?"

Crisp footsteps approach from the hallway. This must be Hinckel's wife. Any hope that this woman might prove an ally blows out of the room as the woman sweeps in, palm pressed to a scrawny, heaving chest, dressed like a countrywoman in crisp, open-necked white shirt, a string of fat pearls, and forest-green wide-legged trousers. She takes Marguerite's fingertips.

"*Enchantée*," she says, in a breathless, childish voice. "Do forgive my tardiness. A dear sweet creature was dropped at the kitchen door in the dead of night—half-starved. I've been run off my feet."

"A child?" says Marguerite.

A flicker of unpleasantness passes over Lina Hinckel's face. "A pup," she says. "Precious little thing." The Bereichsleiter makes an expression of marital despair. His wife drops her chin, shakes her straw-coloured curls at her husband, and pushes out her bottom lip. She will be calling him Papa next. Marguerite shifts in her seat.

Three maids deliver miracles to the table. A stew with meat, roasted vegetables, potato gratin. Marguerite inhales. It takes every gram of strength not to dip her finger into the sauce.

"Does it have a name?" says Anna.

Marguerite leans around the vase. Anna is addressing Hinckel's wife.

"I beg your pardon?" says the older woman.

Anna clears her throat. "The pup. Does it have a name?"

"Not yet," says Lina Hinckel. "It is not clear that it will survive." She appraises Anna and the miserable dress, takes up her napkin, and gives Marguerite a bright smile.

"My husband tells me you are old friends, Mrs. Bernot. Let's hope you prove more reliable than the last girl."

"I have not been a girl for a very long time," says Marguerite, and I am not your husband's friend.

"That much is clear," says Lina Hinckel, and claps ringed fingers to her lips. "Oh, not that I meant— Only that—"

"Mrs. Bernot is of sturdier Saarland stock," Hinckel says to his wife, and tops up her wine. "She has offered you some French lessons, my dear."

Lina Hinckel tilts her head at Marguerite.

"How very sweet of you," she says in her baby voice. "Paris is my second-favourite city."

"I'm no teacher," says Marguerite. "But I— If you wanted to practise conversation or . . ." She trails off, at a loss. What could this woman possibly want to learn? How to order a glass of red and a *plat du jour*? She would be strung up with her husband before they made it ten steps into liberated France.

Lina Hinckel's laugh is a tumble of ice cubes in a glass.

"Don't be embarrassed, dear," she says. "High German is such a difficult language to master—particularly when one's own native tongue descends from vulgar Latin. I am sure we can learn a lot from each other, Marguerite. Are we to use first names? If we are to dine at the same table, then I suppose we must."

Has Anna registered the dig? She is running her finger across a stem of budded cherry as if it were dipped in gold.

"Is there a gardener here?" Anna says, almost to herself, then to Hinckel. It is the wife who replies.

"Gone," she says. "It has been a trial finding people to get the place up and running again. If they're trained, they're a hundred years old. If they are young, they are feeble-bodied or feeble-minded. Why, Anna? Are you offering to clip the lawns?"

"I noticed the greenhouse," says Anna.

"That's none of your affair," says Marguerite.

"Falling to pieces, I'm afraid," says Hinckel. "It must have been marvellous in its day. An air of the circus about it—all that metal and glass."

"I could clean it up," says Anna. "Is there an apothecary in the village? I could get some herbs going, mix some teas. Is there a kitchen garden? There must be."

"Resourceful, isn't she?" says Lina Hinckel to Marguerite, and takes up her wineglass. Those hands have never so much as deadheaded a rose, let alone scraped around in the dirt searching for tubers.

"Do you know something about plants, Anna?" says Hinckel.

"I do," says Anna, and fails to contain a smile. Hell reserves a special punishment for pride, Daughter. "I led the Lauterbach BDM foraging group and earned a medal for my herbal tea collection. It wasn't so easy in Elversberg, where I didn't know the forest and the weather was so dreadful, but the apothecary was grateful for what I could offer him—"

"Anna," says Marguerite.

"I'm going to share a secret with you, Anna," Hinckel says, resting his forearms on the table and his eyes on her daughter. "I prefer coffee to tea."

"But the Führer says caffeine is—"

"He does indeed," says Hinckel. "But there are worse toxins, and I have received this morning a small but fresh supply of coffee."

"Perhaps I can convert you," says Anna. "Mother, tell him about my chicory root tea." At last she looks to Marguerite. The smile falls from her face.

"I will most certainly try it," says Karl Hinckel.

"I hear that you and your mother have experience with potatoes, dear," says Lina Hinckel. "I do enjoy a new potato."

How does Lina Hinckel know about the potato fields? What was it Marguerite had said to Hinckel in the car at Neunkirchen? *I grow potatoes.* Have they already made fun of her, the peasant toiling in the field? Is this how he mitigates the affront of bringing another woman to her table? Two, if she counts Anna, who insists she is not a child.

"It takes nearly three months to grow potatoes," says Marguerite. By then, the war will be over, the Nazis finished.

"You ladies are the experts," says Hinckel. "The cook has been rather spoiled by the deliveries from our friends at the Ministry, but your idea is a sound one, Anna. Consider yourself hired. And so, *bon appétit.*"

He raises his glass, takes a slug of wine, and eats. Are they out of their minds? The Russians are nearing the Oder in the east. The Western Allies are pressing in from the south and west. Germany is on the brink of collapse, and Anna wants to make tea, Lina Hinckel wants French lessons, and Karl Hinckel—what does he want?

Marguerite cuts a piece of meat, places it in her mouth and, yes, it is overcooked and oversalted—but it is all she can do to stop herself from groaning out loud.

*Bon appétit, Marguerite.* In France, high-born families never say *bon appétit* because civilised people dine simply for pleasure. Only beasts are slaves to their appetites. And here is the truth of it: We are all beasts in the end. We do what we need to survive.

A quieter, deeper part of her cries out for her husband. Is he still fighting a hopeless war? Is he injured, a prisoner of war, or dead? And where is Max? Where have they taken her son? Is he at a table somewhere dining on fresh meat and potatoes, laughing at something Hans has said? Or is he sprawled in a ditch, frozen, broken—

The mantis makes its slow passage along the length of a branch. Nothing for you out there, poor shortsighted creature. Just a precipice hovering over a sea of knives.

Later that evening, she crosses Lina Hinckel in the downstairs hallway. The other woman thrusts out her bony arm to block Marguerite in a cloud of stale rose.

"I am not the only one in this house who collects strays," the woman says. Where is the baby voice now? Gone, gone, gone. The eyes are brittle with malice, a stick arm blocks Marguerite's passage. Marguerite shifts to her left. The other woman shifts with her.

"I did not ask to come here," Marguerite says.

Lina Hinckel's lip twists.

"The difference between my husband and me is that he has not a gram of sentimentality," she says. "You will soon enough be back out on the street or wherever he found you. You and your *hure* daughter."

Marguerite itches to smack the smile from that gutter mouth. Instead, she steps in close to the other woman, taking satisfaction in standing a good fifteen centimetres taller.

"Look how scared you are," she says. "And you are right to be."

The other woman pauses, a barely perceptible recoil, and Marguerite is certain she has hit a nerve.

# 10

The train rattles west and the wind snaps and nips at Max and Hans while they construct themselves an alcove with bags of cement. When they are done, Max dusts parched hands on his coat pockets and pulls his grandfather's map from his pack. This is the map he and Anna used to lay out on the living room floor, marking troop movements with tiny flags. Now Hans helps him spread it out on the floor of the alcove, taking care not to tear the creases.

Their route across southern Germany will be at least five hundred kilometres. If they can stay on this train until Ulm—if the train has not been derailed or strafed or commandeered, and if they have not been arrested or shot—they will be more than halfway home.

"Three days, four at most," says Hans, and brushes his hands together as if that's all there is to it.

If Hans does not make it home, it will be Max's fault, and Max may not be able to bear that.

Hans casts him a look. "What?" he says.

"Nothing."

"Max, tell me. What is it?"

"Just thinking about home."

"There's a dangerous thought."

"Will there have been much shelling in Lauterbach, do you think?"

"Hard to say."

65

"Because I worry."

"I know."

The unsettling words of Mrs. Giesel's strange visitor return to him. Another city flattened, she had said. *It's revenge for what we have done to the Jews.*

"I worry that Lauterbach has gone the way of Ulm, and Pforzheim, of Munich," says Max.

"I see what you're saying, and I'm no general," says Hans. "But if you're the German armies and you've got a decent river, which is the Saar, and all the forts and bunkers and cannons of the Westwall to shelter in, why would you put up a fight in the streets of Lauterbach, nose to nose with your enemy?"

"I've thought about that," says Max. "So the risk runs more the other way, doesn't it? That it will be German guns that destroy Lauterbach when the Allies come through."

"It does seem that way."

"I'm trying to calculate how much hope I should allow myself," says Max.

"Well, let's say every second house in Lauterbach is blown to pieces, which is about as bad as it could get—"

"I'm not sure bombs work like that."

"General picture," says Hans. "So odds are that either your house or mine will be standing."

"Fifty-fifty is what you are saying."

"Fifty-fifty. Yours or mine."

Max feels about in his pocket for the silver coin and sees his godfather.

*Take it with your eyes this time. Your hand will follow.*

"Heads it's your house standing," says Max. "Tails it's mine."

The coin spins and Max traps it on the back of his left, then lifts his right. Hans winces.

"Looks like you'll be sharing with Anna and me," Max says.

"She's got a fierce side, your sister."

"Only because she likes you," says Max.

Hans clouts him, then looks intrigued. "Does she now?"

"Not like *that*. She just hates you less than she hates the others. You'd have more of a chance with Hedy Lamarr," says Max.

Hans pats his top pocket where the actress's photograph sits over his heart.

"My Hedy. When she meets me, there will be a lightning bolt, a thunderclap. She will be powerless to resist."

"Shame there will be nothing left of her but a scorched hat and a lipstick case," says Max.

Hans laughs at that, thinks about it, and laughs again.

The sickening, heavy fear lifts. Max folds the coin back into the cotton of his godfather's handkerchief and knots it. He feels Hans watching him.

"Are you ever going to tell me what happened the day he died?" says Hans.

"You know what happened." The memories flicker: Argos bolting through the garden, Charles dragging himself back to his feet, the terrible crack of bone, the bloom of blood on his godfather's shirt.

"I know what they did to Charles, but something else happened. I know *you*, Max. I've known you more than half my life. Why won't you trust me?"

"Thirteen years isn't much of a life, is it?"

"Max."

"Leave it, Hans."

The doctor hisses at him across the years. *Coward.*

At Traunstein there is a long stop to wait for coal. The rain is drilling sideways, so they decide to stay hidden in their recess, prepared to feign sleep if the guards are inclined to brave the weather and search every car. At previous stops, hauling cement bags and appearing busy has helped them through the inspections. That, and the slip of paper the woman gave them at Freilassing. But the temperature is falling with every hour, and the rain only makes it worse, and cement has worked its way into Max's blisters, searing his flesh. It doesn't take much to convince Hans that they should stay hidden for this stop. He only wishes they had some food.

To distract himself from the hunger, he digs out the envelope of postcards he had collected on his way to the KLV camp in February. The first he had bought was at Karlsruhe, where a newspaper vendor stood with a box cart beneath the ruins of the train station. Six post-cards were fanned out beside the stack of newspapers—the top one a Baroque palace fronted with tree-lined carriage ways, formal gardens, smaller trees in planter boxes, ornate streetlamps, and a statue of a bearded man at the centre of it.

"It's historical, that," the vendor had said. "Nothing much left of the *Schloss.*"

Max had reached for it, but the vendor growled a warning.

"Two pfennigs."

"I wanted to see when the photograph was taken," said Max.

"One for a look, two to have and hold from this day forward," the vendor said.

Max did not want to waste two precious pfennigs on such a trifling luxury, but he pressed the coins into the vendor's hands.

*Das Karlsruhe Schloss. Photographed in 1937*, the photograph read. Max counted the chimneys and the windows, the number of trees clipped into neat cones. In the nearest corner he made out a child crouched next to a lump that might be a dog. He stared into the photograph and found that the child's clothing had turned a bright shade of yellow, the sky was now the deep blue of late afternoon, and he could feel the softness of the grass underfoot. All the while, at his shoulder, the skeleton walls and empty windows of the ruined city rolled past.

After that, he searched for a postcard at every stop. At Pforzheim and Stuttgart, Ulm and Augsburg. And during those dreary weeks at the relocation camp, when he was not marching or cleaning or hiking or listening to Gruber's dreary readings of *Mein Kampf*, he would take out the cards and place himself in these untouched places.

*       *       *

Now, he draws out an image of a chalet in the forest, snow layered on its roof and a pair of skis leaning against the carved timber balustrades. This was what he had imagined the day the teacher Weck told them their relocation camp would be in the mountains. So much for imaginings.

He writes his mother's name and address at the old woman's house in Elversberg, taps the pencil against his bottom lip. What might Mama and Anna be doing now? Are they in a bomb shelter, feeling the rumble of American tanks pass overhead? Poor Anna. As far as she was concerned, Germany was impenetrable, even when the National Radio reported foreign troops closing in. The Allies would be not just turned back but destroyed. Germany would never fall. She carried her certainty like a crown. One day soon, she will see for herself those foreign soldiers on German soil, and what will happen then?

He writes.

> *Dear Mama and Anna,*
> *I was at this place.*
> *With all my love,*
> *Max*

He puts the postcard away and takes up his notebook.

*Vachendorf, Übersee, Bernau am Chiemsee.* He challenges Hans with jet fighter facts, the weights of bombs, the calibre of rifles, the features of German and enemy tanks. They invent a memory game out of objects abandoned beside the tracks—items once thought essential, and later, when the weight became too much, expendable. Violin case, bag of books, cradle, brown slipper, broken perambulator, hat box.

He writes *Prien am Chiemsee, Bad Endorf, Stephanskirchen, Clarenheim.* The train passes a group of women unhitching a wagon from a dead ox, a flock of geese driven by a boy and a three-legged dog, a doomsday warning in thick black paint.

The homesickness and hunger are a constant drag on his insides, but the deepest source of the dread churning inside him is the fear of what will happen when they are caught. Because they will be caught. It is a miracle each time they pass through a station unchallenged. They cannot stop now, not until he is home. Not until he looks into the eyes of his mother and sister and says what must be said. And when he thinks of home, what does he see? Foreign tanks and troop carriers. Mortar fire and flame. Mountains of cold rubble and broken glass.

He relieves himself from the train car and is about to return to the alcove when the train passes a dozen or more emaciated labourers in prison stripes blinking up at him. They remind him of the Russian prisoners at Lauterbach trudging to and from the mines and the iron-works. He glimpses familiar faces in the rain-soaked refugees trudging west. His mother, his sister, his father. And Charles. Always Charles.

He climbs back under his blanket and tarpaulin, takes the damp notebook, and writes *Lochhausen, Gröbenzell, Olching, Hattenhofen.*

Hans sleeps, and rain batters the damaged roof and slaps the tarpaulin. Max passes the time by estimating the volume of the alcove they have constructed from the cement bags. He had excelled at People's Arithmetic. *If it costs eight marks a day to feed and house a family of useless eaters, and there are four such families in a small German town, how much does the town spend per day, per week, per month on useless eaters?* The teacher, Mr. Baumstark, had a particular interest in the French exploitation of the Saar. *Between 1919 and 1935, more than two hundred million tonnes of German coal were taken by France, one hundred and fifty-seven million tonnes of which came from the Saar. If a single coal wagon can carry ten tonnes of coal, how many wagons of coal were confiscated per year, per month, per day?*

The rain drums and drips around them. They pass through another dead city of rubble mountains and widow walls. The sirens are howling when the train pulls into the damp ruins of a station. An inspector leads them to a shelter where they wait out the distant explosions. They learn they are in Ulm. They might be anywhere. The rain and hunger and fatigue have clouded Max's thinking. He has stopped writing in his notebook, has lost track of where they are. He has lost track of time.

A checkpoint has been set up at the station entrance just beyond an emergency kitchen. Local police question everyone attempting to enter the station, while two more senior men, one in party uniform, the other in the grey-green of the Waffen SS, stand to one side, smoking cigarettes, scanning their faces. Who are they looking for? The smell of cooked onion sends a flood of saliva into Max's mouth, but joining the queue for food risks attracting police attention. He pats his coat pocket—the travel permit is still there. Is it genuine? He is not inclined to test it here. Max locks eyes with Hans and he agrees. They saunter back to the freight car. They have every right to do this. The paper in Max's pocket says so, but still, his heart canters. He throws his rucksack into the freight car, leaps up, and reaches back to pull in Hans.

"Halt."

A train guard hails them. Who are they? What are they doing? Where are they going?

"Stuttgart is no village," the guard sneers, when they have told their story and handed over their papers. He eyes their filthy uniforms. Cement dust has mingled with rain to coat them in streaks of grey mud. Hans has a stripe of it across one cheek and all through the hair he is forever pushing off his forehead. "How do you intend to find your troop?"

"Train station, sir," says Hans.

"Is that so?" says the guard. "From what I hear, there is a crater where the Stuttgart station once stood."

He marches them to the checkpoint—not to the police, but to the senior men. The party official frowns at Max's and Hans's handwritten travel permit.

"The Volkssturm has no authority over *Jungvolk*," he says. He crushes the document in his fist, and lets it fall into the slush.

# 11

Heilbronn, Baden-Württemberg
March 1945

Bookshelves grin, toothless here and there, from the library that serves as Karl Hinckel's office. The previous owner, it seems, had a taste in literature that did not sit well with the Reich.

The job is real enough. Answer the telephone when the line is working. Organise files when there is paperwork to organise. Type letters. Order the maids to make coffee if there are visitors: real coffee for high-ranked officers, ersatz or herbal tea for the rest.

Hinckel tears open his own hand-delivered messages and telegrams with a silver eagle–embossed paper knife he keeps in his top drawer. He passes most of them directly to her for filing in the metal cabinet of hanging files beside his desk, or for typing a response. Only twice has she seen him place a document in the safe under his desk. God alone knows the horror of the secrets he keeps there, because the correspondence he *allows* her to handle catalogues the staggering and faltering of the Third Reich in its death throes.

The Westwall holds but with heavy losses. Catastrophic airstrikes continue on western defences. Another city has been levelled. Another airstrike on fuel stocks, weapons stores, airplane factories. Another failed Luftwaffe mission. Paralysing shortages—of coal and food and men, fuel, rifles, tank, wheat, meat, coffins, amphetamine, potatoes, ammunition. And into the void, new excesses. Plagues of rats and flies.

Outbreaks of dysentery and typhoid. Floods of refugees. Deserters. Defeatists. Looters.

What does Hinckel think when he reads the latest dispatches? He dictates terse replies, his features sickly in the wash of the emerald glass desk lamp. Here is a man who knows how to compose his face.

That first morning she had listened to his briefing in all its scrupulous detail and waited until he looked up at her.

"I will do it all and do it well," she said.

"And so?"

"And so, are you going to help me find my son?"

"Your son?" He had cocked his head at her.

She fought to keep her face neutral.

"This small matter," she says. "This small matter of my son is dear to me, Bereichsleiter. It is dear to my heart. For someone with the connections you have, it would require not a great investment of time: a letter, a phone call when the line is running. If you think a letter might do it, I will type it for you and hand it to the messenger myself— I fail to see what amuses you."

Karl Hinckel was holding up his hands in mock horror.

"Stop! Stop it, please. For pity's sake, Marguerite. Have you lost your sense of humour too? I am teasing. Of course I have not forgotten. Even as you stand here meek as a lamb, the wheels are turning." His index finger traced a circle in the air.

She should have felt relief, but her instinct was to mistrust him.

"You have made enquiries already? You have news?"

"Patience, Marguerite," he said, and took up his pen. She remained where she stood.

"What I am doing here?" she said, and gestured at it all—the typewriter, the files, the pens and pencils and stamps. "What do you want from me?" And now that the words were released, she was afraid of his answer.

He pushed back his chair, stepped around the desk, and set himself in front of her. Her heart threw itself against its cage, but she matched his stare.

He took her chin between his finger and thumb, lifted it, jerked her face from side to side, appraising her as if she were a table vase—interesting in some minor way, but of little value. "Exactly what I tell you to do, Marguerite."

Dread slid into her belly, heavy and dark, and she did not look away, because if this is what it would take to bring Max back, to get him to safety, then so be it. Women had done worse to keep their children safe.

A smile cut up one side of his face and he released her.

"You are not the woman you once were. Your daughter, on the other hand—there is a filly who'll buck."

She raised her hand to strike him, but he caught her forearm. She reached for his ear with the other, intending to rip it off, but he was stronger. Now both her arms were trapped in his grip.

He laughed, and she lifted her foot to slam it into his shins, but he released her arms and shoved her back with so much force she was in the air for a moment before her back hit the floor. As she lay there, winded, his boot appeared next to her face, reeking of nugget. *The front is coming and still he shines his shoes,* she thought, even though the pain was sending tears to her eyes. The boot drew back and she braced for the kick. She felt only a gentle tap against her shoulder.

"*Au travaille,* Marguerite," he said. Back to work.

She felt a breeze as he passed, the hush of his boots on the rug. The library door opened. She panted thimblefuls of air and rolled onto her belly. She understood in that moment that if she could not find a way to get Anna away from this place, she would have to kill him.

She is permitted to walk in the garden and takes every opportunity to scout the boundaries of her prison. There are armed men all over the property. The chauffeur never strays far from Hinckel; the remaining six patrol the gate and grounds.

When she walks, one or two men break off to tail her. Are they grateful for this dreary watch? She has the sense they are bored out of their minds. Do they dream of manning the guns, riding a tank into battle? Given that all are young and fit for service, the only explanation for their presence here is that they are under Hinckel's protection—the sons of important men.

Still, the guards' boredom is a gift because it blinds them. They think she is a woman entranced by nature, fascinated by a splash of moss on a rock while she is assessing the strength of a branch that overhangs the stone boundary fence, mapping the possible footholds in a crumbling section of wall. They allow sufficient distance to fall between them that, if she wanted, she could scale that wall and disappear into the woods.

But why should they bother pursuing her? They know where her daughter is, where she always is.

Marguerite taps on the greenhouse door. How quickly it has become Anna's domain. She pulls open the door and winces at the screech.

"Those hinges could do with some oil," she says.

"Tomorrow's job."

"You've been busy."

Anna is kneeling on the floor unravelling the tendrils of a root-bound shrub. She blows a lock of hair off her face. A smear of mud runs across her chin.

"I'll only be a minute."

"Don't stop on my account. I was just wandering."

The stained glass detailing in the dome recalls the famous art nouveau Metro entrances in Paris. Green grapevines run in asymmetrical circles, sprinkled with leaves in all the colours of autumn.

The first time she followed Anna in here it was shambolic: tipped and broken pots, shards of glass, overgrown vines, and every unbroken pane of glass covered in mould or moss. Now some of the smaller breaks are patched and taped, and Anna has found an old door to lean against the largest missing pane. She's scrubbed the glass on the south-facing wall to bring sunlight to the seedlings. Six trays are already lined up on a bench cleared of debris. It is all becoming quite glorious.

Anna holds out an earthenware bowl filled with bright rose hips.

"What a find," says Marguerite.

"I should offer them to the apothecary," says Anna.

"I'm not sure there is one."

"There's always an apothecary. I'll speak to the caretaker. He's been finding all sorts of things for me," says Anna. Her eyes settle back on the rose hips. "Shall we keep a few? They'll make such a lovely tisane." Her bright smile sends a ripple through Marguerite's heart. Wake up, Daughter.

"Sounds fair."

"The gardeners knew what they were doing. All the seeds are in individual jars, labelled and dated," says Anna. "There is German mint, German chamomile, German sage—"

"German pineapple?"

"Please don't."

Anna has grown up with the slogan *Blut und Boden*. Blood and soil. The secret to good health lies in a diet of pure German food cultivated by pure Germans in pure German soil. The same rules apply to medicine. Germans should not hanker for modern medicine produced by Jewish pharmacists in foreign places from suspect ingredients. Only pure and natural German medicines will do—manufactured by German apothecaries from German plants and herbs foraged by German children. Outside the Reich, every tree, every flower, every blade of grass and spike of wheat that grows is inferior, contaminated in some way. When really, the only thing contaminated is her daughter's mind.

Around and around she explores the escape routes. Each time she comes back to the same barricade: Max. If Karl Hinckel really is trying to find him, could bring him to her, how can she leave?

She scans every document that passes her desk for information that might lead her to Max. A KLV camp is strafed—could it be his? Another is abandoned after typhus takes hold—is it Max's? Three boys blow themselves to pieces climbing over an unexploded bomb. A boy is incinerated after throwing gunpowder sticks onto a campfire. The face she sees every time is Max's.

She has pieced together the facts about the 12th SS Panzer Division of twenty thousand youth sent to Normandy in June and lauded for their fanatical bravery. Just six hundred of twenty thousand boys survived the first six months. The story that stands out is a one-sentence report about a group of five who were executed as they attempted to surrender to the enemy. The inference was clear—their own comrades had shot them in the back.

An army of children, Charles had said. Children can be cruel enough, but steeped in hate and separated from the moderating influence of parents and priests, who knows what horrors they are capable of? God protect Max and Hans and keep them safe. They will look after each other. Their friendship is uncommonly deep. Neighbours had warned her against Hans, brought up the tragic circumstances of the father's death and the mother's rumoured weaknesses. But how was any of that the boy's fault? He is impulsive, boisterous, sometimes idiotic, but there is no questioning his bond with her son. They fit like lid and jar. Stronger together than either could ever be alone. And if they were ever to be separated?

It does not bear thinking about.

If only she had the name of a village, the number of the KLV camp, an address to search for. What she would give to receive a letter from Max. But the post has stopped, and while a powerful Nazi has messengers coming and going all day long, who would run messages from a children's camp in the mountains?

# 12

Ulm to Schwäbisch Hall, Baden-Württemberg
March 1945

The rejected travel permit sinks into the slush while the party official scans Max's and Hans's identity papers. The guard who detained them remains at their side. Worse, the SS officer has sauntered over to listen in. Without looking up, the party man orders them to repeat their story.

There had been many hours on the train to decide what they would say in this situation, and they *had* decided, but Hans is nervy, and when he's nervy he chatters. He's doing it now—embellishing, exaggerating.

The official takes a long draw on his cigarette and lets the butt drop, just a few centimetres from where the travel permit lies. He releases the smoke in a stream levelled at Hans's middle coat button and lifts his eyes.

"Stop talking, please. Your accent is making my ears bleed." He turns his attention to the papers. " 'Hans-Peter Schlesier and Maximilian Bernot,' " he reads. "Two little Saarfranzosen far, far from home. I will speak very slowly so that you might understand me."

Thick flakes of dandruff are visible in the oily black hair between the official's hat and the tops of his ears. It's not difficult to scrub your scalp clean with the ends of your fingers. Max might have been four or five when his father showed him how to do it properly. And here this man stands with his medals and his badges but he does not know how to wash his hair.

The official turns to the SS man and lifts his hands. "You see what I have to deal with? Imbeciles and miscreants everywhere. Understandable that the Führer wanted the mines and the mills, but did we really want these half-breeds poisoning the water?"

"We both speak German," says Max. It is not safe to be angry with men such as these, but he remembers the speech his mother taught him all those years ago, proving his Germanness, ignoring his French blood, pretending to be one thing when he was—when he *is*—both.

The official laughs but the SS man talks over him.

"If I might interrupt." It is not a question.

"Of course, Herr Kriminalrat," says the official. Max feels Hans straighten. A Kriminalrat is a detective with the Kripo, the Kriminalpolizei. The worst kind of SS.

"You said you 'received word' that your troop had gone ahead," says the detective to Hans. "From whom?"

"I—" says Max. The unhurried gaze of the Kriminalrat switches to him.

"I?" says the official, mimicking Max's tremulous voice. "Where is this perfect German I am hearing about."

Max digs the nails of his thumbs into his index fingers to steady himself.

"I asked a train guard, sir," he says, trying to keep his voice level. "He advised that the train that had just left was indeed westbound for Stuttgart."

"Your troop leader and teacher left word with this guard?"

"Not specifically but he was fairly certain—"

A shout reaches them from beyond the checkpoint, a blast of gunfire. A group of BDM girls who have joined the queue are spinning around, craning to see something outside Max's line of vision.

A crash explodes behind him. He whirls, but it's just the train engine releasing steam. The remaining train guards are spacing themselves along the platform, trying to see where the shots came from.

"*Fairly certain?*" says the detective.

"It was dark, sir," says Hans. "The station was overrun. The authorities had their hands full with the migrants trying to storm the trains. We didn't want to get in the way—we just want to get to Stuttgart and rejoin our troop."

"An inexplicable destination, given your location. Why not send you north?"

"The orders changed several times. To start, we were supposed to catch a train from Tittmoning—"

"Whatever the orders were, you weren't following them, were you?" says the detective. "You were hiding in a toilet."

"I was terribly sick, sir—" Hans raises his eyebrows and begins to confabulate, but Max is back in that toilet at school in Ludweiler, puzzling over the contamination of his blood, the flaws in his character, his future marked out with failure from the moment of his birth. The doctor was right. Why keep fighting the tide?

"You don't look sick now," the detective is saying to Hans. "Although there's a smell about you, it's true. A whiff of something sweet. Something like Eidelweiss."

Max freezes. The Eidelweiss Pirates are a notorious youth organisation that have stepped up its anti-establishment activities since the advance of the Allied troops. A few months earlier, six Pirates, all boys aged sixteen to eighteen, were hanged publicly in Cologne, part of a group of thirteen accused of murder and terrorist plots.

"Whereas this one," says the Kriminalrat, indicating Max. "If you told me *he* had been retching into a latrine all night, I might believe you. Are you going to fall over, boy?"

Max hears steps approaching and cringes, anticipating more gunshots, a blow from behind.

"Herr Kriminalrat." It's a saluting police officer, breathless and gleeful. "We've got them. One of the lads recognised them from the photograph. They tried to run but we've got them both."

"Alive?" says the detective. The officer shrugs.

"Mostly."

"Go," says the party man. "I can manage a couple of lost Pimpfe." The detective draws in his cheeks, examines Max and Hans again, and follows the officer. The guard who detained them steps forward to address the official.

"Sir, I believe these boys to be runaways."

The official lifts a hand to silence him. "And if they were, what use would they be? One's about to shit himself. The other suffers from verbal diarrhea—"

"If you would—"

"Return to your station."

The official reaches into his chest pocket and shakes a cigarette out of his pack while he watches the guard march back to the platform. The train is moving off. Max feels a pang of loss for their cement bags, their alcove.

Hans opens his mouth to speak.

"Ah, ah," the man says, raising his cigarette in warning. "Not another fucking word. Or I will call him back and let him decide what to do with you. Understood?"

The pair opposite them might be sisters. Aged ten or eleven. One has an angry bruise on her cheek. She notices Max and lets her hair fall over her face. Bald fields roll out either side of the train and a coil of smoke twines from a farmhouse. Max checks his compass.

"Northwest," he says.

The party official has put them in a passenger car with about thirty BDM girls who have been moved from a bombed KLV camp.

"Why don't they just tell us where we're going?" mutters Hans.

"We should be grateful it's not the front."

"How do you know it's not the front?"

"They don't send girls to the front." The girls opposite—in fact, all the girls in the carriage—are subdued. Some are sleeping already, most rock silently with the movement of the train.

"Maybe that's the last laugh—sending the Saarland boys to the front with a bunch of girls."

"You shouldn't have annoyed him."

"You shouldn't have shit yourself." Hans laughs and Max shoves him with his shoulder, checking the faces of the girls opposite. One is sleeping, the other's head is rested against the glass, staring out at empty fields.

"Anyway," says Hans. "I can see your sister at the front. She could do with one look what a hundred boys could do with a grenade launcher."

Max laughs, shakes his head, and laughs again, because it's probably true. "She ordered a mouse out of the kitchen once, and it obeyed."

"The mouse?"

"My aunt was squealing and trying to get up on a chair when Anna jumped up, opened the back door, and started shouting at it. 'Get out of here. *Out.*' I remember it was winter and all the freezing air was coming in, and my aunt was panicking and Mama was telling Anna to close the door, but Anna just kept yelling at the mouse: 'Go on. Get outside. Mice belong outside, not inside.' And it went. It actually ran outside. I suppose it was easier to freeze to death than stay there listening to her."

Hans is laughing. "Who needs the super weapons?" he says. "Who needs jets and rockets when we could launch Anna Bernot of Lauterbach? What we need is a loud hailer the size of Saarland and—"

"Russians running left, English running right."

"Americans turning the tanks around—"

"Forget the tanks—run for your lives."

Still laughing, Max reaches into his chest pocket and brings out a photograph of his family. This is not a posed image taken by a professional photographer with his mother touching her hat or his father out of sorts in his Sunday suit. It was taken in the potato field before the war. The women are in old dresses and headscarves, the men in work trousers and shirtsleeves. Hot, dusty, dirty, they are without question *themselves*. He and Anna and Little Josef are in front, squinting into the camera, nursing giant cups of milky coffee, the filthy soles of their boots facing the camera. Aunt Cécile is laughing and Mama looks pleased. Has she made a joke? Papa and Uncle Josef are side by side, same hand on same hip, looking more like brothers than they ever did in the flesh.

If he had a magnifying glass, Max might see his godfather reflected in his own eyes, because Charles was the one holding the camera. This is what he liked to do, capture these special moments, even if it meant dirtying his city shoes. What would he think if he could see Max now? If he had seen what Max was doing as the two black Mercedes rolled down the long hill through the Warndt wood to Lauterbach the night Charles came back.

"Go, Max," his mother had said. "You have to go now."

"You have a big family." Hans is leaning against his shoulder, looking at the photograph.

"You never talk about yours," says Max. "You must have grandparents, cousins . . ."

"My mother's mother is in Homburg, and I have an aunt there but I don't remember her," says Hans. "My father didn't see his family after he moved to Saarland."

Max checks Hans's face. He has never revealed what Luscher said about Hans's father the night Charles died. Nor has he questioned the story Hans told him once about his father being killed by a lion—though even at the time he considered it unlikely.

"About that lion attack," Max says.

Hans meets his eye.

"Are you sure you want to know, Max?" he says at last. Max senses that there is no right answer to this question, but Hans is talking again, quietly so the girls cannot hear. "Are you sure you want to know what he did to himself? What he did to us? How we found him with his head blown all over the firewood it had taken me two days to stack?"

Max reaches for the right words, but nothing comes, so he rests his eyes on the passing fields and tries to quiet his chattering heart. After a time he says, "I quite liked the lion story."

Hans snorts and shakes his head. "He used to wake up thrashing and screaming and thinking he was in a trench somewhere, then he'd stop speaking for days and stay in his bed, and if you tried to talk to him—"

Hans stands abruptly, pushes past him, and strides to the rear of the car. Max follows him out onto the gangway.

"I'm sorry," says Max. "I shouldn't have—"

"He was a *coward*," Hans shouts over the wind and the clatter of wheels on track. "He abandoned us. The priest wouldn't say Mass. My mother— It changed her. It changed her forever."

"Hans."

"Why couldn't he stand up, Max? Why couldn't he brave it out and get better and stay with us?"

Max sees his own father in his miner's jacket and helmet, reaching for the briquet, the metal tin containing bread and cheese to be carried deep into the mine for his morning break. His mother never released the tin until his father had kissed her. "Bring it back, Anton," she would say, her eyes holding his. Papa would place his palm on her ear and kiss her again. His father was a giant. An oak. Impossible to imagine him turning a gun on himself. Impossible to imagine him dead.

Dusk descends, the sisters sleep, and the train crawls into fog. It feels as if they are knocking their way through the ribs of a colossal white beast. An oval of condensation on the glass grows and shrinks with each breath. He draws a series of lines into it: a gallows, a stick figure of a man suspended from the rope. Using his little finger, he draws a short horizontal line above the man's mouth, then wipes the image away.

Through the cleared glass, an immense silhouette appears. The train rocks closer and the shapes begin to make sense. Snapped girders strain upward into the grey, as if grasping for their missing roof.

The engine screams its dying blast, and Max follows Hans onto the raked-over shingle of a temporary station platform. Beyond the murmuring of the girls spilling out of the train and the crunch of their boots on the stones, a rhythmic pounding rises from his left. He blinks into the gloom, eyes stinging. *There.* Haloed in the light of a swinging lamp, a row of marionettes emerges. Prison rags hang heavy on bony arms, stick legs. One man is bent in half with the weight of another across his shoulders. The carried man's arms drape like lengths of rope.

How is it possible that those fleshless legs are supporting a second human being? But they do, and continue to, step after step.

SS guards harry the prisoners with rifles. Between the lines, Max makes out a woman carrying a basket. A ripple runs through the lines of prisoners. Hands reach and pull and pass. The men press something into their mouths, eating with the noises children make—low grunts of pleasure.

"Thank you, madame," one man calls, his voice hoarse. "God bless you."

One prisoner glances his way, and there is a line to his jaw that recalls Charles, darkness where his cheeks should be. Lidless eyes stare hatred at him.

*Nice watch*, says the man who is not Charles. His smile is a black hole.

*"Mama, I would like a wristwatch."*

*The kitchen smelled like summer. His mother was pouring plum preserves. Max reached for a jar, and she flicked his hand with the tea towel.*

*"Hot."*

*He snatched back his hand. She placed the wide funnel into the jar and lifted the ladle. Steaming crescents of yellow slopped inside. She crouched to bring her eyes level with the rim and trickled in the syrup until it was at just the right level.*

*"Jòò?" she said. "Wristwatch, is it? What will it be next? A diamond ring and a tuxedo by order of the young prince?" She ran the cloth around the rim. The jam pan blipped.*

*He was ten. His mother knew nothing about the young war hero visiting Max's school who—at only nineteen—was already wearing a tank destruction badge.*

*"Blind, halt, destroy," the soldier had said. "Any one of you could do it. But you have to be cunning, and you have to be fast. It's no game for old men."*

*When he saluted, his sleeve had pulled back to reveal a wristwatch.*

*"I would look after it well," Max said to his mother, "and wear it every day to school and to Jungvolk meetings." He waited until she met his eye. "Like all the other boys."*

*Mama set the ladle down. Hot syrup spilled into a molten puddle.*

*"I would not want to stand out, Mama," he said. "As being different." The lie set itself in the air like a sticky, swollen horse-fly, and the syrup continued to spread.*

*Without waiting for an answer, he took himself outside and called Argos. He scruffed the dog's muzzle and sighed, surprised to discover he had been holding his breath. She would buy him a watch. He was sure of it. He should be happy. He was happy, but he was also gripped by a sickening feeling. As if he had eaten something dirty.*

And now the prisoner's face is clearly not Charles at all. Whatever injustice this stranger accuses Max of, he is mistaken. Max is no part of the misfortune, the misuse that this man has suffered, and though it is foolish, he wants this fact acknowledged. But the prisoner is staring at the heels of the man ahead. Who knows what crimes he has committed? What acts of savagery? He is a prisoner, after all.

Charles's hollow face returns to Max, hair full of lice, filthy clothes, the sole of his shoe flapping loose. What was his godfather's crime? Escaping from a labour camp. Carrying Jews across the border.

*They are working people to death. It is murder on a scale—*

He recalls the words of Mrs. Giesel's peculiar visitor, the day after he was strafed in the field at the relocation camp. *It's revenge for what we have done to the Jews.*

*Max had been shovelling snow in the courtyard when a wagon drawn by a glum chestnut horse groaned in from the south. The driver was a purposeful woman with long limbs and a wool coat heavy enough to bury her. She dropped into the snow and, arms*

*extended like a tightrope walker, teetered toward him. Her ridicu-*
*lous shoes were the colour of piglets, a thin strap cutting across*
*the creases of her thick woollen tights.*

*Mrs. Giesel emerged, and the visitor threw up her arms.*

*"Alive!" she says. "I heard you were dead in a ditch, sobbing*
*boys everywhere, cows un-milked, Silesians looting the kitchen."*

*"Greta Engel, you heard no such thing," said Mrs. Giesel. Her*
*gaze dropped to the woman's shoes. "What in God's name are you*
*wearing?"*

*"Wear the shoes, kiss the boy, drink the victory bottle. It's now*
*or never, darling. Champagne must never go to waste."*

*Mrs. Giesel's eyes flicked to Max, and she introduced him as*
*the boy who stared down an air gangster.*

*"Brave boy," Greta Engel said.*

*"As if he were a cat," says Mrs. Giesel. "Dripping with lives."*

*"Would you do me a favour, fearless Maximilian from the*
*Saar?" Greta Engel said. "Would you find my poor dear horse*
*something to eat? He doesn't much like the cold."*

*Later, he had gone to the kitchen to steal another look at the*
*woman under the pretext of reporting on the horse's comfort. He*
*stopped at the doorway when he heard the two women discussing*
*the destruction of the city of Ulm.*

*"Name me a city they haven't destroyed," Greta Engel said.*
*Her back was to him, and her mad pink shoes were resting on a*
*chair. "The stories coming out of Dresden . . ."*

*Mrs. Giesel was bent over the fireplace, jabbing at the coal*
*with a poker.*

*"People are saying it's revenge," said Greta Engel. "For what*
*we have done to the Jews."*

*"You shouldn't listen to gossip," said Mrs. Giesel.*

*"They say it was a bumper cauliflower crop in Poland."*

*"Greta."*

*"Monster cabbages. It's the ash, you see."*

*"For God's sake—"*
*"Hundred per cent blood and bone."*
*"Greta!"* Mrs. Giesel stood to face her friend and saw Max. He
pretended that he hadn't heard.

The man who isn't Charles is swallowed up now, by the fog and the
darkness and the heavy, dragging steps of all the other striped men.

# 13

Heilbronn, Baden-Württemberg
March 1945

"Hello?" The maid Liesl enters the library with a handful of envelopes.

Marguerite snaps upright. How long has she been staring at the candle? The wax is spilling over the brass holder, threatening the paperwork. A rush of cold sweeps over her right foot as the pup rolls away onto its back.

All these messages. The couriers still find their way through the cratered roads and treacherous skies, risking God knows what for Hinckel, who walks with his wife in the garden.

"Thank you, Liesl," she says. The girl stays. Her eyes are lifted at the corners. Too pretty for her own good.

"That is not my name," says the maid. "I am Antoninia."

"Oh," Marguerite says, sounding out the singsong syllables of the name. Antoninia.

"Tonia is okay," says the girl. "He gives all the girls German names." She is speaking German. Imperfect, but effortless.

"All the girls?"

"There were five. Now three. And me." She leans her backside against Marguerite's desk. The submissiveness has evaporated. She takes up a candle and tilts it to allow a single drip of wax to roll its length. Marguerite reaches for it as you would a spilling cup from a child, but the girl does not relinquish it. Marguerite's heart jumps. If she pulls any harder and the girl lets go, the candle will jerk and spill hot wax. Marguerite softens her grip.

"We don't want to start a fire," she says. The girl glances at the candle and sets it down.

"This is not good place," says the maid. Antoninia. Not Liesl.

"There are worse places."

"True," says the girl. "But this is hot corner of hell." She screws up her face and shakes her fingers. Hot enough, in other words, to burn. She is so close that Marguerite can smell the bitter saltiness of her armpits. This conversation feels dangerous, conspiratorial. She should end it now, but curiosity wins.

"You speak German," Marguerite says.

"Know the language of your oppressors," the girl says. "My grandmother taught me this."

"But why pretend not to?"

Tonia gives her a pitying look. How has Marguerite not seen it before now? The misunderstandings, the errors. Linen changed on the wrong bed, too much salt in the coffee, breakfast delivered to the wrong room. *Still the Slavs fail to grasp the fundamentals.* Petty rebellions, but rebellions, nonetheless. More than Marguerite has dared consider.

The low light cast by the candles is stultifying. It is tempting to open a window and let some sunlight through those blackened panes, but the breeze is a precocity Hinckel cannot tolerate: a threat to the symmetry of his paperwork. And since the electricity has been off for three days, she is confined to candles, even by day.

"You are Russian?" says Marguerite.

"I am from Belarus."

"Oh, I—"

"Can't tell the difference?" Tonia says. "There is no difference to German soldiers. They put us on trucks with plenty of Russian and Polish girls to come here and be your dogs." She stretches out the toe of a scuffed house slipper and presses it against the pup's silky ear—with just enough pressure to make the dog groan sleepily and roll onto its side. "Not like this one. Street dogs."

"You had me fooled," says Marguerite.

Tonia shows her tidy, stained teeth. "This is bad place, but yes, it is not worst place. Some girls are breaking rocks or putting powder in bombs or working on their backs for twenty soldiers a night."

Marguerite blanches at the vulgarity and stands.

"The war will be over soon enough and you will be happy to go home, I imagine," she says.

"You are funny," the girl says. "Why would I do that? Look at how you people live. You have everything. There is nothing for me at home but Russians and ghosts and hunger and work. Real work. Work that would break your skinny back."

The truth rises and shakes Marguerite. The girl is a prisoner. A slave. Marguerite knows this. She has known it since she arrived, and yet has never allowed herself to know it.

"You would stay here?" she says.

"Germany, sure, but not this house. Not him. He will be dead soon enough."

A door closes somewhere nearby; a footfall in a stairway.

"I don't think this conversation is a good idea." Marguerite takes up a stack of papers and knocks the bottom ends together. Hinckel might be five minutes; he might be three hours.

"This conversation is very good idea," says the girl. "Your daughter has big voice, but she is not strong. If he touches her, she will break like twig."

For a moment Marguerite does not understand. Then she remembers Hinckel's words. *There is a filly who'll buck.*

"No," she says. "No, he wouldn't—"

"He would. He will."

"You know this?"

"I know this. Every girl who has worked here knows this."

A bell sounds somewhere and Tonia pads away to the hall. She can be no more than a year or two older than Anna, but what horrors has she suffered? Far worse than separation from her family, transportation to another country with no income, no freedom—yet she fights back

91

in her own way, with those trifling acts of sabotage. A part of Tonia remains untouched and free. She is *doing* something.

And what is Marguerite doing? Her mind is running itself ragged, inventing outrageous, audacious acts of courage to keep her children safe, yet what is she really doing? What she always does, which is nothing.

*They took Maximilian from her in mid-February.*

*A weasel-faced youth had delivered the news to the widow Liszt's house. Max was to be relocated along with all the boys in his troop from the school at Neunkirchen.*

*Throughout the war the Reich had trumpeted its Children's Relocation to the Countryside programme. The camps, the citizenry was informed, were in the great national tradition of pastoral outdoor recreation, offering a respite for children "inconvenienced" by the terrorist air actions of enemy nations. Alpine chalets and lakeside hotels, rural hostels and ski lodges were requisitioned through the expanding Reich where lucky German boys and girls could enjoy full board and schooling at no cost to their parents. Here, under the guidance of Hitler Youth leaders and party-approved teachers, they would receive an intensive National Socialist education and engage in a range of outdoor pursuits: gliding, skiing, hiking, swimming, orienteering, wrestling, trench digging, target practice, weapons loading. And the happy bonus? Mothers relieved of the responsibilities of caring for their children would be rewarded with more time to assist in the brave German war effort. Relocation was not voluntary.*

*"Zero seven hundred hours at the train station tomorrow," the boy repeated and saluted. This dullard, who should have been at school failing at algebra and girls, had found his place in the world, sticking it to the elders he saw as weak, sentimental, and responsible for Germany's failures in and after the Great War.*

*Youth belong to the Führer. How many times had she seen that on a poster, and here was the proof of it. Never mind that Max came from the Red Zone and had already been evacuated. Never mind that the Reich had already taken his father.*

*Marguerite stared back at the boy until he executed a military half-turn and marched off.*

*Madness. Any journey was madness. German transport was targeted day and night, and refugee trains were no exception. The foreign planes would be drawn to that train like falcons to a chicken. Her thoughts shifted to the poor souls from Lauterbach who perished in an air-raid shelter at Sankt Wendel. Not only was the refugee train bombarded, as well as the station, but the shelter too. The survivors—all women and children—were trapped there in the dark and could not be reached before the air ran out.*

*No. No, no, and no. She could not put Max on a train. The war would be over in a matter of weeks. The only sensible course to do was put out the white flag and wait for the tanks to arrive, not to be sending children all over the countryside. She rested her back against Mrs. Liszt's door and made chaotic plans. She would hide Max in the cellar. She would hide him in the walls, in the attic. She would take her children and head into the night. She would find someone to help; someone she could trust. She would plead with party officials, sell her wedding ring and her coat and herself if necessary. She would disguise Max as a woman and walk the children home.*

*She would do none of these things.*

*She would lie awake all night, and in the morning she would pack his bag and take him to the station and put him on the train.*

*If he touches her, she will break like twig.* Panic is scrambling her thoughts. Max is already gone. Will she lose her daughter too?

Is this the penalty of having grandiose dreams for her children? Just because a boy grew up in Saarland, she used to say to Anton, doesn't mean he must follow his father, his grandfather, his great-grandfather into the mines. Let Max choose. And Anton agreed. Not every husband would have.

She had hopes for Anna too. These she had been more shy about sharing, not certain how he would react. Why should Anna's future be in the kitchen and fields alone? She is smart—more than that. She has a gift. Anna was only four or five when Marguerite gave her an old botanical book picked up at a flea market in Saint-Avold. The French and Latin were beyond the child of course, but the illustrations captured her. By the age of nine or ten she knew the names of her favourite plants in French, Latin, and German. She created alphabet games with Max to memorise the plants and their properties. *Ma petite botaniste*, Marguerite used to call her, and she had allowed herself to imagine her daughter as a grown woman in a white coat working in a laboratory in the Botanischer Garten und Botanisches Museum in Berlin or the Jardin des Plantes in Paris. Regarded with respect, even envy by her male colleagues.

Such ideas. What does she wish for her children now? The life they were born to. A local life. An unremarkable life. Any life at all.

The quickest way to the greenhouse is through the empty kitchen, where a kettle simmers on the stovetop. Marguerite pauses to fill a pot with hot water. She will have an excuse to drop in: a request for an herbal tincture.

"Help yourself." The cook is standing at the pantry door, fists on boxy hips.

"I hope you don't mind," says Marguerite.

"Why would I mind a Saarfrench helping herself from my kitchen?"

"It's hot water," says Marguerite. "Not guinea fowl."

"Foreigners are causing enough problems around here without having them *inside these walls* poking their noses in, trying to show people up."

Here is the truth of it, then. Anna has shamed the cook by getting a kitchen garden up and running while the cook warms herself by the fire. But who is the greater fool? The front will be here before the first radish is ready to eat.

"*Si tellement agréable de te revoir*," she says to the cook, and lets herself out the door. So lovely to see you again.

\*    \*    \*

Anna is not alone. Marguerite watches through the glass as her daughter points out a tray of burgeoning seedlings to Karl Hinckel. There is space between Hinckel and her daughter, but not enough. The ease to her daughter's bearing suggests an alarming familiarity.

Hinckel notices Marguerite before Anna does, and a smile slides up his face. He leans around Anna to pull open the door. Is he showing how close he can get?

"What have you brought us, Marguerite?" he says. She remembers the steaming pot in her hand. Tempting to throw it in his face and observe the oily smile transform into a scream.

"Perfect," says Anna. "What do you fancy? German spearmint?"

Marguerite sets down the pot and steadies her hands on the bench.

At dinner the room reeks of wet fur and stale rose. Lina Hinckel is telling a vacuous story about something the dog rolled in and the great effort required to get it clean. Where did she find a supply of scented soap infinite enough to waste on a dog?

You might think Hinckel had never in his life heard a story so diverting, never seen a woman so enchanting as his ghastly wife. Yet when Lina turns her head away to order the maid to pour more wine, his eyes flick across the table, to Anna.

"I had to change every piece of clothing I was wearing—" Lina Hinckel follows her husband's eyes and stops speaking.

"To you, my dear," he says, and lifts his glass to his wife.

Across the table, Anna's cheeks are flushed—is it the wine, or has she pinched them? Her hair shines. She has taken extra care to brush it out before dinner. They have to leave this place, but Karl Hinckel, seven gunmen, two hundred kilometres, and two armies lie between here and home.

*The wheels are already turning.*

If she gets Anna away, what might Karl Hinckel do to her son?

# 14

Schwäbisch Hall, Baden-Württemberg
March 1945

Hans is shaking him awake.

Yellow light washes the room and with it, memories of the previous night—a half-hour march in the dark into an old city with leaning walls and dripping overpasses. A young woman had left them at the front door of a half-timber house where they had trudged upstairs behind an old woman bent so low with a dowager's hump she had to crane her head back to scowl at them. She led them through a dim corridor lined with portraits of men and women with the same dumpling faces to a bedroom just large enough for two narrow beds, a low table with a tarnished brass lamp, and a small chest of drawers.

The air-raid sirens are growling to life. A thunderous crack rattles the window. Cannon fire. Now the scream of aircraft in a steep dive. Night fighters—directly above. Max is upright, pulling on his boots, colliding with Hans at the doorway. The old woman, face ghoulish in candlelight, watches them sprint past her door.

The heel of his hand barely touches the banister; his feet fly. Hans is across the foyer and already out the door.

The alley is flickering orange and gold. In the narrow strip of sky between overhanging buildings, a searchlight sweeps. The drumming clamour of engines and guns threatens to drown out the air-raid siren. They follow the light to a central square where the upturned faces of fifty or more people are washed with gold.

The bombers are already here—Max hears the growl, feels the thrum in his chest. The night fighters skirmish—spinning in and out of the searchlights like agitated wasps around a stampede of beasts. Cannons chatter. He sways and has to check his feet to find his balance. Which are the German fighters? Which are the English, the American? The familiar rumble of the Mosquitos is there and the deeper purr of the Flying Fortresses, but now a new scream enters the fray: jet fighters. There is no hope of seeing them, but the shriek is everywhere. High in the eastern sky, two fighters are on a vertical climb, one chasing the other; fire pours from the rear craft's nose, tracers lighting the sky. There is only one way out of this manoeuvre. One fighter will stall first and fall away, giving the other the opportunity to drop onto its tail and blast it out of the sky. His head weighs heavy on the back of his neck; his heart rattles with the guns. The planes slip into darkness.

Again a jet streaks by, cannons hacking. A Flying Fortress teeters out of formation, blue and orange flames on its left wing. It hurtles sideways, trailing fire. Max roars, smashes his fist in the air. A few moments later there is a flash in the northern sky. Something bounces off his shoulder. Hot cannon cartridges rain onto the square.

Long after the sky has darkened and the air has quieted, Max and Hans scour the square and the surrounding streets, gathering up warm steel and brass.

The old woman pulls the door open to them when they return at first light.

"They live," she says. Her breath makes clouds in the freezing air. "What? Did you think I was so old that I would not notice two boys in my care had run outside in the midst of an air raid?"

"We weren't the only ones," says Hans.

She flicks the words away with her hand and turns back into the house.

"I know boys. Fly at the sun and laugh when your wings get scorched."

They climb the stairs to their room, the old woman's words jabbing at Max. The bleakness of her tone reminds her of the butcher's wife. Mrs. Weiler. What had she said?

*Don't lock your heart in a box.*

Where is she now? He cannot recall how or when exactly the Weilers left Lauterbach. He'd believed for a long time that Charles had had something to do with their disappearance, after Anna had trusted him with the secret.

*"You have to swear."*

*"I swear."*

*"Properly. With blood."*

*"Whose blood?"*

*She had rolled her eyes at him.*

*He found himself a pin, pricked his little finger, and squeezed out a droplet on which to swear, trying not to show her how much it hurt.*

*"Uncle Charles used to drive Jews in his taxi across the border."*

*"He never did." Jews, he had learned, were like poisonous mushrooms. A single one might kill a whole family, could spread like the plague, taking over whole villages and towns, entire countries.*

*"It was perfectly legal," Anna said.*

*"What does perfectly legal mean?"*

*"Allowed. They didn't want to stay in Saarland after it became part of Germany again."*

*"Did they make him do it?" he said.*

*"Maybe."*

*"Did they pay him?"*

*"Probably."*

*"In gold?"*

*"Gold and diamonds and sapphires and silver plate and ruby rings."*

*"Why didn't they drive themselves?" She did not know.*

*"Why did they not take a cart or wagon or walk?" She did not know.*

"*Did he take the Weilers? Is that where they went? To Paris?*"
She did not know.

Over time, a picture of the Weilers' departure formed in his
mind. They were crowded into the rear of Charles's smart burgundy Citroën. A wooden chest brimming with jewels lay in the
trunk, his godfather's forearm rested on the window frame, a cigarillo between his fingers, leaving a wispy trail from one country
into the other.

Stupid, the things he used to imagine. Charles's journeys
were in the early years after reunification, long before the border
closed, long before the war. The Weilers were still in Lauterbach
at the start of the war, weren't they? He's not sure. And where did
they go? Nowhere good—he is sure of that.

The last conversation he can recall with Mrs. Weiler was the
day Hans cut himself when they were playing deep in the Warndt
Forest, before the land mines.

They had lived and breathed the stories of Old Shatterhand
and Winnetou. He can still see the horses' skidding hooves throwing up a fine curtain of sand in the Arizona sun, as Max, the
cowboy, called a warning to Hans, the Apache.

"Snake," said Max, indicating the flat silhouetted head rear-
ing up from a tree root, and behind it, the quivering, rattling tail.
A woodpecker's sad drum and call ceased, as if it too was holding
its breath. The boys shouldered their rifles.

"Never saw a rattle that big," Hans whispered.

"On three?"

Hans counted it down and they fired at the same moment, then
ran to examine the corpse. Shot clean through the middle, leaving a perfect trophy head with drooping fangs. Or perhaps just a
flat knot at the end of a coiled branch, eyehole drilled by a bark
beetle.

They ran, Argos frisking and sneezing at their heels, to a
clearing where they had constructed a wigwam from an old sheet
and a pile of sticks.

Hans let out a shriek and Max spun, ready to confront a horse thief, a coyote. But there was real blood on Hans's leg.

"S'macht wé?" asked Max. Stupid question. Of course it hurt. "Now listen. You're snake-bit."

Hans didn't move. Max shook out a handful of wild raspberries from a handkerchief and pressed it to the cut.

"And now, the antidote." He blew a leaf from a raspberry. Hans grimaced and took the berry, his face twisted in mock horror.

"You've poisoned me, dummkopf. How many of these have you eaten?"

"Seven?" said Max.

"You've killed us," said Hans, and pretended to choke. Max dropped to his knees, joining Hans in quivering, laughing death throes until they lay still as logs on their bed of moss.

The smell of woodsmoke called them home. Max insisted they detour through the garden behind the Weilers' butchery.

"You shouldn't go there," Hans said, but followed anyway. A goat tied to a tree bleated a protest, but the dog was interested only in the hanging shed. Through the oily glass, a headless carcass was suspended on a hook, a pool of dried blood under its neck. A few steps farther, smoke seeped out under the smokehouse door. It had not been used since Mr. Weiler's arrest. The open rear entrance was obscured by rubber curtains. Max felt the sticky weight of one in his hand and pulled it to the side a little to catch a glimpse of tidy rows of knives lined up next to sparkling chain gloves.

The curtain swept to one side and here was Mrs. Weiler, carving knife in fist, face set on murder. He stumbled back and stood on the dog's foot. Argos let out a yelp, and Max ducked. Mrs. Weiler narrowed her eyes and lowered the knife. Her hair was wrapped in a bright red scarf and her husband's dark leather apron reached to her ankles.

"Is Lea here?" Max said.

"Lea, is it? Who wants her?"

"It's me, Max." Had she lost her mind?

"Max, is it? Surely not! I thought you were his long-lost twin, snatched away by bark beasts and whatnot, covered in dirt and leaves, robbed of his comb and his soap and his usual excellent manners. Oh and look, here's another creature."

"I am Max Bernot," he said. "I have no twin. That's Hans-Peter Schlesier."

"It speaks again!" she said. "What a miracle it did not lose the powers of speech in the wilderness."

He smiled, confused. The Weilers, he knew, were Jews, though he was not sure what kind. Bolsheviks? Or poisonous mushrooms? They were not the ones who plotted to lose the Great War, because Mr. Weiler was a proven war hero, had shown Max his Iron Cross, had let him stick a magnet to the piece of shrapnel embedded below his collarbone. Most importantly, Mr. Weiler and his daughter, Lea, did not mind sharing a little hot beef with Max and Anna, who used to be Lea's friend. Since he'd gone away, the smokehouse had been closed up—until now. Would Mrs. Weiler be as generous as her husband? He feared not.

"Do you need any jobs done?" he said on a whim. "Deliveries? With Mr. Weiler away and everything."

"And everything," Mrs. Weiler said. "If I needed a job done, why would I ask you?"

Max looked to Hans for support, but he had dropped to a crouch to examine his wound, little finger up to its elbow in his left nostril. Argos was pawing at the hanging shed door. "I can run," he said. "Faster than a greyhound."

"Can you indeed, and at what price?"

"Not one pfennig," he said. Her eyebrows seemed ready to launch themselves off her head. "But a slice of beef would be nice."

Hans wiped his finger on his trousers, stood, and saluted.

"Heil Hitler," he said.

Mrs. Weiler looked up at the sky, back down at Max, and retreated into the butchery. He shrugged at Hans and prepared to leave, when the curtains parted and there she was, a fold of waxy paper in her fingers holding two slices of steaming beef. Max reached for it, but she was scrutinising Hans.

"Hans-Peter Schlesier," she said. Hans clicked his heels and fixed his eyes on the meat. She dangled it to and fro, a steaming pendulum, and spoke in time with it. "It's all Hitler this and Hitler that and Hitler the other. Well, is Hitler God, Hans-Peter? Is it Hitler you pray to before you go to bed? Hitler who decides that the next thing you pull out of your nose will be your tiny brain?"

Hans was shaking his head. Left, right, left, right. A dog following a bone.

"Good," she said. "Good, then."

She pressed the meat into Max's hands. He thanked her and asked what she would like delivered. A rush of air escaped from her nose.

"Delivered!" She clasped her hands together and tapped them on her chin. "Let me think. A hat with a feather? A smart new suitcase with leather straps? An American visa? A ticket on a transatlantic cruise liner, upper deck? My husband returned to me?" Then her tone softened and she pulled a dried leaf out of his hair. She rubbed it between her fingers, and it dispersed. "Will you look at that? Quick! Make a wish."

He closed his eyes to come up with the cleverness Anna would—infinite wishes, a genie in a bottle—but could not get past that beef, and how it would taste when he sank his teeth into it, and so that is what he wished for. He felt a touch on his cheek, and Mrs. Weiler was kneeling before him.

"I have no need for deliveries, Max Bernot. I have a need for customers. Rarer than testicles on a cow these days. But you can do something for me. Don't be in a rush to grow up. Don't lock that gentle heart of yours in a box."

The puzzling words were said with such seriousness, her eyes searching so far into his, that he pulled away. He ran with his best friend and his dog to the rear of her garden, where he squatted

*beside the tomato beds and nibbled at the meat, trying to make its
salty, smoky tang last forever, and imagining a small pink heart
jumping in a cold steel box.*

The bent old woman feeds them a breakfast of damp bread covered in
fried onion, but Max's appetite withers under her stare.

"You're to report to the train station for clearing work," she says.

"Was it hit last night?" says Max.

"Last night, last week," she says. "As long as the jets are at that air
base, Schwäbisch Hall is a target."

"What jets?" says Hans. "Where?"

Jets are part of the Führer's technological plan to win the war with
super weapons. Max has heard them often enough, but seldom closer
than a streaking speck in the sky.

"Train station," the old woman repeats. "Easiest way to find it is via
Markt Square."

Max tails Hans across an alley, through an underpass, and into
the square where they had watched the night fighters. At its top end,
wide towering steps lead to a huge gothic church. At the bottom is
the town hall with moustachioed doors and windows, a clock tower
topped with a golden orb, and swastikas quivering from every window.

"Victory is not won through idleness." A limping man struggling
with a laden wooden handcart is scowling at them. His stubbled chin,
hands, and coat are smeared with soot. Max reaches to steady the cart
and the man slaps his hand away.

"Do I look like a cripple? Why are you two loitering?"

"We've been assigned clearing work at the station," says Max.

The man tilts his head toward the town hall. "Left at the Rauthaus,
across Hangman's Bridge, left again." He pulls up the handles of the
cart and moves off, pitching left, metal clattering with every step.

A stone demon grins down at them from the bridge tower, rope
draped around its neck, cap resting over horns and wicked, hooded
eyes. Sickness twists through Max's belly.

"We can't stay here," he says.

"I know it," says Hans.

"I've checked the map."

"And so?"

"If we walk via Heilbronn, it will be only a hundred kilometres to the Rhine."

"And then?"

"We find a way to cross."

"One bridge at a time."

"One bridge at a time."

A shriek rises from nowhere, more piercing than a siren, louder now, and louder. The sky is empty apart from a few wisps of cloud. Where is it? *Where?*

Hans shouts, "*There.*" Three silver jets razor the blue.

As quick as he sees them, they are gone. He lets out a whoop and Hans is shouting too, but their voices are swallowed up by the shrilling sky.

# 15

A few days later a damp young messenger arrives at the door. One of his boots is shredded, a knee and a shin glisten pink, his Jungvolk jacket is torn, and the knuckles of his right hand are ripped open. His face, unscathed save for an angry red pimple tucked beside a nostril, is a study in stoicism. Behind him, the bike is on its side, front wheel askew, mud and tufts of grass in the spokes.

"Oh dear," Marguerite says.

The boy shakes the rain from his hands, pulls his satchel around, eases out an envelope, and waves it at her.

"For the Bereichsleiter," he says. Judging by the air in his chest, this might be the most important message this boy has ever run. He's being brave, bless him.

"Good for you," she says. "Come in and we'll see to those scratches."

He snatches the envelope out of her reach. "I am to deliver it to the Bereichsleiter himself."

"The Bereichsleiter is not here," she says. "He's gone to Stuttgart."

The boy droops.

"Have you come far?"

"Ludwigsburg."

"Good Lord, that must be thirty kilometres, and you probably crossed him on the way. What happened to you?" she says. The boy's hair is plastered in blunt tails over his forehead. Did he cut it himself?

105

Where is his mother? Dead, of course, or in some distant place, because what mother would allow a boy to be out in the open in this weather? What mother with a grain of sense would let her son out of her sight?

"Pedal caught a rock just out of Eglosheim," he says.

"Blasted rocks. Jumping out at you." Why is she teasing him? She doesn't know this boy, but his need to be brave, to be indispensable, is so like Max. Of course he didn't see the rock. He was probably scanning the sky, or peddling in a blind panic, or trying to outrun the rain. Fear or inattention or avoidance of discomfort—none of these faults is acceptable in a German boy, whose demeanour should be modelled on the ancient Spartans.

He is close to fainting.

"Let's find somewhere for you to sit down," she says. His chin wobbles. Kindness will do him in. Briskness is what he needs. "Quick now. We don't have much in the way of medical supplies, but we can give these wounds a wash. An infection will put you out of action and you'll be no use to anyone."

He limps after her to the kitchen. The cook looks up from her stool, cheeks full of food.

"I'm here to steal some boiled water," Marguerite says. "For this young man's war wounds." The cook glares at Marguerite and examines the boy.

"Heil Hitler," she says, and gives him a half salute. She disappears into the pantry and returns with a biscuit. "Take this, little bear, and sit yourself down." The boy stares at the biscuit as if it were made from emeralds.

The scrawny pup wanders in and sits itself at the boy's feet, gazing at the biscuit with the same expression.

The cook takes up a broom and lunges for the pup, then pulls up short. The boy has buried his head in the dog's velvet muzzle.

"Don't waste a crumb of biscuit on that mutt," she says, but puts the broom away.

The boy whispers into the dog's cheek, the dog drools, and Marguerite gets to work on the boy's shin with a cloth and a pan of water. She could weep for him. Does he remember a time before war, when the worst to fall from the sky was a shower of hail?

"Not a good time to be on the road," Marguerite says. He tucks the biscuit into his breast pocket and goes back to stroking the dog.

"Eat," says Marguerite. "You're far too pale."

"I will keep it for my brother," he says.

"How old is your brother?"

"Eight. He's got a cough."

"Do you have medicine?"

The cook reappears from the pantry and waves two more biscuits at the boy.

"Here you are—for you and your brother for later," she says. "Now eat, before you faint and make a mess of my floor." She busies herself wrapping the biscuits in a scrap of brown paper.

Marguerite plucks a piece of gravel out of a graze and the boy flinches, then looks embarrassed.

"Sorry," she says. "How old are you?"

"Twelve."

"Young to be carrying messages so far."

"It's the fuel shortages," he says.

"But surely an older boy—"

"They're all gone."

"Gone where?"

"Stuttgart, to join the Volkssturm."

She wills her heart to steady itself. Charles had warned her, and he is the one whose body lies punctured and shattered in the cold earth.

*They're creating an army of children.*

"A couple of these grazes need a poultice," she manages to say. "Stay here for a few moments while I get my daughter. She's a walking apothecary."

She lurches outside and holds up her face to the misting rain. Charles had been her twin in a sense—the sibling she never had because she was so much younger than her own brothers. He was both brother and sister—protective but also a confidant. They vowed they would travel the world together one day, but it was Charles alone who went, and brought back shining pieces of it to show her.

*He had turned up unannounced one afternoon—typical of him—in the early days after reunification, polished as a clothes mannequin in his smart jacket, eggshell-blue shirt, and burgundy silk cravat. His linen trousers were in perfect creases, tasseled shoes gleaming.*

*"Good God," he said. Marguerite touched her headscarf. She had just come in from the fields.*

*"It's practical," she said.*

*"You look like a peasant."*

*"I am a peasant."*

*"You're too lovely to dress like one."*

*He kissed her twice on each cheek—Parisian-style—and she rolled her eyes, but it was so very good to see him.*

*"A gift," he said, and presented her with a copy of the new book sweeping France:* Gone with the Wind. *She turned to thank him, and he was staring down the street, making no attempt to hide his disgust. The village, her village, sagged under his gaze. It wasn't just the soot and sameness of the houses. It was the swastikas folding and unfolding all along the renamed Adolf Hitler Strasse.*

*"How do you stand it?" he said.*

*"You get used to it."*

*"It's a bad business."*

*"Don't you start."*

*"Start with what?"*

*"I had the priest around yesterday," she said.*

*Charles pulled out a cigarillo and she nudged him to offer her one. He lit it for her, and she drew in the rich smoke. Her head swam, and it wasn't unpleasant there in the sunshine with her favourite cousin. If she closed her eyes she could pretend they were*

*in a different place, a different time—puffing on stolen cigarettes*
*behind Tante Marie's pigpen.*

*"What did he want?"*

*"The priest? To tell us how to run our lives."*

*"That's his job, isn't it?"*

*"It's politics, Charles. Max's new school—"*

*"That would be the* Adolf Hitler *School?"*

*"Stop," she said. "It's actually quite something, so modern. New*
*books, new desks—"*

*"But?"*

*"Teaching the principles of National Socialism too enthusias-*
*tically, too fanatically, in the priest's words. He wants Max back*
*at the parish school."*

*"Why would you have a problem with that?"*

*She had snapped at him.*

*"Come on, Charles. You know what our parish schools were.*
*The Nazis are putting money into these new schools. Real money.*
*What do we actually owe the church? We could have made the*
*difference in the plebiscite, but the bishops made it clear how*
*they expected Catholics to vote. We live every day with the conse-*
*quences of that."*

*What she didn't say was that the Adolf Hitler School was an*
*elite school for elite children, that Max had been chosen, and what*
*mother could turn her back on that kind of opportunity?*

*"You're not buying Hitler's deal with the Pope?" he had said.*

*"You've heard of the new concentration camp up at Buchen-*
*wald?" she said. "They tied a priest upside down and left him to*
*die. Priests are being locked up all over Germany for speaking out*
*against the Fascists."*

*"That's hardly new."*

*"Exactly. What protection can the church offer? The best place*
*for Max right now is to be in a good little German school lining*
*up with other good little German boys playing at soldiers until*
*this is all over."*

"Not every German is so safe," he said.

She felt a stab of guilt at that. Many of those who had sought refuge in Saarland before reunification were now fleeing to France by any means possible.

"It's kind what you're doing for those people."

"The Jews? It isn't a kindness, Marguerite. It's a service."

"How much do you charge?"

"None of your business."

"I rest my case."

The Reich was encouraging Saar Jews to emigrate in those days, so there was no secret about what Charles was doing—but Marguerite's instinct had been to keep it to herself. Some of the women she once counted as friends were now jostling for space around open windows to hear one of the village radios blasting out Hitler's speeches. Grown women were carrying Hitler's portrait in their purses, had adopted the "German greeting," saluting all day long; an army in aprons. Even her neighbour Hedda Luscher—thin as a hairpin, face a squeezed lemon—was giddy for Hitler. She had showed up beaming on Marguerite's doorstep one morning with a gift: a photograph of the Führer in a box frame decorated with a garland of intricate paper roses.

"I noticed you didn't have one." The woman was bursting with anticipation, awaiting Marguerite's rapture.

"Bless," Marguerite had said, taking the portrait between the tips of her fingers. "Aren't you sweet?" When the woman had scuttled off, she had called to Anton. "Look what Hedda has brought for us, chéri. Where shall we hang him? Or should we put him against the wall?" He had laughed at that. They both had.

Then Max had come home and dragged Charles off. If Anton was the root holding Max secure in his world, Charles was the starlight that let him dream. He had been dazzling that night, scandalising the children with stories about the fashionable clubs of Paris where you might see a dress embellished with pure gold, an enormous fan made of peacock feathers, a woman dressed as *a man, a man dressed as a woman. He told them of children their age making thirty francs a day on street corners, performing gymnastics or magic tricks or playing instruments while their parents argued about art and politics and gastronomy in smoky cafés where American jazz blared.*

*But beneath the colourful tales there was a bleakness that caused her stomach to grip. It was rare to see him in one of his low patches. When the children were in bed, Anton poured another glass of Mosel. Would the wine be too rough for Charles? Too provincial? If he thought so, he didn't let on.*

*"How are Josef and Cécile?" Charles had asked Anton.*

*"Good, good," said Anton. His brother's French citizenship had been granted, and he had applied for a visa to return to Lauterbach and help in the fields when he could. "Most refugees have been relocated to the middle of France, but Moselle is in need of miners, so he's just across the border, with a decent job and a good house."*

*"And you?" asked Charles.*

*"Just the same," Anton said. Marguerite caught the firmness in his tone. Did Charles hear it too? "Still maintaining and fixing the pumps, but I'm a supervisor now, so there's a little extra in the salary. Life goes on."*

*"Not tempted to join your brother?"*

*"Politicians and borders change with the seasons," said Anton.*

*"Josef thinks differently."*

*"Indeed, Josef thinks differently, which is why he is there and we are here." Anton took up the cork and pressed it back into the bottle.*

*Oblivious to the signal, Charles kept pressing. "They say that Hitler is serious about this Thousand-Year nonsense, that he's set about making an army of children, indoctrinating them, turning them into automatons who will obey without question."*

*Anton brought his hand down to the table.*

*"They? Who is 'they,' Charles? Your communist friends in*

111

Paris? People who live outside these borders, swallowing a steady diet of anti-German propaganda? In this country, in this house, it is normal for children to obey their superiors. If you had children of your own, you might be better placed to offer counsel. How can you know what it is to belong to a place when you flit like a bird from one place to another?"

Charles sat with that for a moment, long enough for Anton to soften.

"Forgive me, Charles. These are strange and difficult times. We are trying to find our way."

"I understand, Anton, but Hitler's mad enough to start a war. Why keep Marguerite and the children here when the French government would welcome good work—"

"Stop it, Charles— Do I look like a prisoner to you?" Marguerite had said. "And are you really going to wish another war upon us?"

Charles laughed and held up his hands.

"Quite right, Marguerite. God forbid. And God have mercy on your jailer."

"On that we agree," said Anton, and that was that.

Later that night, Anton had nestled into the crook of her neck.

"My prisoner." She could hear the smile in his voice. "Surrender or suffer."

She laughed and twisted around to face him. He had more collier's stripes now—the nicks and scrapes into which coal dust has settled and scarred grey—but still he was the man she married: dark-ringed blue eyes, that slow smile, a soft-spoken giant you could lose yourself in.

"Do you think Charles might be right?" she said.

"Charles has an appetite for drama."

"But the children are so caught up. What if—"

"What if? What if? What if by the time Max is old enough to be a soldier, Hitler is gone and some other jumped-up dwarf is the *political* plat du jour?" *Anton put his lips to the skin beneath her ear. "Speaking of the* plat du jour."

"*Are you suggesting I am no more than a plate of chicken, Husband?*"

"*Chicken?*" *he said.* "*Not at all, Wife. Something much sweeter than that.*"

*And all thoughts of Adolf Hitler and his army of children were discarded along with a nightgown and a pair of homespun knitted socks. They had not discussed it again for a long time, and by then it was too late.*

Anna chats with the messenger, whose name is Ralf, while she mixes up a handful of dried herbs with boiled water, soaks the cloths, and applies them to his hand and leg. She works efficiently, checking often with the boy to make sure she is not hurting him. He has eaten not just the biscuit but a chunk of bread and a piece of salami. His colour is much improved.

"It will be dark in a few hours," Marguerite says. "Time to go."

"I am to give the message to the Bereichsleiter himself."

"You have done your best. When he returns, your message will be waiting."

She takes him to the office and shows him where to place the precious envelope under the paperweight on Hinckel's desk. After she has waved him off, she returns to examine it. It is sealed, stamped, and marked PERSONAL.

*The wheels are already turning,* Hinckel had said. Could it be that the contents relate to Max? She holds up the letter to the light of the desk lamp—the envelope is good-quality linen—not the thin, pale-green paper used by the party for regular dispatches. Could she find a blade sharp enough to lift the seal? She pictures herself lifting the flap of the envelope, pulling the letter clear, reading the words within.

*The schoolboy Maximilian Bernot is living in a mountainside hamlet. He sleeps peacefully at night, undisturbed by bombers. By day he attends lessons with his childhood friend—*

It is hopeless. If she managed to open the seal without damaging the wax or the linen, how could she reseal it without detection? A drop of sealing wax underneath the existing seal might be enough to do it, but what if the new wax were to spill outward or cool a slightly different colour? She could practise with Hinckel's sealing wax, but the thought of his returning without warning makes her heart turn over.

She leaves the letter where it is.

PART TWO

*Kingdom*

# 16

Max and Hans watch from the bedroom window as a noisy troop of local Hitler Youth march through the streets of the old town. Fists pound on darkened doors, edicts are declared, paperwork flourished.

The old woman appears in the doorway a few minutes later holding a mimeograph between thumb and forefinger. She tells them that they must scrub their rooms, strip their beds, and leave no trace of their visit. Due to the early hour of their departure, she will be unable to furnish them with breakfast.

Hans takes the paper from her hand, and she leaves them to digest the details.

They must report to the train station at seven the following morning with a rucksack weighing no more than twelve kilos, clothing and provisions for three days, and a blanket. Heil Hitler. They are to join the Volkssturm after all.

They spread out the map on the floor between their beds. It's tearing along the creases now. The road home looks to be about three hundred kilometres due west, intersected by the Rhine a third of the way along.

"We could leave right now through the wood at the back of town," says Hans.

"We could, but someone might see us. Even if they don't, we

would have to walk an extra sixty, seventy kilometres. We have to get on the train, Hans."

He calls up his mother's face, eyes wide and startled from the men marching black boots through her kitchen. She looked to him, to Max. In that swift half-second appraisal, a question was asked and answered. Before he could deny it with a shake of his head, she turned her back on him. Then the shout, the shot, the dog, the door, the crack, the bloom of blood. The flat haze of his godfather's eyes.

The crumple of shells is closer still; the skies churr with enemy planes. He will make her hear the truth. She might still find that he is to blame. But he will try.

Hans folds up the map with just the right amount of care.

"If we get on that train, we'll end up at Stuttgart in the Volkssturm."

"We get off the train before Stuttgart," says Max.

"And if we get stuck on the train?"

"Not like you to worry about the details."

"Not like you to be so sure of yourself."

"Then we fight our way through to the other side or die doing it."

He does not like how that sounds.

Max is fourteen now. He had not remembered until two days after his birthday and has not mentioned it. Hans will only make a fuss, which will make Max feel worse. He had imagined he would be home by now.

Hans looks up from folding the last of his belongings into the rucksack and says, "Mud."

"What?"

"There's a lot of mud in soldiering. People never talk about it, but soldiers can think of nothing else. Your feet rot in it, it gets into your ears, your arse, your teeth. It jams the guns, and when it gets really bad it drowns the men, drowns the horses."

"How do you know?"

"Papa said he would have killed ten men just for a bath. Would have died for one. Some of the biggest medals went to men who went off on some hopeless errand to take out a gun or rescue a wounded comrade when, really, they couldn't stand the war anymore and knew that a bullet would get them out of the trenches one way or another."

Max considers his words. His own father had been too young to go to war. "Hans—you don't think— I mean this war is different, isn't it? This is not the same war as your father's war. It won't be like that for Horst and Rudy and all of them, will it? It wouldn't be like that for us."

"Only one way to find out," says Hans, and tightens the straps of his rucksack. "Soldiers, then, if need be."

"If need be," says Max. "But we will get off the train."

In the morning, a rumpled party official and swaggering Hitler Youth leader look unimpressed at the groggy bunch of would-be soldiers. The old men—several wobbling from drink or nerves or both—are separated from the boys, who jostle around the platform. One pretends to teeter on the edge, and three others spring forward and take hold of him, suspending him over the tracks. When he screams and flails, they haul him back and he recovers himself with a shaky laugh.

The leader sounds a whistle and makes a final roll call. Sixteen boys are missing. *Sixteen.* A number so astonishing that one or two shift their feet, cast their eyes back the way they came. There is angry talk of delaying departure, marching through town to rattle cages and flush the cowards out from under their beds. But the party official stresses the urgency of the orders. He will see about the missing ones.

Max and Hans wait as long as possible before boarding. They attempt to station themselves on the gangplank, but the youth leader shoves them inside the crowded carriage and takes up the post himself.

They pass through frosted farmland, dead fields. A crashed Ju 88 fighter lies nose down in the dirt, weeds rising around its belly. The train pulls into a station just as someone unwraps a sandwich. The pungency of salami mixed with stale sweat sends saliva rushing into Max's mouth. He pushes out to the gangplank, gasping frigid air.

The youth leader is gone.

He reaches for the door to the next carriage. A soldier with his arm in a sling snarls at him to close it. He backs out, checks the platform. At one end, a train inspector hoists a suitcase onto the train for a woman on crutches. At the other, head down like a thief, the youth leader is marching north, toward home.

"Bastard," says Hans, at his side.

"Those boys need to know what he's done."

"Those boys aren't our friends. We are not the ones who have left them, Max."

But it is not strangers that Max imagines when he looks back at the closed carriage door. He sees Horst, winking his spectacles up his cheeks, lips pressed into a flat, hopeful smile.

"Did we round anyone up?" says Hans into his ear as the train begins to move again. "Did we order anyone to fight? Did we pretend we were the big men? The heroes? Whatever you and I might do or not do won't make any difference to what happens to those boys."

"But we did pretend, Hans," says Max. "It's all we talked about. Maybe we've got this wrong and we're the worst cowards—running away in the end, when it matters most."

"They're the ones who have it wrong," says Hans, shouting now that the train has gained speed and the wind moans around them, tugging at their caps. "They care more about fighting than they do about living, because that's what we've been told all our lives. It's all anyone ever wanted from us. All *he* ever wanted."

As the train rushes its human cargo toward Stuttgart and its mustering yards, Max knows Hans is right. For so long, Max held faceless enemies responsible for the worst things: the bombing raids, the inexplicable successes of the Allied armies, the inexplicable failures of the Wehrmacht and Luftwaffe. Flawed men who operated beyond the eyes and ears of Adolf Hitler. But the ones who locked up Uncle Josef came in the name of Hitler. So did the ones who murdered Charles, who revoked his father's military exemption and sent him to war. And his friends' desire to fight for their leader and country? This can be laid at Hitler's feet. This is what he asked of German children. It's what he demands. And now that defeat is certain, what Hitler is really asking is that they die for him.

"I hate him," he says. "I hate him. I could stick a knife into him. I hate him for what he's done to us, to our friends, to our families, to *everything*."

"So?" says Hans.

"What?" Max shouts into the wind.

"Stick it to him by living," says Hans. "Are you ready?"

And he is.

The train slows. A platform rocks into view. Two men in old military coats lug a trolley of blankets past women perched on a suitcase. Max hikes his rucksack higher and arranges his face into what he hopes is an expression of confident intention.

The train stops.

# 17

Heilbronn, Baden-Württemberg
March 1945

The Bereichsleiter is late. It is after eleven at night and Lina Hinckel is restless. She moves around in the corridor above Marguerite's room, marches up and down the stairs—a sentry without an army.

Marguerite did the same thing in the days the Gestapo used to visit in the early years after reunification She could not stand still for the dread of hearing the growl of those cars. Outside her door, outside the church, the butcher shop, a black Mercedes would glide to a stop, two men would uncoil themselves from the rear, straighten their jackets, and either climb her steps to rap at her door, or call her over to answer their questions in the street. A space grew around her, where her community once stood. A discomfort in friendships that had been effortless. The fanatics mostly ignored her, which was a relief, but her neighbours, Hedda Luscher and her weasel husband, Joerg, took a different approach—speaking to her often, slashing at her with manners so impeccable, you didn't know you'd been cut until you tasted blood.

In the end, it was Anton who was arrested, three years after the plebiscite, on a charge of currency crime. That was all they could come up with, having searched every centimetre of the house. He kept a fold of Saar francs inside a rusted tobacco tin tucked behind a loose brick next to the fire. Anyone who lived on the border kept a stash of francs somewhere—the authorities seldom came looking unless they wanted you for something else. Currency crime was a catch-all—the high value of the franc an insult to the Reichsmark and therefore the Reich. Anton had served his sentence in an underground factory producing aircraft cannons, and by the time he came home the war had started.

The Nazis' interest in her family did not end there. Anton's brother, Josef, was arrested within a year of the German occupation of France and sent to prison for crimes against the Reich. He's been there four years, if he is still alive. It's an age since they've had news. Her family is scattered. Her parents, last she had heard, were somewhere in the Pas-de-Calais. Most of her relatives had fled the borderlands ahead of the German invasion; a few had returned and taken up work offers in the new territories to the east. Still others were exiled and forced into labour camps—Charles among them. Would he still be alive if he had stayed at that camp? He might be in the hands of the Russians by now. Could that have been any worse?

Upstairs, Lina Hinckel paces and turns, paces and turns. She will wear a hole in the floor, drop clean through it and come face-to-face with Marguerite. That would be quite the comedown. What, after all, is Lina Hinckel without her husband? Just another woman tossed around on the tide of war. Marguerite cannot drum up a morsel of pity.

"Morning." Anna stands over her holding a steaming mug. Marguerite rubs the sleep out of her eyes.

"What time is it?"

"Just before eight," Anna says.

"I feel as if I've been hit by one of those damned planes. Did you remember to lock your door?"

"Mother."

"Did you sleep?"

"Here and there. You?"

"Here and there."

"Is he back?"

"Not yet. Mrs. Hinckel sent me to get you."

"What does she want?"

"A French lesson."

"Jesus Christ and all the saints. I'd rather eat my young."

"Mother!"

Marguerite reaches for the mug. The tea is a deep red colour and smells both sweet and musky.

"What have you made me?"

"You tell me."

"I would swear it was berries if I didn't know you had rose hips."

"Very good," says Anna. "And what else?"

She smiles and a curtain lifts. Marguerite sees Anna as a stranger might, as Karl Hinckel might. Yes, she is too thin, her bones too close to the surface, yet there is a fine beauty to her, a radiance. It is not difficult to imagine Hinckel's hand reaching for her daughter's waist, sliding up toward her breast—*stop*. This is what happens when you lie awake half the night. Hinckel is not in the house, and her daughter's door was locked. Anna stands before her unmarked, untouched.

"Sleeplessness becomes you," says Marguerite, taking a careful sip of the drink. "It's not mint. Fresh, though. I like the combination." She tastes the tincture again. "No. You will have to tell me."

"It's thyme," says Anna. "For protection."

Protection. Best you make more of it, Daughter. Make it strong and drink it by the litre.

She meets Lina Hinckel in the salon, after passing by the library to see that the letter still sits where she left it. The woman reclines on a sofa, wearing a violet dress with a deep neckline and a double set of fat pearls.

"What time does the garden party start?" Marguerite says in French.

"What?" Lina Hinckel responds in German.

"I thought it best to drop you in the deep end," says Marguerite, still in French. The pup flops onto its back at her feet and she reaches down to scruff its neck. Its back leg mimics the movement of her fingers. Sweet Argos did the same thing, punctuating each scratch with an encouraging tap of a back paw.

"Sit," says Lina Hinckel. "I suggest we start with something simple."

"*Un deux trois?* A, B, C?"

"Speak German. I am talking about my husband."

"Your husband?"

"What are you doing here? What is your history with Karl?"

"Talk to your husband," Marguerite says. "If you don't want a French lesson, I have work to do."

Lina Hinckel rises to meet her. She is in a fury.

"I asked you a question."

The laughter is out before Marguerite can stop it. "Do you really imagine I have designs on your husband? If he were the last man on earth I would drown myself."

"That's your story."

"No story," says Marguerite. "I knew your husband briefly many years ago. If I never saw him again it would not have troubled me, but I ran into him in the street in Neunkirchen the day before I came here—"

"*Liar.*" The word falls like a cleaver. Lina Hinckel's tone curbs Marguerite's instinct to argue.

"What makes you so sure about that?" she says.

The other woman's hand swats away the words.

"He told me you were coming weeks ago, when the other girl left."

"But that's not—" Marguerite breaks off. She retraces the day outside the Welfare Office. The queue, the rain, the coat. *Marguerite? Is that you?* Not the coat, then. He had known it was her. But how? He didn't even know her married name.

"I ask you again: What are you doing here?" says Lina Hinckel.

"How many weeks?" says Marguerite.

"What?"

"How many weeks ago?"

"Two, three. I don't know."

"I have not seen or heard of your husband for twenty years until

I ran into him on the street in Neunkirchen the day before I came here."

"You're lying," says Lina Hinckel, but she is not so sure of herself now.

"He came for me," says Marguerite, more to herself than the other woman. When she looks up again, Lina Hinckel is gone.

*Marguerite had met Karl Hinckel in the summer of 1922 when she was seventeen and working as a junior secretary at the town hall in Völklingen. The Great War had been over for almost four years and Völklingen was now in the Territory of the Saar Basin—under French administration since 1920 as part of German war reparations.*

*At the time, Germany was in the grip of the worst hyperinflation. Two hundred billion marks might buy you a loaf of bread if you were lucky. Those with the good fortune to live in French-administered Saar were paid in Saar francs, the currency printed by the coal mines administration. It carried the same value as a French franc, so Marguerite was happy to join the many border French who took up jobs in the territory.*

*That time, that life—she can still feel the lift in her heels each day as she walked to the old border, took the tram up the hill through Lauterbach and Ludweiler, over the Saar River and into the old town, dwarfed by the blast furnaces and coal towers, the huge suspended conveyor system of the ironworks. She loved the job: the clear parameters of the work, the ring and clatter of typewriters, the low voices of her fellow workers. She was accepted into this adult world without question. Most of all she liked the pay—the crisp fold of notes tucked into a brown envelope. She had to hand most of it to her father, but still, she felt like an independent woman.*

*She liked Karl Hinckel too. He was a clerk—good-looking in a conventional way: polite and assiduous in his attentions. They sat together at lunch, he walked her to her tram on occasion, accompanied her to a few dances, but his fascination with the Brownshirts was growing to a fixation, to the point he could talk about little else. There was a premature marriage proposal which they had both laughed off, then he left Saarland to take up a new job in Munich.*

*If she had never heard from him again, that would have been the end of it.*

The candle flame throws unsteady shadows onto the wall behind her bed. What could she have done differently? How might she have behaved that could have prevented all this?

The letters started arriving from Munich within days of Karl's departure. At first glance they were the newsy letters from a friend who'd found new purpose in a growing political movement, yet the tone of those precise phrases made her uneasy. There was a presumption of intimacy, hints at a future together. She was young and, she sees it now, flattered. She had written back, careful to make no promises. Then Charles had visited, read one of the letters, and was appalled—as much at Karl's politics as at the tone he saw as proprietary. She stopped writing. Karl's letters stopped too. Instead of relief, Marguerite had felt jittery. For a time she feared he would return to Saarland, that he had already returned. She would see his face in a buzzing café, the penetrating glare of a coal-blackened miner. It was never him, of course. In time, the feeling had faded, and she believed he had forgotten her.

What had he said in those letters that might help her make sense of this? He had written about Munich, his work at the town hall, his rise in the party. He had droned on about the rallies, the inspiring speeches of Adolf Hitler. If anything, his letters spoke of passion for Fascism, not Marguerite Guibert.

He had used her maiden name when he saw her in Neunkirchen. Had he done that deliberately? To deceive her into thinking he knew nothing else?

She wraps her shawl tighter around her shoulders. If he knew her name, how difficult would it have been to learn other things? Hadn't she thought he knew something about her children the day she saw him in Neunkirchen? And if he knew about them, how difficult would it have been to find her address?

It comes to her then—the *Blockwart* who came to Mrs. Liszt's door with his habitation report and his pencil, noting down the names of all those who would be sleeping there. Even in the chaos, the block wardens grasp their last strand of power. Such insignificant bureaucrats help the authorities keep track of who is where every single day.

And still Karl Hinckel does not return.

Late that night Marguerite slips down the hallway and tries the handle to Anna's door. It releases with a light clank. Unlocked. A cold thread runs up her spine and she pushes the door open, hears Anna's slow breath, and releases one of her own.

She sets down the candle on the bedside table where there is a glass of water and a book about fungi Anna has found in the library. Marguerite had permitted only one book in Anna's suitcase for evacuation— the old French botanical encyclopaedia. How could she have said no to her daughter's most valuable possession? The library has been almost as precious a discovery for Anna as the greenhouse. The widow Liszt had not a single book in her house other than her Bible. Marguerite had the sense she saw reading as extravagant. If a woman was to sit, why would she open a book when she might reach for a needle and thread, or peel some onions? Her neighbour Joerg Luscher had the same idea about music.

*Playing the piano is all over for you, Mrs. Bernot.*

She rests her eyes on her daughter. Anna has always looked fearless when she sleeps—bedding pushed aside, head flung back, arms stretched behind her—a wingless angel. Fearless yet vulnerable: a maiden in a dark tale, dreaming of silks and steeds while her pale throat and steady heart are wide open to the assassin's knife.

Marguerite pulls the quilt up over Anna's shoulder and her daughter stirs.

"Mama? Max is on fire."

The breath drops out of her. No. No, no, no. It means nothing. They are five years into a war. The fears we push aside all day long break out in sleep, that is all. If anyone were to sense Max in danger, it would be Marguerite. She would know it. Max is not on fire. He sleeps like his sister, in a painless slumber, tucked in a cocoon of feathers in a warm bunk nestled into trees far from the cannons, and there he will remain until it is safe to come home.

*The night he died, Charles appeared at her kitchen door. It was November. His face was drawn in pits and shadows. Behind his bare head, the stars. The air tasted of frost.*

*"I'm sorry," he said. The steel of the doorknob drove the cold into the heel of her hand.*

*How could this be? Charles was away in a labour camp a thousand kilometres east in Silesia. How did he get here? Between Lauterbach and the ironworks alone there must be a dozen bomb craters in the road. Regional trains were reserved for military personnel and supplies. Smaller roads were overloaded, smashed to pieces.*

*"I'm sorry," he wept.*

*Her heart cracked open. She pulled him inside, tried to embrace him, but he flinched and fell into a chair, shielding his face. Panic engulfed her. The terror worsened every day. People were being executed without trial. Thieves, deserters, hoarders— anyone who spoke out against the party or spoke up for peace or surrender. The penalty for harbouring a fugitive might be arrest. It might be a bullet. There were rumours about orphaned children being given as gifts to childless Nazis. Charles could not be here. She pressed the heel of her hand to her chest to quiet her flailing heart.*

*Who might have seen him? Could her neighbours be awake at this hour? Her house had become her prison: her neighbours the watchtowers, the searchlights. What had happened to the Lauterbach she knew before the war, before reunification? What happened to the friendships borne out of poor harvests and difficult births and stillborn babes, of wayward husbands and accidents in the mines, of money shortages and outbreaks of whooping cough? She had felt part of this place. But now, the exchanges with women she used to know well have become guarded. What is friendship without the freedom to complain, to share a secret? Connections shrivelled and withered. She trusted no one. Except Anton, of course, though the regime wedged its way between them too, because if you filter your words with your spouse for long enough for fear of being overheard, if you avoid the subjects most begging to be discussed because there is no possible resolution, then one day you find yourself skimming across the surface of each other, performing an awkward dance, uncertain how to break back through.*

The sound of a car engine brings Marguerite to the window. The driveway is lit by headlights. Hinckel is back. A long time later, when she hears his tread on the floor above, she creeps down to the office and checks the desk. The letter is gone.

In the morning she discovers Anna in the salon listening to the National Radio crackling out its victory news over the drum of rain on the eaves. Foreign troops are stalled at the Westwall. Germany's defences are impenetrable.

"I'm going to build a greenhouse when we get home," says Anna.

"Are you indeed? Glass doesn't come cheap, *Schatz*."

"It doesn't need to be so grand to start with. Max will help. One day I will have one like the Bereichsleiter's. Bigger than our entire garden, filled with plants from around the world."

"Will you indeed? I remind you that that greenhouse does not belong to Karl Hinckel. None of this does."

"This place was empty and had been for an age."

"Empty of people, but not of their property." And their ghosts, for all we know.

"I'm fixing it up, making it lovely again. If the people come back, they will be pleased. All I am saying is that if I get good at this, really good, the Ministry of Food and Agriculture might see what I am capable of—maybe private benefactors too."

"Benefactors? Anna, what are you—"

"I have a talent." There is a challenge in her stare that impels Marguerite to deny it.

"You work hard."

"He says if I turn my attention to the scientific side—the genetics and plant breeding—I could go to university and make a serious contribution to Germany's self-sufficiency. I could become . . ."

"Become what?"

"Known."

Do you recall what the Bible says about flatterers, Daughter? Marguerite will not say this, because Anna will bat the words away. She will refuse to hear it.

"Why don't you just say it?" says Anna. "Actually, you don't need to. It's written all over your face. You don't think I can do it. Well, he does. He encourages me. He admires me. It's more than you ever do, and that's what makes you angry."

Something snaps inside Marguerite.

"Look at yourself in the mirror, Anna, and ask what he really wants."

Anna blinks at her. "Why would you say such a thing?"

"Because I am an adult and your mother and I am not blind."

"He thinks I deserve the opportunity to shine, to make a difference." Anna's voice is choked with pride, injury, rage.

"*Deserve?*" says Marguerite. "And what about every other girl your age? What do they deserve? What about the other girls in this house? Do they deserve to be slaves? Slaves to him?" It's more than she meant to say. Her breath is ragged.

"You are twisting my words, which you always do." Anna stalks to the door, then hesitates. "What about you, Mother? Do you deserve to have your meals served by slaves? Your sheets changed by slaves? Your clothes washed by slaves? Is that what *you* deserve?"

"I deserve none of it. I want none of it," says Marguerite. "I did not choose to come here." She remembers Charles, sitting on her front step when he was still beautiful and whole, watching the swastikas unfolding down the street. How easy it is to get used to things that would have once horrified you. "The sooner the weather breaks, the sooner the American tanks will be here, and we can be gone from this place."

"Germany is rallying."

"Germany is collapsing."

"Do you *want* Papa to die?" Anna's eyes are wild. "Is that what you're praying for? Do you want to see your children murdered by Russians or English or whoever gets to us first? Will you be happy then, to have proved yourself right?"

"Do you want to know what I pray for, Anna? I pray for your father to save himself, to take his chances as a prisoner rather than to die fighting an unjust, criminal, hopeless war. But if it costs him his life to bring an end to it, to save his children, he would accept that, and so would I. We would give our lives ten times over to save yours."

Anna's face shifts. "You are wrong," she says. "You are wrong about everything."

How is it possible that this proud young woman was the same infant who used to lay a tiny fat palm on Marguerite's breast? It was a private joke between mother and baby, the way Anna would stop feeding until Marguerite looked down and was rewarded with a huge, lazy, milky, secret grin, after which Anna would close her eyes and get back to feeding.

You are loved, Marguerite wants to say. You are loved beyond what you could ever let yourself believe. But she does not want her words laced with poison and spat back at her.

What will it take for Anna to stop believing? For ten of her sixteen years, Adolf Hitler has soaked into her skin, her bones, her head, her heart. Hitler speaks to the egoist in every child. You, my children, will rule the world. Your parents are scolds, idiots, and bumblers who stood by and let Germany's enemies rip her apart piece by piece.

Hitler is so much a part of Anna that to hate him would be to hate herself. And when the day comes, when she sees him for what he is, for what he has become, what will remain of her daughter?

*       *       *

Marguerite resolves to search Hinckel's office. There must be reports or documents to prove to herself and to Anna that there is more to their presence here than Hinckel is admitting to. There must be a clue in the letter Ralf delivered. Does it concern Max or herself? Either way, the need to find it feels urgent, desperate. She should have opened it when she had a chance.

# 18

Ludwigsburg, Baden-Württemberg
April 1945

Two quick steps onto the platform, and they are fugitives. Avoid the eye of the train inspector, the women trickling ladles of thin soup. Don't stare at the two guards sharing a cigarette and ogling the backside of a young woman bent over a bawling child. The train whistle wails—sending another bolt of fear through Max. Eyes are on him. He feels it on the back of his neck. *Don't turn around.*

A poster on the wall. *Wer eine Niederlage will, will unseren Tod.* He who wants our defeat wants our death. Is that true? Does he, Max, wish death upon the German people? He wants an end to the war. Is that the same thing? He feels a touch on his arm and braces, ready to fight, to run, to strike out. But it is only Hans, indicating the road beyond the station entrance. Together they march out. Confident, purposeful, terrified.

The town gives way to open farmland, and with every step away from the city Max breathes easier. Weeds sprout among a few straggling plants from previous crops, alongside the frost-burned shoots of turnip and a handful of wild asparagus. He jumps the fence to retrieve it and a memory flares.

He is in the kitchen at Lauterbach, a strand of asparagus in his hand. Fine as a skewer, the bright green shoot is not his to take. It is a delicacy, one of a small bunch collected by Anna to be shared and savoured. But

Anna has stepped out and his mother's back is turned. He sinks his teeth into it. *Snap.* The outrage echoes around the kitchen. His mouth fills with the fresh tang. His mother, quick as a skink, snatches the rest from his hand.

"Thief!" She laughs, showing him the whites of her eyes. "What next? Arson? Murder? Shall I deliver you to prison myself to save the magistrate the trouble later?"

They head north, following the road to Heilbronn. It's quiet for the most part, except for an ox-drawn cart carrying a load of corpses. A white-haired woman presses a handkerchief to her lips without a glance at the bare legs greyed with dust and sticky blood.

They reach a forked intersection where a messenger in a ripped Jungvolk jacket is pumping up a tyre on a battered bicycle. His knee and shin are bandaged and one of his boots is so badly torn that his sock is visible through the shredded leather.

"Any news?" calls Hans.

"Rhine's breached," the boy pants. "Our boys are on the back foot but fighting hard."

"Cheers," says Max.

"Heil Hitler," says the boy, and lifts the pump by way of salute.

"*Drei Liter,*" Hans says. The boy doesn't notice. No one ever does.

They strike out northwest. Max feels the few pfennigs left in his pocket, thudding alongside his wrapped silver coin. A dog lying in a patch of sun lifts its head to examine them and flops back to the grass. It lies in a perfect C except for the tail, spread out like a fat feather duster.

*Argos.* The pain doubles him over.

Hans sees the dog and sighs.

"Best dog in the world, Argos," says Hans.

Max sinks his teeth into his lip. Best dog in the world.

*His mother's voice was calling from the house, but Max was un-touchable in the rickety pigeonniere. It was sometime early in the war, and Moselle was part of Germany again. Now that the border was gone, Tante Cécile and Little Josef were permitted to come and go as they pleased.*

*The four of them—Max, Anna, Hans, and Little Josef—feasted on forest berries in the pigeon house, coughing out dust and bits of leaf. Max lifted his collar to wipe his chin, remembered his uniform, and used the back of his hand instead.*

*Anna had been the first to wear a uniform. Max, as the oldest of the boys, was next, then Hans, and now Little Josef. Max pulled his dagger from its sheath and checked the blade. Perfect.*

*"If you were a soldier," said Max, "would you rather get hit by a bomb and lose your leg, or get stabbed in the eye and go blind?"*

*"Bomb," said Hans.*

*"Stabbed," said Anna.*

*"But you'd be dead," said Hans.*

*"No she wouldn't," said Max. "Just blind in one eye."*

*"The knife would go in your brain," said Hans.*

*"Not necessarily," said Max.*

*"Then stabbed," said Hans.*

*"Stabbed," said Josef.*

*"Anyway," said Hans. "Girls make terrible soldiers."*

*"I fight better than you," said Anna.*

*Hans laughed and made a face.*

*Max heard a soft bark. On the ground below, Argos was stretched out beside a rusted plough, whimpering, dream-running, paws twitching. Now Anna had Hans pinned in the straw. Hans was stronger but trying not to hurt her—using his left hand to snatch at her hands, his right to tickle her ribs. Josef grinned through a mouthful of red. Hans yelped and leapt back, rubbing at his shoulder and glaring at Anna, whose hair was full of straw.*

*"Biting is dirty," said Hans.*

*"Fighting is dirty," said Anna.*

*A shadow passed, a shift in the light. Max crawled over to a window. The straw spiked and tickled his knees. The sunlight was*

*playing his favourite trick—dipping under a line of storm clouds
and spreading gold across all that should be in shadow.*

"Look, the light of angels," he said. He spread his palms on the
hot bricks. The wood and the potato mounds and field-side cot-
tages of Lauterbach were coated in gold. From up here he could
see the barbed wire of the Russian labourers' camp. He would
go back with Hans tomorrow and climb the oak to play sniper.
That one cut the legs off a priest, Hans would say. Fire. That
one hanged a baby. Fire. That one cooked an old woman and
served her to her husband for dinner. Fire. Max knew the stories were made up, that the foreigners were watched day and night
by armed guards, that there was another camp, a serious place,
for reeducating those who worked too slowly, or refused to work,
or attempted sabotage or rebellion. Yet still he avoided coming
face-to-face with the Russians at the mine entrance or on the road
to or from the ironworks. He did not want to smell the filth on
them or feel the cold fury in their eyes.

"Children!" His mother's voice was beneath them now. "Do you
want to be up there when the storm breaks? You will be cooked
alive and served to the pig for dinner."

They stuffed fists in their mouths, snorting and kicking
each other into silence. Mama would no more follow them
up those unreliable stairs than throw off her dress and dance
naked around the potato field. Max pulled everyone into position around the trapdoor, commando-style, heads over the edge,
camouflaged by the darkness behind them. And there was Argos,
sitting upright, his nose a signpost. The dog barked—a single
helpful "boff."

"Traitor," Max hissed.

"Maximilian Bernot! I can hear you!" his mother called.

Lightning brightened the loft for a moment, and Mama let out
a yelp.

"When you are running around the fields with your pants on
fire, don't ask me to fetch the water," she called, her voice growing

*fainter.* "*It will be God sending you a message!*" *A low thundering rattled the bricks.*

"*We will not tolerate traitors,*" *said Anna.*

"*What will we do with him?*" *said Hans.*

"*Tie him up,*" *said Max.* "*We'll take him into the wood and build a concentration camp and teach him what loyalty means.*"

*Josef sat up and wrapped his arms around his knees.*

"*Don't hurt Argos.*"

*Anna rolled her eyes.*

"*It's a game, Josef,*" *said Max.*

"*Why do you wear your uniform all the time?*" *said Josef to Max.* "*Everyone else takes theirs off after parades and meetings.*"

*Max checked himself. Still presentable apart from a little dust and a few strands of straw. The first heavy taps of rain bounced off the roof tiles and the hard-packed earth around the loft.*

"*Maybe it's different for the French,*" *he said.* "*Here it's an honour to wear the uniform.*"

"*Why are you speaking German?*" *said Josef.*

"*Because I'm German,*" *said Max.* "*Why should we always speak the Platt?*"

"*He's not God, you know,*" *said Josef.*

"*Who?*" *said Max. But Josef was easing himself down the narrow steps, his boots thumping on the ground just as the first raindrops smacked into dust. Argos was already gone; like Mama, he was terrified of thunder.*

*That was the day Aunt Cécile told them that Uncle Josef had been transferred from prison to a concentration camp at a place called Buchenwald.*

If Max could go back to that time he would say he was sorry. He didn't know about Uncle Josef when he made the stupid joke. He didn't know he wouldn't come back from prison. He thought he'd be released when his sentence was done, as his own father had been released after serving his time in the labour camp. Yes, Papa was thinner, with a cough that took a long time to get better, but he *came back.* Uncle Josef had never come back. Four years it must be now. Is he still alive? Or is he like Charles and Argos? Dead in the ground, eyes filled with soil.

If Max could go back, he would bury his head in Argos's muzzle and whisper sorry over and over to him too. Best dog in the world. His mother took him to a neighbour the day before the second evacuation and had him shot.

And what would he say to Charles? What will he say to his mother if he ever has the chance to explain himself? Will the words desert him again, leaving her to believe the worst?

Is this how it will always be? Death circling, jabbing, striking at him—forever testing him. The doctor saw so clearly what Max tried to ignore for all those years by being the hardest worker, the strongest marcher, the loudest singer. It was all make believe. His weakness cost Charles his life. It may have cost Horst his as well. How many more? How many?

A few kilometres on, a shout echoes through a lane to their right. Two boys in torn shorts and dirty shirts are playing soldiers. Stick-rifles drawn, they shelter behind a sparkling motorbike and sidecar—beloved by someone—and chatter out the sound of machine-gun fire. Hans takes two lumbering steps to the shelter of a street sign, draws a finger pistol from his pocket, and fires a shot at the kids, who promptly return fire.

"Hans," Max says. "Come on." But Hans throws himself out into the open, shoulders recoiling left and right. With an agonised flourish, he drops to the ground. Max wanders over to the corpse, and kicks at its boot.

"I hope you're satisfied," he calls to the children. "You Tommy bastards killed my best friend."

"You're the Tommy bastards," a child shouts back.

"What?" The corpse sits up. "Do you know the punishment for executing an officer of the German Wehrmacht? Get us some food or it's the firing squad."

Two giggling faces emerge. A boy and a girl, it turns out, though both wear shorts and cropped hair. Their names are Till and Hilda and they lead Max and Hans to a high fence at the rear of a three-storey school building. The gate is barricaded, but Hilda pulls it open with ease. The lengths of timber overlapping the sides of the gate are not attached to the fence—only the gate itself. A clever trick. A garden is lined with burgeoning vegetable rows. Potato plants are beginning to flower.

An older girl of around seventeen steps into the garden, rifle in her hands. Her dark hair is short, and she wears a man's shirt and trousers. She quiets the children without taking her eyes off Hans and Max.

"Well?" she says.

"Do you know how to use that?" says Hans.

"Do you want me to demonstrate?" she says.

Hans tells the story they have settled on. A strafed train. A lost troop. A mission to get to Stuttgart.

"Is that true?" She silences Hans with a jab of the rifle in his direction. "Not you, Chatterbox." She lifts her chin at Max. An instinct tells him not to lie, but he can't think what to say.

"Best you get on," she says. "Head south along the main road. You'll reach Stuttgart in half a day."

A call comes from inside the house. A third child arrives with the news that the block warden is on his way. Max catches Hans's eye and the older girl notices.

"Would you like to meet the block warden?" she says. "Thought not. Runaways, I suppose? Come on, then." She waves them into a classroom where the chairs are stacked on desks and a dozen mattresses are lined up on the floor, each with a folded quilt and pillow. "Choose a bed and try to look sick." She knocks off their caps. "Jackets off. Quick."

A few moments later footsteps approach and he hears the older girl's voice.

"What have you brought our orphans today? A crate of pineapples? A fresh round of cheese? Your timing is impeccable—we have picked up a couple of new strays. No names yet."

Has she given them up so easily?

"Forgive me if I don't follow you in," the girl says. She's right at the door. "The stink coming off them. I hope it's not typhoid. I've isolated them in here for now. They were planning to meet their troop in Stuttgart in that state, but they're not going anywhere until they stop shitting soup. If you'll forgive the expression, Herr Gartman."

Through half-closed eyes, Max gets a look at the block warden. Narrow shoulders and a low, round belly. Hans moans. Max is inclined to kick him for overacting.

The warden reverses out of the room. A few minutes later the girl is leaning on the doorjamb, slow-clapping.

"Bravo," she says. She pulls up a small wooden chair, sits, and rests her elbows on her knees. "Spit it out."

"We're going home," says Max.

"And where is that?"

They tell her.

"And the front?" she says. "How will that work? You just wander through the German armies, tiptoe across the firing lines, wave to the English on the way past, yes?"

Fatigue washes over him. A simple puzzle to be solved piece by piece disintegrates with her words.

"Tell me," she says. "If a bullet going through your front meets a bullet coming through your back at the precise same time, what would happen? Would they bounce back out or stop dead in the middle or go sideways?"

"Bounce," says Hans.

"Hans," says Max.

"If you want my opinion," says the girl, whose name is Vera, "you should stay put for a few days and the front will cross you."

# 19

"Marguerite." Hinckel waves his fork at her across the dinner table. They are dining on *Eintopf*, the economical national dish made of meat scraps and vegetables. This one is better than most, thickened with barley. "Did I mention that I have received news of your son?"

Her heart tips.

"Max?" says Anna. "How do you—"

"You have a son?" says Lina Hinckel, but her eyes are on her husband.

Hinckel sinks his fork into a piece of turnip and places it in his mouth, taking his time to chew. Marguerite would like to snatch the fork and impale his hand to the table.

"It seems," says Karl Hinckel, pausing to swallow, "that Maximillian and his compatriots spent several weeks at a KLV camp not far from Salzburg before they were called to join the Volkssturm."

Her stomach twists at her son's name on Hinckel's lips.

"How old is he?" says Lina Hinckel.

"The People's Army?" Marguerite says. "In Bavaria? What duties would he be expected to perform?"

"You have never mentioned this," says Lina Hinckel.

"Whatever is required," Hinckel says. His wife folds her napkin onto the table and pushes back her chair.

"Karl," she says. A lock of hair has fallen free from one of her pin curls.

"I'm sorry, my dear," he says. "What was that?"

"My son is barely fourteen," says Marguerite. "Since when do we call fourteen-year-olds to be soldiers?"

"Fourteen indeed," says Hinckel. "I would have given my right arm to be a soldier at that age."

"He is a *child*," she says. Hinckel is inventing this. She's heard of sixteen-year-olds bluffing their way into military service. But not *fourteen*. Surely not. And here's where she has a doubt, because to a fanatic, what difference is there between fourteen and sixteen? If he is tall enough to wear a uniform, strong enough to pick up a gun, they will put one in his hands.

"Every citizen has a role to play in defending the Reich," says Lina Hinckel. "Why should your son be any different?" She walks the length of the table, places her hand on her husband's shoulder, and leans down to kiss him. Before Marguerite has time to look away, before she has realised that this is no good-night peck, but a deep, wet, crass display of ownership, she glimpses Karl Hinckel examining her across the back of his wife's collapsing curls.

"In any case," he says, when his wife has left the room. He dabs his mouth with the serviette. "He was indeed called, but he did not arrive. Your son is missing."

"He will be trying to get home," says Anna. She has followed Marguerite to her bedroom. "They'll think it's a big adventure."

"They?"

"Max and Hans."

"He never mentioned Hans."

"Why would he? It's Max he's trying to find, but I bet they are together." Anna chews on her lip for a moment. "What is wrong with that woman?"

"Lina Hinckel?" Marguerite shrugs. "Like attracts like."

"He's nothing like her," says Anna. "There's nothing inside her

143

head. She's only interested in hair and cushions and those stupid clothes."

"And her husband, Anna. She is very much interested in her husband."

"What does *that* mean?"

"It means there is nothing good in holding the attention of Karl Hinckel."

"Why do you do that?"

"Do what?"

"Pour scorn on everything I do. Is it so hard for you to believe that someone might see good in me without—"

"Do you really imagine he is interested in your *tea collection*? He'll say anything. He's only—"

"No, *you'll* say anything. Why do you have to turn something good into something corrupt, rotten? How can I even look at him after what you—"

"Good. Don't look at him, don't talk to him, stay away from him."

She must take Anna away from here, but if there is the smallest chance that Hinckel still has the power to bring Max to her, how can they leave? Karl Hinckel might be inventing everything; he might be hiding the truth. Either way, she has to know. Tomorrow she will start the search. She had tried earlier in the day when he stepped out of the office, but she was shaking so much she dropped the first file before she'd read a single line. She put it back together and rushed back to her chair, expecting Hinckel to burst through the door.

Tomorrow she will try again. Tomorrow she will be braver.

She wakes with a jolt. Charles is banging on the door. She fumbles for the lamp, but it's not where it should be. Nothing is where it should be. She remembers where she is and falls back onto the pillow. How many times must she relive it?

*Once she had the door safely closed, she reached for Charles and saw why he pulled away from her. His hair was crawling with lice.*

*"Sit," she said, and poured him a glass of water, set about cutting some bread. She would feed him first, clean him up, then find somewhere safe for him to go.*

*"They're working people to death," he said. "It's murder on a scale—"*

*The hallway door flung open, and there was Max, blinking into the light.*

*"Charles?" he said.*

*Marguerite knocked a chair over in her haste to quiet him. He tried to get around her and she blocked him again, held a finger to her lips and demanded his attention until he nodded. Half a dozen expressions flickered across his face as he took in his godfather—joy and surprise, yes, but she also detected a recoil— fleeting, barely perceptible, and understandable given Charles's physical state. Max recovered and threw himself at Charles, who fended him off, told him embraces would have to wait until he'd had a bath. There was nothing to worry about. Max would tell no one. He was loyal, obedient, dependable. But that recoil played over in her mind. Was he not equally loyal, obedient, and dependable to his youth leaders? To his teachers? Charles was a fugitive. Was Max capable of betraying him? Of course not. Of course not. But the truth was, she could not say. This was the price then, of keeping your children safe. They became strangers to you.*

She becomes aware of the chirrup of a robin. It doesn't feel like morning. She finds her way to the window and pulls back the curtain. The moon takes up too much sky, monstrous and rust-coloured. The oaks stretched out in the dirty light look hungry. The bird calls again, and a shudder runs through her. This is no harbinger of spring. The poor bird is confused. Expending precious energy into the night to herald a false sun. She could weep for the poor, doomed creature.

She wraps herself in a robe, and creeps up two flights of stairs to the attic.

A shadow moves near the west-facing window, and Marguerite steps back in fright.

"Only me," says a soft voice. It is Tonia.

"The last time I saw the moon that colour I was a child," says Marguerite.

"The last war?"

"Yes."

"Can you hear it?" says Tonia.

Marguerite listens past the jabber of the confused robin and makes out a low clumping, like bricks dropping into snow. She knows it well from those last days in Lauterbach. Mortar.

"Not far now," Marguerite says.

"The other girls have left," says Tonia.

"Who? How did they leave?"

"They went with three of his men."

"By choice?"

"By choice, with big promises," says Tonia. "Safe passage to Switzerland."

Marguerite closes her eyes. "And those poor girls believe that."

"One of the men believes it himself. He thinks he's in love."

"There is hope, then."

"He will end up in a ditch when the other men want a turn with his girl."

"You don't know that," says Marguerite.

"You really don't know what men are capable of, do you?" says Tonia.

"I wouldn't say that, but perhaps I have been very lucky."

*Les soldats reviennent.* The soldiers are coming back. It was Marguerite's grandmother who opened her eyes to what men are capable of, when Marguerite was younger than Anna is now. She had been at her grandmother's bedside as Mémé's quiet journey toward death had been capsized by memories she must have lost or kept secret for decades.

"*Les soldats reviennent.*" The soldiers are coming back.

"There are no soldiers, Mémé. The war has been over for months. It's me, Marguerite."

"Marguerite?"

"Yes, Edwige's daughter. It's 1919, Mémé. The war is over."

"Kill yourself, child. Quick now. Before they return."

Marguerite had run from the room but found herself unable to repeat her grandmother's words to her mother. Had Mémé been violated? Clearly not in the war that had just ended, so the previous war? The Franco-Prussian war? She would have been in her twenties. Who were the violators? Napoleon's men? Prussian men?

For a woman on the border, anything was possible.

How is a mother to counsel her daughter in such matters? We learn from our mothers how to feed a family on scraps, calm a fussing baby, draw infection from a wound, cool a fever, coax a chicken into laying, but where is the preparation for this? Rape is the oldest weapon of war. Where is the wisdom handed down on that subject?

What would she, Marguerite, do to protect Anna from foreign soldiers? Would she offer her own body? A thought, unbidden and cold, occurs to her. They might choose Tonia over Anna, for her exotic beauty. This is how war builds a wall around the heart.

"What?" says Tonia, and Marguerite remembers her question.

"I'm sorry, Antoninia."

"Sorry for what?"

"For all of it. For what has happened to you. For what this country has done to you. I am sorry for being part of this, Tonia, for accepting the unacceptable. If you had told me before this war that any of this, that I—" Her tears, in the absence of Tonia's, feel tasteless.

For a time, Tonia says nothing, and when she speaks, Marguerite has to lean in close to make out what she is saying.

"Have you ever seen a two-year-old who has starved to death, Marguerite?"

The question needs no reply.

Tonia says, "She looks like a little brown nut dried up in its shell." And then: "I have known worse than this."

They listen to the approaching front. Please, God, let it bring salvation.

There are many places Karl Hinckel could secret away documents—the tall metal cabinet, the other drawers of his desk, the stacks of box files that must have been transported from his previous headquarters. The safe box is bolted to the floor under his desk. Only once has she seen him open it in recent days—to retrieve a thick envelope for the driver Gunter. He had replaced the key in a chest pocket of his uniform jacket.

The first place she searches is the top left-hand drawer of his desk. When he goes to lunch with his wife—Anna and Marguerite take breakfast and lunch in the kitchen—she waits a few minutes, then opens the hallway door. The passage is empty.

She has the retyped letter in her hand, ready to be waved about if he were to enter without warning, but still the blood is thumping in her ears. She places herself at the side of his desk—she will not be caught behind it—and leans around to slide open the top drawer. Something metallic rattles. Bullet cartridges in a cardboard box. There is also sealing wax and his stamp, a fold of matches, and an engraved silver cigarette lighter, a paper knife. No papers.

She closes the drawer and drops back into her chair, panting, and spreads out her unsteady fingers. Can she really do this?

A handful of winter aconite sits in a vase. Anna must have brought it in earlier in the day. Picking flowers for her mother is a childhood habit she has never grown out of—but seldom the ones you expect. She would walk past a perfect rose to cut a stick of rosemary that has grown into a circle, would ignore a magnolia bloom to shear a branch with three fur-covered silver buds. Precious, fragile girl.

Yes, she will have to do this.

For several days, each time he leaves the library she checks another drawer or a file—never rushing, always listening, ready with an excuse, although she is not sure she will have the strength to use it if he should walk back in without warning.

Her hands shake all the time now—even when she's typing out those dry explications of ever-shifting chains of command, instructions to do what cannot be done, fix what cannot be fixed. These communiqués conjure up their own world in which the war is present, yes, but in an abstract sense: a bureaucratic irregularity to be remedied by each new round of protocols.

She continues her circuits of the garden—mapping out escapes that seem both more possible, given the reduced number of guards, and less so, given that Anna would refuse to go. Marguerite includes the greenhouse on her circuit because Anna is always there, working alone or with the caretaker, patching a broken windowpane, staking bright seedlings, lugging soil in an old barrow.

She finds Karl Hinckel with her daughter only once. Their heads are bent together over the countertop. Anna speaks and Karl Hinckel listens. He watches, motionless as a cat stalking a bird.

One morning while Hinckel walks in the garden with a party official from Stuttgart, she places the last hanging file back into the cabinet. On a whim, she reaches down between the files, runs her fingertips through the dust of the drawer base. She feels movement and snatches back her hand, catching her thumb on the sharp edge of a metal binding. Was it a spider? A cockroach? She shudders. Blood begins to seep from her thumb knuckle, and she brings it to her mouth, trying to draw out the pain. She tastes copper and salt and thinks of Anton, and the sob is up and out before she even realises it is coming.

An image comes to her of her husband dozing in his chair in a patch of sunlight, legs splayed, one of the socks she knitted for him half pulled off his foot. Max was a few days old, curled like a comma on Anton's chest. Anna slept in the crook of his arm. It struck her that if she were to die now, her children would be loved and protected by this man for as long as he drew breath.

Might there not be a single minute in this endless war where she gets to step off the screeching carousel and have someone, anyone, *Anton*, fold her up, kiss her hair, and tell her that all will be well?

*Ça ira. Ça ira.*

She manages to get back to her desk and presses the heels of her hands to her eyes.

All that remains to be searched now are the box files—thousands of papers, judging by the way they are collapsing in on each other—and the safe. She will never get near his jacket pocket but there *must* be a spare key. Might he have given it to the driver Gunter or to his wife? Too much temptation for an employee, and Karl Hinckel is a man who keeps secrets from his wife.

She pulls a book from a shelf, and another, looking for an alcove, listening for a rattle that might signal a hiding place. But there are hundreds of books in the library, thousands. It's a waste of time.

On her way back to her desk, she notices a ball of light blue paper in Hinckel's bin. She stoops to retrieve it and hears a footfall. She lets it drop and hurries back to her desk, to resume her typing. Above the ting of metal against paper and platen, she hears Karl Hinckel enter and pause. Can he hear her scurrying heart? She returns the cartridge with a firm clack and ring, acknowledges him with a nod.

Hours pass before she has the opportunity to retrieve the dispatch and smooth it out over her desk. The Upper Rhine has been breached. The Westwall is penetrated. Foreign armies are pouring into German soil. Heilbronn will be under attack within days.

# 20

Max and Hans help Vera pull down the swastikas. They are heavy with damp, stained with mildew and bird droppings.

"We should bury them," she says.

"What should we wrap them in?" says Hans.

"Are you planning to dig them up again?" She gives him a long look, tilts her chin at his armband. "That too. And the shirts, and your buckles, and all of your badges. I hear the English have a thing about Germans. They think you're going to sneak up and throttle them in their sleep."

She reminds him of Anna, except he cannot imagine Anna screwing up her uniform and digging it into the dirt. She would have argued the point, wanted to pick up a rake or a garden spade and fight the enemy herself.

Vera's father is a soldier somewhere in the west. Her mother was the schoolmistress until she died a few months earlier, having already taken on three young orphans who had been students before the school closed.

"And they keep coming," she says. "The Block Warden is threatening to report us, but he's in love with me, so I turn on the waterworks and he scuttles off to find me more food. He won't like the look of you, though."

"Does he really bring you pineapples?" says Hans.

She blinks at him, then at Max, and back to Hans.

"No, Hans. No, the Block Warden does not bring me pineapples. On a good day he brings onions. On the very best day he brings six real eggs."

Max turns his back to pull off his shirt, which is torn on one sleeve, and filthy round the collar and cuffs.

"Not much time," she calls from the corridor.

He shakes out the sleeves, folds the shirt in half, and again. It is harder than he expected to let it go. He will keep the dagger.

Max eases open the latches and the window creaks open. A triplet of starling chicks nesting in the gutter squawk out a hopeful cry. The road is quiet after two days of steady traffic—the tanks and guns and trucks and foot soldiers of the great German army in retreat. When will their pursuers arrive?

His jaw aches from chewing the hard bread served up with Vera's thin but tasty spring vegetable soup.

"What are you sighing about?" says Hans.

"Cheese," says Max.

"A chunk or the whole round?"

"Stop it."

"Aged or new?"

"Stop it," says Max. "You're a terrible friend."

"Your only friend."

"There is no comfort in that."

"Yet here you are, lost in hilarity, and all thoughts of cheese forgotten."

"Until you bring up the subject again."

"But you're cheerful about the cheese now," insists Hans. "Before you were morose."

"How long have we been locked up here?"

"A hundred years."

The anticipation is an itch he cannot scratch. It makes him want to sprint up a hill, to blow somebody's head off.

\*    \*    \*

Max closes his eyes, holds the postcards in his left hand, and draws one out with his right. It is an image of the Rauthaus at Ulm, purchased from a vendor with a wooden leg and an incomprehensible murmur. The old German flag flies from the town hall—no swastikas, no posters of the Führer or declarations or warnings of this or that offence. No broken window or demolished wall or boxes of papers blowing into the wind.

He recalls the words of Mrs. Giesel's strange visitor. *Ulm has been flattened. It's revenge for what we have done to the Jews.*

He turns over the postcard and writes.

> *Dear Mama and Anna,*
>   *I have been to this place.*
>   *With warm hugs and kisses,*
>   *Max*

Hilda appears, two liquid candles extending toward her top lip, and shoves a piece of paper at Max—a leaflet dropped by the Allied forces, warning them, the German people, not to fight, that their safety is assured if they surrender peacefully.

White sheets drape from windows along the length of the street. Defeat was once impossible. It meant annihilation, the end. But now, in the silence, in this weightless, timeless in-betweenness, in the brightness of those lengths of white cloth, he senses a change, a fragile awakening.

He needs the foreign soldiers to arrive, then leave, so he and Hans can get back on the road. Two hundred kilometres to home.

Mama and Anna might already be there. And Papa too. Or is he injured, or a prisoner somewhere? Better that than the alternative.

The first Allied tanks arrive mid-morning. Vera has locked the younger children into a windowless room in the centre of the school. Max and Hans keep watch upstairs, under an oath of silence.

Max rests his binoculars between two slats of the blind as the troop carriers growl through the street below. Most of the soldiers are in

French greys, but one group of foot soldiers stands out—the legendary Moroccan Goumiers in vertically striped cloaks woven in the colours of the desert. Along with their rifles, bayonets, and grenades on cross-body harnesses, they carry curved knives on heavy belts.

"Any necklaces?" says Hans. Great War legends tell of Goumiers fashioning chains out of human ears sliced from their victims.

Max adjusts his binoculars and rubs at his ear, imagining the tip of one of those curved knives pressed to his own temple, slicing downward in one brutal cut.

A few of the North Africans wear turbans beneath metal helmets; one has an arm draped around a colleague. Some look joyous, others murderous. One is the rich brown of fresh-watered soil; another the pale ochre of a scrubbed new potato. They look nothing like he expects them to. They look nothing like each other. A Jeep passes at speed— a single Goumier leaning on a mounted machine gun at its rear. A thick plait flies from the back of his helmet.

A shot cracks, and a hanging basket across the road erupts into dirt and leaves. Scores of guns rise, barrels aimed in every direction. A shout goes up. Someone laughs. Another shout. Another basket explodes. This time Max sees the shooter: a French soldier on foot with a large swastika draped over his shoulders. An angry order is barked out and the shooter lets his gun fall to the limit of the shoulder strap, opening his arms in mock surrender. The swastika slips and the soldier recovers it and knots it around his neck.

It is the end and it is the beginning.

For two more days they stay out of sight while the troops pass, playing knucklebones and cards with the little ones, carrying water from bath to kitchen. Hilda attaches herself to Max: a sniffing shadow.

On the fourth day Vera sends Hans and Max out with instructions to find out who is in charge and bring back some food.

The main Platz is deserted: a couple of bullet holes are blasted through a portrait of Hitler, a door is kicked in and the entrails of a house spill out: a bread bin and part of a meat grinder, an atlas with half its pages missing. There are no foreign soldiers, no food coupons, no food. Nor are there SS officers or Hitler Youth or a single German in a uniform.

"Hans," he says.

"What?"

"Do you feel that?"

"Feel what?"

"Where we stand right here, at this moment, the war is over. It's done."

"Huh," says Hans. He tips back his head.

"What?" says Max.

"Waiting for the sky to fall," says Hans. He stays like that for a moment, then lowers his head, widens his stance, presses his hand to an imaginary pistol. "If the Nazis are gone and the French aren't hanging around, then this town is ours for the taking."

"Let's take it," says Max, and tilts his Stetson.

Hans scans the Platz, feigns alarm, and fires on an unseen enemy in an alley.

Max peers into the shadows. At first it appears to be a dog, a submissive smear of crouching brown. He takes a step, and the shape becomes a young woman, bony knees tucked to one side, splayed against a stone wall. A hole is torn in her brown wool stockings.

The woman's hatless head begins a slow rotation and drops forward. Her hair is in a tangle and her cheek is smeared with mud. One of her eyes is bruised and swollen closed. She tries to get up. Her skating, slipping legs remind him of a newborn foal. They remind him of Charles, in the dirt, unable to stand, but she has not been shot. There is, in her face, a blankness you see in a bird that has flown into a window or been played with by a cat. A stillness that at first glance appears bold until you understand that a light has been switched off.

A droplet of blood rests in the corner of the woman's mouth. Max takes his time to approach, searching for words to make her less afraid. A shoulder lifts. She turns her face away, presses herself against the wall.

"Would you—" he says. A lump has jammed his throat. "Would

you like to come with us?" But she is indicating no, the smallest of shakes, the way you might dislodge a fly from your hair. He should fetch help; he should not leave her here, but he is afraid of this woman. Afraid of what has happened to her.

"I'm sorry," he whispers. He raises his empty hands to show her that he carries no gun or stick or knife.

Her chest rises in a huge, shuddering sigh.

What can he do but leave her?

# 21

Each day Marguerite searches one or two shelves of books, drawing out each one and shaking it open in the hope of finding a spare key to the safe. Should she be more selective, scanning titles for ones meaningful to Hinckel? But she is no student of National Socialist–sanctioned literature, let alone Karl Hinckel's personal taste.

The box files are more difficult to manage—heavy and awkward to remove from the stack, difficult to replace. She does not dare touch them when Hinckel is in the house, but for two of the last three mornings he has travelled to the city to attend emergency meetings, and she has been able to make a start.

Her system is to empty the contents of a single box file into her desk drawer, return the box to its place, and go through the contents page by page in the drawer, ready to close it and return to her work if she hears him coming.

So far there have been only dreary administrative reports related to his previous role in Karlsruhe, yet Karl Hinckel knows something about Max—she's certain of it, and there must be proof of it somewhere. He knows something about her, too, something that has led him to her after all these years. If she could find it, then Anna might understand that he is someone to be feared, not admired.

One morning she is in the office when she hears a shout from the garden, a car accelerating, then a shot.

157

Hinckel snatches up his pistol, releases it from the holster, and runs down the corridor. She reaches the front door to see one of the Mercedes speeding along the driveway, Gunter in pursuit on foot. He pauses to aim the rifle low and fires. The car heaves to one side and thunders into one of the oaks. The horn blares—a shrill, wavering bleat. Gunter approaches, gun raised. He uses his left hand to yank at the handle of the driver's door, which remains closed.

The caretaker appears to Marguerite's right, hands covered in dark soil. Smoke pours from the wrecked car and the horn continues its tremulous blare as Karl Hinckel reaches Gunter. The two men speak, and Gunter manages to wrench open the door. He reaches in and the horn falls silent as he drags the driver from the car. Marguerite recognises him—one of the last remaining guards. He's a reedy, arrogant boy, but she would not wish this on him. He is on his knees. Hinckel barks at him and the boy covers his face with his forearms. Hinckel drags him up by the collar, throws him against the rear door, and aims his gun at the guard's chest. The guard slides to his backside and lifts his head to stare at a place far above Hinckel. Is he speaking to his God, or resting his eyes one last time on the sky, low and heavy beyond those barren branches?

Hinckel's arm jerks once, twice, and a moment later the short cracks reach her, and echo in the distance. Before the dead man has finished falling, Hinckel has spat an order to Gunter. He turns back and kicks the dead man with so much force that his body jolts for a third time.

She sees Charles's broken body at her garden gate and feels the bile rise into her throat. Murder. These people are murderers. This country is run by murderers.

Hinckel looks up toward the house, to Marguerite. He has lost his cap, his hair has shaken free, and the gun is still in his hand. He starts walking.

"Karl!"

Lina Hinckel rushes out of the front door in a blue silk robe and matching slippers with a puff of quivering fur above her toes. She glides down the steps, silk billowing, breasts rising and falling untethered beneath a low-cut gown. Karl Hinckel transfers the pistol to somewhere at the back of his trousers and smooths his hair.

"Are you hurt?" she calls, and throws herself at him, limp in the arms of her knight. She reaches up a hand to touch his cheek. "What has happened, Karl? What have they done?"

He peels her off.

"Back to the house," he says, taking the stairs two at a time. "Go and get dressed, woman."

The caretaker pulls a weed out of the mouth of one of the concrete cherubs. "Kill as many rats as you want," he mutters. "It will not change the course of the ship."

"You." Hinckel leans over the heavy banister, directly above the caretaker. If he heard the comment, he shows no sign of it. "Gunter will need help."

The caretaker nods his agreement.

"Back to work, Marguerite," says Hinckel. When he has gone, she steps in close to the caretaker.

"I have to leave this place," she whispers. He straightens and pulls away with a warning frown.

"Not yet." His tone is a surprise—firm and clear. "He will not hesitate. Hold your nerve and he's the one who will be gone soon enough." There is, in those deep-set eyes, curtained by weathered folds of skin, an authority she has never seen before.

"I wish I had your faith," she says.

"It's not a question of faith. It's a question of timing," he says. "Even his idiot driver is starting to wonder what he's doing here." She hears boots on the gravel signalling Gunter's approach, and the caretaker is himself again: eyes downcast, shoulders stooped. An old man of no consequence flicking dead leaves from the crevices of a stone cherub.

"Get the shovels," Gunter mutters. The caretaker is right. He is no longer so sure of himself.

Tonia arrives with the cook to serve the evening meal. Hinckel has made no mention of the dead man, let alone the disappearance of the girls and three of his guards. He has only his chauffeur and two others now, and Gunter does not look happy about being relegated to patrolling the grounds day and night.

Tonight's stew is presented in fine china bowls painted with yellow roses. The quality of food is declining faster than it should, considering the supplies that were in the pantry only ten days ago. Is the cook running a black market operation from the back door? Marguerite would do the same, given the opportunity. Food is currency.

Lina Hinckel sips from a spoon with an expression of bland serenity. What a model of German stoicism, she is, eating the *Eintopf*. And that's what people have taken to calling the Volkssturm, the People's Army. Old meat and greens.

"Liesl," Lina Hinckel says. "More bread for the Bereichsleiter." The "bread" is made from potato flour and crumbles away from the knife.

Liesl, who is really Tonia, extends the silver tongs to deliver a disintegrating slice to Hinckel's plate. Her sleeve pulls up to reveal darkness along the inside of her wrist. Three colours of blue. Inky, reddish, purple. Brunfelsia. Yesterday, Today, and Tomorrow is its common name. A bruise for every day.

Across the table, a look passes between Anna and Tonia. What secrets are they sharing? Have they developed a friendship? It seems unlikely given Tonia's self-sufficiency, but she's a girl, after all, and what do girls do but live and breathe secrets?

Marguerite has not had an opportunity to speak to Anna about the death of the guard today. Has Tonia already mentioned it?

"What are we going to do about you, Anna?" Lina Hinckel takes a sip from her spoon and aims it at Anna. "You are fading away. Time to freshen up your hair, put some colour in your cheeks. Shall we have some fun tomorrow, just the girls?"

Anna's eyes snap to Marguerite's.

"Your mother has work to do, dear," says Lina Hinckel, observing the silent plea. "But I have a little time tomorrow."

The water in the crystal jug shivers. The front is fewer than five kilometres away. What vapid dreamland does this woman inhabit?

"Your generosity never fails, *Liebe*," Hinckel says. Husband raises glass to wife. Lina Hinckel gives him a coy smile and returns to evaluating Anna as you might a cow that has dried up. Anna's spoon tilts and the sauce dribbles back into the bowl. Has she even tasted the food? Tonia has the crystal pitcher in her hand. She reaches for Lina Hinckel's glass.

"I have an idea for what we can do to give your hair a lift," says Lina Hinckel. She lifts a hand to touch one of her own curls and the pitcher drops from Tonia's hand with a splintering crash. The older woman leaps up, shaking off crystal fragments and water.

"For God's sake!" Lina Hinckel slams her ringed hand into Tonia's head.

A gash appears on the maid's temple. Tonia stoops to pick up a shard of glass.

"Get out," Lina Hinckel says in a low voice. Then, more forcefully. "Out!"

Tonia rises, blinking, hand-wringing. The novice again. She is so very good at this. Did she drop the pitcher on purpose? Marguerite feels a surge of affection toward the girl, because if she did it on purpose, she did it for Anna.

Lina Hinckel is patting at herself with a linen napkin.

"The girl is an *imbecile*, is that not the word, Marguerite? *Im-be-cile*."

Beside her, Tonia lifts a hand, traces three vivid lines of blood across her cheek, and examines her wet fingertips. If her bearing were not so passive, it would be a declaration of war. Is Lina Hinckel responsible for the bruises on Tonia's wrist? Are they *both* brutalising her?

Anna is on her feet. The tendons fan out from her neck, and she stares at Lina Hinckel with an intent that is frightening.

"Sit down, Anna," Marguerite says.

"Leave it," says Lina Hinckel, waving a hand. The dullard imagines that Anna has risen to help clean up.

"Liesl will take care of it," says the Bereichsleiter.

Anna presses a palm to her belly, a gesture suggesting she might explode if she were to eat a single mouthful more, yet her food is cooling, untouched, in its elaborate bowl. She sits.

"Do you know," Anna says. "I might offer my help to the cook to-morrow if it's all the same to you, Mrs. Hinckel. Some of my herbs are almost ready and a meal like this could be made so much nicer with some fresher—"

"Cook is doing the best she can," says Lina Hinckel.

"She never sets foot outside—"

"Anna," says Marguerite.

"There is nothing to eat out there," says Lina Hinckel.

"You just have to know where to look. Asparagus will appear any day now, and you should see what is sprouting in the greenhouse—"

"Rabbit food won't fill anyone's stomach," says Lina Hinckel, but her husband waves his spoon.

"Forage away, Anna," Hinckel says. "I might join you if I have time. You can show me what you know."

Lina Hinckel places her spoon on the tablecloth. An indistinct lump of vegetable rests at its centre, and a muddy stain oozes into the damask. Marguerite tries to catch her daughter's eye, but Anna's attention is on her own spoon, making diminishing spirals in the stew.

After dinner, Marguerite finds Anna in her room and begins to tell her about the murder of the guard.

"Karl told me," Anna says. "That man was making threats against him, against all of us."

"*Karl? Karl* told you?"

"We are all living in the same house," says Anna, but her cheeks are flushed.

"Did *Karl* tell you that he executed that poor man? No attempt to arrest him, let alone—"

"There's a war on, Mother, in case you hadn't noticed."

Marguerite backs out of the door, away from this creature. She has asked God for too much in this war, been too selfish in her prayers. Maybe this is her punishment.

\* \* \*

The messenger Ralf shows up again in the morning. His wounds are healing; he's fixed up his bike and is in good spirits.

"What have you got for us?" says Marguerite. He pats his satchel. Is there news of Max in there? "Let me guess—for the Bereichsleiter and the Bereichsleiter alone?"

The boy nods.

"May I see?" she says. He opens the flap and shows her the contents: the same white linen stationery as the last time. "You're in luck this time. I will take you straight to him."

Karl Hinckel is all smiles and praise for Ralf until the boy lifts the envelope from the satchel.

"Leave it there," Hinckel growls, indicating the desk.

"Heil Hitler," Ralf says. Hinckel responds automatically but is intent on the letter. She leads the boy away. They have not reached the end of the corridor when there is a loud thump, the crack of glass breaking.

A few minutes later a car engine turns over and she hears the crunch of wheels on gravel as the Mercedes heads down the driveway.

The door to the office is open. The remains of the table lamp are spread across the floor. Marguerite kneels to pick up a shard of green glass and there, under the desk, is the letter, handwritten on heavy linen paper.

*My dear Karl,*

*Once again allow me to extend my deepest sympathies on the death of your youngest son in service to the Reich and Führer. It will certainly be a comfort to you that Armored Rifleman Walter Hinckel had recently been awarded a War Merit Cross (1st class).*

*As to the matter of your request, I have carried out further investigations into the disappearance of your eldest son, Captain Wilhelm Karl Hinckel, and while I am able to provide a few further details of Captain Hinckel's last flight, I regret to inform you that I can offer you little in terms of hope that your son might have survived.*

*Captain Hinckel's commanding officer took the opportunity to mention that your son was both a skilled and courageous pilot whose ability to respond under pressure allowed him to extract himself and his men from several situations which appeared desperate. Nevertheless, Second Lieutenant Allinger has reiterated that the fires in both the cockpit and starboard engine of Captain Hinckel's HE 162 appeared simultaneously, and he is of the opinion that the cockpit was itself struck by cannon fire. If Captain Hinckel had indeed survived, which Second Lieutenant Allinger believes unlikely, he would have had mere seconds to exit the aircraft before the cockpit was engulfed. Please be advised that the pilot provided these troubling details only at my insistence, and because he did not wish you to hold false hopes.*

*Needless to say, had your son somehow survived the destruction of his aircraft and was able to deploy his parachute under heavy flak, he would have landed deep inside enemy territory. I have sought information through the limited channels available to us and have no reason to hold out hope that he is in enemy hands.*

*I remain at your service.*

*With German greetings, Heil Hitler.*

"What are you doing?"

Lina Hinckel is in the doorway taking in the broken glass, the upturned lamp, Marguerite on her knees. She lets the letter fall away where it will not be seen. Her cheeks burn. Neither Karl nor Lina Hinckel have mentioned their sons. Is this why? How could Marguerite have read the news before the boys' own mother? Her instinct is to explain herself, but she recalls the lightning sweep of Lina's ringed hand against Tonia's head and says nothing.

"What has happened here?"

"The lamp," says Marguerite. "Your husband knocked it."

"Where has he gone?"

"I— He didn't say."

"What is wrong with you? Get off the floor."

Marguerite rises. To lose two sons—it happens often enough in war, but it is no less terrible. "Lina, Mrs. Hinckel . . . I am so very sorry." She searches for better words, but it is hopeless when the woman is staring at her with such contempt.

"I don't care about a lamp. I asked you where my husband was going."

"No, I mean—I mean your sons," says Marguerite.

The other woman snorts.

"My sons?" she says. A jagged blue vein appears on her temple.

Marguerite picks up the letter and Lina Hinckel snatches it from her hand. She runs her eyes over it and hands it back with a cold smile.

"Spare me the false sympathy," she says. "They were not my sons."

# 22

Josef Goebbels growls from the radio while Max folds his tarpaulin into a neat oblong, corners matched to corners, and rolls it into a tight cylinder in the cool of his canvas pack, next to his blanket. Tomorrow is Hitler's birthday, but Goebbels's traditional celebration speech is a mournful affair: world destruction, annihilation, the final battle. Children of the Reich shall become known as Werewolves, bringing terror to the enemy. With a keen set of eyes, they can become a spy. With a rifle: a sniper. With a packet of matches: an arsonist, a saboteur.

*Victory or extermination. Fanatical resistance is required.*

Max has polished his binoculars, bundled his matches into waxed cloth, and secured his knife and scabbard in the front pocket of his bag. He gives his watch eight careful clockwise rotations and checks the time against Vera's wall clock.

She switches off the radio and folds her arms.

"Unexploded bombs, looters, mines, escaped prisoners. Did I mention foreign soldiers who think the best German is a dead German? Not to mention drowning, if this weather keeps up."

The more dramatic her soothsaying, the steadier Max feels. After what seems like weeks immersed in a cauldron, pulled down into the currents created by some invisible spoon, he has crawled out to the edge and can see a way out. His legs itch to get moving, to get home, to jog up the back stairs, throw open the door and start talking, and not stop until the truth is out.

"Stay off the main roads at least," Vera says, and presents them a chunk of bread, two tins of beef in sauce, and six precious, crumbling biscuits.

Outside in the dripping garden, Hilda blinks rain out of her eyes and stares after them.

It is roughly two hundred kilometres to home. Not so very far. Nowhere near as far as Charles travelled when he escaped from the labour camp in Silesia and made it to Lauterbach, which should have been his refuge.

And what or who will be waiting for Max? Vera was right—the front has passed but the war is not over yet. There might be nothing left of his home, his family, no one left to listen.

*Light was leaking from under the kitchen door. Max opened it and blinked into the glare.*

*"They are working people to death. It is murder on a scale—"*

*Shapes formed into people. A figure rose. A chair fell. His mother. And next to her—filthy and aged a thousand years: Charles. Without his smart clothes and combed hair and flesh on his bones, he was so like the grim, filthy Russian labourers that for a moment, Max felt disgust.*

*Charles never saw it, because he was staring, wild-eyed, not at Max, but at Mama. Max had recovered himself and run for Charles, who had waved him off, promised Max a volley of kisses, a tsunami of embraces, once he'd had a good wash.*

But now Max thinks back to that fallen chair, his mother on her feet, her hands pressed into the air in front of her, he is certain that she would have seen it. The rain hisses off the road, and a bomber stream thrums beyond the clouds as they walk. Ten, twenty, thirty kilometres to the east, the fighting continues. Here, it is over. It feels as if time is suspended and they are marching between the old world and the new. The rain falls, his breath rises and falls, his feet lift and fall, lift and fall. There is only Max and Hans and the road. Each step brings them closer to home, or whatever is left of it.

A billboard is collapsed on the roadside—an image of the Führer with the eyes shot out. Who is Adolf Hitler to the invading armies? An enemy. A stranger. What can it have been like to grow up without knowing him? His face is as familiar to Max as his own father's. The Führer has always been there—glaring out from magazines and newspapers, posters in the street, portraits in the chapel and classroom and shops, at every Jungvolk meeting or march. There were many times when Max saw the Führer's face more often than Papa's—during Papa's time in prison, of course, his long shifts in the mine, all the meetings that sent every member of the family in different directions, not just in the evenings but on Saturdays and even Sundays. Hitler's voice was always there too—passionate, electrifying, even through the radio wires. Papa is a quiet man given to saying little. Less than you might wish for. Hitler would utter more words in a single speech than Papa might say in a month.

"I saw him once," says Max.

"Who?" says Hans.

Max indicates the desecrated billboard. "The year of the plebiscite."

"When he brought the armies to Saarbrücken? You were there?"

"With Papa."

"Did he see you?"

"Who, Hitler?" Max remembers marching, being inflated with a feeling akin to love. "I don't remember much. Just a lot of rain."

Their steps knock a soothing beat on the rain-soaked road.

"When did you stop believing?" says Max.

Hans laughs and flashes his eyes. "In fairies?" he says. "Or ghosts?"

"In *him*."

Silence.

"Hans?"

"The same day as you. The day your godfather—The day they came for him."

"They brought him low, Hans."

"It was a bad business."

"There's more to it. When Charles came to our house, I was supposed to— She asked me to do one thing, just one thing to help him, but—" The words jam in his throat.

"It doesn't matter now."

"It will always matter. I have to get home. I have to make her understand."

"Then let's walk a little faster. How long to go?"

"A week?"

"Less if we move?"

"Yes."

"Then let's move."


When he lifts his eyes again, the rain has eased, the countryside has crept up. To their right, flat fields lead to stepped vineyards running along the slopes of a small mountain. American trucks and Jeeps line the road leading to the ramparts of an old fortress at the summit.

They shelter under a row of rain-blackened oaks glowing with fresh leaf, and watch the invaders move up and down the mountain road. A figure appears from the west with the stooped, rocking gait of someone with a bad hip. Long minutes pass until the old man reaches them, wool cap glistening, a package in heavy canvas tucked under his arm. He grunts a greeting and lifts his head to the dripping oak.

"You running with a gang? I have nothing except my books."

"Just us," says Hans. "Walking, not running."

"Walking where?"

"Home."

"Ha," says the man, and he looks, warily, it seems to Max, toward the mountain swarming with foreign troops.

"You know that place?" says Max.

"Hell Mountain?" says the man. "I know it."

"Not much of a mountain," says Hans, and the man croaks out a dry laugh.

"Five minutes to the top, twenty years to get back down. There lies the joke. That place has been a prison since my grandfather was three cheeses high, but the things going on up there lately would make your hair stand on end."

"What sort of things?" says Max.

The old man's face hardens. "How would I know?"

They leave him there under the trees and head out into the misting rain, dog-legging through an untended beet field strewn with German military clothing.

Max sweeps the rain from his cheeks with a sodden coat sleeve and recalls the look on the old man's face. Surprise hardening into suspicion. He's seen it before on the face of his mother. It's seared into his memory.

*"Max, I need you to go and wake the priest."*

*"What for?"*

*"What do you mean 'what for'? Do as you are told."*

*"Why do we need him?"*

*"He knows people."*

*"What kind of people?"*

*"We have to get Charles to France. Now go."*

*"But Charles should stay here."*

*"Max."*

*"He's half-dead, Mama. We—"*

*"Go. Don't talk to anyone other than Father Peter, tu piges? No one. If you speak of this to anyone, you put Charles in the most terrible danger. Not just him. You, me, your sister, your father. Everyone. Do you understand? You have to swear to me."*

*"I swear, Mama, but what about Papa? Papa will know what to do."*

*"Papa's shift doesn't end for another four hours. There is no*

*way to bring him up without making a fuss. Father Peter will help. Now, go."*

It was insanity. Charles could not be sent into the bitter night with torn shoes and a filthy shirt—hatless, freezing, starving to death—in the company of terrorists and brigands.

"If you want to send Charles away so badly, then why don't you get the priest?"

"Because I am French," she said. "Because I am watched. Because there will be people who are interested in where I might be going at this hour. But you, Max, you are a good little German, a devout follower of Hitler, quite above any suspicion."

Her tone cut him. He had sensed for a while that she found his Jungvolk stories irritating. If he told her about his efforts to earn a new badge or repeated a battle story shared by a Hitler Youth hero, she would cut him off, send him to fill the coal scuttle or some other tedious chore. Now he saw that it was more than boredom or irritation. It was deeper than that, something he didn't have a word for.

His mother's face changed, and she began to cry.

"Max, please. Please do this without having to understand every detail. This is Charles. Your godfather. The man you love most in the world after Papa. Please, please go, for his sake. Go now."

The fear in her face loosened a memory from when he was very young, the night his father was arrested. He'd woken to blinding light, monsters in the bedroom, skulls on black caps, the stink of sour cheese and wet leather. The monsters were men who were tearing his room apart, searching. Anna was curled in the corner of her bed whispering her floral alphabet. Acanthus, Bitterwurz, Christophskraut, Digitalis. Mama was speaking German to a man with rain on his spectacles, pleading with him to leave the children alone. The man had Max's silver coin on his black leather glove. Up spun the coin and down it fell to the rug. Lothar's beady eye glared up at Max from between faded tufts of green. The men left soon after and took his father with them.

*He saw now in his mother's eyes that if they returned, it would be Charles they came for.*

*"Go, Max," his mother had said. "You have to go now."*

They rest in a cattle shed with the side blown out of it. Max dries his hands on his trousers and rifles through the postcards to find one of a Bavarian farmhouse, picked up at Augsburg on the voyage east.

*Dear Mama and Anna,*

*I send you greetings from Eglosheim where we are staying in a schoolhouse. It is a pleasant town. With love and hugs.*

*Max*

# 23

Sleep skids out of Marguerite's reach. She runs her palms over eyes gritty with fatigue, the sound of a piano sonata repeating in her head. A Chopin melody her mother used to play while Marguerite sat with her back resting on the piano leg, watching her mother's foot lift and fall on the tarnished brass pedal.

The need to hear it, to *play* it, is irresistible, and she takes up her candlestick and a fold of matches, creeps down to Anna's door—still locked—and makes her way to the piano room.

The match flares, and she holds it to the candlewick. A narrow face looms out of the night, eyes deep in shadow. She blanches, but it is only a mirror. She steps closer and holds the flame to her cheek. She looks a hundred years old and she is thirty-nine. It is not the new strands of grey or the lines in her brow that repel her from the mirror now. It is that look she carries. *Un air dur,* her mother would call it. A woman who has weathered more than the usual storms.

She sets down the candle on the piano top, lifts the lid, and is stabbed by a memory: the last time she played the piano. Rain was throwing itself at the house, wind billowing the curtains, while her children danced with Hans, circling and stamping madly, careful to avoid the lamp the wind had knocked to the floor, while she hammered at the keys, her hair in ropes, her housedress soaked, weeping for Charles and

Anton. One killed and the other sent to war in the span of one ghastly morning.

Her breath comes out in a ragged sigh. If she could have that time again, if she had sent Charles straight back out into the night, would it have changed anything?

*Charles was in her kitchen, a fugitive. He could not stay. The risk to the children, to Anton, was too great. But where could he go? Anton was deep in the mine, not halfway through his shift. Who could she turn to?*

*Just once, in the early days of France's occupation, Marguerite had overheard a parishioner make a snide comment to another about the priest's "friends" in France. The other woman had scoffed, but the alarm on her face told its own story. Marguerite had pretended not to notice.*

*Fetching Father Peter herself was out of the question at that hour. She needed to find clothes for Charles, prepare him a meal. She would kill one of their last chickens and make a feast to carry him through the difficulties ahead.*

*So she had sent Max. She had not expected to waste precious minutes convincing him to go. This was Charles, after all, his beloved godfather. Only when he had stepped out into the night did it occur to her how much she was asking of her son. Loyalty was one of his strengths, but when had he ever had to choose between family and faith? Because that is what his indoctrination had become, a corrupted type of faith.*

*She was still plucking the chicken when she heard the racket. Who was this battering at her door? But she knew. Already she knew.*

*Anna was in the kitchen, head swivelling like a carnival clown. Charles was up and running for the door to the garden. Marguerite snatched up his coat and called a warning, but he had already slipped on the first frosted step. His legs flew out from under him, and he landed hard on his back.*

174

*Three scorched demons stormed the room. Black uniforms,*
*black caps, black guns.*
*And behind them,* with *them, Max.*

The piano keys are silk beneath her fingertips. She closes her eyes to find the tune, and the door handle turns. Karl Hinckel steps into the room holding a cognac glass. She pulls her robe tight and rises, almost knocking over the piano stool.

"I wondered who was burgling the salon," he says.

"Sleep has abandoned me," she says. *Where is his wife?* She takes a few cautious steps, putting the piano between them, and picks up the candlestick.

"Insomnia is for those with a guilty conscience. Or so my father insisted." Is it his conscience that keeps Hinckel up with the owls, or the death of his sons? He pulls the door closed. "A man who never had trouble sleeping."

Marguerite's heart flails. If she were to scream, who would hear? More to the point: Who would come?

"I was just going back to bed," she says.

"No you weren't." He takes off his jacket and drapes it over a settee.

There is a good weight to the candlestick. Would it be enough to knock him down? Does she have the strength? Could she get close enough?

"Go on." He gestures at the piano and sinks into the sofa. "Play." His tone reminds her of the bruises on Tonia's arms. Her forearms itch.

She slides out the piano stool and lowers herself onto it. Playing the sonata is out of the question, but when she reaches for an alternative, the first few notes of "Cradle Song" find their way through her fingers. She lifts her hands. This is another precious scrap of her past she will not share with Karl Hinckel. She used to play it when Anna and Max were infants, and fractious in the evenings. Anton would lug them around, face down on his forearm, humming along. They were quick to settle in his arms. And so was she. He knew how to soothe her jangled nerves.

Tears blur her vision—pointless tears because she wants him back now, in this room, not just as a buffer between her and Karl Hinckel, but to remind her who she is and where she comes from and what is true and where her heart lies, because she is adrift.

"Play," Hinckel says.

She recalls the words her neighbour, Luscher, spat out into the rain the morning they sent Anton to war. *Playing the piano is all over for you, Mrs. Bernot.*

Play. Don't play.

These men and their appetite for telling Marguerite what she can and can't do. Play. Don't play. By appearance Luscher and Hinckel have nothing in common, yet they both like to be admired, and Marguerite does not admire them. Play, don't play. This is how they punish her. She hates them for it.

She rises and closes the piano lid. Hinckel remains in his seat, one knee crossed over the other, a hand tracing circles in the velvet arm of the settee.

"I'm going to bed," she says.

"My wife tells me you have been reading my private correspondence."

She hesitates. She could ignore him, walk away right now, but it doesn't feel safe to turn her back.

"I should not have read it. I am sorry."

"My sons were decorated."

"And that is a comfort to you."

"Does that surprise you?"

"It would not comfort me."

"You don't understand the first thing about nationhood."

"What do the deaths of your sons have to do with nationhood?"

"Everything."

"Germany is falling. Even if you imagine this war to be justified, every life lost is an egregious waste."

"You have no inkling what it is to be proud of your race, your blood, your history—"

"People are not seeds or cattle. They can't be categorised. Certainly not where I come from. Not on the border."

"You picked your side, Marguerite."

"What is that supposed to mean?"

"If you felt so strongly, you could have followed your husband's brother to France."

"What do you know about my husband's brother?"

"I know whatever I choose to know."

A nerve grips the base of her spine.

"Why should we leave our home, our land, the place my husband's family has lived for generations?"

"It was a choice, nonetheless."

"Why am I here, Karl? Because I turned down your marriage proposal twenty years ago?"

He laughs, and the chill makes her flinch. "Still the egoist you ever were. I never proposed marriage to you, Marguerite."

She blinks at him. Does he actually believe it? The proposal had felt like a business proposition, not a declaration of love. He was fixated on politics, increasingly outraged at the punishing terms of the Versailles treaty, the conspiracies without and within, the vultures picking at what was left of Germany's corpse. He intended to move to Munich and wanted her there to support him during his rise within the party.

"I remember differently."

"I left you because you had no ambition," he says. "You were parochial. You couldn't see past your next payday, working in the typing pool of a provincial town hall."

"I turned you down because you wanted me to be a breeding sow for the party."

"So you became a breeding sow for a Saarland coal miner? A drudge with field-worker's hands. As I said, Marguerite: no ambition."

"If only your party faithful could hear you now. What it must have cost you to pretend all these years that you saw the great worth in miners and peasants." Her voice is hard and strange to her. "You call me an egoist, but it is your own ego that will not allow you to remember

177

proposing to me. If it was you who left me, then explain what I am doing here. Explain why you are threatening my daughter, keeping us in this house, claiming to be searching for my son. If this is not some elaborate game to punish me for what I did or didn't do when I was nineteen, then what is it?"

"You broke the law, Marguerite."

"What?"

"You broke the law. Your name crossed my desk, and I was intrigued. The Marguerite I knew would never have been part of a movement, would never have had the inclination to harbour a fugitive, let alone the courage—"

"What are you talking about? You mean opening my door to my cousin? My own flesh and blood who was half-dead from what you people had done to him?"

"Your role was somewhat less heroic than the paperwork led me to believe," he says. "Still, I was curious to see who you had become. Then my secretary collapsed into hysteria the very week I tracked you down. Two birds, one stone. No broken heart, Marguerite. No hard feelings. Nothing more than curiosity—closely followed, I am sorry to tell you, by deep disappointment."

She bows her head and extends her arms in a mock curtsy.

"When this war is over—and listen to that mortar, Karl, because the end is coming—I will return to my grubby coal miner, and my potato fields, and my little house. If you survive the end, what will you do? Without your uniform and your title and your slaves and bodyguards— what will you be? What medals will your precious Führer bestow upon you for hiding in the countryside, drowning yourself in cognac and brutalising women?"

A tiny muscle beneath his left eye twitches. He is twisted up with nerves, and for a moment she is gratified, then concerned. Too late, she steps back, but he is on her. He grabs the collar of her robe and tears it off her shoulder. She drags herself clear, collides with a lounge chair and pulls herself around the back of it. He lunges again and she ducks out of reach, keeping the chair between them.

He hesitates. She has played this game many times with her children and her husband, weak with laughter. Now rage and fear are making her heart rattle.

"What would your sons think if they could see you now?" she says, because she knows how this will end and she has nothing to lose. "Would they be proud of their father? Or would they have become like you? Maybe it's better they did not live to understand that their lives were thrown away in a war started by you and your cronies. You might as well have shot those poor boys in their cribs."

He yanks the chair toward him, and she leaps for the door, but he has her. He drags her back and throws her face down on the settee, pinning her with his body. She tries to strike back with her feet, her elbows, to smash the back of her head into his face. He gets hold of her left arm and she uses the right to grip the back of the sofa, but he wrenches her hand free and drags both hands high up her back. The pain is searing, and she screams. Then, a miracle. Her hands are free. She twists around and sees that he is working at his belt buckle. She manages to drag herself a little farther along the couch when a heavy blow knocks her sideways. A flat ringing sets into her ears and then a knocking.

Not this. Please God. Not this.

He strikes her again, but the door is opening and it is Tonia, blessed Tonia, the archangel Tonia, backing into the room with a silver tray in her hands. She seems not to notice the struggle she has walked into, frowning with the effort of not tipping over the crystal decanter and matching glasses. Hinckel releases Marguerite, and lurches away. She falls back, pulling her shredded gown up over her shoulders.

"I am here for make drink," Tonia says, with a brilliant, triumphant smile. "I hear nice music. I think: *Good. I will take drink.*"

If Tonia sees his rage, she does not let on, brave girl. Beautiful, brave girl.

Hinckel lifts the decanter from the silver tray and hurls it at the fireplace. Glass and cognac splatter. Ashes hiss. He pushes past Tonia and is gone.

"You," Marguerite whispers.

"Me," says Tonia.

Marguerite reaches for her robe and pulls it tight around herself. She steps toward the girl and tries to thank her, but Tonia interrupts.

"You should go to bed now."

"Not yet," she says, and plants a kiss on Tonia's forehead, and another for luck. Tonia wipes it away with her forearm. "Go and wake Anna and lock yourself in there. I will be up in a moment."

She reaches for Hinckel's jacket, which rests where he left it on the sofa. She knows it will be in there, but it is still a shock against the tips of her fingers. Fear claws at her. *You do not have to do this, Marguerite.* She closes her fingers around the key and draws it out of the jacket pocket. *Yes, I do.*

The library door groans open. The dark reaches for her. She fights the urge to back out. Is someone in here? Only the hiss and creak of trees at the window, the thudding of her heart.

She fumbles for the matches, and they spill onto the carpet. One is all she needs. She feels around on the floor, finds one, and strikes it. The flare is blinding. *Hurry.* The wind lifts a branch onto the window, but she will not run. The key fits and turns with a light snap.

She pulls open the door of the safe.

Mostly, there is money. Thousands and thousands of Reichsmarks bundled up in stacks as thick as her thumb. How is it possible for one man to accumulate all this? Not since the twenties has she seen currency in this quantity—but in those days it was worthless. Underneath is a plain brown file. It slides out, causing a few packets of money to topple.

The folded edge is torn at both top and bottom. This file has been opened, many times. Handwritten in faded pencil in the top right corner are the initials MG. Marguerite Guibert.

# 24

Max is tying a length of sacking around his right boot to keep the flapping sole in place when he hears the rumble of a convoy. He is perched on a pile of rubble that used to be a school. Below, a Jeep comes into view carrying three soldiers; the one in the rear grips the handles of a mounted machine gun. Two trucks follow. More beyond.

"The rucksacks," says Hans. Max leads the way, crabbing down the rear side of the debris. The ruins tremble with the advance of the convoy. Max ducks through a hanging door to a classroom. A handful of gravel patters above somewhere. Through the gap where a door once stood, their packs are clearly visible next to the road but in the shadow of a collapsing wall.

"Shit," says Hans.

"They're looking for snipers, not rucksacks."

A brick bounces from a sorrowful chimney on the other side of the road. And another. The chimney shimmers, groans, and folds in on itself just as the first truck rolls past. The backs of scores of Allied soldiers pass by, faces turned into the dusty air where the chimney used to be.

At the convoy's rear, bareheaded prisoners in Wehrmacht and SS jackets slouch in open troop movers. One among them stands out. There is a loftiness to him, an air of the untouchable, even without his cap and his hair so windblown. This is a man Max would have feared.

181

A foreign soldier tousles that wild hair, and the Nazi snatches his head away, his torso rocking with the pitch of the truck on the potholed road.

Max and Hans head north through the ruins, taking quiet lanes, avoiding the checkpoints and the lines of homeless with their miserable loads.

By the time the sun is directly ahead, a low disc of silver in heavy cloud, they have reached the forested hills on the back route to Karlsruhe.

Max wakes shivering to a brighter morning, a stick of hay cutting into his cheek and the sound of Hans sneezing. It had seemed a smart idea the previous night to dig themselves into a haystack, but now his skin and hair prickle with dust and dew. The field shimmers red with corn poppies. If each one shelters a fairy, as Anna used to say, there is enough magic here to transport him home.

"Dead Man?" says Hans. He's holding out the open can of beef. The gravy resembles dark mucous, but a few spoonfuls soothe his stomach. They had resolved to leave it until morning, to provide energy for walking.

"Hans," Max says, and hesitates.

"*Jòò,*" says Hans.

It is good to hear the Platt. They have been in the habit of speaking German for so long now.

"I swear I can hear my name being called, and once the thought is there, I can't shake it."

"Who's doing the calling?" says Hans.

"My godfather mostly. Sometimes it's our friends from the train at Sankt Wendel. I can't believe they're gone."

"I don't like to think of it, Max."

"The worst is when I hear the ones who are alive, who *should* be alive. It's Horst, or my mother, or father, or Anna. I worry that they're dead too. All of them. That when we get back, there will be no one. A thought like that has a way of sticking, you know?"

"My father," says Hans, "is a quieter sort of ghost. He only comes in dreams, smiling like one of the saints."

"Sounds peaceful."

"You might think so, but my sleeping self has a question, and no matter how many times I ask—even if I scream it in his ear—he refuses to answer, and it makes me hate him."

"What's the question, Hans?"

Hans sneezes and wipes his sleeve across his eyes. "Look at us," he says.

Max laughs, as much as he can when his throat is locked up so tight.

"Do you know what I think?" says Hans. "I think the Messerschmitt 262 jet is the greatest aircraft in the world." He sniffs and spits. "Did you ever fly one, Captain Bernot?"

"Indeed I did, Captain Schlesier," Max says. He plucks a piece of hay and transforms it into a fat cigar. "Blasted hell out of a bomber stream once."

"Sounds like a fine day at work, Captain Bernot. How many did you take out?"

"Difficult to say, difficult to say," says Max, and sends three perfect smoke rings out into the field. "I was halfway to London by the time I stopped firing and Lancasters were raining from the sky."

"Not easy to pilot," says Hans. "The legendary Silver."

"Only the best can manage it," says Max. "Slow to take off. Slow to put down. Makes you a sitting duck for those Tommy bastards."

"Shall we fly one home from here?"

"Excellent idea."

Hans is quiet for a moment.

"How far now?" he says.

"Half a day's walk to Karlsruhe."

"And then?"

"Cross the Rhine, and we'll be home in a few days—or an afternoon if we get ourselves a lift."

"Let's go, then." Hans is up and dusting the hay off his backside. He reaches for Max's hand and hauls him up, and his energy is infectious, but Max hears that voice again.

*Max*, Charles calls. *Max. What have you done?*

He closes his eyes and sends a silent message to his mother across what remains of this ravaged country. *It wasn't me.*

*The night was cloudless and bitter. Max had almost slipped on the first of the frosted steps and paused to button his coat and plunge his hands into his pockets.*

*Charles was still in the bath. It would take twenty minutes to walk to the church. Who were these people who were going to hide Charles in France? The armed brigands who roamed the forest and called themselves Maquisards? How could his mother put Charles into the hands of such men, send him out on such a night in such a state?*

*Max sank onto the stair landing. The moon cast a strange brightness and the shadows, so much darker and deeper by night, seemed to reach for him as he tried to concentrate. The safest thing would be to keep Charles here, wouldn't it? To hide him in the coal cellar or in the attic or in the woodshed or under Max's bed. No one would know.*

*Through the lower branches of the cherry tree that stood between their yards, a cigarette crackled and glowed.*

*"The Bernots are up with the birds today," the neighbour Luscher said, his voice a murmur.*

*Startled, Max raised a hand in greeting.*

*"The unbidden guest is ever a pest, eh, Max?" The cigarette made a circle toward the west, toward Carling. Acrid smoke sat in the air like poison. "Tippity tap tap."*

*Max rose, taking hold of the banister. Had Luscher heard Charles at the door?*

*"Turning up at the most inconvenient time, yes?" Luscher said. Why was he up at such an hour, wearing a hat and coat?*

*Max's foot found the first stair.*

*Luscher lowered his head a little, to see Max better through the branches.*

*"Max?" he said.*

*Max's foot found the second step, and the third.*

*Luscher had smiled at him through the dying leaves. "I think you had better come with me."*

From a forested hill, Max and Hans watch barracks burning unhindered on the eastern outskirts of a small town. The roads hum with ambulances and trucks, a few wagons, but mostly the homeless on foot with their wretched loads. Enough of a crowd to disappear into.

A quiet foot track leads between overgrown gardens. Just one is well-tended. Is it worth jumping the fence for a handful of baby carrots? An old man steps outside and lets out a cry. Max raises his hands.

"Could you spare some food please, sir?" says Max. "We will work for it."

"Are you *trying* to get arrested?" he says. "They're rounding up all the boys. One or two lads have been taking potshots, posting pamphlets. The foreign soldiers are livid. All that rubbish about Werewolves. Go back the way you came before you get yourselves locked up."

"What are they burning over there?" says Hans, undeterred. Smoke blots out the sky beyond the old man's roof, spinning all the colours of darkness.

"You wouldn't credit the horror they are accusing us of," the man says. "Raging at us. We are Christian people."

Before Max can ask what he means, the man retreats.

Pain needles his heels and the balls of his feet, but they press on through overgrown forest tracks and neglected farmland.

"I'll be there," says Hans. His voice is a surprise. Max has been listening to the creak of branches and the chattering of the birds for hours.

"Where's that?"

"Lauterbach," says Hans. "If there is no one else. I'll be there."

"Just you and me," says Max. He feels a pang of gratitude. How long has Hans been wondering how to cheer him up?

"Running the show," says Hans. "You can be the mayor, with your looks and your middling brain."

"And you can organise the peace celebrations," says Max. "With your sparkle and your gift for words."

Hans tips at the waist and makes an elaborate flourish. "Hedy Lamarr."

"What does Hedy Lamarr have to do with it?"

"She'll be desperate for an invitation. She'll host the cabaret and bring one or two of her less beautiful friends so you will have someone to talk to. Because Hedy will only have eyes for me, Max, and that will be hard on you."

"Thoughtful of you," says Max.

"The cabaret could be the grand finale of the chocolate festival."

"Chocolate festival?"

"Of course."

"A chocolate festival in Lauterbach, population of two?"

"You're forgetting Hedy and the girls," says Hans. "We'll get one of those chocolate fountains. We'll turn Adolf Hitler Strasse into a river of chocolate and take our baths there and duck our heads under it and drink and drink until we're drowning in it."

The crack of a stick in the trees brings them to a stop. The canopy hushes them. A woodpecker taps out a warning, and Max hears a gentle thundering. A fat boar and her farrow are rocketing straight for them. Max shouts and Hans lifts his arms. The boar squeals and changes direction quick as an arrow. Her three piglets, absurd in their seesaw gait, sprint by at full screech.

"Lunch!" Hans roars, and is after them. Max follows at half the pace, the laughter having robbed him of his strength.

# 25

Marguerite lifts the envelope from the safe with a shaking hand, and her wedding band knocks against the steel frame—the sound ringing out into the night. She braces, expecting to hear a door opening, rapid footfalls. The house holds its silence. She tips the envelope and dozens of photographs spill onto the floor. She holds one to the light of the candle. Then another. And another. Her face is in every image.

Here she is on the bike with Max, an infant in the basket. Here she emerges from the bakery in conversation with the baker's wife. Here she leans her head on Anton's shoulder at the tram stop at Ludweiler, crouches on her front step with her hand on Charles's knee, speaks with Father Peter outside the church, weeds the garden—oblivious to the invisible eye of the camera.

Nausea rolls through her and she reels back, pressing her hands to her abdomen to stop herself from retching. She has to get all this back in the safe, get herself out of here, but another part of her is mesmerised, trying to make sense of what she sees.

She recalls that unsettling time after Karl Hinckel stopped writing, the feeling that he was there, just outside her line of sight. He had been watching, or had had her watched, for at least five years, judging by the most recent photograph in which Anna is three or four years old.

She reaches into the safe for a larger envelope. Inside, a collection of letters and reports are clipped to a cover letter dated in January.

*Sir,*

    *As requested, the documentation in relation to the suspect BERNOT, Marguerite, née GUIBERT, is ATTACHED. Whereabouts unknown. Suspect relocated to NEUNKIRCHEN with children BERNOT, Max, DOB 08/13/31, and BERNOT, Anna, DOB 11/05/28, in early December. Informant reported to Neunkirchen police 12/08/45 that BERNOT, M and children had failed to arrive at designated accommodation, and this was regrettably not followed up due to a large number of similar reports. Investigators now checking HABITATION reports and WELFARE OFFICE records for further information.*

    *I remain yours, etc.*

The trees creak outside the office window and a floor makes an answering groan somewhere above. Only a gust of wind, but her heart is cantering. Is he coming? Is he creeping along the hallway right now? No. Karl Hinckel is not a man who tiptoes in his own domain. If he is coming, she will hear him.

She brings the candle closer and flicks through the documents he has kept hidden. Most are copies of Gestapo reports from the days after reunification—outlining Josef's attendance at political rallies, activities, his departure to France, and Charles's taxi journeys across the border. Anton's links to the union and other social democrats are laid out with records of the interviews with Marguerite, with Anton, with Josef when he had visited before the war. There is a letter from Anton's supervisor begging to reinstate him to his former position despite his criminal record, and a report detailing Anton's friendship with a man thought to have links to the Maquis.

The last document appears to be a dry administration report on food supply, transport issues. She flicks the page and sees her own name circled; a series of neat stars scratched into the margin of the letter.

    *A fugitive from a Silesian munitions camp LEVEQUE, Charles, reported at BERNOT residence, Lauterbach. Shot while trying to*

*escape. Resident BERNOT, Marguerite (née Guibert), interrogated
and released.*

She goes cold. *Charles.* Her skin prickles and she spins around, but
the door remains closed. She places the file back into the bottom of
the safe and lifts out a packet of fifty Reichsmark notes that have fallen
from its stack. There must be five thousand marks here at least. Would
he notice it was missing? She slips it deep into the pocket of her dressing gown, then snatches a second one, and is about to lock the safe
when she sees a telegram pressed into the back of the compartment.
She reaches for it, hand trembling.

*BERNOT Maximilian LAST CONFIRMED ADDRESS
TITTMONING STOP SEPARATED FROM TROOP
FREILASSING STOP CONFIRMED BOARDED TRAIN
BOUND FOR ULM STOP NO FURTHER INFORMATION.*

Hinckel had told the truth about Max, or some version of it. But
how did Max get separated? Is he sick or injured? What has he done?
She runs her hand across the telegram, over her son's name, replaces it
and locks the safe, then turns to Hinckel's desk. She pulls open the top
drawer, lifts the cartridge of bullets from the drawer, and presses it into
her pocket. Now she will have to get her hands on the gun.

It is after two in the morning when she knocks on Anna's door.

Into Anna's silence Marguerite speaks, and her daughter's eyes track left
and right as if she were reading the documents, studying the photographs, witnessing the attack on Marguerite, the threat against herself.
It is a long time before she responds, and her voice is devastating in its
coldness.

"Are you satisfied?"

"I beg your pardon?"

"You were right. About him. About his interest in me. All just a
tactic to get at you, to punish you."

"Anna, I don't—"

"Spare me."

"Be as angry as you want with me, with him, but swear to me you will do everything to avoid him. It is not safe for you to be out in the greenhouse alone."

"I am never alone in the greenhouse," Anna says, missing the point.

"What are you taking about?"

"The caretaker is always around. If I can't see him, I can hear him." She frowns.

"What? What is it?"

"I think he's keeping watch over me."

Hours later, unable to sleep, Marguerite treads to Anna's door, takes hold of the handle to check the lock and hears her daughter's voice, low and urgent. She hesitates. If it is him, she will need more than her bare hands. The floor creaks under her steps and she takes up the first heavy object she sees—a Hitler bust made of marble.

Tonia is perched on the end of Anna's bed, speaking in a rushed whisper. They fall away from each other at the sight of her.

"Tonia has brought me a blanket," says Anna. How quick she is with a lie.

"Frost come tonight," says Tonia. "Room is cold one."

"Why are you speaking like that, Tonia?"

Tonia smiles. "You can go to bed," she says. "Everything is good."

Everything is not good. But it comforts her to know that Tonia is in the room with her daughter. What are they whispering? Tempting to listen at the door, but Marguerite is not sure that she wants to know.

It is barely light when she hears Lina Hinckel pacing back and forth in her room. What is she doing up there? Pressing her curls? Marguerite will give her something else to think about.

Lina Hinckel pulls open the door wearing an oriental silk robe over a low-cut nightgown that reveals her bony sternum, jutting clavicles. "What do *you* want?"

"I need to talk to you," says Marguerite.

"I am occupied." She tries to close the door, but Marguerite presses both hands against it and pushes her way through.

"Now is better."

"Get out of my room."

Marguerite uses her back to slam the door. Lina recoils, then gathers herself, scraping the hair off her face and straightening her robe. The room is as crammed as the back room of a furniture store—every surface crowded with crystal, candlesticks, *chinoiserie*. There are countless Matryoshka dolls, ornate silver pillboxes, miniature crystal animals, and so much polished silver.

"Not until you've heard me out," says Marguerite. "Sit."

Lina Hinckel chews on the inside of her cheek, then sinks into a turquoise chair with a mustard-coloured cushion that matches a sofa Marguerite has seen downstairs. The woman is a magpie. She has gathered up bright objects from all over this house. None of it is hers.

"I've come to appeal to you."

"I can't imagine why."

"I want you to help me leave this place with my daughter."

"Why on earth would I do that?"

"You have made it clear you don't want us here."

"My husband has been gracious enough to offer you a position, a roof over your head, a place at our table—and this is how you reward him?"

"He has made a threat against my daughter, against me."

"Oh, boo-hoo." Lina Hinckel rubs her fists into her eyes.

"Where is your heart?"

"What good is a heart?"

"If not for me, then my daughter. I entreat you, one woman to another. The next time your husband is away from the house, you could find a way to occupy the guard so we could slip away. We only need—"

"I will not begrudge him his sport," says Lina Hinckel.

Marguerite takes a moment to make sure that she has understood.

"There is something wrong with you," she says.

"Not at all, Marguerite," says Lina Hinckel. "I simply know men. They are like dogs. They turn wild if you don't give them a treat now and again, and once they've had it, they go back to licking your hand."

In the morning, Anna is gone from her room. She is neither in the kitchen nor in the library. Marguerite breaks into a run as she approaches the greenhouse, and almost weeps with relief to find Anna bent over a tray of seedlings, hair loose, a dead leaf caught in the flat crown of her hair.

But her daughter's eyes are red-rimmed and swollen.

"Child," says Marguerite. "I told you not to come out here—"

"Not a child," says Anna.

"Yes, yes, yes," says Marguerite. "And if I live to see you grow a dowager's hump and lose every tooth in your head, you will still be my child. I do not call you that to make you small but because you are mine and you are a part of me more precious than you can ever know."

"I thought he admired me," says Anna.

"He would be a fool if he didn't."

"All that talk about university, benefactors—I might as well dream of meeting a prince."

"You don't need a prince, Anna. You certainly don't need a monster. All you have learned so far has come from your own endeavours, your own passions. I don't know the first thing about university, but I do know that there are female scholars. When the war is over, when sanity is restored, we will look into it. I can't make you any promises. I don't know how any of it works, but we can ask people, we can write letters."

"What is wrong with me? Every girl I know dreams of having seven children and earning a Mother's Medal."

Marguerite takes hold of Anna until she lifts her gaze. "Not me," she says. "I never dreamed of Mother's Medals for you. Before the war, when so much still seemed possible, I used to imagine you working in a great botanical garden in Paris or Berlin wearing your white coat, impressing all the men with what you knew."

The tension drops from Anna's face and a series of expressions cross it—surprise, pleasure, then doubt.

"It's true, Anna," says Marguerite. "Allow yourself to believe it."

And God forgive her, but Hitler had played his part in Marguerite's hopes for her daughter. She had dismissed so much of his bluster and vitriol, but when he spoke of the children, of the opportunities that would be available for those from humble places, humble beginnings—what mother could resist?

"And now?" says Anna. "What do you imagine for me now that everything is destroyed?"

"Who knows what will grow out of the ruins, Daughter?"

The door rattles and the caretaker wanders in.

"Good news, Miss Anna," he says, and extends toward her daughter a narrow spear of bright green asparagus.

"Where?" Anna says.

"Southwest field," he says, and nods at Marguerite. "Madame."

"Look at my seedlings," Anna says to him. "I swear they have grown a centimetre overnight."

"You have the knack of it," he says. "Has the label fallen from this tray?"

Anna bites her lip. "I've done it again. I keep forgetting to label them."

"We don't all have your memory," he says. "You have to give the rest of us a little help to know what is what."

"What is this?" Hinckel is at the door of the greenhouse in full uniform but unshaven. One of his buttons is undone. "Why are you not at work, Marguerite?" he says.

She sees him as he was last night, panting, a trickle of sweat running down his temple, tearing at her nightgown.

"I don't feel well," she says, and it is true.

Anna greets the Bereichsleiter with a half salute.

"I'm making Mama a tincture," she says. "I need to remember where I've put the peppermint. Get yourself back to bed, Mama. I'll bring it shortly."

"I believe I know where the peppermint is," says the caretaker, and he wanders off into the depths of the greenhouse.

Hinckel is gone most of the day and does not return until they are seated at dinner, where Lina Hinckel is making steady progress on her third glass of wine.

"Darling," he says, kissing his wife, throwing off his coat and resting his pistol and holster on the sideboard. He calls for Tonia to pour wine. He still hasn't shaved, and his hair has come free of the usual meticulous rows. Has he been drinking? He is not usually so casual with his gun. She could get to it in three quick steps, but then what?

Tonia lifts bottle to glass. The label is water-stained, and a rag of cobweb drifts from its base.

"What made you choose this wine, Liesl?" Hinckel says.

Tonia stares at the bottle as if the correct answer lies within.

Marguerite would have to get the gun out of its holster, point it in the right direction, and be ready to shoot before he's out of his chair. Is it loaded? Would she be able to tell? Gunter might be right outside, and what is Lina Hinckel capable of if she feels truly threatened? Then there is the matter of the other guard, and what will happen to her daughter if she fails.

"I am sorry, sir," Tonia says.

"I did not ask for an apology, Liesl," Hinckel says. "I want to know what made you choose this wine."

"Is not good, sir? I find other," she says, but before she can move, he has her by the hair, dragging her to her knees. Her head is at a terrible angle.

"I did not ask you to find me another one," he says. "I asked why . . . you . . . chose . . . this one." With each word he yanks at her hair. She gasps but does not cry out. How brave she is.

"It is with bottles you show me."

"Are you sure about that, Liesl? Look at this label." With his other hand, he holds the bottle to her face. "Mukuzani, from Georgia. Have I ever expressed an appetite for Bolshevik wine?"

Lina Hinckel makes a face and sets down her glass.

"Quite right, darling," she says in her child's voice. "I thought it was off."

The maid reaches up for the bottle and Hinckel whips it out of her reach.

"Perhaps you chose this wine because you wish to taste it." The girl shakes her head, as much as she can with her hair caught so tightly in his fist. Hinckel drags her head back so that her mouth is forced open. He smashes the top off the bottle and a flare of red spreads onto the white damask.

Marguerite feels Anna's eyes on her. What can she do? Challenging him is out of the question with that gun on the sideboard, but doing nothing makes her a part of this.

"Do you want to taste it, Liesl?"

"I will find other, sir—" But the wine is flowing over Antoninia's mouth and into her nose, across her cheeks and into her hair, reddening the white collar of her uniform as she chokes and swallows and coughs. A splatter hits Hinckel's face, and he shoves her to the floor. He dabs at his face, rearranges the napkin, and glances at Antoninia, as if surprised to see her there, gasping and gagging on her hands and knees.

"Hurry now, Liesl. Our dinner is getting cold." Only when she is upright at the door does he call: "Fresh glasses, please, and clean yourself up before you come back in here."

Anna puts down her knife and fork. Neat squares of German turnip and German carrot and German potato are gathered to one side of her plate as if they have been laced with poison.

Tonia is back a few minutes later—face washed, shirt changed— with a different bottle. Hinckel examines the label and gestures at her to open it and pour.

"Now, Marguerite," he says. "I have been meaning to tell you we have located your son." A fleck of red rests on the sallow skin under his left eye. "He has turned up in Munich and I have arranged to have him sent here without delay."

She does not trust herself to speak.

He claps his hands together.

"Are you not pleased, Marguerite? Tracking down wayward boys is not an easy business at the best of times. What could be more satisfying than reuniting a lost son with his mother?"

He's lying. She's certain of it. He will never be reunited with his own sons, so why would he reunite her with her own—unless he means to harm him? And by what means did this information arrive? The telephone lines are out; for days the only communiqués passing through Hinckel's office have been war emergencies.

"Thank you, Herr Bereichsleiter," she says.

"I have to warn you, Marguerite, that he has won himself no favours by running away."

He takes up his glass and studies the colour of the wine. He takes a slow sip, moves it forward and back in his mouth, closes his eyes, and swallows.

"Oh, don't worry yourself unduly," he says. "I am sure he is all in one piece, but our youth take a dim view of *Kameraden* who abandon their friends to save themselves. I'm sure it will be nothing more than a little roughhousing—nothing a healthy young man won't survive."

He is a snake. If she had that gun, she would point it straight at his chest.

"Darling," says Lina Hinckel, and leans over with a napkin to dab the wine from her husband's face.

"I have a question." Anna's voice rings across the room.

"Anna," he says, his tone bright, cultured, the gentleman again.

"If we are not to drink the wine of our enemies, why is French wine so often on the table?"

Marguerite closes her eyes. *Dear God, not now.*

"An interesting question," Hinckel says. "We do have a soft spot for the wines of our old foe. But I would remind you that champagne, that very best of French wine, is produced on German land. Contested over the generations, certainly, but German *terroir* nonetheless. Is that not so, Marguerite?"

Marguerite does not trust herself to respond.

They drink. They eat. Marguerite imagines the weight of that pistol in her hand.

# 26

East of Waldbronn, Baden-Württemberg
April 1945

The same cuckoo has been pursuing them for an hour, calling so persistently that Max is not sure if the call is real or an echo playing over in his head. He stops to check the compass. They are making steady progress west through the northern reaches of the Black Forest, sticking to the shelter of the trees where they can, though the rain has eased.

Hans takes hold of his sleeve. "Listen."

The sharp rise of voices reaches him. They continue through a stand of beech to where the forest opens out to a field overlooking a long valley. The far side of the field is ploughed in neat rows except for a single furrow weaving toward a hamlet nestled into the sloping forest edge a few hundred metres from where they stand. The plough rests there, horse still attached and nibbling on the outer branch of an apple tree. A sheet hanging from a clothesline has lost a peg and is dragging in the dirt.

"I don't like it," Hans says.

A tang of yeast cuts the air. Max drops to a crouch and takes out his binoculars. Hunger drags at his insides.

"We need to eat," he says, but his skin prickles.

They slip back into the darkness of the forest and make their way toward the hamlet, pausing at a lane leading past an old well with a gabled roof and a heart carved into it. The slow rocking of the bucket suspended on its rope recalls another sort of hanging.

The voices are louder now—rising and falling in merriment or anger. Max and Hans bypass the lane and take a concealed route behind a cattle barn to a hedge.

It is a brawl, not a celebration. Two men throw lazy, mis-aimed blows while six others, armed with rifles and sub-machine guns, circle in a noisy, ragged dance. They are gulping from flagons, stumbling, steadying, swilling. The air is heavy with yeast and the ground gleams with broken glass. A dark trail runs from the centre of the scuffle to the double doors of what must be a brewing shed. A body lies in the entrance, rifle still in one crooked arm.

This is a place where law does not exist: where you can kill a man and hang around to drink his beer without fear of arrest.

Max and Hans return the way they came and have just reached the crossing when a shout goes up. A gigantic bearded man is aiming a torrent into the well; penis in left hand, rifle in right. The man lifts the gun in greeting and shouts a few words Max does not catch. The man overbalances, checks his fall with the rifle butt, then worries he has pissed on his own boots. He looks to Max again, and the laughter dies. The problem, Max sees, is the expression on his own face.

The man lifts the gun and aims the barrel.

A sharp blow to his backside propels Max forward. He whirls. All Hans's teeth are showing. What the hell is he doing? The man is laughing again, but the gun is still raised. Hans takes a wide, slow swing. Max dodges.

And now he sees.

They are to be Dick and Doof. Fat and stupid. A couple of comedians who have helped themselves to the ale. Hans reverses and lowers his head, a bull preparing to charge, and Max flails and stumbles back behind a garden wall. Then Hans is sprinting, urging Max to go, go, *go*.

With every step Max expects the bullet to tear him open, but feels only fire in his lungs and power in his legs and, at last, the forest-cooled air wrapping him in its safety.

"Holy Christ," says Hans, bent in two, hands resting on knees. "That was lucky."

"Not that lucky—didn't get any food, did we?"

"Can't eat if you're dead."

"True."

"How far to go, Max?"

"A few more days."

Or weeks or months or years. The hunger grinds at his insides. He walks and dreams of apple tart and beaten cream and roasted pork with braised carrots and potatoes cooked in lard until their skins turn golden and crisp. He dreams of his godfather Charles, who must have known this hunger. When Max placed the bread and jam on the table before him the night he returned, he looked ready to bite Max's arm off.

*"I think you had better come with me."*

*Max had hesitated there on the stairs while Joerg Luscher took another deep drag on his cigarette. He must have seen or heard Charles at the door, but he couldn't have known who it was in the darkness. Should Max ignore him? Run back up the stairs right now to warn Mama and Charles? No. No, that would just confirm Luscher's suspicions.*

*"Quietly now," said Luscher.*

*Max had descended slowly while his mind sprinted ahead trying to find the means, the words, to extricate himself. He could invent a story, convince Luscher that it had been he, Max, at the door, but Luscher already had him by the arm in a fierce grip. Together they ascended the neighbour's stairs. Each step was a mountain to be scaled, fear and dread dragging him down. I will be good, Herr Doktor, he once promised the doctor, and himself. Good and loyal and brave. Max felt none of those things.*

*A single candle burned on the kitchen table where Hedda Luscher sat in her dressing gown and slippers, her hair in a long plait resting over one shoulder. She saw Max and her eyes widened. A look passed between husband and wife.*

Max shivered. *The light from the candle was the only warmth in there. The fire was unlit. What had Hedda Luscher been doing here, alone in the cold and the dark?*

*"You'd better go," Luscher said to his wife. Her gaze dropped to the table and she did not move.*

*"Hedda." Luscher's voice was low, but Max heard the fury in it. Still Hedda Luscher did not move. Max did not trust himself to breathe. He felt in her stillness a protest, a possibility.*

*"Time to go, Hedda." This time she could not withstand him. She rose and left the room, pulling the door closed behind her. The fear winding through Max's limbs took a firmer grip.*

*The kitchen smelled of lard and stale onions. A pair of pots sat on the stovetop; dirty serving spoons balanced on top. Mama never excused Max or Anna from the kitchen until every dish had been dried and put away, the bench washed and polished. He'd often wished his mother wasn't such a stickler, but here, in the Luschers' grimy kitchen, where the stink of last night's dinner was suffocating, he longed for the gleam of his mother's kitchen.*

*"Take a seat, take a seat," Luscher said, pulling out a chair. Narrow black eyes glimmered in the candlelight and that smile was not to be trusted—too wet, too wide, too much bottom lip. Luscher smeared a heavy lock of hair back onto his forehead.*

*"I can't stay," said Max. "I have to . . . I have to go to my friend's house."*

*"So early in the morning, Maxi?" Luscher's tongue darted out and ran across his lower lip with a tiny click and slap that sent a shudder through Max.*

*"Hans and I have volunteered for clearing work at Völklingen," said Max. "The ironworks was spared the latest bombing but—"*

*"Trams don't run until six."*

*"We're going to run there," he said, desperate now. "We have to get fitter for our silver Jungvolk badge. We have to—"*

*"Ahh, the famous Jungvolk badge,"* Luscher said.

Farther inside the house, hard shoes struck against wood, then carpet. They grew louder. The kitchen door opened and Hedda Luscher appeared, all dressed, with her hair tied back and her coat on, one hand on the door, the other carrying a hat. Luscher let out an angry breath, but she spoke anyway.

*"Joerg, what are you—"*

*"Off you go now,"* Luscher said.

*"I just—"*

*"Off you go."*

She glanced at Max, started to say something.

*"Hedda,"* her husband warned.

She pulled the door shut and her footsteps carried back along the corridor. The front door rattled, then closed.

Luscher turned back to Max. *"It's a very bad idea to lie to me,"* he said. Max went cold. *"Go on now, take a seat."*

Max knew where Hedda Luscher had gone. He knew who she would bring. He had to go, now, right now, to warn his mother, to warn Charles.

*"Interesting,"* Luscher continued, *"that a boy such as Hans-Peter Schlesier should be considered eligible for any honours at all given the burden his family has placed on the Reich over the years. One can only be grateful that Saarland returned to Germany before any more deranged little Schlesiers could slither out into this world. Imagine the cost of that."*

A strange thing happened then, so strange that Max felt it necessary to step outside himself and observe, fascinated, as his other self began to shrink.

*"Have you ever seen any sign of it in your friend?"* Luscher continued. *"The father's mental condition? I'll be honest with you, Maxi. Michael Schlesier did not take the sterilisation well. I don't believe he worked another day in his life. Cost the taxpayer a pretty penny, let me tell you."*

The Max that was outside himself recalled Hans that first day in the bathroom, scanning his nose for evidence of inferiority. He pitied the Hans of then and of now. He pitied himself, too, that young idiot trembling in a cubicle at the thought of a trespasser in his blood. How pathetic they were. They knew nothing. All they wanted was to be who the Führer wanted them to be: whole and pure and, most of all, good.

"Sit," said Luscher.

The skin of the shrinking Max drew in and his flesh flattened, his bones compacted, and this reduced version of himself lowered itself onto Joerg Luscher's chair.

"You're not much better, if we're speaking honestly, Maxi," said Luscher. "You're of the age now that we can speak man to man, no? Do you really consider yourself eligible for German honours when one considers your parentage? A common criminal and a conceited, self-important Frenchwoman?"

The candle flared and for a brief moment, Max expanded again. Joerg Luscher was a good National Socialist. A good party man, he'd heard people say. But what single thing was good about Joerg Luscher with his stupid wife and his dirty kitchen and his greasy hair and sticky forehead and filthy smile?

"Shut up," Max said.

"And that uncle of yours. Still at Buchenwald, is he? Writing his letters? All that fighting talk before the plebiscite—too blind to see the writing on the wall. It should have been no surprise to your father that he scuttled off to throw his lot in with France, but I hear it caused quite the kerfuffle in the Bernot house."

How much hot wax was pooled in the candle? Would it be enough to scald him or blind him, at least for a moment?

"Shut up."

"And now, Maximilian Bernot, who's knock-knock-knocking on your mother's door in the middle of the night? No law-abiding German, that's for sure."

He would need to be quick—throw it at Luscher's eyes, run for the door, let himself out, and rush through his yard to Mama and Charles to sound the warning.

Luscher laughed.

"Oh, dear Maxi, what are you thinking?" He drew the candle out of Max's reach. "You could no more stand up to me than your mother's country could stand up to the Reich. Weakness is in your blood. It's in your bones."

And with that Max shrank again, faster this time, until he was no bigger than one of Anna's cast-off dolls. This Max let his head droop. The doctor had been right. Max had tried to prove him wrong. He'd worn the uniform, learned the songs. He'd tried to be the fastest runner, the loudest singer, the sharpest marcher, the most obedient student, and what good was any of it? The flaw lay at the heart of him, the blood that carried impurity and weakness and failure to every part of him.

Luscher talked and the minutes ticked over into an hour, and soon Max heard the rumble of vehicles.

"Marvellous," said Luscher, rubbing the palms of his hands together. Outside, doors slammed. Luscher sat back in his chair and raised his eyebrows at Max. "Well, off you go, young man. Off to see your mother."

Max rose and took a step toward the back door, but Luscher shook his head. "Not that way, Maxi. Front door, please."

Max ran, tripping on the hallway rug, and threw open the Luschers' front door. The stars were gone. A slither of dawn was disappearing under the heavy sky. Was that thunder? But it came from his own front door.

His feet barely grazed the Luschers' front steps. He sprinted down the path, turned left, and left again along his own path, his own stairs. He followed three men along the hallway and into the kitchen where his mother stood at the door to the garden, a coat in her hand, feathers hanging in the air around her, the whites of her eyes bright as she took them in. Three armed men in black coats and, directly behind them, the traitor Max Bernot.

*The* look *she gave him. It will forever burn in him. Before he could deny it with a shake of his head, a pleading word, she turned her back on him and tried to close the back door against those men, against him. One of the men threw her aside and flung it open. Another took the garden stairs, lifted his pistol.*

*The hissing bullet.*

*The scudding dog.*

*The swinging door.*

*The second shot.*

*The crack of bone.*

*The red bloom.*

*For a long time he didn't remember more than that. A squall had blown in, and rain was battering at the glass. Anna was curled up in the corner of the kitchen reciting her plant alphabet.* Acacia, begonia, chrysanthemum. *Their mother's forehead was on the table. He sat next to her for a time, but she did not speak, did not lift her head. Her hand lay limp in his.*

*He went out again, this time to find Hans. Together they walked to the mine entrance, sheltering in the lee of a shack, and waited for his father.*

*When the cage ascended and the men spilled out, Papa's face lifted at the sight of Max and Hans.*

*"It's Charles," said Max, and couldn't say more. It was Hans who told him what happened, and only what he knew, which wasn't everything.*

*Papa cut him off.*

*"You left your mother?" he said to Max. "Your sister? You left them alone?"*

*His father did not wait for an answer. He ran, helmet in hand, briquet bouncing in the leather satchel on his hip. By the time they reached the Adolf Hitler Strasse, the Feldgendarmerie were waiting, steam spewing from the exhaust of the distinctive black car.*

*Papa stopped running and Max caught up. His father was out of breath and had to shout to be heard over the gale and the stinging rain. He was no longer angry. He said what fathers say to better sons about taking care of their mothers and sisters. The words dissolved over him as they had another time he'd been stung by his father's anger, when he'd imagined himself a soldier boy and had proudly joined the marchers in the rain at Saarbrücken.*

*"Max?" his father said. "Max?" Two men in long coats were stepping out of the car. Papa pulled Max to his shoulder, rocked his head briefly side to side. "You're a good boy," he said. "A good boy."*

# 27

The rain is trying to get into the room. It drives at the glass and batters the eaves. Marguerite's bones have taken root and are pulling her through the mattress to the rug, to the floorboards. Somewhere, a chiming clock sends blades into her head. How many chimes? Difficult to concentrate. Where is she? A candle burns. It is night. She is in her bedroom at the Bereichsleiter's house on the outskirts of Heilbronn.

She tries to sit up. The room tilts. How long has she slept? What is the time?

"You want more water?" It is Tonia's voice beyond a blinding torchlight.

"Off. Turn it off." Her own voice sounds foreign, slurred. "What time is it?"

"Don't worry," says Tonia. "Rest."

Yes, she will rest. She lets the pillow take her back.

The rain batters at the window, demanding to be let in.

*She is in the kitchen, plucking a chicken. Charles will have a proper meal before he leaves, before he is smuggled into France, secured in a safe house. Anton will come home from his shift, and they will dine together on a delicious casserole.*

*Who is this, battering on her door, demanding to be let in?*

But she knows. Three scorched demons storm the room. Black uniforms, black caps, black guns.

And behind them, with them, Max. Has he brought them here? Where is the priest?

A chair falls against a wall. Anna is screaming. Charles is on his feet and limping out into the garden. She throws the door closed, feels herself hurled sideways. The door swings open.

"Halt." There is no urgency to the call. At the top of the steps the murderer takes aim. Charles gives up fiddling with the gate latch, scrambles over the top. The murderer fires. Charles jolts. The dog careens through the garden, yelping. Or is it Anna who makes that noise?

Charles slides down the gate and his eyes lift to hers. There is a lifetime in that look. Her heart contracts. A dark rose unfurls onto his shirt. He takes hold of the gate and pulls himself up, stumbles, then stands again.

Another shot. He is thrown back. His head strikes the cattle trough with a ghastly crack. Please God, that he was already dead and did not hear the sound of his own neck break.

Anna picks up a heavy copper pot from the oven. Behind her, one of the demons raises a pistol. Marguerite runs, trying to use her body, her insufficient arms, to shelter her child.

Beyond Anna, Max's back is to the wall, his eyes rings of white, palms jammed to the sides of his head as if to drown out the sound, the most dreadful sound coming out of his mouth.

"Please," Marguerite says to the gun. "Please."

The killer steps close, lifts her chin with his thumb. At this proximity, she could tear off sneering lips with her teeth, smash her forehead into his nose, reach down for his gun and fire it into his chest. But she will not, because he will take or kill her children.

"You French." His spittle lands on her cheek. "When will you ever learn that you are beaten?" He releases her and gestures to the third thug, who swings around his machine gun, gouging *the butt into the corridor wall and dragging it as he walks back through the hall. The* WELCOME TO OUR HOME *cross-stitch panel splits and falls, followed by the ship painting, and the framed photographs of a much younger Max and Anna and Little Josef. Down they all come: smack, splinter, snap.*

*Charles's brown tasseled shoe lies on its side on the kitchen floor, leather sole peeled away; a tongue drooping out of a gaping mouth. How it must have distressed him to wear it.*

*The world pulls away. It feels as if she has lost her footing and been hurled into the air, weightless, staring at the endless glory of the stars, all the time bracing for the smack of bone on ice.*

The rain has stopped. She is alone. Where is Anna? What is the time? Below her bedroom in the Bereichsleiter's house there is a shout, followed by heavy, running steps.

She pulls herself up, waits for the room to settle. The nausea has reduced to a dull pain, but the room is still turning. She is in bed in all her clothes. She swings her feet to the floor. There are more urgent footsteps below. Her mouth tastes bitter. The tisane Anna made for her earlier is gone, replaced by a glass of water. She lifts her head. Better. She takes a sip, swirls it around her mouth, and swallows.

What time is it?

On your feet, Marguerite. Her body feels weighted, clumsy. She takes up the candle, shuffles to the door and into the passage. A shock of cold air hits her and the flame dies. An outside door is open.

At the top of the stairs she calls for her daughter. The banister is freezing. Is there a door open? Or does she have a fever? That would explain the dizziness. She takes the stairs. Careful. At last, some light. Candles in the foyer. Who is that?

Slumped in a chair, wrist pressed to his chest, the whites of his eyes glowing, is Karl Hinckel. Even in the half-light, he is a ghastly colour. What has happened here? Has he been *shot*?

Karl Hinckel looks like death.

# 28

A sharp thud in the right shoulder knocks Max awake. The O of a rifle barrel is pointed at his chest. At the end of it, narrowed eyes, a hawk nose, and gaunt cheeks sooted with whiskers. The gunman's jacket is ripped, his trouser leg matted with leaf drop and soil.

Hans is leaning back on his elbows, blinking into the rifle of a second man so small that from a distance he might be mistaken for a child. Up close he is all leathered skin folds and a fat moustache. A third is going through Hans's rucksack. He is younger than the others with a peculiar, caved-in mouth. He pulls out a grenade, and his lips stretch open into a wide, fleshy chasm. Not a single tooth to be seen.

The previous afternoon they had found a stash of weapons in a field strewn with war litter. Spinach seedlings sprouted between turned-over tanks, trucks broken down or out of fuel, and mountains of empty shells.

Hans had spidered up an American tank, hauled open the hatch, and reeled back, retching into the mud just as Max caught the throat-catching stink of rotting animal. They'd jogged to the western corner of the field where a dozen plain timber crosses marked fresh graves, and it was not far from here that they made the discovery.

Three packs of American army rations lay in a foxhole along with a clutch of grenades and two filthy rifles, one of them jammed. They tore open the rations and gorged themselves on crackers and chocolate, canned meat, packaged cheese, and sugar cubes.

The food was a drug that made everything funny: the lettering on a box, the texture of the stringy cheese, the wrapping on the roll of toilet tissue. When their stomachs were full, they re-counted the weapons: one M1 Garand rifle, one Browning automatic rifle, seven grenades. No ammunition.

Max had picked up a grenade and weighed it in his hand. The American ones were nicknamed pineapples for the pattern of the deep grooves circling the cast-iron shell. He got to his feet and slid out the pin, and drew back his arm, envisaging the arc it would trace toward a tree fifteen metres distant. This would be a champion throw—and there was a part of him saying *hurry now, this is live ordnance*—but not a throw to be rushed. His shoulder led, his arm followed, his torso swivelled. There was a marvellous weight to it. He let go. The explosion jolted the earth and sent birds shrieking into the sky.

They filled their bags with the remaining rations, shouldered the guns, packed the grenades around a blanket, and carried the bag deep into the forest where they created their own wooded battleground, firing into treetops to bring bolts of timber rocketing into the enemy. They set trip wires on the forest-floor, booby-trapped corpses, stole up on sleeping men to garrote them or hurl a grenade into their dugout. This is how you send your enemy mad, raving and howling back to whatever hell he came from.

Breathless and hot-cheeked, they lay on their backs in a clearing, boot against boot, heroes a thousand times over. High above, the canopy slipped sideways under its river of clouds.

"Weren't we supposed to be kings of the world?" Max said. "With our own little country to rule over? A palace and a stable full of horses and ladies to serve us coffee on a silver tray with a silver jug and silver spoon and silver sugar bowl. And cake."

"What sort of cake?"

"Every sort of cake."

He felt Hans's boot knock against his own.

"Who's to say we're not already kings?" said Hans.

"Kings of what?"

"Kings of here. Of each other. Kings of this patch of forest and these most excellent American rifles. It's not so bad as kingdoms go."

Max listened to Hans's breathing deepen and watched the astonishing stars through the gaps between the trees. A pair of foxes struck up a screeching duet and he was glad of Hans's company. He fell asleep dreaming of polished silver, of the ancient kingdom in his pocket.

The man with the gun on Max barks in a guttural language—he's the leader. Toothless grunts a reply, lines up the binoculars beside the rifles and grenades, and continues his search. Max's own binoculars and knife lie wrapped up near his feet. He had been too tired to pack them away but had shoved them under the tarpaulin to keep off the dew.

"*Luc*," says Toothless, "*tu te rends compte?*" The words fall into place. French. A heavy accent, slurred with drink. The man is expressing disbelief. He brandishes a brown shirt. Hans's Jungvolk shirt. Folded the regulation way without a crease out of place.

Did Hans dig it up from Vera's garden? Or did he never bury it in the first place? Hans gives no clue. The shirt might as well be a snake, judging by the way he looks at it. Toothless shakes it out, and Hans's dagger thuds onto the dirt.

"What luck, stumbling upon a couple of young Nazis planning their next attack," says the leader, the one called Luc.

"We're not Nazis," Max says in French. "We are just trying to get home."

The leader blinks at him

"You are French? You don't sound French."

"My mother is French. We are from Saarland, next to the border."

"This true?" the third man says to Hans, kicking his boot.

"His parents are from a different place," says Max. "He doesn't speak much French."

Hans looks so morose, Max would take pity on him if he didn't want to choke the life out of him.

"Why does he have the shirt?"

"We all had to wear them," Max says.

"Not now."

"No."

The leader kicks his boot again. "Ask him why he kept it."

"He wants to know why you kept the shirt."

Hans shrugs. Hot fury flares through Max.

"How is it you know French?" says the leader.

"I told you; my mother is French. My grandparents are French. I have cousins and aunts and uncles who are French; my godfather is—was—French. He was shot by the SS."

"That's quite a story."

"It's not a story," says Max.

"What about your father?"

"A miner," says Max. "Until he got drafted."

"What kind of miner?" says Toothless. He has dropped Hans's bag. All of his attention is on Max.

"A supervisor. He was in charge of maintaining—"

Toothless flies forward, arm raised. Heat explodes into his temple.

"Supervisor, is it? What kind of supervising? Would that be supervising foreign labourers? French slave workers?"

Max braces to be hit again. The man shimmers. Blackness encroaches. He brings up his knees, lowers his forehead. Voices reach him through a deep ringing.

"Let's give him a taste of supervision."

"Leave it, he's a kid."

"Give him one in the back of the head—for the father."

"Waste of a bullet. Let him swing."

The world moves in a slow circle.

"Tell us about your mother," says the leader, the one called Luc. "This honourable French woman who married a Nazi."

"Like to meet her," says Toothless with a wet grin.

"Sounds like a bomb," says the small man.

"She's not a Nazi," says Max. "She hates the Nazis. They put my

French relatives in labour camps. My father's brother moved to France, and they put him in a concentration camp years ago. They murdered my godfather—"

"Which concentration camp?"

"Buchenwald."

"They'll say anything," says Toothless to Luc, shaking his head. "*Putains.*"

"What do you mean? What is it?" Max says.

There is a doubt on the leader, Luc's, face. "Are you sure about that? Buchenwald?"

Toothless swears again. "He's seen a newspaper or heard about it. Cunning little bastard."

"Tell me," says Max.

Toothless spits, aiming for a spot a few centimetres from Max's boot.

"Shut up, Léon," says the leader without taking his eyes off Max. "A camp at Buchenwald was liberated a few days ago—or discovered, you might say. The Nazis were long gone."

His dread thickens.

"*N'importe quoi,*" says Toothless. Bullshit.

"He doesn't know," says the small man. Is that *pity* on his face?

"Please," Max says.

"He doesn't know," says Luc. "Tell him."

Toothless tells him and he doesn't cushion the words. They arrow into Max—a catalogue of horrors. Piles of emaciated bodies stacked like cut branches. The choking stench of burnt and rotten corpses, of human excrement. He speaks of torture and beatings, disease and filth, horrifying medical experiments, starvation, execution, humiliation. Allied soldiers offering food in kindness to half-dead survivors, only to witness them die in agony, their bodies too weak to cope.

*Josef.* His father's brother. Little Josef's dearest father. His uncle. A gaping jaw, a wasted body stacked in a pile. Nameless, naked, forgotten.

He weeps.

\*     \*     \*

The men take the weapons, the last of the rations, and Hans's shirt, binoculars, knife, and blanket. They leave Max's bag mostly untouched, stealing only his scarf and a spare pair of trousers.

When he is certain they are gone, Max shakes out the tarpaulin, and a grenade thumps onto the forest floor.

"We could have used that," says Hans.

"I wouldn't have had time to get the pin out."

"Still," says Hans, "who would you have picked?"

"Toothless," says Max.

"Yes," says Hans. "Jammed straight into that empty mouth of his."

Max buries the grenade in his bag, nestled into the tarp.

"Will you tell me, please," says Hans. "What they said to you?"

Max busies himself with packing up and clearing the campsite while he repeats what he has been told to his friend, this time in German.

They continue west, more wary now, pausing often to filter the natural cracks and rustling of the forest from other, more threatening, noises.

"How many times did we climb the tree next to the Russian prisoners' camp?" says Max, remembering the early days of the war, before they were evacuated from Lauterbach.

Hans shakes his head. Too many times to count.

"They weren't all Russians," says Max.

"They looked like Russians."

"Papa worked with some in the mine. There were French, Italians. Belgians too. And they weren't all soldiers."

"What difference does it make? Your uncle wasn't in there, Max. And it wasn't like that at Lauterbach. Not like he was saying."

"It was bad, though, Hans." Hans doesn't respond. "Wasn't it? It was bad."

"How long have we been walking?"

"A hundred years."

Twice they plunge off the path and hide themselves in shrubbery, behind fallen trees to avoid gangs of men. The rations are gone, food pickings are meagre. They're filling their water bottles in a brook when Hans spots a shoal of perch. They sacrifice an hour's walking to trap two fish and descend deep in the forest to set a small fire and cook it. They eat standing up, drooling over the sweet, flaking flesh and crispy skin, kicking dirt over the fire.

The sun is sinking into the tree line when they set out again, the glints catching them through birch pillars.

"My mother worked hard to pay for that shirt," says Hans.

"I know."

"I should have got rid of it."

"It doesn't matter, Hans."

"I'm sorry for the other thing too."

"What other thing?" Max kicks a pine cone away from his foot and regrets it because it's not just blisters that torture his feet, but his toes pressing against the end of his boots. How does his body continue to grow when the whole world feels suspended, caught between one time and another? The war is finished here, but not there. He and Hans have left one place, but not yet arrived in another. It's possible that everyone he has left in the world will be waiting at home to greet him, and also possible that they are, every last one, dead.

"Your uncle Josef," says Hans. "I liked him. Like him. He is probably on his way home."

"He's been in there a long time," says Max.

"Do you know what his crime was?" says Hans.

Max searches the treetops for a scrap of memory, hears only the scuff of their boots on decomposing leaves.

They enter the southern outskirts of Karlsruhe through minor roads, past a cluster of still-standing houses, a row of businesses with the doors and windows blown out: a printer's workshop, a stationer, a bookbinder. The sky lowers and Max tastes metal. Thudding rain soon turns the city black. Mud finds its way through his useless boots to menace his blisters.

"Let's find somewhere to dry off," says Hans.

"If we can get to the other side of town, we will be at the Rhine."

"An hour will make no difference. Come on. My feet are bleeding."

A trail of sodden papers covered in bloated text leads to a desk lying upside down in the street. They fill their water tanks from its upturned belly. Across the street, the words *Hitler is your enemy* are scrawled in English across a door hanging ajar. All those years of English lessons were meant to prepare them for the day Germany would occupy England. Now the opposite is true. The door opens with no resistance. The rain pounds the street, drips from muddy planter boxes. Max calls a greeting into the dim entry hall.

Nobody home.

They stretch out on a bed in an upstairs room with a view across the main street.

"Have you ever felt a bed so soft?" says Hans.

"A king's bed," says Max.

"Would a king take his coat and boots off?"

"The servants would do it for him."

"I'll wait for them to arrive, then."

"Good," says Max. "After a rest."

A low wind growls through the house. They might have done a better job of closing the door, but the bed holds him snug and rain patters against the window. He is too tired to move.

"You haven't got a tin of pears in your pack, have you, Max?"

"Bound to be," says Max, letting his eyes close.

"Shall we leave it there for the moment so we know it's waiting for us?"

"We'll appreciate it more."

The rain calls him home to billowing curtains, a lamp on the floor, his mother's hands at the piano, and the three of them—Anna, Hans, and Max—stamping and spinning, bent over in desperate, weeping, mirthless laughter.

He wakes to the roar of heavy engines.

"Trucks," says Hans, already at the window.

Outside, a woman emerges from a door, pushing open an umbrella. Three children spill out behind her to hail the arriving soldiers. Up and down the street, doors open.

The rain-soaked foreigners shine like gods. Their teeth are bright tablets of white. They pass neat packages to outstretched hands. The adults are cautious, sullen, some curious. The children are shameless, cheering beggars.

A wide, duck-footed man emerges from a foyer buttoning a coat over a bright waistcoat straining across his belly. The commanding nature of his gestures suggests importance. A call is repeated along the convoy and the trucks growl to a stop. An American soldier unfolds his long limbs out of a Jeep and pushes forward to hear what the man is saying. He is clearly having trouble hearing over the rumble of engines and hiss of the rain.

The fat man shakes his head and lifts his gaze. His arm rises. His finger points.

# 29

Karl Hinckel has aged twenty years. His eyes slide away from Marguerite, indifferent.

She drops down onto a stair like a child.

What is *happening*?

Lina Hinckel is marching through the foyer, pup at her heels, balancing a hat box on a large toilet bag. Tonia follows, carrying two heavy suitcases. Outside, a car is running.

"For God's sake *move*," says Lina Hinckel. "He needs a hospital."

Hospital? Has someone *shot* him? Has she, *Marguerite*, shot him in her sleep? Her mind is lined with sludge. Nothing makes sense.

The pup jumps at Lina Hinckel and she kicks it away. It rolls and squeals. Anna scoops up the animal, whispers into its cheek. *Anna.* Where did she come from?

"Keep it," says Lina Hinckel. "You'll make a handsome pair of mongrels."

So much for her sentimental side.

Lina Hinckel returns from the car to help the driver drag her husband out of the chair and onto the front steps.

"Help us," she shouts, and the other guard steps inside to half lift, half drag Karl Hinckel out the door.

Can he feel Marguerite's eyes on him? Will he turn to face her, this waning king?

He does not.

Doors thunk, and two vehicles roll away along the gravel, lights extinguished. Where will they take him? The nearest hospital would be Heilbronn if it's still standing.

The front door clicks shut. Anna releases the struggling pup and brings her hands to her face—a gesture of disbelief, or is that *satisfaction*?

"Good girl," says Tonia, and notices Marguerite.

"Thank you," says Anna, and throws her arms around Tonia.

"Talk to your mama."

Anna stiffens, lets out a long breath, and turns to face Marguerite.

"What happened to him?" says Marguerite.

Anna presses her lips together. Marguerite knows the look too well.

"*We* happened to him," Anna says. "Tonia and me."

"What are you talking about?" The knowledge comes in the same instant. "What did you give him?"

"A little aconite, a few foxglove leaves. Not enough to kill him. Just enough to make his heart a bit . . . unreliable."

"Boom-shicka-boom," says Tonia. "Very nice jazz beat."

The pair of them, the poisoners, are sparkling. Do they imagine themselves immune from punishment?

"And when the doctors find out he's been poisoned?" says Marguerite. "When he comes back with a firing squad?"

"By the caretaker's reckoning, the nearest major hospital that is *not* in a battle zone is Nuremberg," says Anna. "The foreign armies will be here any day. Why would he come back?"

"Did you say the *caretaker*?"

"Very intelligent man," says Tonia.

"You didn't tell me what you were intending, and you told the caretaker?"

"What would you have said, Mama?"

"I would have said murder is a sin as much as it's a crime."

"Is he dead? He didn't look dead to me."

The room tilts again, and Marguerite closes her eyes to steady herself. The truth jolts her out of the torpor.

"Anna Bernot, did you give me a sleeping draft?"

Anna bites into her bottom lip. Worried, yes, but she's still looking as if she has won a race.

"You would have tried to stop me—and even if you gave permission, which you would never have done, you would been a bundle of nerves and given it all away."

Marguerite rubs her fingernails through her scalp. Who knows us better than our own children?

"I suppose I should be grateful you didn't get your potions mixed up." Ridiculous to think it, let alone say it. Anna would never make such a mistake. "And Lina? How is she still walking?"

"One looks like a heart problem," says Anna. "Two looks like poisoning."

"I wanted to poison her," says Tonia. "Double dose."

"Good God," says Marguerite.

"Now we are free," says Anna.

Marguerite snorts. A Frenchwoman, a Belarusian, and a German girl in the middle of nowhere in the middle of the war, the front on its way. She uses the banister to get herself upright and takes careful steps toward the kitchen, glaring off Anna's attempt to steady her.

Anna's face falls. The brightness has evaporated. She was expecting praise. Marguerite reaches for her daughter's arm and hooks it into her own.

"How about you help me into the kitchen," she says.

"Mama—"

"Anna, you did a brave thing," she says as they walk. "I'm going to need a little time before I will say that it was the right thing, but it was brave, and it was *very* clever."

Anna blinks, tries to hold down her smile. She looks just like Max.

Marguerite kisses her daughter's shoulder.

"And now I need a warm drink," she says. "And if it's all the same to you, I prefer to make it myself."

She puts kettle to tap and opens the faucet. Nothing comes out.

# 30

Max and Hans drop out of their accuser's sight and crawl to the hallway. Nothing there but a wide armoire, empty aside from a few dusty dresses that must be a hundred years old. Below, the door slams against the wall. Foreign words travel up to them, the scratch and clatter of handheld radios.

At the end of the hallway, a ladder leads to the attic, the obvious hiding place, but Hans is climbing into the wardrobe.

"*Hans.* We might be able to get out through the roof." Max scrambles up the ladder and presses against the trapdoor. It's jammed shut.

The soldiers are throwing open doors, searching, bellowing words he cannot make out.

"For God's sake, Hans. Get *up* here and help." He pounds the trapdoor with his shoulder. A shower of paint flakes blinds him. He blinks his eyes clear. The house shakes with the movement of those boots, making steady progress toward the stairs. Hans adds his weight to the trapdoor, and it rips open.

Max hauls himself up. He weighs a tonne—his backpack is wet, his trousers are wet, and everything sticks—but he is inside now, and spins to help Hans up and through. They ease the trapdoor down, and as it closes, Max glimpses a treacherous shower of paint flecks and dust drifting down to the hall runner below.

It takes precious seconds for his eyes to adjust. A small square window split into four filthy panes casts a dull glow onto frantic dust and dead-end walls.

The thumping boots have stopped. The soldiers are below. Hans's eyes are black holes. A command rises from below in urgent German.

"Out, out!"

Hans scrambles away toward the window, but it is pointless. They will never squeeze through and, judging by the pitch of the roof, there is nowhere to escape to other than a fall to the street below. The floor between them erupts. Timber splits, the air sings, and hot metal thwacks into ceiling rafters. Max rolls into a ball, heart hammering. The gunfire stops and a dozen needles of brightness rise from the attic floor, spotlighting trembling dust motes and a panicked spider scampering up a thread.

"*Kamerad! Kamerad!*" Hans yawls, but another burst of bullets is unleashed. Above them, a loud crack, and a net of cobweb descends. Max rips it out of his lips, his eyes, his hair. His mouth is full of dust.

More shouts from below.

"Flag," wheezes Hans; his hands are on the trapdoor. "Come on, Max. Anything."

There is a shirt in Max's bag, not white, but it will do. He reaches for his rucksack. How many kilometres has he walked only to die here in a squalid attic? His own thoughts amaze him: splitting off like this. One Max is terrified: ripping open the bag, feeling for a shirt and finding only useless binoculars and a blanket and a map and a tarpaulin. The other is in a cold rage at the unfairness of it, the *gall* of it. The men below have invaded his country. They want to kill him without knowing his name, where he comes from, where he is going, what he believes. It is unfair. He hates them for it.

His hand closes around the cold steel of the grenade. Every hair on his body is electrified. Why not? It is a simple act, to pull a pin from a grenade. He will wait for Hans to open the trapdoor and will let it fall. He can silence those roaring voices, still their guns. He will be killed for it, but it will be an honourable death. Why not do what he has prepared to do all of his life? If not for Adolf Hitler, then for his country.

"*Max.*" Hans's voice is almost a scream. It is not possible that he can see the grenade in Max's hand through those pillars of brightness, dozens now, illuminating swinging spider silk, the light snow of cement flakes, the troubled dust. They are finite in form but infinite in content; teeming with life, with grace.

A thought comes to Max, and later he will wonder how such clarity was possible amid the noise, the terror. Did God himself cast his eye over a dead city to a terrified boy and send him that thought? The thought is this: if he kills the soldiers, he kills Hans. His friend. His dearest friend. A brother in every sense except blood.

A sigh passes through him. A dreadful weight lifts.

He sets the grenade onto the black attic floor and feels inside his pocket. The handkerchief is still there, knotted around the coin. No longer white, and a paltry flag, but it's the best he has.

Hans is dragging the trapdoor open. More cruel light. Max picks and pulls at the knot in the darkness. It's tight. Too tight. He gets his nail into the knot, gets a grip at last, and yanks it free. Something light bounces once, twice, and sinks into darkness. No. *No.*

"*Max!*"

Max thrusts the handkerchief into Hans's outstretched hand and wheels on all fours to pat down ceiling boards draped in centuries of dust and the webs of long-dead spiders. *No.* He moans, fumbles for his pack, and finds the torch. He hauls it out and flicks the switch. Dead.

"Yes, yes! Okay! Friend!" Hans is calling in English. He waves Charles's handkerchief at the men below and stretches a foot down toward the ladder. Max leans over into the dazzling light; indistinct shapes resolve into men, rifles. There is no mistaking the order to descend.

Max whirls back to the attic floor, blinded again. He has just a few seconds while Hans descends, but the light shafts created by the bullet holes only intensify the darkness between.

He sees, again, Charles's face in Lauterbach a few hours before he died; sorrowful as a calf, as he tried to toss the Lotharingian coin and it fell from his hand to the floor. A pain slides under Max's ribs and he extends a foot onto the ladder.

Rough hands pull him down into confounding light and noise. A wall of khaki. Guns, American uniforms, dripping helmets, grim faces, all of them black.

He reels back and pain shoots through his head. He has smacked it on the ladder. Three of the soldiers are laughing, but the fourth man's expression makes his skin prickle. Tawny fur is stitched onto the inside of his collar. He wears an extra stripe on his shoulder badge—a corporal. His eyes are dark chestnut ringed with black. The eyes from a box in a classroom. *Number fourteen.* These eyes are neither lidless nor panicked. They carry authority.

Max's bones have liquefied. He is nothing more than a layer of weak, pale skin.

These are the men he has seen only in caricature—the kidnappers, the cannibals, the fools—never in the flesh.

*Is she swimming up your leg right now?*

The corporal says a few low words and a soldier steps forward. Powerful hands pat down his torso, squeeze his arms. They stop at Max's wristwatch and tap it. The soldier, who has a sparse, pencil-thin moustache, says something that sounds like a question. He turns Max's wrist, unbuckles the strap, removes the watch, and drops it into his pocket.

The search continues and Max remembers the dagger on his belt. Too late. The soldier pauses. The sheath loosens and falls away. The soldier draws the knife and brings the blade to Max's neck. It catches against the delicate skin of his Adam's apple. *Ta pomme d'Adam. Ta pomme d'Adam.* His heart thrums out the words.

"Private Griggs," says the corporal. The knife falls away from Max's throat and the soldier returns it to its sheath.

"*Vielen Dank,*" he says, attaching the sheath to his own belt. Thank you kindly. He pulls from his pocket a neat, rectangular packet, winks at Max and flicks it up, spinning into the air. Max snares it and is gratified to see the surprise on the soldier's face.

*The eyes are everything. The hand will follow.* This is what his godfather taught him the day ten years ago when he gave him the coin, the day Max snatched it out of the air for the first time.

The soldier grins, impressed, and repeats the action with a second pack. Max catches it again. A dog performing tricks. Two packs of gum for a dagger and a wristwatch. Fair trade. He does not care about the watch. Does not care about the knife. He wants the coin. He wants Charles.

The lanky American soldier outside is a lieutenant who speaks German. He listens to the corporal's account and barks a series of questions at Max and Hans but is not much interested in their responses. Young fanatics calling themselves Werewolves are proving a nuisance to Allied troops in the newly occupied territories, he says. These boys can't be allowed to wander the streets carrying out acts of sabotage and murder—this said with a glance that suggests he thinks them capable of neither. Max senses they are a problem the officer does not want or need.

"If we wanted to fight we'd be fighting, sir," Max tells the officer. "It's why we ran away. If we could just get over the Rhine, we will be out of your way. We only want to get home."

Something in those words seems to strike a chord, because the lieutenant has a brief exchange with the corporal, then brings hands to hips, resolved.

"The corporal here will put you on a transport unit leaving shortly for Strasbourg. That will get you across the river. From there, you can take your chances."

The six-wheeler rattles through the wasteland of Karlsruhe. In the open rear of the truck, Max chews American gum and watches the soldier Griggs smoking cigarette after cigarette, studying the ruins. Has this American ever seen a German city untouched by bombs? Can he imagine such a place? The devastation doesn't shock Max the way it used to. He notices, instead, a ginger cat stretched out in a patch of sun, tongue caught between its teeth, a row of bright socks pegged out on a line.

He had not been so immune on that long journey to Bavaria with Hans and their new troop of Neunkirchen boys just two months ago. The memories come to him in grey sketches: a ruined city cloaked in ash, smoke threads over a stunted skyline. Every time he closed his eyes he saw Charles, a battered and ruined body where his godfather should be, and every time he opened them, a fresh horror. They had spent an afternoon helping stack dead soldiers from a strafed armoured train—though Rudy made a joke of it by strangling himself with the severed arm and constructing three-legged men. They'd washed their hands in a spoonful of petrol, climbed into an ancient bus, and never mentioned it again. The same silence followed the sight of the three men suspended from streetlights at the station at Munich—cobblestones stained yellow beneath dangling feet, placard swaying from each broken neck.

*Deserteur. Plünderer. Defätist.*

"My turn," says Hans.

Max pulls the gum from his mouth and hands it over—they have resolved that each stick will last a full day—and leans over the side of the truck to see what Hans is staring at.

The shores of the Rhine are chewed up with track marks, overturned tanks, exploded rafts, and collapsed sections of pontoon bridges. To his right, a massive steel bridge zigzags through the water, crumpled like damp cardboard.

The truck mounts wide metal tracks leading to a pontoon bridge. A cheer rises and an American Jeep rattles along the riverbank, a dead boar strapped across the rear. The soldier in the passenger seat balances a machine gun on his lap and toasts his cheering comrades with a champagne bottle.

They cross the river and turn left at a field where peasants are bent over bare grapevines. The next field is a churning mud path torn up with vehicle tracks and abandoned vehicles. A French flag ripples above a roadside café where the proprietor has set up a few tables outside with a sign advertising a special *menu* for soldiers.

With the Rhine still on their left the spike of a church rises a good distance south. It can only be the famous cathedral of Strasbourg. Max's French grandfather once told him that for hundreds of years it was the tallest building in the Christian world. A beacon for the faithful.

"What do you think Anna's doing now?" says Hans. It's a surprise to hear her name, though Max thinks of his sister every day.

"Manning a flamethrower? Up a tree with a sniper rifle?" They both know the Allied soldiers have already passed through Neunkirchen. Anna, like everyone else this side of the front, will be adjusting to the new order, or lack of it, and the new leaders, or lack of them.

"She might already be home, Max."

"She might. I hope she is. Though I can't picture home like I could before, Hans. Nothing's as clear as it was. What if it's gone, all of it, and I have no memory left of it?"

"It's the forest I miss," says Hans.

"Ruined," says Max.

"What's a few land mines? You and I can get to work the minute we get home. We'll come up with much less tedious ways to clear them. I'm thinking hammer-throwing, chicken in a trebuchet, advance party of Grott brothers."

"The Grotts aren't that bad."

"Then why are you laughing?"

"Chicken in a trebuchet," says Max. "Waste of a good chicken."

"Never said it was a good chicken."

A pause.

"You all right, Max?"

"I'm all right." Max pats the front pouch of his rucksack. Only three unwritten postcards remain. He chooses one of Schwäbisch Hall, bought from a one-armed bookseller in the old town. A rowboat drifts under the Devil's Bridge, appearing to float over the old buildings reflected in the still water.

He flicks the card over, rests it on his backpack, and writes.

# The End *and* the Beginning

*Dear Mama,*
*I have visited this place.*
*Sending warmest greetings and hugs,*
*Max*

Hans is quieter than usual, jouncing with the movement of the truck. He's taller now, heavier in the jaw, with more hair sprouting on his outer lip. It's not so hard to imagine a time when they will both be grown men. Will they play backgammon outside Möllers' guesthouse in the tradition of the old men of Lauterbach, entertaining each other with stories of these times? Will they exaggerate the fearlessness and strength of their youth?

Later, when he does recall these moments, he will wish that he had paid less attention to Hans's bobbing head and more to what he thought might happen when they got to Strasbourg, the medieval city which is no longer a part of the Thousand-Year Reich, as he remembers, but a different country altogether.

# 31

The caretaker is attempting to liven up the rusting pump on the old well—a Herculean task given his age, the lack of materials, the risk of being bombed, and the want of fuel for the generator. With Hinckel gone, he seems infused with new energy.

Marguerite gathers Anna, Tonia, and the cook to the well, and declares collecting water a priority.

"Who put you in charge?" the cook says. There are flecks of food on her bodice.

"No one," says Marguerite. "But we have to prepare. The front is coming."

The cook drills knuckles into hips. "The enemy is being forced back."

"For God's sake, woman," says the caretaker. "Listen for yourself."

The thump and roll of artillery grow louder with every hour.

"We can shelter here if we have water," says Marguerite. "If not, we have to find somewhere else. Shall we get on with it?"

"Look at her," says the cook. "Well, I for one will not be ordered around by a Frenchwoman—a spy, for all we know. I wager it was you who sabotaged the water supply."

"You should stop talking," says Tonia to the cook.

"Nor will I be told what to do by a Bolshevik slut," says the cook.

"Really, you should stop talking," says Tonia. "You are stupid person."

"Oh, she speaks German when it suits her," says the cook. "Crafty little tongue on her."

"I will cut out yours if you don't stop talking, and next I will start on your heart." Tonia's tone is bored, so the cook does not at first register what she has said. Then, her mouth and eyes tighten to form three small o's. Her hand lifts, index finger extends. Tonia grins her tea-coloured grin and widens her eyes at the cook.

"Are you all hearing this?" the cook stutters. "She would murder me and make no secret of it."

"Calm yourself," says Marguerite. "Tonia, apologise to the cook. You're giving her a fright."

Tonia shrugs. "Where would I find a blade long enough to get through the fat?"

The cook lunges. Tonia jumps out of reach, and it might end there, but no, in one quick movement Tonia springs forward, grabs the cook by the ear and twists, hard, ignoring the squeals and slapping hands.

"Belarusian," Tonia says. "Not Russian."

The caretaker clears his throat. He looks pained at this breach of civility, hovering there with his head averted. The women ignore him. Tonia cranes out of reach of the cook's desperate hands. Her demeanour is relaxed, but her knuckles are bloodless. The cook's face is turning purple.

"Antoninia," says Anna, and Tonia meets her eyes. "Let her go, please. She will leave this house and not return. Agreed, madame?"

The cook's head bobbles as best it can.

Tonia lowers her head to speak into the cook's hair.

"No more talking, yes? Go home to your pig shed. No more feeding at the big house." She releases the cook, grimaces at her fingers, and wipes them on her backside.

The cook pulls herself up and stalks toward the driveway. When she is a good distance away, she calls back. "The soldiers will line you up. Mark my words. You'll be pincushions and you'll deserve it. Every last one of you foreign whores. You'll wish they had shot you."

Tonia turns her back. The colour washes out of Anna's face.

Marguerite wants to tell her not to listen to a bitter old harridan, that the woman is talking nonsense, but what guarantee can she give? Anna knows it too.

*Kill yourself, child. Quick now. Before they return.*

The caretaker is unable to get the water running, so they will have to fetch it from the nearby hamlet, where there is a well. They load two handcarts with every jar and vase and pitcher they can find, and the trio—Marguerite, Anna, and Tonia—trudge through a narrow forest track past budding oaks and beech. Wafts of burnt rubber and oil come in on the breeze. Every farmhouse, every cottage and stable appears locked up, abandoned, and yet Marguerite can hear the snorting and shifting of animals, feels observed.

A line of seven or eight women has formed at the well, which is, thank God, giving forth buckets of fresh, clear water. Alongside is a Volkssturm collection truck. *Clothes for the soldiers*, reads the banner tacked up on its side.

From the west, the front growls, ever closer. What is the point of collecting thrice-darned socks and threadbare coats? The People's Storm will be an army dressed in rags. What in God's name will these poor boys and old men use against foreign tanks? Sticks and stones? And Goebbels continues to rant about this militia of boys, these *Werewolves* who will materialise behind enemy lines to do the work of spies and saboteurs, arsonists and assassins.

Where is Max? Where is her son? She wants him within reach so she can hold him down, lock him up, keep him safe, stop him running headlong into war.

An elderly woman passes up a heavy black coat with a gesture that speaks of years of meticulous care. Her dead husband's best coat. Marguerite could weep for her.

A boy takes it without a word and throws it to the rear. A moment later a call goes up and a taller boy appears, forearms jutting from the same black coat. He sashays left, then right. The other boys leap on him, and he folds up with laughter, the coat pulled taut across his back. It would have torn if it were not better made.

The old woman shuffles away.

They are equal parts arrogance and ignorance, these quick-footed, spindly boys with their belts cinched tight. Not a whisper of fear among them. If this war would end, if this war would only end now, they could be spared, every one of these beautiful creatures.

"Got anything for us, miss?" a boy calls to Marguerite. She opens up her empty hands and smiles her regret.

Marguerite's nerves arc and flare in the gloom. Someone scrapes the metal water pail against the stone floor, sending shocks into the roots of her hair. She shifts the weight from her aching left hip. No blanket is thick enough to soften the cellar floor.

For two days, she has spent more time underground than above it, most of it here, with Anna and Tonia, and the caretaker at times. Since the fog and rain cleared, a rift has been torn in the sky and a plague unleashed. Metal locusts prowl the heavens day and night, releasing bitter rain. The air shakes with the unholy scream of the jets. They are safer here than in a city—the worry is the stray bombs that fall far from their targets.

Sleep offers no solace. Sometime earlier in the night she had fallen into a doze and stepped into a crater lined with faces of the bewildered dead. She had jerked awake with such violence her elbow struck the wall and her cry triggered a fuss that took long minutes to calm down. If it is not her own thoughts rattling her awake, it is the screeching water pail or the squawking rooster, or the rattle and throb of bombers and fighters, or the soul-sucking, relentless drip in a damp corner of this pitiless hole in the ground. The wide-open space of the night hours is filled with the most unwelcome thoughts. Is Anton retreating with the Wehrmacht? Or is he dead or captured or injured? Has he deserted and headed home? Where is Max? Is he really on his way here, to Heilbronn? Who is feeding him, keeping him safe, drawing a blanket over his poor ruined face?

*Enough.*

She climbs out of the cellar and up through the house to the attic. The skies over Heilbronn flash ochre and white. The shelling is incessant, implacable.

The stairs creek with light footsteps. It's Anna.

"Did you sleep?" says Marguerite.

"More than you, apparently," says Anna. She runs a finger across a suitcase cracked with age and examines the dust.

"Do you think he is coming?"

Anna looks up. "Max? No. If they had found him at Munich he'd be here by now."

"There might have been a delay, a problem with communication—"

"He was trying to get under your skin."

"But it's possible—"

"He killed that poor girl, Mama."

"What are you talking about? What poor girl?"

"The secretary, the one you replaced. That's why he needed someone, because he had killed her."

"You mean *Hinckel?* How do you know this?"

Anna had been foraging for wild asparagus in the southwest field when she had noticed a disturbance in the mud—some clothing, twisted in the dirt. She leaned closer and saw that there was a wrist, and then the smell—

"I turned and ran straight into the caretaker, and he put his hand over my mouth—no, not to hurt me, to quiet me. He wanted me to know who she was and what that—that *monster* had done to her. We mustn't raise a fuss, he said, because now that the front is so close, these people need to cover their tracks. They need to get rid of the evidence, which means anyone who knows."

"Dear God, Anna. And you saw this girl?"

"Only her wrist. They didn't even dig her a proper grave. Some of the soil had washed off or been pushed off by animals, I suppose—" She breaks off, covering her mouth.

"Did Tonia know about this?"

"She suspected. The secretary was infatuated with Hinckel, who tired of her, but she was horrible to Tonia and all the others, so Tonia didn't really care to find out what had happened. I understand that, I do, but still she was a person, wasn't she? Entitled to live a life."

An explosion lights up a huge ball of smoke rising over the city in a lazy curve.

"How many days has it been now?" says Anna. She's shrinking faster than the Reich. The food supplies are shrinking too, but there is enough to sustain them for a while longer. When so much life is being destroyed, is a person not obliged to cling to it? Should Marguerite hold up a mirror to show Anna what she is doing to herself?

"The battle? Five, six?" The battle for the town, the reports say, is progressing street by street, house by house, room by room—it is bitter, vicious, personal. Every tree in the city must be in cinders by now. Kitchen tables and chairs, shelves filled with generations of memories are burning. How many libraries? How many books? Has the Rathaus burned? All those records of births and deaths and marriages going back through the centuries? A history wiped out.

"What would Hitler think of all this?" Anna has always called him the Führer. There has been a shift in her, and it fills Marguerite with hope. "Mother? I don't mean the public man. I mean when it's quiet. Just him and his thoughts. What does he think about what has become of our country?"

There is so much to say—all the words that have not been said across the years, words that have stacked upon words to form a towering wall between them. But Anna's shoulder rests against her own, warm and close. Words can wait.

"Victory or extermination," says Anna, and presses her forehead against the window. The merciless rain falls. Heilbronn burns.

PART THREE

*Arrival*

# 32

The caretaker arrives mid-morning with a length of bread, a few centimetres of dried meat, an axe, and news. The battle for Heilbronn is over. The city is awash with the dead. German troops are falling back, and Allied troops are moving in fast, racing the Russians for Berlin.

"It's time, ladies," he says. He had been horrified to learn of their intention to walk to the village to welcome the Allied men and offer up Hinckel's office and files.

"The front is a lawless place. You will wait."

"Wait until when?" said Marguerite.

"Until they've sobered up, calmed down, and been knocked into line. That won't happen until some high-ranked brass shows up and declares himself in charge."

"How long will that take?" Anna had asked.

He lifted his shoulders. "I will come for you when it is safe."

They have settled on an alcove in an upstairs salon, which the caretaker will cover with a heavy wardrobe. It was Tonia's idea to coat the floor in wax to make the immovable movable. She and Anna have rolled up a rug for the caretaker to unfurl and cover the tracks. The water is in place—four pails and several pitchers—as well as a toilet bucket and cover, candles and matches, bedding, and all the food left in the house, which is not much.

Marguerite weighs the axe in her hands and the caretaker frowns.

"I am not suggesting you use it as a weapon, madame."

"That's a relief."

"If I were unable to return for some reason, you will need it to cut your way out."

"You're not planning on making some sort of stand, are you?"

He opens his empty palms. "With what, madame? My father's needle-gun hasn't been loaded in seventy years and you have my axe. This war should have been over long ago."

"I would be happier if you came back to get us out—just to know that you are safe. You have done so much for Anna."

"Your daughter is a credit to you," he says.

"She thinks she's immortal."

"Sometimes it is necessary to act," he says.

"You have been good to her. To us all."

A couple of Saarfrench, she thinks. A slave girl from Belarus. Her thoughts are upending her. In the life that is lost to her she would have expressed her thanks with food—a quince tart, a jar of preserves, a soup made from the sweetest spring vegetables. What luxuries they had in those years they had believed so difficult.

"*Stärke, madame,*" he says. Strength.

She is tired of being strong. Tired of being responsible for choices that might end in disaster. She wants her family together. Where is her son? Where is her husband? She aches for Anton to be here, to be her barricade, to hold the world at bay.

Karl Hinckel could not understand why she would marry a coal miner, but Karl Hinckel knows nothing about the human heart. The more you try to hold it down, make demands on it, the more it recoils and jounces away. Leave it be, let it be, and when the time is right it will leap—lightly, but with formidable, matchless power. Such it was with Anton.

The floor trembles. The shells are so close. The Reich is sinking into a sea of blood.

\* \* \*

If she stretches out an arm, a leg begs to be extended. If she finds somewhere to unwind a leg, her arms complain. Her neck cramps, her throat itches. The worst itch of all is the desire to lift the axe, smash it through the wall, and climb outside to gasp cool air and know that she is alive.

The only sound that penetrates is the growl of aircraft. It should be a comfort that there is no grumble of trucks, no boots in the corridor heralding the arrival of men with guns in a lawless country, yet the silence leaves the imagination to do its worst.

Before they came in here, the caretaker had taken a ladder and drilled a series of discreet air holes above the top shelf in the wardrobe. But when the darkness presses in and she can taste the breath of the others, she feels an invisible enemy creeping up the stairs, climbing over the wardrobe to press cloth into those holes—

"Marguerite," says Tonia.

"Sorry," says Marguerite. She stills herself, tries to calm her breathing but the air is too close. She cannot get her fill of it.

"*Marguerite*," says Tonia. "You are like a worm in the sun."

Anna says nothing. Does she feel it too? The stifling darkness, the certainty that the air is running out—it calls her to those poor women and children trapped in the bomb shelter at Sankt Wendel. She and Anna have barely discussed the tragedy. This is how it has been with so many terrible days. What will happen if she holds the darkness up to the light?

"Do you know what chaff is, Tonia?" Marguerite says.

"The metal in the sky?"

"Yes. It makes it difficult for the flak towers to locate the bomber streams. Do you remember, Anna? The day after the evacuation, at Mrs. Liszt's house?"

*Marguerite had been outside when she heard the low growl of aircraft and saw the sky splinter. She called Max and Anna out to her. The air was full of sharp light: thousands of aluminum threads released in advance of the air raids. A large shoal harassed by the breeze startled upward and back into the blue.*

"The bombers will be here soon," said Max.

"I know, Schatz," said Marguerite.

Her children were lit up like saints on the street.

"It's beautiful," said Anna. "Like Christmas."

"Shall we stay just for a moment?"

And they did. Chins tilted, waiting for hellfire.

It had burned elsewhere.

The following day, at the Neunkirchen People's Welfare Service office, she recognised a fellow parishioner from Lauterbach, Elisabeth Lange. In a city of strangers, it was a pleasure to see a familiar face.

"You haven't heard," the woman said. Her face folded in like paper in a flame.

One of the refugee trains had pulled into Sankt Wendel station just as air-raid sirens sounded. The passengers were led off the train—although some young men had insisted on staying on board—and directed across the tracks into a building with a solid bunker and freshly reinforced roof. The bunker was reserved for women and children, so Elisabeth and her husband rushed to another shelter where they could stay together. The raiders came; the train was destroyed, and a bomb landed directly above the bunker where so many Lauterbach mothers and children were sheltered.

"The roof collapsed. Such an explosion. You cannot imagine. It shifted the ceiling of the bunker, but they survived the explosion, you see. That's what everyone is saying. They survived."

Elisabeth brought her fingertips to her lips. Marguerite had an impulse to shake a finger. Ah-ah. To forbid the woman from speaking another word, to walk backward and away to a place where the story ended there, where the women and children climbed out of that bomb shelter and walked back into their lives.

But words were pouring out of the other woman. The men had emerged from their bunker, and the German Maiden's League and People's Storm were there within minutes, but where do you start

*with a two-storey pile of rubble and steel? The roof of the bunker*
*was sealed shut.*

*"How many?" said Marguerite. "Who?"*

*Elisabeth took a deep, shuddering breath. The names sighed*
*into the space between them, wisps of sorrow. Too many. Too many*
*names to hold in memory.*

She and Anna speak those names now, and into the darkness their
memories reconstruct the streets and houses, the chapel and school
and shops of their village, and the voices that once filled it with chatter
and laughter. They are free at last to weep for the dead.

# 33

The truck takes a left at a palace converted into a hospital, traverses a canal and joggles through a street lined with half-timber houses. Tricolours sag. Cobbles complain under heavy wheels. Jazz music keens from the open door of a café where a waitress fans herself with a menu, watching three soldiers drink like champions.

The driver leans out of his window and speaks to a well-dressed young woman picking her way around a deep pothole. She rolls her eyes but does nothing to contain the swing of her hips. A man with no hat and an open sore on his head cycles past, trousers hanging off bony knees, a small white dog grinning out of the basket mounted on his handlebars.

The street opens out to a grand square where the pink cathedral crowds the sky. Its broad lower tower resembles a giant stack of burnt kindling and the windows are emptied of glass, but still the church is a marvel, populated by thousands of intricately carved saints and sinners, angels and apostles, virgins both foolish and wise, and Christ himself from birth to rebirth.

At the feet of the cathedral is another populace, sweat-soaked and sunbaked, sitting on their backsides and stripped of rifles and purpose: the captured soldiers of the great German Wehrmacht.

"*Cette chaleur, ce n'est rien,*" a war-addled preacher howls down at the men from a spot halfway up the cathedral steps. *This heat is nothing.* Compared with the fires of hell perhaps, but still it feels diabolical.

A trio of sweating newsmen rolls a moving picture camera down the nearest line of prisoners. Cheerless, haggard faces lift and grin, and just like that, the years evaporate and they are boys again.

The defeated soldiers are not lined up but sprawled or crouched on the ground. These were the valiant heroes of the Reich. Diminished, beaten, humiliated.

One face catches Max's eye, taller than the rest, his damp hair unruly, a cigarette in the corner of his mouth. Hope flashes, but it is not Papa. Max scans more faces, frantic now, but the truck changes direction, and he loses sight of them.

A few turns later, the truck stops. The driver raps on his door and calls something back. Private Griggs jumps down to speak to the driver and returns with two packs of US Army rations.

"Curfew soon," he says. "Curfew." The word means nothing to Max. Griggs pulls up his sleeve and taps his wristwatch: Max's wristwatch. It looks smaller on this man's dark arm. Griggs releases a little air out his nose. He flips his wrist, unfastens the strap, and offers it to Max.

"*Vielen Dank,*" Griggs says, and winks. The strap is warm and damp.

"Thank you," Max says in English. "Very good."

Griggs extends his hand and Max hesitates, then grips it. The soldier's thumbnail is the colour of milk. How is it possible for a hand to be both black and white? The skin on the soldier's forearm gleams. How might it feel to run his fingers across that skin, to discover if it feels as it looks, smooth beyond measure? But Griggs is staring at him with an odd expression. Max feels a deep flush of embarrassment, thanks the soldier once more, and pulls his hand away.

Red Cross nurses walk the lines announcing that it is too late in the day for assistance, that they must shelter tonight and return in the morning. The emergency housing is an old student hostel called Gallio that must have been a grand affair. He trails Hans through immense carpeted rooms crowded with people fanning themselves with newspapers and hats. There are fewer people in a wide rear hallway. Here stands Hitler on his head. The glass and frame of the portrait, at least two metres tall, are smashed, and the upside-down Führer has been defaced with devil horns, glasses, and a beard. The punishment for this will be brutal.

He must remember for the hundredth time that Hitler is the enemy here. It is easy to forget something that seems impossible.

The heat is already unbearable at the Place de la Gare, and it is barely nine in the morning. Prisoners stomp past in lines. Refugees mill around emergency kitchens and form snaking queues outside the Red Cross tents. A delivery boy balancing a sheep-sized package on his bicycle fights for space among horse-drawn carts, motorcars, and a truck laden with scolding chickens. Two men rest their backs against a rubbish bin, drinking from beer jugs.

"Let's go straight to the station," says Hans.

"The Red Cross nurse said they'd help," says Max.

"The lines are too long. We only need a train to Metz, and we can walk from there."

"We might need travel papers."

"*Papiers.*" A uniformed guard has his hand out. Gendarmerie. Max reaches into his jacket.

"We are trying to get to Thionville, monsieur, to my grandparents' house," he says in French.

"You are French?" says the gendarme. He is puzzled. This is Max's opening, his moment to make his impression. A memory pulls at him. A hot classroom glittering with chalk dust. A nurse with a secret smile. A tinful of eyes. *I am German. My father and grandparents and great-parents are German. My grandfather fought in the Great War.*

"Thought not," says the soldier.

"No, monsieur," says Max. "My grandparents are French, my god-father, my mother. We—my friend and me—are from the border. The Saar."

"*La Sarre*? That would be part of Germany, would it not? By popular vote a few years ago, if I recall."

"What's he saying?" says Hans.

"Is he claiming to be French too? The one who doesn't speak French?"

What can Max do to convince this man who holds the gun and all the power of the Republic of France? Might it be safer to grab Hans's arm and bolt into the crowd?

"Have you ever lived in France?"

"No, monsieur, but—"

"I understand," says the gendarme, and he smiles.

All is well. He will show them to their train, they will travel to his grandparents' house in Thionville, and from there they will make their way home.

The smile drops faster than a falling apple.

"This," says the gendarme, and opens his hand to them. "This is the story of our times. The Boche who remembers that he is, after all, French. The Boche who has a distant cousin who lives in Normandy. The Boche who visited Nice one summer, dreamed of walking the Champs-Élysées, the Boche who looted a crate of champagne and drank every bottle and now considers himself to be a true-blooded Frenchman."

"Max?" Hans looks ready to run.

"How did you get to Strasbourg?" says the gendarme.

"We crossed the Rhine with American soldiers," says Max. "We travelled from a children's camp in the mountains, in Bavaria. We were being called to fight, so we had to run away."

"What's happening?" says Hans.

"So you are Nazi deserters?"

"Not Nazis," says Max with what he hopes is determination, but the panic is rising, and Hans's fear is making it worse. He might as well be speaking Russian to this man.

"Or are you these Werewolf boys," he says. "Here to carry out your mischief and your murders."

"If you would consider my papers, monsieur—"

"We should go," says Hans, and takes a step backward.

"Don't," says Max. The gendarme adjusts his rifle to his front.

"Come on, Max. He can't shoot into the crowd."

"Come with me," says the gendarme.

"We're not Werewolves, sir. We——" But a hundred words, a thousand words, a sky full of words will not shift this man.

"Oh, I grasp it very well," says the gendarme. "Your arse is hanging between two chairs, is that not so? And you shift your cheek according to which way the wind blows."

"We want to go home, monsieur. That's all."

The gendarme lifts his chin, closes his eyes, and considers. Max has a hope, because is he not lucky? Has he not always been lucky? The gendarme holds the documents between thumb and forefinger, sweeps them against Max's nose—left, right, tap, tap, no, no—and arrests them.

From the outside, the cattle car isn't so bad. Some boards are rotting, and it needs a coat of paint, but there is a roof, at least. Three guards take up positions with rifles, a fourth grips the handle and the door screeches open. A wave of heat and urine and sweat washes out. Crammed, sweat-soaked men shout out their protests.

"There's no room."

"Water. Please."

"Have mercy. Please fetch us water."

Max turns to plead one last time, but the guards gesture at him to board. He takes hold of the guardrail and puts a foot on the step.

"Max, what's happening?" The dread in Hans's voice is worse than all of it.

"*Embarquez.*" Max has seen faces like the guards' before, in a fancy church in the city when he was young. While his mother prayed, the apostles glared down at Max, their faces set against him. He had buried his head in his mother's warm blue coat and begged to leave.

Another guard spins his rifle and jabs the butt toward Max.

"*Embarquez.*"

Max boards the train.

# 34

Heilbronn, Baden-Württemberg
April 1945

Anna and Tonia sleep, and Marguerite thinks of Max as she last saw him, at the train station at Neunkirchen.

Steam roiled from the engine, thick as beaten egg, white in the frozen air. Five or six soldiers, unshaven, hollow-eyed, huddled around a drum fire, sharing a cigarette while the class of uniformed *Pimpfe* stamped the cold out of their boots, breathing ghosts into the air. They were jostling, nervy. This was no weekend camp; there was no end date to this excursion.

Max gleamed like a trophy, but Marguerite adjusted his collar anyway and picked a piece of lint from his coat until he frowned and pulled away.

"We will write," said Marguerite.

"The post is stopped," said Anna.

"It won't be stopped forever," said Marguerite.

"We don't know his address," said Anna.

"He will send us his address," said Marguerite. "Won't you, Max?"

"How can he, when the post is stopped?" Anna said, and swiped a drip off her nose with the back of her glove. "Max, how about you stay here with Mama and refill Mrs. Liszt's coal scuttle, and I'll go to the mountains in your place?"

Marguerite had looked skyward, but there was no golden hand

reaching down to slap sense into her daughter. Just heavy skies: more cold, more snow. At least the bombers would be grounded.

A shrill whistle sounded, and the troop leader ordered the boys to board.

Marguerite pulled Max close. He was taller than her now, and would soon be taller than his father, although it had been months since they were able to compare. He did not fight her, nor did he yield. Charles's murder had changed him, damaged him in some way.

She wanted to put him back together the way she always had when he was injured or feverish or throwing up into a bucket. But it's not really mending that mothers do. It's clear to her now. A mother pats and clucks, offers warm blankets or cool compresses, kind words and sustenance, and waits for the child to repair itself. Does prayer play a part? If the events across two wars have shown her anything it is that Marguerite's prayers go unheard.

"Maximilian."

She had pushed her boy, her only son, to arm's length. Through the melt of tears she saw that he was scanning her face, searching, but for what?

*It won't be long,* she wanted to say. *It won't be long.* But her throat had closed over. She kissed him on both cheeks and held his head briefly between her palms. He stepped onto the train, and she wanted to call to him—but then Hans was there grabbing Anna around the waist, swinging her in a high circle. Anna rolled her eyes and pretended to endure it, but she liked Hans's strongman demonstrations as much as he liked displaying them—a safe way for them to show their affection without the intimacy of an embrace. Hans set her down, ducked the gentle swing she took at his head, and kissed Marguerite on both cheeks.

"See you when we get back, Mrs. B."

"Hans," said Marguerite, and her voice failed again.

"Don't worry," he said.

"Remember that you are students, not soldiers, Hans-Peter Schlesier," she said. "You stay in that camp and watch out for each other until it's over."

He threw out his chest and saluted, then followed Max onto the train. She searched the windows, but they were steamed up with the breath of so many others. A hand appeared, clearing a circle, and there was Max's face. The train shrank away, and it occurred to her that he had left without speaking a word.

How could she have allowed him to go? Several other boys had failed to show up at the muster. Their families were prepared to risk it—but they were local boys, with local connections, local places to hide, local relatives to keep them safe. Here in Neunkirchen, she had nobody. She *was* nobody. Neunkirchen might well be part of Saarland, but the farther she was from the border, the more her accent marked her as suspicious. Not to mention the black marks against the Bernot name for whoever cared to look it up. If Max Bernot had not got onto that train, the authorities would have come down on him, on her, on what was left of their family. Putting him on that train was the only way to keep him safe. Or so she had thought. The need to have him back, within sight, within reach, is a ragged, bone-deep tear in her chest that will not heal until he is returned to her.

"Marguerite," says Tonia.

"Sorry," says Marguerite.

"Would you like to light another candle?"

"No, no," she says. "Of course not. I'm sorry."

She wants to be distracted from her thoughts, from the oppressive air in this hole. "Tell us something of your family, Tonia."

In Tonia's silence, she hears a rebuke. *Have you ever seen a two-year-old who has starved to death?*

"Mama," says Anna.

"I mean before—" Marguerite says.

"Before?" says Tonia. "Before the Germans? Or before the Soviets?"

"I don't— I'm not meaning to pry. I just— It would be nice to think there is a family, Tonia. A family who will be waiting for you."

*"Mama."*

"Then you should think it." And Tonia says no more.

# 35

Somewhere in France
April 1945

A train may stop, but the journey is not over. A train may stop, but the doors remain closed. A train may stop and be replenished with rumbling coal and tumbling, fresh water so plentiful that it spills over rusted steel and drenches the dark earth, but not a drop will fall on its passengers. A train engine may quiet, but there is no rest for the ears—from the pings and clanks of stones, from the eye-watering screech of a crowbar scraped along the sides of the carriages, from the jeering and name-calling.

"Murderers. Murderers. Murderers."

The first time it happens, a couple of passengers call out indignant protests.

"I am French, not German!" one man says. "This is an outrage. Liberate us!" But no one believes a Frenchman who sounds like a Kraut. No one is in a mood to ask what terror might compel a French citizen to put on a German uniform and fight against his own country. No one is in a mood to doubt the wisdom of the authorities who have deemed that French collaborators and German civilians should be put on the same trains and sent to the same internment camps.

At the second stop, the same man tries singing the "Marseillaise," but the crowd outside takes it as a provocation, prompting a bustle of movement that cuts him off mid-verse. At the third stop, he stays quiet.

With each stop, the putrid heat worsens. It had been thirty degrees Celsius in Strasbourg, but this feels worse, far worse.

The train continues and the breeze shifts the stagnant air. Max can make out the faces of the men around him—those who have not collapsed. The coughing is incessant. There are three or four in the car who have a deep, rattling cough like the one that took Max's grandmother. Coughing that sounds as if a person's insides are being dragged out. How long has he been in here? Checking his watch is not easily done, bending his arm up through the bodies to bring his wrist to his face. But he cannot resist. He tries to space it out to no more than once an hour. The record so far: eighteen minutes.

His legs are filled with stone. His bladder aches. He has pissed in that stinking bucket once and would have vomited if there was anything in his stomach. His body is desiccated, his mouth lined with salt.

He dreams of piercing a mirror lake with a perfect dive, slicing into the cool, drawing in water through his skin. He dreams of the open tap in his mother's kitchen, splashing careless drops onto the bench. He imagines weeping, *wills* himself to weep so that he can catch a tear and hold it on his tongue and be comforted.

"He's dead." The words, in French, come from somewhere behind. "Get him away. Please. I cannot bear it." A surge runs through the carriage; Max's face is pressed into the damp shoulders of the man in front.

"*Calmez-vous.*" Calm yourself. This voice, lightly accented, is as deep and authoritative as a radio presenter announcing measures to be taken in a gas attack.

"Calm myself? There is a dead man beside me. How many of us are going to die in here?"

"He was an old man in poor health," says the man with the radio voice. "He might have died sitting on his chair at home. If it helps, imagine that he is sleeping."

"I can't bear it."

But the man does bear it. What else can he do? And now, when the train stops, Max waits, everybody waits, no longer for the door to be opened because the door never opens, but for the shouts and the stones and the clatter of steel.

Sometime in the night the train stops again, but this time the engines shut down. The temperature drops, and the freshness is a relief, but how soon fresh shifts to chill, chill to cold, cold to pain.

One or two passengers call for water, for food, for blankets, but it's clear from the unhurried pacing of the guards that they will receive none of these things and will spend the night here.

Darkness descends like a solid mass. He will die in this train alone yet surrounded, pressed in by strangers.

"Hans!" he whispers. "Hans, are you there?"

"All right there, Max?" says Hans. By his tone, who would know he was trapped in hell with a hundred other souls and a dead man, starved of food and water and light? Is he three metres away? Four? "Enjoying the view of the lake?" says Hans.

"Shut it," someone says in French.

"That lobster was a bit salty for my liking," says Hans. "How was the duck?"

"For God's sake." This one speaks German. "Are we not suffering enough?"

The Frenchman curses. "I will kill him myself if I have to listen to another word. Three years of their *putain* language stuffed down our throats, forced to fight in their *putain* uniform and now being taken for Nazis by our own people and locked up with the *putains*?"

"Show some compassion, *messieurs*," the radio man says. "The boy is afraid."

Max is thankful for the darkness.

"When did the Nazis ever show compassion?"

"And you would differentiate yourself from them?"

"Watch yourself, Kraut."

But the man has nothing more to say.

# 36

Heilbronn, Baden-Württemberg
April 1945

"You let us worship him." Anna's whisper cuts through the dark.

Marguerite wants to say: Who? But she knows.

"Do you know what they did to Antoninia's family?" Anna speaks in French, but Tonia sleeps on, her quiet snore rattling through the stillness. She will not hear.

"A little," says Marguerite.

"All the men were killed or sent to camps, and Tonia's family had to choose a child to send to Germany to work. The first time they sent her brother. Then the soldiers came back, and they had to send a second child. That time they chose Tonia."

Tonia stirs and Anna breaks off. Marguerite has the sense that she is weeping.

"Anna."

"You let us worship him."

"We did not encourage it."

"You did not discourage it."

"We did. We tried to. We wanted to, but you were so caught up."

"You could have done more."

She's right about that. Marguerite had not seen or had chosen not to see the depth of it, the diabolical reach of it. Every school lesson, every leaflet, every marching practice, exercise book, magazine, newspaper article, newsreel, and radio broadcast was designed to make the children worship Hitler—and not just him but themselves. Hitler convinced them that their parents, their church were nothing but the chains holding them back from their destiny. He was their parent, their God, their saviour, their hope.

"You would not hear a word against him, Anna, and we had to be careful."

"Careful?"

"Yes."

"You thought we would denounce you? You really believed we were capable of that?"

"It has happened, and don't pretend otherwise."

She had never seen her children as spies in their household—nothing so calculating. It was more a fear of a petulant outburst or a misplaced complaint. What might happen if she scolded them too forcefully, or said no to a wristwatch? What would they say in that moment of anger to a friend seeking favour with a virulent teacher, a youth leader looking for promotion? So much power was placed in the hands of those with so little ability to control their impulses.

"What am I supposed to believe now?" says Anna. "Tell me that. I don't know what is true. I don't know what is real, what is happening, what is *meant* to happen."

"There was a time before Hitler and there will be a time after."

"But what will become of us? What about Papa and Max? How will we ever find Max?"

Marguerite wants to say what mothers say. All will be well, Daughter, everything will be fine. *Ça ira, ça ira.* Yet she hesitates, sensing in that heavy darkness Anna's hunger for the truth.

"I don't know," she says. "This is the end of something, it's true, but not of everything, Anna, not of everyone. There will be difficult times ahead—worse, I imagine, than after the last war—but ultimately your generation will be the ones to decide what happens."

Marguerite slips her arm out of her blanket to reach for her daughter's arm. It stiffens and pulls away.

"Do you know what the cook told me a few days ago? Adolf

Hitler awarded an Iron Cross to a twelve-year-old boy somewhere in the east. Her sister saw it in a military bulletin in Heilbronn, and it wasn't just one boy. There was a long line of them, she said. Brave young boys fighting for the Führer, fighting to the end."

"Why are you telling me this?"

"Why did you let them take him, Mama? Why did you put Max on that train? What if he and Hans have been caught up in it all? What if he's dead?"

"Don't say that. Please don't think it."

"You could have done more."

"Yes," Marguerite says.

She should have done more.

# 37

Somewhere in France
April 1945

The cold has stolen their voices. Mauve light and frosted air washes through the grills. The faces surrounding Max are caved in with exhaustion. Condensation spears Max's nose and ears with minute daggers of ice.

The train moves, and with it a savage wind. He lifts himself up, on legs that feel detached from his body, to see over the shoulders of the men in front. Ragged wisps of cloud trail from low skies. The plummeting temperature is a barbaric trick of nature, because if the heat was unbearable yesterday, this is a cold that will squeeze the life out of you.

Another man died in the night; others have lost their footing, collapsed. Dysentery spreads.

His watch has stopped; his fingers incapable of a movement so delicate as feeling for the crown of his watch and gripping those minuscule ridges.

The train slows. There are voices. The muffled clop and rattle of a horse-drawn cart, and two men greet each other in French.

"What game is God playing with this weather, Samuel?"

"A good question, sir."

"First the heat, then the cold, and now a fresh trainload of Krauts. What will be next? A plague? An earthquake or some such?" A horse snorts. "What's wrong, young man? You're out of sorts."

"I do fear what is coming, monsieur. I really do. Did you read that poor man's account this morning? At least twenty thousand dead, he thinks, in Buchenwald alone. How many others will there be? 'Scientific extermination,' he called it, and now these people, these murderers, are flooding into France by the trainload."

"Calm yourself, Samuel. They'll be kept separate from us, and it's only for a short time, until the troops are through and the war is won, then they'll be gone. Pray for peace, because the sooner the Nazis surrender, the sooner we will be rid of them."

The train moves on and a freezing draught howls through the car. On all sides he is pressed in by trembling bodies, and yet the cold still feeds on him. His bones have turned to ice. If he stamps his foot his leg will disintegrate like a dropped glass.

He runs through his head what the men outside the train said about Buchenwald and the other camps. As long as he can remember, the camps have existed. Some were different from others, some worse, but that was as much as he knew, or thought he knew. Papa had been imprisoned in a labour camp, early in the war, where he worked underground building missiles for the Reich. He seldom spoke about it other than right after he came back with stories about tasteless food and idiotic guards. Many of his mother's Mosellan cousins and aunts were "guest workers" in labour camps in Silesia. They'd sent postcards early on. The Russian prison camp had appeared at Lauterbach sometime during the war. Max had understood that with so many German men fighting, there was a need for foreign labourers to fill the gap. What better use of vanquished enemy soldiers or foreign criminals? That's what he'd thought or had been told. He cannot recall. Uncle Josef had been in Buchenwald since early in the war, and Max had the sense from Tante Cécile that it was a bad place—but twenty thousand dead? Scientific extermination? What did that mean? Those wretched men coming at him out of the fog at Schwäbisch Hall were from some sort of camp, and Charles too.

*They're working people to death.* That's what Charles was saying when Max discovered him in the kitchen. Was he speaking about the camp he'd escaped from, or a different one? Max had not thought to question him, and if he had, Charles would have changed the subject.

Charles. Max would give anything to see him again, to hear his stories about exotic places, outlandish people. Wherever he went in the world, he remembered to bring back a coin. All Max had to do was catch it and it was his. Each coin came with a story, each coin was special, and none so special as the first one Max had ever caught—the thousand-year-old denier that Charles's ancestor had found in the field at Lauterbach the very year that Napoleon Bonaparte was defeated at Waterloo and lost the Saar. Again and again his godfather had tossed it into the air. Again and again Max had tried to catch it and failed.

*What is the eagle's secret?*

*I don't know, Uncle.*

Think. *How does it make its catch?*

*Sharp claws?*

*Before the claws.*

*Going very fast?*

*Think again.*

*I don't know.*

*Before the claws, before the speed.*

*It watches?*

*Exactly. Once the eagle has seen the mouse, there is only the mouse. Its chicks, the other birds, the sounds of the forest, the pain in its wing. Nothing exists for the eagle except the mouse. The eyes are everything. The hand will follow.*

*The eyes are everything.*

But Max's own eyes had failed him. Or perhaps he had failed to look, because he had not seen what was right in front of him.

*They're working people to death.*

*It's revenge for what we've done to the Jews.*

*Don't put your heart in a box.*

*It's murder on a scale—*

*Bumper crop of cauliflower.*

A fresh memory claws at him. He is in the garden in Lauterbach, helping Anna dig fertiliser around the home vegetables. They were complaining about the stink of it, the sticky grit that caught under your nails and made your skin crawl. He rubs his fingers together and cringes.

Blood and bone.

The stock car shudders. Max stumbles and rights himself using the sleeve of the man next to him. He rewraps his scarf over his nose. The coughing around him is deeper with each hour. How many more will die? Will he be among them? He has not heard Hans's voice for hours but does not want to risk the ire of the angry Frenchman by calling out to him again. Hans is probably thinking the same thing. Or maybe he is sleeping, or gravely ill, or slumped dead on the shoulder of the man next to him. Hot panic sinks its claws into his throat.

"Hans," he calls. "Are you still there?"

"*Jòò*," says Hans. "Go to sleep, Max."

"How am I supposed to sleep standing up?"

"Close your eyes."

Impatient voices hush them but the relief is so intense that a smile breaks across his face, tearing the parched skin of his bottom lip.

It might be late afternoon when the brakes scream and the boiler releases a head of steam. The engine is shutting down. Max would give his life to rest for a single minute in the cab of that engine, blanketed in the heat of the coals.

Scores of boots strike timber—is an army marching by? There is a low chatter. Is it ducks? A stone cracks against the cattle car wall; another pings off the roof. Not ducks.

A gruff male shouts in an accent too dense to decipher, and the timber plank screeches outside the door. Rusted hinges moan, light floods in, space opens up, cold envelops him, and Max's legs fold. The heel of a boot crushes his fingers; a knee catches him on the ear. Someone takes hold of his coat and hauls him up.

# 38

"Acanthus." Marguerite's voice sounds foreign to her—a crackle in the dark.

"Bitterwurst," says Anna.

"Boring," says Tonia.

"Has to be a flower," says Anna. "And start with *C*."

"You can have convallaria, Tonia," says Marguerite.

"Dreary," says Tonia.

"Her German goes from strength to strength," says Anna.

"Astonishing progress," says Marguerite.

"Complains like a native."

"I am dead, and this is hell," says Tonia. "It's not normal, this stupid game."

"Quite normal," says Marguerite.

"Perfectly normal," says Anna, and the allegiance feels like forgiveness, like hope.

"What games did you play when you were small?" says Anna.

Tonia laughs.

"What?" says Anna.

"You are funny."

"Did you hear that?" says Anna.

"What is it?" says Marguerite. "Did you hear that?"

"It is nothing. Just your brain blowing out steam," says Tonia.

"Is it time to break out?" says Anna.

"No." Marguerite and Tonia speak at the same time.

"Another round, then?" says Anna, and yelps. It's her turn to feel the end of Tonia's foot.

"I remember one," says Tonia. "Big favourite in my family. It's called 'The Quiet Game.'"

"Very funny," says Anna.

"I win," says Tonia. Marguerite laughs.

"And again."

Time is moving backward, forward, sideways. How many days has it been? Too many. Wretched air, cramped limbs, and the *blindness* of the dark. The waiting and the not knowing. The straining to hear unfamiliar noises, and the dread at what they might bring.

The only food left is a tin that has lost its label and a bottle of bitter olive oil which they take like medicine: a teaspoon at a time, three times a day.

"It might all be over," says Anna.

"We wait," says Tonia.

"We wait," says Marguerite.

"How do you *know*?" says Anna. "Could we at least take the waste bucket out?"

The unholy stink that comes off it each time they remove the lid takes an age to dissipate. Anna knows full well that in order to free themselves of it they will have to break through the wardrobe wall— there would be no coming back in here if they do that.

Where is the caretaker? Where is the front? Has the front passed, or not passed? Is the caretaker waiting for safety? Has he fled or is he dead?

Again and again in the merciless dark, she relives the night of Charles's return. She should have thanked him for all those visits, the stories that took her out of her quiet life and showed her a different world, full of risk and chance, that both repelled and fascinated her. She should have thanked him for loving her children as if they were his own. She should have spirited him away into the night and found a place for him to hide. She should have saved him.

Before the murderers arrived, before Charles had had his bath and was still apologising over and over, her cousin had plunged his hands into his pockets and pulled them out, empty, to show Max. He apologised. This time for traversing a thousand kilometres through unimaginable peril and failing to bring his godson a gift.

"It doesn't matter," said Max. Pride radiated from her son's upright posture, and he drew that battered old denier from his pocket.

Charles stared at the coin, then at the boy who held it. It is no small thing to feel the love of a child. Max had given up trying to hold back the smile. Charles could only cross his hands over his chest as if trying to anchor his soaring heart.

# 39

Poitiers, La Vienne, France
April 1945

*"Sortez! Sortez!"*

Rifle butts slam into cattle car doors. Fierce light. A dense arrow of pain explodes in Max's shoulder. Through raised forearms, he spies a small crowd. A wide-eyed doll stares out from a basket held by a girl of three or four buttoned into an enormous coat. The girl lifts something from the basket and throws. A stone bounces off the fresh-sawn timber of a temporary platform. A woman with a shaved head screams.

Max turns and pushes back, steps on a foot or a hand. Someone cries out. Stones smack and ping off flesh and steel. There are heavier, more ominous thuds, too, low groans of agony.

*"Sortez! Sortez!"*

Someone has him by the back of the coat. He flies backward and bites his tongue. Outside now, his legs won't hold him, the pain in his mouth is brutal, his breath comes in gasps. His tongue swells and feels foreign.

A truncheon appears, held high by a guard whose roar covers Max in spit. What is he *saying*? The guard twists away, distracted. To Max's left is the crowd, contained behind flimsy chain barriers. To his right, the train. All along the platform, guards beat passengers with truncheons. The passengers shield themselves with what they have to hand: rucksack, suitcase, sack, blanket, arms. Another shaven woman shrinks from a guard roaring insults at her. Max feels a sharp thud on the front of his trousers, and he looks up—a ridiculous reflex—to search for the stone-thrower. This unleashes a fresh round of jeers and another volley. Some-one is tugging at his rucksack. He jerks his shoulder forward, an instinct to protect it, and a truncheon descends, smacking through muscle to bone at the base of his rib cage. His breath jams.

The guard jabs his finger at a growing pile of luggage on the plat-form and Max understands that he must take off his rucksack and add it to the pile. He is getting a little air now but feels as if he is breathing through a straw. He shakes off the bag into the pile. Down the line, the arms of the guards cut like threshers.

A woman with two young children and a pram drifts in a hopeless panic. A guard steps in her direction and she turns her face up to him: an appeal. She hasn't seen his foot. It draws back. Max shouts a warn-ing. The pram lifts. It strikes the wall. The woman shrieks and dives. The baby tumbles. Another shout. A second guard hurls himself onto the first and slaps him. The first guard comes back fighting. A stone grazes Max's temple and he crosses his arms in front of his face. Some-where a baby squalls.

*Avancez. Avancez.* Move forward. A blow lands on Max's left side with a hideous crunch. He drops to his knees. The cold of the plat-form burns his cheek. A discarded cigarette butt sends a trickle of blue smoke into the pitiless air.

*Boche, Kraut, Nazi, Schleuh.* The crows are screeching. He wants to scream back at them that he is none of those. How can he be, when in Germany he is a string of other names: *Saarfrench, Westwall Gypsy, Inferior, Contaminated.*

Max feels himself lifted. Far, far below, the train station is no bigger than the tip of a pencil. The whole of France is laid out beneath him. He sets his eye to the northwest and his home.

Up here, in the velvet silence, he can see the meandering line that marks where his own village of Lauterbach in Germany becomes the village of Carling in France. This is the crossing where, before the war, he risked feeling the back of his mother's hand, because he could not resist pausing to stand in two countries at once. His father had told him that the true German border lay to the east of their home, beyond the dragons' teeth and barricades and underground labyrinths and cannons and tanks and armies of the Westwall. But the thin strip of Germany outside the wall was Max's Germany, his own territory. His home, his family, his forest, his church. Undefended by the Reich yet claimed by it. And if he, Max Bernot, is unclaimed by Germany, and unclaimed by France, then who is he? Where does he belong?

A quiet ringing fills his ears. His heart feels loose in its cage. A fluttering bird. A tapping finger. *Tippity tap.* Blackness gallops in. A cushioned silence, merciful and kind. He dives.

Someone repeats his name. The platform is sticky and tastes of pine. Splinters tear at his shoulder and hip. Hands pull at him, and the ground falls away.

"Can you stand on your own?" It is Hans. His cheek is bruised.

Where is Horst? Where are the rest? Gone, gone, gone.

But Hans is here. Hans is still here. Max takes the arm that is offered and pulls himself up the rope that is his friend.

With each swerve and shudder of the truck, his body rings with cold and pain. To keep himself from tipping off his seat at every pothole or corner in the road, he uses one hand to hold the icy steel bench beneath him, the other to grip the freezing tailgate.

They bounce along a bomb-damaged street under a trio of wooden boxes overflowing with flowers and he remembers the night the Gestapo came to the house, into his bedroom, the night they arrested his father for currency crime. While the agents screamed at his mother, emptied the closet, hunted under the beds, Anna curled up in the corner, drowning out all of it with her floral alphabet.

*Acanthus*, Max whispers to himself. *Bitterwurz. Christophskraut.*

A leg presses against his own. He flinches away.

"That was a warm welcome." A voice sounds like Hans but a long way off.

*Digitalis. Erica. Fuchsia.*

"Will there be more of that, do you think, at the hotel?" the voice that sounds like Hans persists, intruding closer now. "I imagine the concierge won't let the rabble past the door. Will we go straight to the room? Or the restaurant? Restaurant, I think. I fancy a schnitzel, but would they know how to make that in France, Max? Max? What local delicacy would you suggest?"

Max shakes his head.

*Acanthus. Bitterwurz. Christophskraut.*

"Max," says Hans.

He starts again.

"Max, *please.*"

Max opens his eyes. Tears are spilling down Hans's cheeks. Max's mouth is disconnected from his throat. He coughs and pain cuts deeper into his ribs.

"What?" says Hans.

"*Coq au vin,*" rasps Max at last. He drags up a smile and tastes blood. "Rooster in wine."

A guard raps on the tailboard with his rifle.

"*Ferme ta gueule.*"

"The guard says to shut up," says Max. He licks the split in his lip.

Hans laughs, then laughs again. "Service is a nightmare," he says. "He won't be getting a tip out of me, that's certain."

The truck slows and they pass through tall wooden gates set in a three-metre-high timber-and-barbed-wire fence. A watchtower rises to his left. To his right, there are three more.

Dozens of low barracks lie on a vast plateau. The bare earth is unbroken by a single tree or shrub—just a few frost-topped mounds and iced-over puddles.

A fleck of white catches on his eyelash. Max holds out his hand. It is the twenty-seventh of April. This is not possible. A fat snowflake settles onto his wrist. The sky is falling.

# 40

It is Anna who picks up the axe. Marguerite doesn't argue. The silence is testing her sanity. In its endless depths she hears heavy footsteps, screams, vehicles, gunfire—all of it real or none of it. She has begun to wish for the soldiers to come, to get it over with, whatever it is.

Anna swings—there is hardly room for it—and strikes. The axe head springs off the wall. They listen. Nothing. She swings, and again the axe bounces. They listen. And again.

Tonia takes it up next, grunting with the effort. On the fifth strike, the wall cracks. On the seventh, she breaks through. When they have cleared a gap wide enough, Marguerite puts a restraining hand on Tonia's arm.

"Let me go first."

"Why?" says Tonia.

"There might be someone."

"If there was someone they would be here already," says Tonia. She shows her brown teeth. "And I'm the one holding the axe." There is a brittle strength to her that makes Marguerite feel both protected and protective.

"What?" says Tonia. "You think I wouldn't use it?"

"Quite the opposite," says Marguerite. "Lead the way."

The light is blinding, and when her eyes adjust to the glare, the house seems ten times larger than before, stretching up and out and

269

away in every direction. For a single, crazy moment, she wants to crawl back into the alcove and put her hands over her head.

Anna and Tonia are horribly thin. Their hair is grubby, their skin too pale, their eyes underlined with shadow. They each need a bath, a good meal, a night in a bed.

Heilbronn is no longer burning. From the attic the sky is clear apart from a twine of smoke from a distant farmhouse. A good sign? But no, anyone at all can walk into a house and light a fire.

"First we wash, then we find out what's going on," says Anna, but Tonia is frowning, finger raised, pointing.

The Jeep is American. Three helmeted soldiers, three rifles, three sets of eyes scour the garden, the outbuildings, the windows of the house, the attic.

Marguerite crouches beside the girls, heart belting. There is no disguising their presence in this house. The smashed wardrobe and the stink of the toilet bucket tell a tale a simpleton could read. She drags her hair into a knot. She must look and smell a fright, which is good.

"Hide yourselves," she says.

"We will come," says Tonia.

"No, you won't. They will have no reason to think there are more of us."

"Mama."

"Anna, you and Tonia have risked enough. Let me do this."

She creeps into a first-floor bedroom, shakes a pillow out of its slip and approaches a window. The soldiers are advancing. There is fear in their cautious, circling steps.

She taps against the glass, the gentlest of taps with the knuckle of her index finger. It is enough. Three rifles lift to meet her.

She wants to drop out of sight, to flatten herself on the floorboards, to run and hide herself from these strangers, these soldiers, these killers. Instead she takes a breath and remains there, in full sight, hands raised beside her face.

*They are battering at the door.*

The stomach drops out of her. Courage evaporates. She cannot do this. She cannot do this. She cannot do this again.

# 41

Poitiers, La Vienne
May 1945

A man from Saarbrücken died overnight. He watched Max from half-lidded eyes, pale jaw open, while two men stripped him of his shirt and picked through his pockets to find a photograph, a compass, a square of chocolate. Were these treasures being gathered up to be sent to his family? Max's heart lifted at the thought of a family somewhere receiving a memento. But one man tore the foil off the chocolate and crammed it into his mouth, prompting a protest from Roger, the white-haired Alsatian who was trying to make the compass work. The chocolate-eater dodged out of reach for the few seconds it took him to swallow, then sauntered to his bunk. The photograph quivered to the ground, forgotten.

The man from the train with the radio voice turns out to be a doctor of sorts: a psychiatrist. A slight, middle-aged man with a downcast face and heavy moustache. He had pushed his way through to the dead man and checked his pulse and led a prayer. The other internees had nominated him barrack representative on that first, freezing day. Max had imagined that this granted the doctor mystical powers to deliver better food and clean water and soap and their belongings, but the camp authorities have ignored all his requests.

The dead man's name was Brecher. When the doors were unlocked for the morning, the doctor and Roger carried him outside, his body sagging in the middle like a rolled carpet. Max had watched them haul him onto the wagon. A fly landed on the dead man's cheek, walked across his jaw and tipped into his open mouth. Max had turned away. Hans was there.

"This is not forever, Max. Just until the war is over." Hans's smile could make him forget the worst things.

"Never said it was." But Hans had read his mind. Max had imagined himself in that cart, stripped of his shirt and wristwatch and photograph of his family in the field, flies crawling into his own mouth.

Max and Hans are the only boys their age in their barrack of one hundred—too old for the women and children's sector. As Germans, they are also in the minority. Most men in this barrack are from Alsace and Moselle, the French side of the border, cleared out when Allied troops swept through.

The ones caught in Wehrmacht uniforms call themselves the *malgrénous*, forced to fight for the Nazis. True for most, not all. Others, accused of different types of collaboration, simply call themselves French. The guards don't care what anyone calls himself. Every internee is a Nazi, no matter where they were born, what language they speak, where their mother comes from. That's the way it is at La Chauvinerie civilian internment camp.

Word reached them the day after they arrived that Hitler is dead; fighting to the end or swallowing arsenic, depending on who you believe. And still the war continues. Bitter fighting in Berlin. Child soldiers are manning machine guns, loading mortars, screaming in astonishment and outrage when shrapnel and bullets and flying bricks find their mark and bring agony where only glory was anticipated.

A sharp clatter on the roof sends a jolt through him. The visitors, Hans calls them. Local men letting off steam about the Nazis in their midst. One of the regulars, with a powerful arm and a voice to match, is making all the usual promises: throat-cutting, testicle-slicing, neck-breaking. The shouts are slurred with wine and the Poitivine dialect Max has come to understand from listening to the guards.

*Murderers. Bastards. Hang yourselves and save us the trouble.*

"Same story?" says Hans.

Max never translates the threats, only the insults. Hans's laughter keeps him brave.

"Shh," Max whispers, straining to pick out individual voices. "Cabbage head? Pig. Nazi." Hans is already smiling.

"Nazi pig's arse, maybe?" says Max. "Something about sauerkraut."

"Sauerkraut," says Hans. Up go his eyebrows once, and again.

Max groans. The hunger draws deep. "Stop it," Max says, wrapping his arms around his abdomen.

"Roast pork," Hans says. "Smoky bacon. Fresh sausage."

"Stop, Hans." The midday broth has left a chasm the size of France inside him. He cannot think for hunger, cannot move, cannot hold a thought for anything but the hole where his insides should be.

Dubois, a stooped and nervy Mosellan, slides off his bunk and wags a trembling finger at them. He has lost his top buttons, and the sagging skin of his chest is tufted with grey hair. He has the air of a madman, not helped by his story about hiding in a cave for three years to avoid being drafted by the Wehrmacht. "Shhhh," he says, finger to lip, and clambers under the bunk. "*Il nous faut préparer.*"

"We need to prepare ourselves," Max translates.

"Batshit will do that to a man," says Hans.

"You boys think everything is a joke," sneers Roger, who occupies the bunk above Dubois. "You think the people out there throwing stones have forgotten anything? Does your little friend know what happened at Oradour? He might like a story about the adventures of one of his heroic Waffen-SS commanders rushing to Normandy on a sweet summer's day in 1944."

Max ignores the Alsatian, pulls a stalk of straw out of his sleeve and presses the cut end to his bottom lip.

"The Nazi commander made a detour to organise a little retribution," says Roger. "Tell him. Tell your Nazi friend they locked the men in the stables and outhouses and slaughtered them. Then they barricaded the women and children into the church at Oradour-sur-Glane, and tried to blow it up."

"That's enough." The doctor has placed himself at the foot of Max's bunk.

"When that didn't finish the job, they threw in grenades, fired into the church with machine guns, but there was a lot of panic," Roger continues, craning around the doctor to catch Max's eye.

Dubois's crooning rises a notch and the doctor growls another warning, but Roger continues.

"Kids bellowing, mothers panicking, trying to pass a child out a window. You can imagine how difficult it was to get a decent shot." He lifts his chin at Hans. "Tell him that. Tell him how long it must have taken to make sure there were no survivors. And then they set the place alight."

Max closes his eyes but the images appear anyway: the panic, the pain, the blood, the shoeless feet of a dead child poking from a quilt, a folded-up corpse in a suitcase, a knee without a foot, an arm without a torso, a socket without an eyeball. The toss of a coin.

"What's he saying, Max?" says Hans.

"More than six hundred and forty dead," says Roger.

"You can't lay it at their feet," says the doctor.

"They may have stuffed their uniforms in a hedge, but we all know what they are," says Roger.

"They're not the only ones who stuffed their uniforms in a hedge," says the doctor.

Roger is off his bunk and holding the other man's throat, forcing him into a bunk frame. The barrack erupts—four or five men surge forward to pull Roger off. They are all too weak, too hungry to fight, but he falls back.

"The bells!" Dubois is groaning from under the bed. "The bells."

The bells. Discordant, insistent, from every direction. Voices rise. A volley of shots comes from somewhere close. Max is back in Saarbrücken. The rain falls, voices rise, and he is lifted. If he were to turn right now, he would see his father.

Hans is off his bunk, has Max by the shirt.

"It's over, Max. The war's over. We're going home."

Hans is whooping and dancing like a fool. Max takes a long, shivering breath and joins him, but the shout turns to a cry, and the cry turns to a howl, and he is on his knees, calling, calling through the barrack, through the walls, through the barbed wire, across the dry plateau, across the fields and valleys and mountains of France.

"Max?" A familiar face appears in the yard later. "Is that you, Max Bernot?"

It is a shock to hear his name, and it takes a moment to recognise Heinz Grott from Lauterbach, father to the twins and exempt from soldiering because he'd lost a hand before the war in an accident in the ironworks. He's lost weight and his hair has turned grey.

Mr. Grott laughs and takes hold of his shoulders.

"Have I changed that much that you have to check the hand? Let me look at you, young man. Just wait until I tell the others."

Others. There are others? "Is my family here?"

Mr. Grott blinks. "Oh no. No, I'm sorry, Max. No, I didn't mean—"

"You said—"

"Others from Lauterbach. No, bless you, Max. I have seen no one else from your family, I am sorry to say. Have you had no news? Listen, come with me."

"Wait," says Max. He is winded. For a moment, he thought they were here. Mama, Papa, Anna. All here waiting for him.

"Come," says the old man. Max follows him on a tour of barracks he has never visited, and there are more faces from home. The men squeeze him and pat him until he winces, and they realise he is hurt and insist on examining his fading bruises. They walk him to the barricades and call across to the women's side. There beyond the barbed wire, are more familiar faces. *Max, Max, Max.* For long weeks, every person he has encountered, except for Hans, has been a stranger. Their excitement, their concern is a balm. Their news even more so.

The village is damaged but standing for the most part. Some residents had been allowed to resettle the western end of the village; others had been cleared and sent here, to La Chauvinerie. No one has had any news of his family or of Hans's mother, which is not a bad sign, they assure him, just an indication of the chaos on the border.

"Listen, a kind woman from L'Hôpital has been delivering a few packages," says Mr. Grott. "We'll have a chat with her if she comes again, see if she has heard anything."

The men share a few small luxuries with Max—a morsel of cheese, a tin of meat, half a packet of cigarettes for trading. He shares everything with Hans, except for the meat. As long as it remains unopened, as long as he does not eat it, his conscience is clear.

# 42

*They are battering at the door.*

Marguerite draws a shuddering breath and makes herself walk. She pulls the front door open a few centimetres and drapes the pillowslip out of it. Someone shouts instructions, but she can make no sense of the words. A sob of fear catches in her throat.

"Okay, okay. It's okay." The soldier at the front has lowered his weapon and is showing her his palms. The fingers tip. *Come outside.* He is older than the others, in his thirties. She steps outside and pulls the door closed behind her.

He speaks calmly but his German is incomprehensible. He gestures toward the house and repeats the question. His eyes are fixed on hers; the other men are scanning the house.

"*Soldaten?*" he says, and this she understands.

"*Drei von ihnen,*" she says. Three of them. She points to him and to each of his men, reciting in English: "One, two, three."

"Ha," he says. "Very good. I am Sergeant Jim Woon."

"Bernot," she says, and takes his hand. "Mrs. Bernot."

"A French name," he says.

"Yes."

"*Vous parlez français, madame?*" he says.

"Of course."

277

"*Vous êtes française?*" You are French?

"That is another question."

His French is a great deal better than his German. An English father, French mother, he explains. He introduces the two soldiers, who are boys—no more than nineteen—and look like they could do with a nap. They had detoured from their route to investigate reports of looting and been unable to find their way back to Heilbronn.

"It's not difficult to get to Heilbronn from here. I can give you directions," she says.

The sergeant removes his helmet and scratches at his hair, which is jet black and speckled with silver. He is too young for grey hair. Has the war done that to him? The soldiers, already bored by a conversation in a foreign tongue, flop onto the steps and light cigarettes.

"You don't have any schnapps, do you?" the sergeant says, nodding toward the men. "It's been a long day."

"What time is it?" she says. He checks his wristwatch and the gesture, so casual and unselfconscious, recalls Max in the early days of that damned wristwatch. He had tried to cultivate that same nonchalance, but the pride and satisfaction were all too clear in the awkward twist of the wrist, the stiff glance downward, the flick of the eyes to check who was noticing. Marguerite, still furious with him for coercing her into buying it for him, had found it irritating. Now it seems endearing.

"Just after five," the soldier says, and notices her smile. "What's funny?"

"Right," she says. "Schnapps is about all I have. Wait here." She retrieves the half-empty bottle from the kitchen and tips a third of it down the sink, remembering the words of the caretaker.

"Will this do?" she says, with a shrug of apology, and hands over the bottle and three glasses. The soldiers are grateful, thank her in German. One jogs to the Jeep and returns with two packs of army rations. These men look ridiculously healthy. Their teeth are blinding. She feels a sharp pang of jealousy. This is how Max should look. *Max.* Where is he? She takes the rations and thanks the soldier.

"Don't get your hopes up," says the sergeant, nodding at the packages in her hand. "*C'est vachement épouvantable.*" It's frankly awful. He's talking about the rations. She snorts at the slang in the mouth of an Englishman.

"*Vachement?* Where did you hear that one?"

"Marseilles," he says. "We have no equivalent in English, but it is my dearest wish that the word *cow-ly* will one day make it into an English dictionary."

"*Cow-ly,*" she repeats. "And what word do the English use when only *vachement* will do?"

"*Dreadfully? Horribly?* Nothing comes close. *Cow-ly* is the better word." The breeze lifts and it already carries the late-afternoon chill.

"Shall we go inside?" he says.

"Can you tell me what is happening?" she says. "On the fronts?"

"You don't have a radio?"

"Not anymore."

"I see," he says. "Hitler is dead, but the Boche are putting up one hell of a fight in places. It's beyond hopeless. It's criminal." He pauses and scans her face. "I'm sorry. I'm not completely clear which camp you're in, so to speak."

"Shall we say the camp of peace?" she says.

"Cheers to that," he says, and lifts his glass.

"Hitler is dead?" she says.

"One can never be sure, but his own people are saying it."

"Too late," she says.

"Five years too late. Ten. Someone should have put a bullet in him in 1933."

"Yet still no ceasefire?"

"The fanatics still hold power right down to the street. My boys cut down a poor man strung up in a village not far from here for trying to save his town, talk down the soldiers, wave the white flag. The Nazis hanged him for it in the morning, then fled in the afternoon. It's all so pointless."

He takes in the lawns and the gardens and the mansion itself. "You have a lovely home."

She snorts. "There are no cherubs holding up the front stairs of my home."

"*Cherubin?*" He looks puzzled. She waves her hand at the stairway and he sees, and grins. "I live in a mining town in Saarland, three hundred metres from the French border."

"That is not what I expected you to say," he says. "How on earth did you come to be here?"

"My home is in the Red Zone. We were evacuated when the front approached."

"That can't have been easy."

"It's not the first time," she says. "You might say our region has been a Red Zone for a thousand years."

Her grandfather was fond of declaring that it was the Celts who were first to chip coal out of the earth near the Saar River to fuel their fires and forge their weapons—and not the Romans as most people thought. After the Romans, the land was tossed between barons and lords, dukes, princes, and bishops—some Germanic, some Frankish. Louis the Sun King had his time, as did Napoleon Bonaparte, the fledgling French Republic and in time the new nation of Germany. The border lifts, the border shifts. It has changed three times in her lifetime and will probably change again now. And she will do what people always do. Hold on. Live, work, worship, endure.

"Madame?"

She looks at his face—patient, inquisitive—and decides to trust him.

"I have a sense that you are a decent man, Sergeant Woon," she says.

"I'm sorry?"

"Are you? A decent man, a good man?"

"Is any man qualified to answer that question about himself?" He pulls a cigarette pack from his shirt pocket and offers her one. It is tempting but having him light a cigarette invites an intimacy she will not allow. "I am not the sort of man who generally frightens women, if that's what you mean."

"And did you walk around your hometown in England with a rifle and grenades hanging from your belt and two excitable soldier boys at your side?"

"I see what you are saying," he says. "Well no. I did, however, shoot a duck on occasion, and a hare once, although I admit to some regret about that."

"I would think that you've shot a few men by now."

"You are not one for small talk, are you?"

"I'm not inclined to turn around the pot, no. Perhaps that's how this war has changed me."

" 'Turn around the pot'? Yes, I see. Waste time."

"You didn't answer my question."

"Let me put it this way," he says, and gazes behind her to the house. "I am not sure who you have there in the house with you, madame, but unless it is a clutch of fanatics, or stragglers staging an ambush, they are in no danger from me, from us. If they are your children, I will do my best to help. A fair exchange for directions to Heilbronn and a little schnapps."

A rumble heralds a high-flying aircraft, and they tip their heads back to search for it. She inhales the tang of the cigarette smoke and, beyond it, a whisper of *Maiglöckchen*. The scent brings her back to Lauterbach in the first year of her marriage, walking into the kitchen to discover a pitcher filled with flowers, cut and arranged by her husband, heralding spring and love and the promise of happiness.

"I would like one of those cigarettes now," she says, and lights it herself.

# 43

Poitiers, La Vienne
May 1945

The war has been over for more than a fortnight but there is still no word about sending them home.

Max lines up for roll call at seven, hunched against the drizzle. Weather exists only in extremes here. Wind moans around the barracks for days at a time, lifting everything that is not pinned down, causing an irritability that spills into sharp words, violence. Frequent tempests sweep through, battering the barracks with so much force the roof threatens to lift. On cloudless days the barracks are murderously hot by ten in the morning, and there is not a single tree to shelter beneath. Perhaps it is always like this in Poitiers in May. Perhaps God really is showing his displeasure. Perhaps this is not God's domain at all, but Max is in hell; four weeks into an eternity, having forgotten the precise circumstances of his own death, if not the sins that landed him here.

Mud slips between his toes. He traded his boots for a larger pair a few days earlier, but the new ones are in no better condition. The lines of prisoners steam like cattle.

The camp commander waddles past, head in the air. They say he is a mayor of a village somewhere in the hills. He calls himself *Colonel* and wears the uniform of one but is mocked for it by certain guards who say that his position is bureaucratic, not military, that he was given his rank by the Vichy government, and therefore it is the rank of a traitor. His son storms around calling himself *Capitaine*, with the uniform to match. The political allegiances are complex in this place, but one thing everyone agrees on: not just the food is rotten here.

A shout rises to his left where an internee, bleeding from the cheek, is being marched through the barracks by the camp sergeant and an Austrian prisoner who acts as an enforcer. Some of the guards are decent enough here—old men or returned soldiers happy to receive a paycheck and get on with their work. The sergeant and the Austrian are the worst brutes, the Grubers of this place, with an appetite for humiliation and cruelty. The caught man is probably the one who escaped from work duties at a rail yard three days earlier. Will he be whipped or blasted with a fire hose in the mustering yard? Or will he suffer one of the punishments carried out in private: hot coals in the trousers, feet rubbed with nettles and thistles, flaming papers applied to the soles of his feet to wake him when he has lost consciousness. The camp hums with rumours.

It makes no sense to Max that anyone who looks or sounds German would try to escape. They are safer in here. The previous week someone threw a grenade into a dormitory housing German prisoners on a local farm. Twelve others were smuggled out of another in the dead of night and found days later dead in a quarry, heads caved in, hands wired behind their backs. A friendly guard told Max it is no secret who the killers are: local thugs, ex-Maquisards who joined the Resistance only when liberation was assured, attracted to the cause for the reasons of pillage, not patriotism. Now they roam the countryside with submachine guns demanding work from terrified locals. Max feels like a chicken locked in a flimsy coop while the foxes make careful circles, studying the fences.

"I've had enough mud," says Hans. "You coming?"

"I'm going for a walk."

"You'll only make yourself hungry."

"I'm already hungry."

They receive tea and a fifth of a flute of bread for breakfast, a watery potato or carrot soup for lunch, the same for dinner. Once a week, there is meat in it: a morsel of black pudding or fat. It's nowhere near enough. Ten corpses were carried out yesterday: diphtheria, dysentery, pneumonia.

Near the canteen, a prisoner is mixing paint next to a canvas propped on a low easel. A guard poses, rifle across his lap. He will have provided the painting materials and probably a morsel of food for this service. Where is the food? The paintbrush roll has a suspicious thickness to it. Is there bread in there? Dried meat? Cheese? His stomach yawns, and he keeps walking.

A couple of wood-carvers from a neighbouring barrack are doing a steady trade. Some of the inmates released each day to labour in a carpentry workshop outside the camp walls have been smuggling in tools and timber. The resulting knickknacks—decorative plates, figurines—are worth a fortune in food or cigarettes or soap. Those without skills or resources to manufacture art or repair a guard's shoes or stitch his trousers can trade only a few belongings. A man in Max's barrack swapped a pair of underpants for soap, the soap for half a baguette. On the women's side, young mothers who have sold off their possessions and cannot find sewing or domestic work for the guards' wives are offering their bodies for a pitcher of milk. And still their babies die.

He rounds a corner behind the infirmary, where a nurse smoking a cigarette is staring through the barbed wire toward the plateau.

"*Flûte alors*, you've caught me." She lets the cigarette fall and uses the heel of her boot to crush the butt into the mud. She is in her early twenties, with short dark hair tucked behind her ears.

"I won't tell," he says. She tries to smile and her chin wobbles. "Are you all right, miss?"

"Me? Oh, I'm peachy," she says. "Another day, another cartload of coffins." She presses the back of her hand to her mouth. "What a thing to say. You must think we are all beasts."

"It's not your fault."

"We are trying, many of us," she says. "I went to the Prefecture myself yesterday to beg for food. They referred me to General Supplies. You could not find more efficient functionaries in the whole

of the Republic than the men running General Supplies. I begged
them—mouldy pasta; beans with weevils—anything at all, I told them.
I warned them. I said: 'This camp is becoming a giant infirmary.' It
runs contrary to all the rules of medicine and humanity."

"Try not to worry," says Max. "We will be gone from here before
it can get much worse."

She bites her lip. "We must have courage," she says. There is a mud
splatter running up her stockinged calf.

*Courage*. She is too honest to offer him hope.

Max studies a postcard that carries an image of the Munich train station at a time when there was a roof, and no craters, and not a soldier
to be seen. A few smartly dressed passengers browse the stalls next to
the platforms while they wait.

He sees his mother as he last saw her at the station at Neunkirchen.

Since Charles's death he had avoided her eye, terrified at what he
would see. She had never accused him, but he felt it in her silence,
in her heavy sighs, in the way she dropped into her chair at night. It
should not have been too difficult to tell her that he had followed the
Gestapo into the house, not brought them. Yet each time he came close,
he burned with shame. Luscher had not held a gun to his head, a knife
to his heart. So why had he not thrown the candle in his face and run?

He had watched her from the train window and thought she might
plead with the inspector to open the door and order Max off the train.
If she did, he would blurt out everything and not stop until she understood that he had not betrayed her. He had not betrayed Charles.

But the platform slid away and she was shrinking, and then gone.

*Dear Mama and Anna,*

*I hope you have received my other letters by now. If not, greetings
from La Chauvinerie. I am in an internment camp! It's close to
Poitiers, though I have not seen that place since we drove through
on our first day. This is like no camp I have ever visited. The worst
thing is the food. If we are lucky enough to get soup, there is nothing*

*recognisable in it. Hans likes to say there are tiny ghosts of meat*
*floating around in there. I've never seen one or tasted it. Yes, I am*
*with Hans! There are others here from Lauterbach. At the beginning*
*I hoped I might see you both here too, but it's better you are not. I*
*pray you are at home and safe and that Papa is with you. Hans and*
*I have been here a month, and it seems longer. We thought we'd come*
*home as soon as peace was declared, but there is no news on when*
*the transports will start. Please make sure Hans's mother knows he is*
*here and quite well. Neither of us have received replies to our letters. I*
*hope that all is well with you, that Papa is home, and that the house*
*is still there. There must be new potatoes by now, and peas. Please do*
*send food if you can for me and for Hans. Ask Father Peter to pray*
*for us. I hope to see you again very soon.*

    *With love and affection*
    *Max*

The photograph is badly creased now, but he can still make out the faces of his family. He had not understood the great comfort that comes from the gentle symmetry of potato furrows and mounds, the slow ebb and flow of the seasons, the long, hot days of the harvest.

If he could, he would dive into that photograph and back into that field. He'd walk among them, listening to their chatter, resting his palms on their hot, dusty backs, and feel the miraculous rise and fall of their breath.

# 44

The sergeant is true to his word. A truck manned with American soldiers shows up the following morning. Marguerite, Anna, Tonia and the pup, who showed up the previous night filthy but inexplicably fattened, make the slow journey to dust and ruins that used to be Heilbronn. Curious relics survive. A billboard advertises a barber's price, a shop mannequin missing an arm wears a German army helmet, and a filthy cat picks its way up a set of stairs leading to nowhere.

"Nice town," says Tonia.

Marguerite follows Anna's eye to a group of women bent over the rubble, strangely intent on poking through the smashed bricks and split timber and dust. What are they searching for? A photograph? A saucepan with a handle? Perhaps they are afraid to stand up, to risk being reminded of the extent of the destruction around them.

The truck takes them to an army base on the outskirts of the city where they are to wait for space on transport heading west. Tonia wanders off, and Marguerite finds them a bench to rest on and work their way through the rations they have been given. The sweet biscuits are so dry that they crumble between her fingers, and she catches them with her knees so she can eat every crumb, but the pup shuffles its paws and how can she not share? She gives it the cheese spread, which is an abomination, then Anna bites into a stick of chocolate and groans like a slattern.

"What?" says Anna.

"Have some dignity."

"Have some chocolate," says Anna. "This is the best food I have ever eaten."

"Don't expect me to cook for you after a comment like that."

Anna breaks off a piece for Marguerite. She takes it and feels it melt into sweet softness on her tongue.

"You see?" says Anna. And she does.

Tonia is back and uses her hip to shunt Anna along the bench.

"Where have you been?" says Anna, handing her a piece of chocolate.

Tonia moves the chocolate around her mouth, stretches out her legs, and bangs together the heels of a brand-new pair of army boots. She looks twelve years old. Anna laughs, and Tonia laughs, and there is a little warmth in the sun. Marguerite recalls a moment like this with Anton, under the cherry tree in the back garden sometime in the middle of the war. He had his hand at the back of her neck, absently untangling a knot in her hair, and she had pushed away the worries and chatted instead about the work that needed doing in the vegetable beds.

He is probably dead.

She straightens up. What is wrong with the human heart? We can tolerate endless suffering, but a moment of happiness is too much to endure, because it can never last.

A soldier shows them to the truck they will board for Karlsruhe and tells them to get their belongings together.

"I will stay," says Tonia.

"No." Anna reaches for Tonia's arm.

"I have a job," says Tonia. "And boots. Also, somewhere to live and good food supply."

"You were gone fifteen minutes," says Marguerite.

"I only needed five," says Tonia. Her teeth are oozing chocolate. The ache of the sadness comes as a surprise. Marguerite does not want to say goodbye, but there is no point in arguing.

"I have something for you," she says, and, careful to check that no one other than Anna sees, she retrieves the two stacks of money, wrapped now in newspaper to resemble two fat sandwiches. Tonia narrows her eyes.

"What's this?"

"A gift. Don't lose it. And take care of yourself. You are not invincible."

"I am okay," says Tonia, and strikes a pose. "I have moxie."

"What on God's green earth is *moxie*?" says Anna.

"Anna," says Marguerite.

Tonia shrugs. "The American said it's a good thing." She takes Anna's cheeks in her hands. "Listen to your friend from Belarus. Are you listening? This is where the world is." She stamps the ground with the heel of a shining new boot. "You hear that? Where your feet are. Not in here." She rocks Anna's head from side to side. "All that thinking, thinking. Walk on the ground, eat some food, grow some plants, do some work, okay?"

"I thought you might come with us," says Anna.

"Crazy girl," says Tonia. She kisses Anna on both cheeks, lifts Anna's suitcase, and presents it to her. "Go."

They share the ride with a troop of soldiers bound for weekend leave in Paris. The men are raucous but sweet—trying for her sake not to stare too much at her daughter. It is difficult to take her eyes off *them*, these beautiful, vital young men. They have survived this war and they will go home to their mothers, and it feels like a miracle.

"Have you seen my son?" she wants to whisper as the truck rattles west on potholed tracks, past teetering walls. "Have you seen my husband?"

Their ease, their confidence, is mesmerising. Somewhere in England or America or Canada, their homes and families wait in safety, untouched by destruction.

*I used to be like you*, she wants to say. *I come from somewhere. There were times when the future and the past did not exist, and we were happy in our way.*

\* \* \*

The blast furnaces and coal tower of the ironworks still stand at Völklingen. The slag mountains are untouched. How can it be that half of the township has been blasted to hell, half of *Germany* has been blasted to hell, but the *hütte* remains intact? Anton once told her that almost every helmet worn by a German soldier in the Great War was made from Völklingen crude steel. In this war, it was more than that, so they say: grenades and tanks, cannons and guns. For all of her married life she has lived with the black dust of the ironworks settling into her washing and her vegetables and fruit trees. It has crept into her house and laid itself down inside her linen chest and clothes drawers and deep into the kitchen cupboards like the foul breath of a soulless creature. A creature that has fuelled two world wars and has lived on to supply the next.

The house still stands. A shutter hangs off a hinge, and a couple of flowerpots are smashed—the remainder overflow with dead foliage—but there is still a house.

Even as she understands there is no one there, she is running, calling for them. *Anton, Max.* Are they here? The stillness and dust and state of the garden all give the same response. She didn't know until this moment how much she had believed they would be here.

She sinks onto the step that Charles slipped off, looks out across the mound where Argos is buried. It is too much. Anna is trying to offer up words, an embrace. It is suffocating. She shakes herself free.

"You're not the only one," says Anna. "I wanted them to be here too."

"Then we are both fools." Anna flinches and Marguerite hears the harshness of her own words. "I'm sorry, Anna, I'm so stupid. I was just so sure, for a moment, that they would be here."

There is a movement in the neighbours' garden. Hedda Luscher stares at her through the bare bean racks. Of course Hedda Luscher has survived the war. She'd survive arsenic soup, and a bomb dropped on her bed. She'd survive arson and earthquakes and a bullet to the brain.

The other woman's hand rises, hesitant. Good God, is she going to salute? But no, she is waving, an excited gesture, an invitation to wait, because she intends to approach.

Marguerite whirls and feels under the pot for the key. Gone. She cannot talk to that woman. She tries the latch. Unlocked. The door opens a hand width and stops dead. She peers through the gap. The piano is in the kitchen. The floor is covered in mattresses—not all of them familiar.

"Help me." Anna helps her force back the barricade, a tallboy tipped on its side. The crockery has been swept, not all of it broken, to a corner of the kitchen. The floor is littered with rubbish, spilled oil, bloodied bandages. Was the kitchen some sort of first aid post? The corridor wall has been split open. Were they searching for valuables? Perhaps they found the silver cutlery and miniature sewing box buried under the daffodils. It doesn't matter. None of that matters.

"Mrs. Bernot?" Hedda Luscher is thrusting her head through the kitchen door like a nosy chicken, eyes jerking this way and that. "Marguerite, it's Anton."

He is alive. In the hands of the Allied soldiers, but alive, uninjured, and expected to be released once he has been interrogated and had his identity checked. Hedda Luscher knows this because she has received a message from her son, who is in the same camp.

*Alive.* Is it safe to believe it? She looks to Anna for confirmation. They are in each other's arms. *Thank you, God. Thank you.* Her thoughts skate to Max and she tries to push them aside, to demonstrate some grace and gratitude for Anton's life, for God's mercy, but it is impossible. Knowing that Anton is safe only intensifies her fear for her son.

"My husband was not so lucky," Hedda Luscher says from the doorway.

Marguerite swipes the tears from her cheeks and is transported back to the morning Charles was murdered. Her feet were bare. Her hair was in ropes. Rain poured into the neck of her dress, itched her navel as she stood there on her front steps watching two black cars melt into the gloom.

*Charles was dead. The Feldgendarmerie had come for Anton to revoke his exemption and send him to the Westwall. The only reason they didn't imprison Marguerite is that the priest turned up with the deputy mayor in tow to plead her case, and Anton's good name, and that of his father, and grandfather.*

*The neighbour's window had groaned open, and she began to weep, because here was a witness to her misfortune. A word of kindness would both comfort and break her. She and the Luschers were not fond of each other, but trivial animosities would fall away when times were truly difficult. Joerg Luscher's thick fingers gripped the sill, and his voice arced out into the rain: flinty and gleeful.*

*"Playing the piano is all over for you, Mrs. Bernot," he said. "You will have to work for your children now."*

*The window slammed shut, and she blinked up at the black glass, lost at first—until the meaning caught up with her.*

*She spun back to the door. Max and Anna were there, and Hans. Max was trying to speak, but the crash of the rain and his hiccoughing sobs broke up the words. He was so lost that she almost took a step toward him, to silence him with an embrace as she had done all of his life, but what would that teach him? What good were tears? Life was hard and it would only be harder, and the sooner her children learned that the better.*

*She pushed them back inside and through to the kitchen. Anna stared at the shards of a broken jug on the floor.*

*"Clear it up," Marguerite said. She wrapped her apron tight and offered kettle to tap, but the water recoiled off to the side. The stupid kettle was jumping like a fish on a hook. She gaped at it. The fault lay in her own, unsteady arm. She set down the kettle and gripped the bench.*

*Was it Joerg and Hedda Luscher who had denounced them? Had they heard Charles knocking at her door? Was their fanaticism so complete that an offence against the Nazis was an offence against them? Or was it more personal? Anton's superior position in the mine, perhaps. Was that enough to be hated for? Or was Marguerite the problem? Too bourgeois, too French in this spartan nation, where all that mattered were work and strength and preparedness?*

"Mama, I need to tell you," said Max.

*She held up her hand.*

"Hért uf." *Enough.*

*Max left the kitchen: head high and straight-backed. Trying to be brave. A memory jolted Marguerite. That very posture. It was Hedda Luscher, walking away down the Adolf Hitler Strasse, stung by what Marguerite had said. She could not recall the conversation, just a prickling of remorse tempered with impatience. She had made a sharp comment, and should have apologised, but the woman's injured air was so infuriating, so pompous, that she could not truckle to it.*

*The fragment was gone. Marguerite was left only with the certainty that Hedda and Joerg Luscher's antipathy, and therefore Charles's death and Anton's call to fight, was her fault. And with this certainty came the rage, that this was all it took now to have your life destroyed: a snub, a slight. Lives hung in the balance over a misjudged word.*

*They could go to hell, the pair of them. To hell.*

*The kettle had rattled, and she'd summoned the three young people to the living room and pulled open the windows. The curtains shivered and rose. Damp air filled the room.*

"What are you doing?" *Anna said.*

*Marguerite had opened the piano lid and took up Strauss's noisy "Tritsch-Tratsch," hands intertwined in the rapid, playful high notes. Her children recoiled as if she were a rabid dog. Hans looked ready to run.*

*She called, loud enough to be heard over the scampering notes and the moaning wind and the rain wheezing in through the windows.*

"Have you forgotten how to dance?" *The curtain billowed and*

*knocked a wooden table lamp to the floor. Anna rushed for it, but*
*Marguerite lifted her hand.*

*"Laisse-la." Leave it.*

*It was Anna who first raised her foot and stamped.*

*"Yes." Marguerite said. "That's it! Louder!"*

*Up came Anna's foot and down again, then quicker, in time*
*with the manic swirl of the notes. Max was blinking, stunned, but*
*Anna grabbed his hands and spun him so fast he stumbled. The*
*pair of them pulled Hans into the circle, while the curtains in-*
*haled and exhaled. Floorboards thundered. The kettle screamed.*
*Charles was dead, and Anton's chair sat empty, and the broken*
*pieces of jug were heaped in a bucket and none of it mattered.*
*None of it.*

"I am sorry for your loss," says Marguerite to Hedda Luscher. She
turns her back and takes in the state of the kitchen. The stovetop is
invisible under filthy pots, every dish either dirty or broken.

"Marguerite," says Hedda.

Best to start with the medical supplies. Marguerite scoops up the
empty coal scuttle and starts collecting bandage wrappings and medicine vials, a couple of syringes.

"I didn't understand—I didn't," says Hedda. "When I saw that poor
man shot in the garden—then Anton was taken. I didn't—"

"That poor man?" says Marguerite, straightening.

Hedda Luscher's chin is puckering. She might actually cry, and if
she does, Marguerite will throw the scuttle and its contents right in
her face.

"But your husband is alive, and that is the most important thing,
isn't it? It's a new start, a new beginning for all of us. It wasn't me who
threatened Max. You should know that. But it wasn't Joerg's intention
for anyone to die. He was terribly upset by the collapse of the German
armies. He hadn't *adjusted*, you see, to the realities of the situation. He
felt that the citizenry must play its part, that it might make a difference,
might give Germany the chance, do you see?"

Here come the tears now.

"Oh, Marguerite, we believed that we were helping in some small way, and now that poor man's face, excuse me, Mr. Leveque's face. It stays with me. And the terrible sound when his neck— It plays over and over and I can't seem to *remember*, I am having trouble recalling exactly what we thought would happen, but we didn't think *that*. Do you see? Those days are gone. We have to start again."

"If you want forgiveness, you're at the wrong door," says Marguerite.

She stoops to pick up a bandage and hears Hedda Luscher's feet tread down the back stairs.

"What does she mean they threatened Max?" says Anna.

"Nothing she says matters. She doesn't matter."

"And so the war continues."

The words find their mark. Marguerite could go after the woman, attempt to express deeper sympathy, ask after her children, but she recalls the look Charles gave her as he slid down the garden gate.

"Your father is alive," says Marguerite. "We need to make things nice for him, and for Max. Find an apron and check the cellar for coal." She tips the contents of the scuttle into the fireplace. "Take this."

She tugs at a board nailed across the back window and manages to wrench it free. The vegetable garden is a bomb site, but it is only May. She will get started with the carrots and lettuce.

# 45

Poiters, La Vienne
July 1945

A gunshot snaps the afternoon air, and Max's eyes flash open. The echo splinters off mildewed walls and dust-caked windows. Close, but not inside the camp perimeter. He rolls his head to the left and breathes again. Hans is here. Back propped against the wall, scanning the rafters.

"It's nothing. Shooting at clouds," Hans says, scratching at his temple, pulling something out and holding it up to his eyes. "Farewell louse, your journey ends here." He crushes it between his fingernails.

The end of an index finger presents itself under Max's nose. A pin-prick the colour of chocolate sits crushed on his nail.

"No? Are you quite sure?" says Hans. "You could do with some protein. You're starting to resemble an upside-down broom."

Hans's skull is trying to escape through his skin—eye sockets and cheekbones straining against the parchment that used to be flesh. The crescents beneath his eyes are violet. He looks older than fourteen. This is how Hans will look when he is an old man. When he is laid out dead in a box. A spider of dread picks its way down Max's spine.

Hans shrugs and puts the end of his finger into his mouth, doing a fine job of pretending that he tastes something good. He shakes the dark hair off his forehead and scratches again.

Alive. Definitely alive. Max's friend, his companion, his saviour on a road that began so long ago.

Another volley of shots is released, closer than the last.

"Don't worry," says Hans. "The guards will let them throw their stones and send them away."

Max reaches down to a sore spot on his backside. He stops when his fingers encounter bone. A vast, growling chasm lies in his belly. Cramps and chills, hunger and nausea roll and shift. Would a drop of water or a morsel of bread soothe his stomach or set off a new wave of retching? His throat is a desert. His tongue is cemented to the roof of his mouth. He is desiccated, dry as a dead mouse he found once under his chest of drawers. His thoughts have drifted. What was he trying to remember? Places and times and faces move in soft currents.

Hans comes into focus. He's folded his eyelids up on themselves to reveal two alarming shelves of slippery pink. His chin hangs loose. He's trying to make Max laugh but looks even more like a corpse and it is too much. Hans cannot die. He cannot. Not after all they have endured.

*Périple.* That's the word his mother would use. *Le périple.* The French word is a better one than the German *Treck.* Theirs was not a laborious trudge from A to B, but a tortuous road, a thousand kilometres of twists and turns.

It is so difficult to concentrate. What does he remember? A bathroom. A bathroom at the new Adolf Hitler School in Ludweiler. A metal case filled with eyeballs. A dark-skinned girl swimming inside his blood. A volcano of soapsuds. Boots kicking foam over black and white diamonds.

Max tries to sit up, but the room begins to turn. The handfuls of damp straw lining his metal bunk offer no comfort, just another reason to scratch.

Hans is gone.

*Hans.* His voice comes out as a harsh croak.

But here is Horst! Rushing to his side in a white nurse's cap, pulling a fob watch from his pocket, squeezing Max's wrist in the other. Max can feel his own pulse tapping between Horst's fingers. He searches Horst's dazzling apron—somewhere beneath the white there is a fragile flicker on the skin between Horst's ribs. *Tippity tap.*

"*Quoi de neuf?*" says Horst. What's new? Can he not hear the men outside chanting insults over the barricades? Why is he staring with such intensity into Max's eyes? The hair on his temples is damp. His cap has a smear of blood on it.

"Horst?" says Max, but his throat is too dry to form the word properly.

Horst places his palm on Max's forehead and his hand is ice. The shock of it makes the room turn again. Wait now, wait. This is not Horst at all. This is the nurse, Edith. Something is wrong with his head.

"Can't seem to hold down my food," Max says. He sounds drunk.

"Food?" Edith says. She pockets her fob watch and takes a careful look at him. "What food?"

Max had opened the tin of meat a few days earlier, rationed himself to two spoonfuls a day. He had intended to share it with Hans. He had *wanted* to share it with Hans. But the hunger was so fierce, the desire to keep it so overwhelming that he had weakened. A quarter of the can was gone, and then half and then—

Hans is back, plonking himself on the floor, knees curving like hard apples under his trouser legs, ragged shirt loose on his sternum. He would not be sitting here if he knew what Max had done.

"What have I told you, Hans-Peter?" Edith says.

"Just visiting."

"He has dysentery, not a sore thumb."

"Everyone has dysentery," says Hans. "What is a thumb?" Hans's French is improving for the most part.

"It is a thing attached to your hands. Speaking of which, when did you last wash your hands?"

Hans pretends not to understand. He's teasing her and she knows it.

She mimics handwashing with great exaggeration.

"You have some soap?" he says.

"Mother of God," she says. "The taps are working today. Use them. And if you must visit, keep your distance."

"I'm strong like a bear, me," says Hans.

"Dysentery has no regard for charm." She produces a pitcher and splashes water into a tin cup.

The promise of relief in its brilliance is more than Max can bear, and he feels tears pooling in his eyes.

She lifts the back of his head, holds the cup to his lips, and releases a thimbleful of liquid. Max washes it around his mouth, frees his tongue, and swallows. It tastes like a clear blue lake. She lifts the cup again, and he grabs at it, almost knocks it out of her hand.

"Just a little," she says. She is beautiful. He wants to bury his face in her neck, roll himself into a ball in her arms and weep because everything hurts less when she is there. She lifts the cup just enough to release a few more drops. The water settles into a crack in his lips, soothing and stinging at the same time. His stomach rolls. A vise takes hold. Hans's face blurs and he is reduced to a splat of black hair and a frown. Put a moustache on him and he'd look like Hitler.

"Heil you," he says, but it comes out as a cough.

"What's the joke?" says Hans.

"He's delirious," says Edith. Who is she talking about?

The men outside the camp are chanting a song. He picks out a few words.

*Ça ira, ça ira.* All will be well. All will be well.

"Hans," whispers Max. "Anything around the kitchens today?"

Hans swipes the hair off his forehead, points his stubby chin upward as if about to recite a poem. The cracks in Max's lips pull open. He tastes the tang of salt and iron. The hunger is a monster—a toothless jaw stretched open from the base of his belly to the tip of his tongue.

"There was a very nice plate of roast pork," says Hans, the idiot, the clown, the magician, because has he not transported Max to the kitchen in Lauterbach? Can he not see the dish right now? Dotted with cloves and juniper berries, crackling in its glossy bed of potatoes, onions, and carrots. Real carrots. Fresh-pulled from the earth, rinsed and placed in the pot. Dazzling, blinding, brilliant orange; a shushing miracle between his teeth. It was his job to go with Anna and find the juniper berries in the wood. Each time he put a berry between his teeth he believed it to contain the secret heart of the forest. The freshness of pine needles and lemon lingered long after he spat out the hard cone and emerged from the damp wood into the burnt, grit-laden air of home.

"After that," says Hans, "there was a half-decent plum tart and a minuscule bar of chocolate. I would have shared it with you, but it was a mere half kilo, so . . ." Hans shimmers.

How could Max have kept food from Hans? His friend. His dearest friend. There is a flaw in his character. A fault in his blood.

"I'm sorry," Max whispers.

"We need to cool you down," says Edith.

"I was so hungry," says Max, and he does not have the strength to lift his hands and cover his face.

"What is he talking about?" says Edith.

"The Dead Man he's been hiding under his bunk," says Hans.

"Dead Man?" she says.

"You knew," says Max.

"Tinned meat," Hans says. "Pretty awful, and quite possibly spoiled."

"I'm sorry," says Max. Hans wavers again.

"Christ in a pudding basket," says the nurse. She lays her palm to Max's forehead. "No need for tears."

"I should have shared it," whispers Max.

"What, and have me shitting soup too?" says Hans. "No, thank you very much. Anyway, you needed it more than I did. Built like a bunker, me." Which is a lie.

"Rest," says Edith. "And don't worry about the roosters outside. It's Bastille Day. They're just letting off steam." She holds up an index finger to Hans. "You. Let him sleep. And wash your hands."

Hans bends into a deep bow, and Edith rolls her eyes, squeezes Max's toes, and moves to the next bed. Max's insides cramp again, and he wants to curl up against the pain but cannot imagine how to move.

"I don't feel good, Hans," says Max.

"You're not looking your best, Max, I'll admit that. But you've still got a certain appeal that might work for a particular kind of girl. A blind one. With a limp."

Max snorts and the pain is a dagger.

"You have to tell my mother," he says.

"Tell her what?"

"It wasn't me. I didn't bring the Gestapo."

"Of course you didn't."

"She thinks I did."

"She doesn't."

"Tell her."

"Tell her yourself."

"I have tried a hundred times. I—"

"When you see her, it will be easy."

"Why are you crying, Hans?"

Another rifle shot sends a jolt through him. A stone cracks off the roof, and he sees his godfather slide down the garden gate. Charles, poor Charles in the mud, his neck snapped, all the life gone out of him. Max reaches for his pocket, pats the flat space where the Lotharingian coin should be. It rises into the air, spinning so fast that king and cross blur and merge.

*Take it with your eyes this time. Your hands will follow.*

The coin bounces away from him into the dark. He hears the roar of soldiers below, sees again the pillars of light, the swinging silk of a panicked spider, the troubled dust. He remembers the moments he held Hans's life in his hands. He has cursed what came after a hundred times, cursed his carelessness and childish panic, but now it makes sense that the coin should rest back there in the dark with the grenade. The coin was the price. The price to pay for Hans's life, and Hans will live. He knows it beyond doubt, and the knowledge is a comfort to him.

Raucous voices lift in song outside the camp, and inside it. Here is a tune he knows well. They roar "La Marseillaise" with jubilant emphasis on certain murderous phrases; phrases he learned in the potato field, when his mother clapped her dusty hands at his horrified response. *Égorger.* To slaughter. *They will slaughter your sons, your wives.*

"No one wants to sing an anthem about flowers and lambs, *Schatz,*" she had told him. "The thrill is in the danger. The threat. The call to be a hero."

And so she had taught him. Line by terrifying line. His favourite was the passage about the blood overflowing the ditches. He sees it now as he saw it then: a thick and bubbling current of ruby red rolling up the dust, coating the pebbles and weeds and dead leaves, rising and rising until it floods across road and field alike. That *sang impur*, the impure blood, meant the Prussian and Austrian invaders threatening France—German invaders, German blood. Yet is German blood not the purest of all?

Hitler is dead. The war is lost. Germany stands accused of murder on a scale for which there do not seem to be adequate words in any language. Whose blood is whose? He cannot hold the thread. It twists out of his reach. Something about blood. Something about earth.

Other prisoners are pulling themselves upright, easing their weight onto ragged shoes. Their clothes are rotting in the filth and merciless heat that lets up for only a few minutes when the rainstorms come through each afternoon. With that, a few heavy drops batter the roof, hard as pebbles, then the rain descends with the weight of an ocean. It drowns out the singers and their stones, silences their rifles. It is the sound of a thousand hands clapping, a forest of cicadas, a waterfall crashing into bedrock.

Max opens his eyes. Clouds of spiderweb tremble between rafter and lamp. Funny. He'd expected to see the sky. He'd like to see the sky. He shifts. He lifts. He blinks as he passes through sticky silk and rough-cut board and rusted iron.

Here now is the rain.

A camp guard, unsteady with arthritic knees and a good measure of Pernot, grunts with the strain of drawing closed the rusting bolt on the last barrack, putting to bed roughly four thousand German civilians, French collaborators, and sundry other suspect individuals: two thousand men, fifteen hundred women, and five hundred children—give or take a few.

It's after nine, and the sun is slouching toward the horizon, but the air has lost none of its heat. The guard gives the kitchens a wide berth and shuffles through the women and children's side of the camp, past the tall, uneven grids of barbed wire separating it from the men's side.

The *canicule* has intensified the stench cloud squatting over the camp, temperature pushing forty degrees Celsius today. Five days without water the previous week have not helped. Attempts to fix the pipes have been lackluster. There should be a riot, but no one has the strength for it. Foul vapours rise from toilet drums slopping with diarrhoea, clothing reeking with sweat and filth, unwashed feet and underarms, breath rank with hunger and disease.

The worst of all the stinks emanates from the mountain of rotting potatoes, cabbages, carrots, and peppers behind the kitchens. Its underskirts quiver with rats, while a mantle of flies hum above it.

Each day food merchants dump their fuming, spoiled dispatches and present crisp invoices to an office to the right of the main gates. They leave with a portion of the sum the Republic of France furnishes the camp with to provide eight hundred calories per prisoner per day and a little extra—fresh milk, no less—for the babies.

The office is locked and empty for the holiday, the camp director's monthly report unfinished on his otherwise empty desk. It is not easy to embroider words fine enough to render unremarkable the deaths of nineteen children, twenty-three men, and two women in just thirty days. Babies born in here never live long.

At last he circles past the infirmary, anticipating a warm word with the nurses, who are forthright and tireless, and never fail to lift his spirits. He tackles the steps one at a time and rests at the landing. There are rumours of a new typhoid outbreak, so he will need a good lungful of clean air before he leans his head in the open door.

He lifts his shoulders, sets his smile, and prepares the greeting he has settled on: *Comment vont mes vaillants petits soldats?* How are we today, my brave young soldiers? Alas, two of the three nurses are at the far end of the barrack, busy as bees. The third, and loveliest, is just a few steps away, but an interruption would not be welcomed. Her head is bowed, hand resting on the frail shoulder of a boy who kneels, weeping, at the bedside of another poor lad.

The guard sags. Some days are so much longer than others. He heads for the stairs and prepares himself for the long walk back to the administration block to track down the coffin cart.

# 46

Lauterbach, Saar Protectorate
September 1945

Marguerite cycles down the Haupt Strasse—it's been months since Adolf Hitler Strasse signposts disappeared into woodpiles all over the country—and sets her eye a good way down the street.

The neighbourhood is busy rebuilding walls, patching roofs, filtering soil, replacing glass, painting over graffiti, replanting vegetables, rewashing linens, sorting crockery. Sappers are working in the wood, digging up the mines, detonating unexploded bombs. Potholes are being filled, rubble cleared, bricks reused. Busy, busy, busy. And wherever there are people, there is talk. Incessant talk.

*It cannot be so. As God is my witness. I have it on good authority.*

A parishioner walking by with her son smiles, a sympathetic press of the lips. Her hand betrays her real thoughts though, by flying out, fingers splayed, to check the tall presence next to her, the son returned home. The empty air at Marguerite's side howls Max's absence. She must bear it because to do otherwise would be to suggest his absence is greater than the other absences, when really it is a drop in an ocean.

The human ruins trickle in from the fronts, the prisoner-of-war camps, the displaced persons camps, the *other* camps. Auschwitz-Birkenau. Bergen-Belsen. Buchenwald. Dachau. Josef, sweet Josef, died eight days before the camp at Buchenwald was discovered. Cécile is convinced that his body was in one of those photographs taken with forensic precision by Allied soldiers: dozens of naked, skeletal men heaped like wet laundry. Impossible to imagine, impossible to stop imagining. How can Marguerite rail about her losses when there has been murder of that magnitude? That such things could happen. It is too much to take in. Too much to understand.

She passes the boarded-up shop that was once the butchery. The Weilers disappeared in the early years of the war. There are rumours about where they went—one of the worst of the camps, it is said. Marguerite had not understood the great danger they were in. And if she had understood? Each time she passes the old butchery she imagines the Weilers tumbled together in one of those horrifying mass graves, one of Ruth Weiler's elegant scarves dragging in the earth. She, Marguerite, did nothing to harm Ruth Weiler, nor did she help her.

Perhaps they are two sides of the same coin.

A woman from church looks back to her roses without a greeting. Certain people hold opinions about Marguerite. Unvoiced but clear enough. Why did she not send Max back to the church school when the priest demanded it? Why did she let him go to that Hitler Youth camp? Why did she not hide him away? Why did she not bring him back from that godforsaken internment camp once the war was over?

She tried. God knows she tried. She received word in early June that Max was being held in France. As soon as she had been able to speak with Anton, she packed a small bag and joined the lines at the border post. German citizens were forbidden from travelling outside the country, but might an exception be made for a French-born mother trying to reunite with her son? The soldiers were courteous but firm. Three times she tried, and the third time the officer recognised her from an earlier attempt and took the time to explain that there was no process for exemptions. All their manpower was tied up repatriating French displaced persons, or DPs, as they were now known, the lost millions.

"Your son will be fine, ma'am," he had told her. "The Red Cross checks all those camps. He's probably better off there than here right now."

In July, American troops left, Saarland was again placed under French administration, and French border guards had no sympathy for a Frenchwoman married to a Boche.

She nears her house and spies someone sitting on the front step. A young man. A boy.

*Max.*

She forgets to use the brake. Her feet scuff the road, catch on the pedals, and she falls, trying to free herself from the bike, calling his name.

But it is not him. It is not Max.

Hans is pulling her up, straightening her dress, picking up the bread, putting the bike to rights. "I'm sorry. I'm sorry. I didn't—"

"I thought—" she says. He is taller, a little heavier in the jaw, his Adam's apple more pronounced, but in every other sense he is diminished. Dangerously thin. Murderously so. He brings to mind a hatchling, its bones jangling about in a delicate sleeve of skin. He is lucky to be alive. Max was not. That is all.

"I'm sorry," he says. "I'm so sorry."

"Don't you be sorry, sweet Hans. Please don't. I'm so silly. Of course it's you. Of course it is. It is very good to see you." She wipes the tears from his beautiful face.

His heart is broken too.

"I've brought his letters," he says. A bundle rests on the step, bound with twine. "I thought you'd like to read them."

The letters. She's trembling like a pup. Good God, she had wondered. She had cursed the war and the bombs, and the postal service for giving up. Now here they are, and she cannot bear to look.

"Come, come inside," she says, and embraces him again. She had not understood until this moment how much she loves this boy. "Your mother? How is she? She must be over the moon."

"Good, good," he says. "She told me to come straightaway."

"She's been very kind," says Marguerite.

"You're bleeding," he says, frowning at her ankle.

"So I am. Tell you what—you wait in the kitchen and fill the kettle.

I found some coffee at the market yesterday. I'll hunt out a bandage and be with you in a moment."

Upstairs, in her room, her back to the door, she slides to the floor. *Max.*

So many times she has seen him—on a passing tram, in the face of a French soldier, a grainy picture in the newspaper. If she is not seeing him, she is dreaming him, dreaming him back. A bureaucratic mix-up, for instance, or a case of mistaken identity, or a turn of events more supernatural: a dead boy so determined to live that he shakes off dirt and death and marches home, eyes bright and smile wide, straight into her arms. Alive.

*Alive.*

How many times has she imagined holding him close, inhaling the scent of him, the *life* of him, oblivious to the rising bedlam outside— the neighbours rushing into the street, arms lifted heavenward, hailing God and Jesus and the Virgin herself for the miracle of a lost son re- turned from the dead? How many times has she imagined whispering into his ear. "I knew it. I *knew*. I knew you would come back to me."

Such miracles have happened. They *have* happened. They have happened to others, but they will not happen to her.

Her feet carry her down the stairs and back into the kitchen where the bundle rests on the table. Hans places a coffee before her. He is more man than boy now.

The clock ticks, reminding her of interminable dinners at Karl Hinckel's table. Is he one of the Nazis strung up or shot or facing prosecution for his crimes? And what of his vile wife, Lina? She has heard nothing and has no wish to.

How the days have dragged since she and Anna returned home. The cleanup wasn't so bad. At least there was coal and the kitchen was airtight. They slept there for those first few days with little to eat, but they were warm. Anton returned a few weeks later. He had deserted as Allied troops crossed the Saar—but not before distributing every gram of food to his compatriots. The Americans held him for a time before questioning him and sending him home. He is outside now with Anna in the garden, shoring up the bean racks. She will fetch them. She will fetch them in just a moment.

"Did you forget the bandage?" Hans says, puzzled. Her ankle is bleeding unchecked.

"I just needed to have a little cry," she says.

Hans releases an unsteady breath. "I have some things to tell you, Mrs. B. You might need another one."

"Oh dear," she says. "Perhaps you'd better try singing it."

He flicks the dark hair off his forehead and laughs. For a moment he is the old Hans. He tells her a story Max told him about the day Charles died.

"But I never blamed him, Hans. How could I have?"

Then it comes to her. Three demons in black marching into her kitchen and with them, Max. For a heartbeat, no more, she *had* thought he was with them, that he'd *brought* them. And had dismissed the idea as quickly in the horror that followed. But Max had seen her judgement. Seen it, felt it, absorbed it like poison. He had not understood that a hundred different thoughts had spun through her mind in her panic and terror. Why hadn't he *asked* her? Why hadn't she *remembered*? An ache pierces her abdomen. Max. *Max.*

"He wished he had pretended not to hear Luscher," says Hans. "That he'd kept walking, or fought back, or stopped her, the wife, from going to the police."

"But what could he have done, Hans? There was never going to be enough time. Even if he had fetched the priest, the front was approaching so fast. Who knows how long it would have taken to make contact with the Maquis?"

Another memory returns—the night before Max was sent to the camp.

"Don't make me go," he had said. She had already dismissed every possible scenario for keeping him off that train and did not wish to go through it all again.

*"You will do as you are told."*

*"I need to talk to you. I have to—"*

*"No arguments. The best thing, the safest thing to do is go."*

*"You want to get rid of me. You can't stand to look at me."*

*"What nonsense are you talking? Do you want the authorities to pay us another visit?"*

*She saw the injury in his face, but there was nothing she could do, and she was too exhausted to say any more about it.*

"I really never blamed him," she tells Hans.

"I told him that," he says. "I tried."

"Yes," she says. "I imagine you did. He has always been hard on himself, our Max."

The clock wheezes and clangs out the hour. She hears quiet laughter from the garden, where Anna will be lecturing Anton on where to tie wayward vines, and how to best tie them. Hans's eyes lift and Marguerite feels the strength of will it takes him to stay in his seat. She should let him go, should call them in, but she is not ready because her heart is peeled open, and in this silence, in this peace, she feels Max in the room.

She reaches for Hans's wrist and squeezes. A plea. A selfish woman's plea for just a few more moments. Then she unknots the twine of the package he has brought her and lifts out the first postcard: a chalet surrounded by snow and pines, steep slopes of a mountain range rising beyond. She flips it over. No message. Just her name and address in Neunkirchen in Max's impeccable hand, and the name and address at the Relocation of Children to the Countryside camp in Bavaria. Each line is underscored with a ruler, twice, in heavy pencil. The postmark is February—impossible to make out the exact date, but it can have been no more than two weeks after he left on that train.

The prestamped image of Hitler is accompanied with the phrase: *The Leader knows only struggle, work, and care. We want to take what we can off his hands.*

May he burn in hell.

She traces a finger across her own name, pencilled with exactitude, so like Max, and the address written with such care. No greetings. No embraces. Just empty space. Was there no time? Was it too dangerous? Was he afraid?

She closes her eyes. Of course he was afraid. Everyone was afraid. She had wanted to leap on that train after him, drag him off and take him back to Mrs. Liszt's house. But she told herself that he would be safe in the mountains. She was wrong, as she was wrong about everything. It was not, in the end, the Thousand-Year Reich that killed her son, but the Republic of France. She will never forgive her country. She will never go back.

Thumping steps outside rattle her thoughts. It's Anna, taking the stairs two at a time, always in a rush. Here she is now, and Hans is out of his seat and lifting her, swinging her in a circle, the pair of them squealing, and just as quick, falling into laughter at the din they've made. Anna is shaking her head at him, astonished, delighted, then—when he sets her down—uncertain, a little shy. It's Anton who rescues her.

"Hans-Peter Schlesier," he says from the doorway, scoffing at the offered hand, dwarfing Hans instead in a hug that accentuates the boy's fragile form. "I heard the fuss Anna was making and thought there must have been a fire in here."

"Don't exaggerate, Papa," says Anna. She looks like she's won a prize. A tide of pink is sweeping up Hans's neck.

"Look," says Marguerite. "Hans has brought his letters. Max's letters."

A light green card juts out from the bundle. She frees it and there he is. A small photograph pasted onto a death certificate, tilted anticlockwise, giving an air of mischief to the face frowning down the lens. The word *décédé* is pencilled across the brief typewritten facts. Deceased.

Max stares back at her. He does not look afraid. The date of his entry to the camp: April 29. Nine days before the war ended. Date of death: July 14. Bastille Day.

Anna is at her side in an instant, damp breath in Marguerite's hair. Hans pulls up a chair on the other side, and Anton is at her back, leaning on her shoulder. She lifts her hand to cover his. She feels encircled, steadied by them. More than that. She feels buttressed.

"There he is," Marguerite says.

"There he is," says Anna.

"I was with him," Hans whispers. "At the end."

"Good," Marguerite says, and she wants to thank him, but it is no longer possible to speak.

# EPILOGUE

Mont-Saint-Michel, France
Summer 2019

Look at them out there, across the mud. Travel-weary and slack-jawed, trooping from coaches and cars onto the promenade, squinting into those tiny, shiny little boxes, trying to frame the un-framable. He is a tourist of sorts himself, of course, but it is the sheer number of them that sends a hollow rattle low in his gut, a jitteriness about crowds that he has never overcome. That and their confectionary-coloured clothing and ghastly sport shoes.

He scrubs at his cheeks and his whiskers are noisy under his palms. *Wake up, old man.* The car—a rented tin testicle—howls like a lawnmower when he eases it back onto the road and lifts his hand in a loose gesture of appeasement to the honking driver behind him. He crawls along until he finds the salt-parched sign pointing away from the marvellous abbey spindling skyward from its cradle of granite and toward the *Ossuaire Allemande.* Such a curious word, *ossuaire.* Softer on the tongue than the German *Beinhaus.*

He turns right, out of the traffic, and moves through ancient flood plains divided into neat rectangles of gold, fields of durham wheat and maize, and here he is at the foot of Mont d'Huisnes, a mound more than a mountain, with nothing to crow about other than a vantage point from which to view the Mont-Saint-Michel and its collection of twelve thousand German skeletons from the Second World War.

What an uneasy affair it must be for the people of these few quiet hamlets to be so outnumbered by the dead—not their own ancestors, but their invaders and oppressors; the murderers dug up from the battlefields decades after the fact and entombed in steel and stone. How many French have ever wandered through here, curious at what a German military ossuary is doing here of all places? How many would know that it is not only the chalky scraps of German soldiers stacked up in rows; that there are the delicate metatarsals of dozens of infants, the broad, flat pelvises of young mothers, the dense femurs of fast-growing adolescents all neatly boxed up in this southwestern tip of Normandy far, far from home? The scandal of La Chauvinerie internment camp has faded along with the French newspapers whose pages it once dominated. And why shouldn't it be forgotten? The losses at La Chauvinerie were a pinprick of blood compared to the ocean bled in the German camps.

It has taken a long time to get here, not that it was hard to find the place, once he put his mind to it. Seventy-four years it took, and a single phone call to the German War Graves Commission.

The gardener, surprised by a visitor, is a chatterbox, lifting his chin to show the point up beyond the necropolis where one can take a short path through the trees and gaze over the patchwork fields to the abbey, the bay, and the Channel beyond. The view pleases the gardener, but not the tomb.

"*C'est austère, sombre,*" he says with a glance up the hill. "Gives me the creeps. But there you are. See for yourself."

The old man nods and casts his eyes to the stairs. He will get up there, but his knees will not like the journey back down.

"Don't waste words, do you?" The gardener's comment follows him up the stairs. Did he forget to wish the man a good day? He is so intent on getting to his destination, he had walked away without a thought. He stops.

"Why would anyone waste words?" he says, and swipes his hair off his forehead.

"You looking for a relative? We get a lot more Germans than we used to," says the gardener. "Your French is better than most."

"I learned a little," he says. "After the war." A part of him wants the gardener to know the decades of service he dedicated outside of his teaching career—attempting to forge closer bonds between two nations nursing their wounds. Small-scale, local efforts, but it gave him some satisfaction. For all the good that it did.

The flags are flying again, the rabid talk has returned. He trembles for his great-grandchildren and yet, and *yet* he cannot help himself. He has a hope. This young man before him is curious, open, kind. Most people are, at the heart of it, kind. "I was fourteen when the war ended."

"You are one of the last, sir. There are still a few down in Manche." The gardener tells a story, too fast for Hans to follow, about a British spy, a hiding place, and an elderly grandmother dropping dead of shock. "Can you imagine?"

"I do apologise. My French is a little rusty." He attempts a smile but cannot sustain the weight of his cheeks. When did it become difficult to smile? Is there no part of him into which gravity has not sunk its teeth?

"Of course, I beg your pardon." The gardener is embarrassed. "*Bonne visite, monsieur.*" He trails off to his sparkling van, his pressed workman pants glinting with a multitude of zips and buttons, and Hans feels a rush of warmth for the man, particular in his habits, a little peculiar, but a gentle man.

His eyes throb. His sternum feels bony under the heel of his hand.

*Courage, old man.*

The mausoleum is hidden from the surrounding fields of almost-ripe corn by a lush woodland garden, alive with the crisp click of cicadas and a kingfisher keening for its mate. Hay sweetens the air and a whisper of salt—the English Channel just a few wingbeats away.

He climbs the stairs of pebbled chip and ducks through an arched opening in a low brick wall—a nod to the crude brickwork of the parish farmhouses. Is it his own nerves or has the temperature dropped? He hurries now. Where does this come from, this eagerness? After all this time, what is the rush? But his feet keep lifting, his groaning hips and knees following orders.

Ahead of him a simple concrete cross stands in a circular lawn. Curved around it is a two-storey vault cut into the hillside. Strict stacks of stone bricks, bare concrete walls. No statues. No crooked cross here. No words of glory. What a contrast to the American cemetery at Saint-Avold with its towering angels and flags, its victory maps and sprawling lawns of white crosses.

He walks from door to door, room to room, searching identical, symmetrical *chambres*; marble-lined doors, impeccable brass plaques, a few miserable mementos—a dead posey, a creased photograph.

His breath catches. There it is.

A name. A name and sixteen numbers. A name and sixteen numbers on the door of a box, in a vault of one hundred and eighty steel boxes in a tomb of sixty-eight vaults.

Maximillian Bernot. Date of birth. Date of death. The remains of his oldest friend, his dearest friend.

*Your only friend.*

If he were to prise open the heavy brass door, what would he find? A stack of bones topped by a skull of perfect symmetry once measured by a virulent Nazi in a hot classroom in the Adolf Hitler School in Ludweiler? Or the remains of a stranger? How could one set of bones be discerned from another in a mass grave?

The cold brass sends a shock into his swollen finger joints, but he does not flinch.

"One or two things to tell you, old friend. Horst made it through. We met up many times after the war. Stephan, too, and Rudy. A few of us took to visiting Tittmoning after our kids were grown up, stayed at the inn— Do you remember Mrs. Giesel? She treated us like her lost children, fed us like kings. It wasn't all bad there, was it, Max? I ran into Gruber years later. He clipped my ticket on a tram, the miserable bastard—didn't remember me and I didn't remind him. Horst became a musician, can you imagine? Anna thought the world of him."

Out on the lawn, a thrush skips along a clipped edging, rooting for worms and flicking out clods of wet earth. Hans eases himself down the wall, stretches out his aching legs, and sees Max as he first saw him in that bathroom long ago, soap lather dripping from his hands, his worried face breaking into a smile.

# NOTE TO READERS

This book is dedicated to Edmund Baton, whose remains are interred at the German Military Cemetery at Mont d'Huisnes in Normandy.

*Edmund at school, courtesy of the Baton family*

Back in 2015, the German War Graves Commission, better known as the Volksbund, didn't make much of the fact that hundreds of German civilians are interred at Mont d'Huisnes along with all the soldiers, but it did tell a version of Edmund's story and it went like this:

Edmund Baton ran away with a friend from a youth camp in the Bavarian Alps in the final weeks of World War II. Their plan was to get home to Lauterbach in Saarland. They made it to Ludwigsburg, where they hid for eight days because of heavy fighting. Edmund then convinced American soldiers to take them across the Rhine to Strasbourg and from there the pair intended to travel home by train. They were arrested on the way to the station and taken to central France, where Edmund died in an internment camp on July 14, 1945, of hunger. He was aged fourteen. Crypt 59, Grave number 90.

I read and reread those brief sentences. The eldest of our three sons was thirteen at the time, just a little younger than Edmund when he set out on his journey. I tried to imagine my boy in Edmund's shoes. Any of our boys. Impossible.

I knew then I wanted to write this book.

It had to be a novel. I knew that from the start, because I was sure that only scraps of information would remain about Edmund's real life. My research would instead focus on time and place, building a world into which I could imagine his story, because seventy years after his death, Edmund would probably be no more than a face in a photograph, an uncle unmet. How wrong I was about that.

Which brings me to Joseph.

A single tantalising thread about the Baton family had been published by a Lauterbach municipal website that mentioned a man called Joseph Baton, a retired teacher who had received high honours for his lifetime of service in fostering Franco-German relations. Joseph Baton lived in Creutzwald, France, but had been born in Lauterbach, Germany, the same town as Edmund, in 1930, a year earlier. Could this be a surviving relative? I sent a short message to the council asking to be put in touch.

Three days later, the name Baton appeared in my inbox for the first time.

"Creutzwald and Lauterbach are two towns separated by the border between two countries, Germany and France," Joseph Baton wrote (my translation from his French). "My family's history is a cross-border story and it is with great pleasure that I will talk about it. There you are, contact is made." *Voilà, contact est pris.* I loved that forthrightness from the start. ("I googled you," he would say later. "Didn't find much.")

Joseph's next message contained the revelation that he was Edmund's first cousin and close childhood friend. Their fathers were brothers.

"The difference is that Edmund's parents were German and lived in Germany, and my parents were French and lived in France," Joseph wrote. "Only a few kilometres separated us, but there was a border between two countries to cross. And this is where the history of our region comes into play. You have to go far back into the past to understand."

And there was more.

Edmund had an older sister, still living, just across the border in Germany.

Joseph provided me with her name and address and recommended I write to her on paper because, unlike him, she did not use email.

Further, Joseph (once a teacher, always a teacher) recommended I make "internet searches" on Lotharingia, the Germanic Empire, the Kingdom of France, the Duchy of Lorraine, and the history of Saarland.

Right, then. Homework.

Three months later I was back in France, in Joseph's living room in Creutzwald, with a list of questions in French and a marginally improved understanding about Lotharingia, the Germanic Empire, the Kingdom of France, the Duchy of Lorraine, and the history of Saarland.

In the room were Joseph, his wife, Jeanne, and Edmund's sister, Elisabeth Paulus (Lilli). The cousins were ready to talk about Edmund and all three were happy to share stories about their own childhoods that spanned the Great Depression, the rise of Fascism, the reunification of Saarland with Nazi Germany, the start of World War II and the end of it.

What followed in that meeting, and the many that came after, was

*Joseph Baton at the American Cemetery at Saint-Avold,*
*courtesy of the author*

the most extraordinary gift to a writer. I was a stranger from the other side of the world with a solid background in journalism but no experience in writing a novel. In order to imagine this world, I needed to know everything. Not just all they knew of Edmund, but the wider world in which they were raised. There were the big questions regarding indoctrination, persecution, and oppression; and little ones, such as what did they eat for breakfast? What did they do after school? What did they wear? Did they have a bicycle? A dog? A wristwatch?

Joseph, Jeanne, and Elisabeth placed their trust in me, answering every question to the best of their recollection, showing me the photo albums and Edmund's many postcards and letters.

The interviews were in French. It must have been a particular challenge for Jeanne and Joseph, both retired French teachers, to hear me murdering their beautiful language. That first time, Joseph took the list of questions out of my hand and set about correcting the grammar, bless him. At one point, Jeanne asked after the proposed title for the book. At the time I was thinking, *The [Something] Road.* Off she riffed, like a high-speed talking French thesaurus: Le Chemin Difficile, Le Chemin Tortueux, Le Chemin Serpentin, Le Chemin Sineuex. I enjoyed those meetings so much.

One of the most powerful moments was when Elisabeth placed in my hands the letters her brother wrote from the internment camp. You don't need to understand German to read the story they tell. One is in a neat, firm hand and indeed the tone of the words is exuberant, excited. Edmund has survived a great adventure. He's full of news, full of hope. The second is faint, shaky, illegible in parts, and desperate in tone. "Do everything you can," he writes. "Ask the priest to pray for me." He was already in the grip of a fever.

So, what of Max's story is based on Edmund's story? The pair have the same birth date, religion, French-German parentage. They both have an older sister, although Anna's and Marguerite's characters and story are entirely invented. Max's love for his family, his warmth and likability, are based on what his family and friends recall, and what his postcards and letters show.

Edmund was indeed evacuated to the Bavarian Alps in early February 1945—but not Bad Reichenhall as the Volksbund believed, but a small hamlet near Tittmoning. And that wasn't his first time in a Children's Evacuation to the Countryside (KLV) camp. He spent most of 1943 in Silesia, where his frequent, affectionate postcards home demonstrate the intensity of his homesickness.

*One of Edmund's postcards home, courtesy of the Baton family*

*Edmund's last letter from La Chauvinerie, courtesy of the Baton family*

The details of Edmund's attempt to get home in 1945 were the most difficult to pin down. There is no account of his whereabouts from late February 1945 when he was at that KLV camp in Bavaria, until late April 1945 when he shows up in Eglosheim, north of Stuttgart, having travelled seventy kilometres by train, according to one of his letters.

A study of old rail maps of Germany led me to lovely old city of Schwäbisch Hall, which is roughly a seventy kilometre train journey from Eglosheim. That's where I placed Max, but I can't say for sure Edmund was there. The story of the Hitler Youth leader who rounded up those young recruits and then abandoned them on the way to the muster at Stuttgart is based on an anecdote told to me at Schwäbisch Hall.

From Eglosheim, Max follows Edmund's path through Enzburg, to

Karlsruhe, across the Rhine with the GIs, into Strasbourg, and into the hands of local or military police.

Max's difficult train journey from Strasbourg to Poitiers is based on firsthand accounts of passengers, including Edmund, a train guard from Poitiers, and a report by the soon-to-be disgraced director of La Chauvinerie civilian internment camp, complaining about the state of health of those on the train and warning his superiors to expect more deaths. He bemoaned the fact that there were newborns, heavily pregnant women, and elderly people on the convoy, who could hardly be considered a threat to the Allied armies then pushing on toward Berlin—the ostensive reason given for clearing them from the border areas. He made a fair point.

Max's thoughts and beliefs are, of course, invented, but the family did provide clues and introduced me to some of Edmund's childhood friends, including one delightful woman who confessed to having had a crush on him. She recalled she wasn't the only one. All remembered him as quiet and gentle in nature. He was proud of his Jungvolk uniform, and that wristwatch as well—a rarity in those days, especially on a child. It would be naive to imagine that a child raised in Germany at that time could resist the indoctrination they were subjected to through

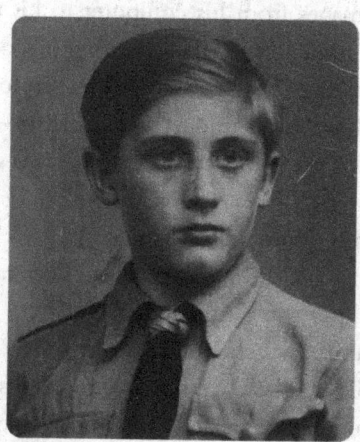

*Edmund in uniform, courtesy of the Baton family*

their schooling and after-school activities, although in Edmund's case, the persecution of his own extended family must have clashed with the messages he was fed at school and Jungvolk meetings.

Edmund's father was indeed arrested for currency crimes—a catch-all for suspected individuals who were guilty of nothing more serious than keeping Saarfrancs in the cupboard. Elisabeth believed their father was arrested a second time during the war and sent to work in an underground missile factory.

The Josef Bernots in this book retain the first names of the father and son their story is based on, at Joseph Baton's request (In France, the name is spelled Joseph; in Germany it's Josef). Joseph Baton's father left Saarland after the 1935 plebiscite and became a naturalised French citizen, was arrested by German authorities for political reasons in 1941, and transferred to Buchenwald in 1942. His death, reported by camp authorities in the final days of their reign, was blamed on *"pleurésie et faiblesse du cœur."* Pleurisy and weakness of the heart.

Weakness of the heart. Remember those words.

You've probably seen the images taken by American soldiers when Buchenwald camp was discovered in April 1945, a few days after Joseph Baton's father died there. I thought I had seen them too, but I didn't really see them until I sat in Joseph Baton's lounge room and he projected a series of images from his computer to his television. I didn't know what was coming and had been teasing this octogenarian about this most excellent grasp on technology. The photographs he wanted to show me were those stacks of emaciated corpses—piled six or seven high—at the door of the camp crematorium, onto a lorry trailer outside.

"My father's body is probably in there," he said. "I am sure of it."

How many times had he stared at those devastating photographs, searching for a glimpse of a familiar face?

Many of Edmund's French relatives were sent to work in German labour camps in Silesia. The character Charles is inspired by one who was a taxi driver and drove many Jewish refugees across the border into France following the Saarland's reunification with Germany. The same relative escaped from a Silesian labour camp late in the war, made it as far as Lauterbach, a journey of roughly a thousand kilometres, only to be arrested and sent to Dachau. The family believe he was denounced by a neighbour. He survived.

On the subject of Edmund's death, Edmund's family believe he died from eating spoiled food. The Volksbund records the cause as "hunger." The records of La Chauvinerie blame "dysentery and weakness of the heart." Perhaps it all amounts to the same thing if you consider the ghastly conditions at the camp, which provoked a national scandal when prison guards blew the whistle in August 1945.

An outraged opinion piece in the regional newspaper *Nouvelle Republique du Centre Ouest* in October 1945 stated that the death rate for adults in La Chauvinerie was seven times higher than other internment camps. A meal was a few carrots in thin soup, a loaf of bread split between twenty-four men. Emaciated internees were like "ghosts floating in khaki greatcoats, with slow gestures, feverish looks." There were thefts of personal property, arbitrary searches, violence, and, though rare, torture of detainees.

It was the children that bore the brunt of the appalling conditions. "Various causes [of infant death] are cited—epidemics, impossibility of isolating the contagions, bad milk, lack of hygiene, etc.," the newspaper declared. "Of course we didn't kill them. They weren't even let die of hunger, strictly speaking. But the lack of organisation and supervision, the insufficiency of the means made available to nurses, the administrative negligence, in a word, led to this appalling result: a mortality of 100 of 100 newborns."

If France, the newspaper opined, did not observe the rules of simple humanity, by what right, and in the name of what morality "would we pose as judges and accusers of the executioners of slow death camps?"

An aberrant internment camp in France cannot be compared to the systematic murder carried out by the National Socialists in numerous camps. The principle is what scandalised the nation.

Whatever the precise cause of Edmund's death, the date recorded on his tomb at Mont d'Huisnes is July 14, 1945. It was only when I came to write this author's note that I noticed a discrepancy. A diagonal pencil line runs across the page of his camp record, with the words Décédé le 13/7/45 au camp. The numeral *13* is almost illegible, written across the printed CHA of the word *Chauvinerie*. A report by the camp director dated July 16, 1945, in which Edmund's name is misspelled "Edmond" states that he died on July 14, 1945, at 8:30 a.m. I had always believed that Edmund died on Bastille Day 1945 and could not bear to change this element of Max's story, but I am now sure Edmund died a day earlier.

That moment of the chaff shimmering like Christmas lights before the bombers arrived is a retelling of Elisabeth's experience.

The tragedy of Sankt Wendel, in which so many Lauterbach women and children died is true. Wooden crosses bearing all their names are displayed in the Catholic church of Lauterbach.

There were difficult moments in some of the interviews. Memory is fickle. Stories change with each telling. I was not always able to verify the facts. Some subjects had not been discussed in seventy years.

"You didn't know because we never told you," Elisabeth said to Joseph at one point. When I asked her later about the tensions the war must have caused within the family, she waved off the question and told a story about watching Joseph's mother, Léonie, cross the fields that first summer after the war. It was hot. The window was open. Her aunt announced that Joseph, her husband, was confirmed dead at Buchenwald. Elisabeth could still see Léonie and her own mother sitting there weeping together on the garden stairs in that terrible heat.

Unpicking the history of La Chauvinerie was made a great deal easier thanks to the work of retired historian Professor Jean Hiernard, archaeologist Sonia LeConte, and their colleagues from the University of Poitiers who brought the forgotten scandal of La Chauvinerie back to light with a series of publications after the remains of the camp were rediscovered in 2008.

I am indebted to Professor Hiernard for his time and generosity. The Archives Départementales des Deux-Sèvres et de la Vienne in Poitiers has compiled and cross-referenced the documents from the various internment camps to facilitate easy access and foster further research.

Dr. Erik Windisch, an amateur historian from Schwäbisch Hall, met me off the train to show me where the German jets were built in a bunker outside the old city, and to look around his aircraft museum. It was Erik's recollection that inspired the scene of Max and Hans watching the night fighters from the square in the old city.

The nurse Edith in this book is inspired by an unnamed camp health worker who later testified she was so concerned at the food situation at La Chauvinerie that she took herself to the food authorities, then the prefecture, protesting at what was happening "contrary to all the rules of medicine and of humanity" and pleaded "for some beans, even infested with weevils, pasta, even if it were mouldy, to feed the unfortunate people of this camp."

It's important to state that La Chauvinerie was established as a camp by German authorities in 1940 after France's capitulation. At that point most French soldiers were deported to German labour camps, but French Colonial troops were considered unsuitable under Fascist ideology. An existing barracks was commandeered, and new ones built for a camp that would ultimately house more than seven thousand detainees—the majority of them soldiers from Senegal, Morocco, Algeria, the Caribbean, Madagascar, Indochina, and Tunisia. The former Senegalese president Léopold Sédar Senghor, a poet, was detained there in 1941 and wrote of the terrible cold, lack of sanitary facilities and adequate clothing, the spread of diseases like tuberculosis, and racist attitudes of the German guards. There were other camps in the region detaining Roma and Jewish people. La Chauvinerie was handed back to French authorities in February 1942 and reopened three years later to house German civilians cleared from the French-German borderlands, along with French collaborators—anyone considered "suspé."

I have tried to be as historically accurate as possible, but in places I have changed the timing of an event to fit the narrative, such as the German prisoners executed in the quarry and those who died when a grenade was thrown into their dormitory. In fact, those events occurred after Edmund's death.

Writing is hard. Research is easy. It was perhaps going too far to spend as much time as I did discovering which troops were where and when so I knew who Max would cross, and what they'd been through. I probably didn't need to know about the weather in such detail, but I did not make up the unseasonable heat waves and snow in April. There were so many "aha" moments that only a research geek will understand—the sudden availability online of the weekly reports of the Allied Expeditionary Force, for instance, which gave accounts of how things were on the ground in the territories Max was walking through.

There were many times I became bogged down in detail, and at those times, I would hear Joseph Baton talking about that border that cut a line through a region that had shared a thousand-year history, culture, church, language, and blood. A border that cut a line through a family and an entire community.

"We were a people," he said many times. "We were a *people*."

# SOURCES

Many books were useful in researching this book, but the one I keep returning to is Erika Mann's terrifying warning to the world: *School for Barbarians: Education under the Nazis*. First published in New York in 1938, it reads as if it were written today—a chilling dissection of how the Third Reich set about indoctrinating a generation of children.

To understand the individual experiences of the children of the Third Reich: *A Hitler Youth in Poland: The Nazis' Program for Evacuating Children during World War II* by Jost Hermand; *Witnesses of War: Children's Lives under the Nazis* by Nicholas Stargardt; *Hitler Youth: The Duped Generation* by H. W. Koch; *Hitler's Beneficiaries: How the Nazis Bought the German People* by Götz Aly; and *World War II through the Eyes of a German Child* by Reinhold Pflugfelder.

For a close look into the final stages of the war in Germany and the immediate aftermath: Ian Kershaw's *The End*; Richard Bessel's *Germany 1945: From War to Peace*; Nicholas Stargardt's *The German War: A Nation under Arms, 1939–1945*. Also, *Armageddon: The Battle for Germany, 1944–45* by Max Hastings. For the wider picture, a great place to start is Anthony Beevor's *The Second World War*.

Victor Kemplerer's diaries and essays provide astonishing detail into the daily experience of Jewish people under the Third Reich: *I Will Bear Witness, A Diary of the Nazi Years, Volume 1 & II* and *The Language of the Third Reich*.

W. G. Sebald's tiny volume *On the Natural History of Destruction* is a series of essays that explore the consequences for the German people of the mass destruction of their cities.

For novels that explore the child and youth experience in Nazi Germany, Anthony Doerr's *All the Light You Cannot See*, and Marcus Zusak's *The Book Thief* set the standard, as does Catherine Chidgey's wonderful *The Wish Child*.

# ACKNOWLEDGEMENTS

My heartfelt thanks to Elisabeth Paulus and Joseph and Jeanne Baton for your generosity, hospitality, and trust.

Thank you to the many people who have provided vital assistance in the research of this book, including: Professor Jean Hiernard, Dr. Nicholas Williams, Marie-Thérèse and Reinhard Hager, Dr. Erik Windisch, Benjamin Haas, Patrik Paulus, Anita Goetthans, Hermine Glück, Alain Jeanne, Hella Bauer, Annette and Ian Larsen, Roland Geiger, Nicholas Michael Koziol, Daniel Stihler, and Horst Schmadel.

Associate Professor Paula Morris from the University of Auckland: thank you for letting me onto the course and for teaching me all the good stuff. Thank you to my MCW cohort for helpful feedback in those excruciating workshops and for creating a strong and supportive environment in which to learn the craft. Thank you to those who spent many hours reading various versions of the manuscript and providing feedback to help me improve it—Paula Morris, Tom Moody, Stephanie Johnson, Erik Windisch, Hella Bauer, Laura Moss, and Genevieve Gagne-Hawes.

To Tonya. Thank you for the inspiration. Antoninia's sass and goodness are all yours.

A particular thank-you to Laura Moss, for good advice, and for not laughing the day I told you I was thinking about writing a novel.

To Giles Milburn from Madeleine Milburn Literary Agency, and Adrienne Kerr at Simon & Schuster. Thank you both for your faith, vision, and the many, many hours of work you have put into helping me get this book into shape.

# Acknowledgements

My family and friends have been constant and patient cheerleaders for this book. Thank you.

My parents, John and Judy Holdom, set the scene for this writing caper by being fanatical readers, filling the house with books, and by helping to establish a community library so that no child of Awatuna was ever short of a book to read. I am so grateful.

To Connor, Liam, and James: thank you for the time I stole from you. You found unique ways to repackage the interruptions—stealth, humour, trickery. I loved finding the notes squirrelled away in my research folders.

Thank you to Steve for unwavering support and faith, and particularly for the door.

# ABOUT THE AUTHOR

K. J. Holdom is a New Zealand writer who lives in Auckland. A former journalist, she holds a master's in creative writing from the University of Auckland, where she won the 2018 Master of Creative Writing Prize for best manuscript. *The End and the Beginning* is her first novel.